A LETTER FROM SICILY

A Letter from Sicily

A novel

by

CHRISTOPHER AMATO

Adelaide Books
New York / Lisbon
2021

A LETTER FROM SICILY
A novel
By Christopher Amato

Published by Adelaide Books, New York / Lisbon
adelaidebooks.org
Editor-in-Chief
Stevan V. Nikolic

For any information, please address Adelaide Books
at info@adelaidebooks.org
or write to:
Adelaide Books
244 Fifth Ave. Suite D27
New York, NY, 10001

ISBN: 978-1-954351-36-3

Printed in the United States of America

Dedicated to the immigrant

Chapter One

1877

They were gaining on him. He could hear their labored breathing, their footsteps pounding close behind. He could almost feel their eyes tunneling into his back.

"Saverio! Stop now and we'll go easy on you."

He wouldn't stop. They would have to catch him first. Nine-year-old Saverio was running from the school bullies, three of them, including the leader Marco and his two henchmen. They were only a year older, but Marco was a head taller than Saverio.

He was no match for them, but he did have one advantage—speed. He might be the fastest kid in school. If he could outrun them a little longer, the teacher would be outside to call everyone in from break time. Maybe by the end of the day the bullies would invent a new problem, find another victim, a fresh score to settle with someone else.

At most, Saverio figured he was ten seconds from clearing the olive grove next to the school, then he'd probably be safe. He didn't see the *rastreddu*, a tool used to reach the ripening olives high up in the trees, hidden in the brush. When his foot caught on the teeth of the rake, the hunt was over. Saverio tripped and went tumbling to the ground.

They set upon him like lions on their prey in the African savannah.

Marco pulled Saverio to his feet and backed him against a tree. "Why do you have to make it hard on yourself?"

By now, most of his classmates were gathered and eager to witness some punishment. Saverio knew Marco liked him, but he understood that as the leader of the gang, Marco would have to make an example of him, if for no other reason than to maintain absolute authority.

Marco demanded something quite simple, really. He suspected Saverio had a crush on Rosa, a girl from school. An ordinary conversation earlier in the morning had evolved into an argument. Challenged in front of the others, Marco finally ordered him to admit he loved her, but Saverio never liked being told what to do. He was stubborn that way. Even if it was Marco doing the telling. So stupidly stubborn.

When Saverio refused, the battle was on and now the hunters had their quarry. Marco's sidekicks twisted his arms behind him around the trunk of an olive tree.

Marco said, "Okay, say you love her. Say it."

Saverio wasn't giving up without a fight and tried to twist free from his captors. That was a mistake. Marco punched him in the gut. The struggling ceased.

Marco's first lieutenant, Barbaro, a short brutish boy with thick eyebrows and a perpetual frown, kept a firm grasp on one of Saverio's arms and edged his ugly, dog-like face close. "The boss said to say it, you say it!" he shouted in Saverio's ear.

Marco said, "Say it. Say you love Rosa now."

The other kids, big and small, chanted, "Saverio loves Rosa, Saverio loves Rosa."

Marco held up his hand and the chanting stopped. "And say you want to kiss her too. Say it."

The chanting began again, this time morphing into a silly tune, "You love Rosa, you love Rosa, and you want to kiss her."

There she was. Almost hidden in the crush, Saverio saw her. She was neither singing nor chanting. She simply watched the scene unfold with her lovely green eyes.

Marco held up his hand again, silencing the group. "Okay, you better say it now or else."

When Saverio remained silent, Barbaro punched him in the face. The swelling around his eye was instantaneous. But Marco hadn't authorized this aggressive action, and there would be repercussions later for Barbaro in private away from the rest of the group. He scowled and ordered his underlings to release Saverio.

Barbaro furrowed his eyebrows and faced the horde, encouraging them to shift their attention instead to Rosa. He pointed and they turned on her, singing a new song suggesting she loved Saverio. Unaccustomed to being mocked, it didn't take long for her to start crying.

Saverio considered leaving, but her tears would have forever tied him to this spot of shame if he did nothing. His eyes found hers. Enough was enough.

"Stop it, Barbaro, leave her alone."

When mutt-face only sang louder, Saverio socked him right in his sack, bringing the boy to his knees.

Saverio shouted so everyone—the tallest to the smallest—could hear. "Yes, I love Rosa and I want to kiss her on the mouth."

The truth was set free.

Marco nodded.

Saverio walked away.

Rosa's tears dried and a tender smile appeared.

The afternoon heat was oppressive, and the sweat stung her eyes. She dug deeply into the loam in search of evening's dinner. The plants grew best in loose earth where the potatoes would have room to grow, but she knew the deficient chalky soil wouldn't yield much—still, she hoped to find a few handfuls of the small root vegetable. Dropping three more spuds into the basket, she crawled on hands and knees to the next plant.

Rounding the corner of the house, familiar footsteps approached. Salvadora wiped away the sweat from her face with her forearm.

By now the flesh around Saverio's eye was a puffy medley of green, black, and blue.

"Oh, God, what happened to you?"

She jumped to her feet and tried to examine his eye, but Saverio pulled away.

"Saverio, did you get in a fight?"

"Not really."

He bent over and grabbed a tuber the size of his fist from the basket. Kicking it with the side of his foot, he snatched it in midair and took a bite.

"You need to wash it first."

"Okay." He spit on the other half, wiped it on his pant leg and ate the rest.

"Will you tell me what happened at school?" his mother asked.

"*Matri*, do you want some help scratching up a few more?"

"If you won't tell me about your eye, you can talk to your father when he gets home."

He dropped to his knees. "I will."

His hands plunged deep into the dirt.

Salvadora loved her only child more than anything in the whole world. A bit sullen at times, she knew he had a good heart. Leaning over, she kissed the top of his head.

It was early evening. Salvadora sat at the kitchen table dicing vegetables on the scarred wooden chopping board. She heard her husband summon their son to come outside. Stepping close to the entrance of the house, she cracked the door open, anxious to understand what had happened. Saverio stood in front of his father, Alessandro, who was seated on a tree stump next to the side of the house.

"How was school today?"

"I don't know."

His father dropped the last of the cleaned paintbrushes into a bucket he held between his legs. "Well, who should I ask, do you think?"

Saverio stared at his feet and kicked at a jagged rock jutting above the surface of the ground that now seemed to capture most of his attention.

"I guess you want to hear about my eye."

"Are you ready to talk about it?" He set the bucket filled with brushes and tools aside.

"*Patri*, these older boys chased me while we were playing outside. Marco and his friends held me against a tree and other kids from the school kept saying, 'You love Rosa, you love Rosa, and you want to kiss her.' Then they started singing it. They tried to make me say it and, when I didn't, one of Marco's friends hit me. I got mad because they made Rosa cry, but Barbaro still wouldn't stop singing it, so I hit him. Then I said to everyone, I said, I said—"

Alessandro tugged on Saverio's shoulder, pulling him close to his chest.

As Salvadora watched and listened from inside, a lone tear rolled down her cheek.

Saverio stepped back, turning away from his father to stare at the ground again.

"I said, I looked at Marco and I yelled, 'Yes, I love Rosa and I do want to kiss her.'" He turned back to face his father. "Will I be punished for fighting?"

"Come here, Sav." Alessandro hugged his son again. "No, you won't be punished. I'm proud of you for standing up for your friend, Rosa."

Inside the house, Salvadora pressed her closed fist to her mouth to keep from making any audible noise. Overcome with emotion, she bit into her hand with such force, she had to check to see if she had drawn blood.

Alessandro said, "Next time, remember to keep your arm up a little more, okay?" He held his arm to his face with a closed fist covering his left eye.

Laughing, Saverio launched an attack on his father.

After a barrage of light punches, Alessandro said, "Okay, I surrender. I surrender the hill to you."

"Yes, the hill is mine!" shouted Saverio.

They looked at each other for a long moment.

"No more fighting, right?"

"Yes, *Patri*. The fighting is over."

Salvadora used her apron to wipe away the tear. She was about to step outside when her husband spoke again.

"What's in your pocket?"

"Oh, today a boy brought this American magazine to school. He said I could bring it home to look at for one night."

In spite of its ragged condition, Saverio had been fascinated and couldn't stop staring at the richness of the photographs and the intricate detail of the drawings.

He pulled the furled journal from his back pocket and shared with his father the idea of using pictures to advertise the family painting business.

Alessandro smiled. "I know everyone in Marinella, and everyone knows me. Why do I need to do this advertising?"

Saverio explained as well as any nine-year-old could that his father needed an edge over his rival. He held the magazine open for his father to see. "*Patri*, look here. I thought maybe we could write your name on the side of the wagon and a picture of a man painting a house."

Salvadora smiled at her young son engaging in spirited debate with his father.

Alessandro said, "Why do I need my name on the wagon? People know my name and, besides, I paint walls, not wagons."

As he spoke, his deep-set brown eyes flashed a smile of sorts with the black, bushy mustache spreading across the tanned and rugged face.

Saverio persevered. "*Patri*, I can paint the picture with bright colors, I can. My teacher told me I might even be an artist someday."

"I believe you. We can talk more about this later, but now it's getting dark. We should go in and eat, otherwise your mother will think we aren't hungry."

They raced inside, running headfirst into Salvadora on the other side of the door.

She said, "Oh, I was trying to get the heavy pot down, but couldn't reach it."

Saverio darted away.

Alessandro grabbed the pot inches above Salvadora's head and asked, "Is this the pot you wanted?"

She swatted him on the chest with the apron.

"No, I don't want the pot; I wanted to listen, okay? And I love our little boy."

Alessandro wrapped his arms around her. "Listen, he's going to be fine. It's me you should worry about."

She lifted her face toward him. "Why? What's the matter with you?"

"Today I hurt my back carrying the pails and tools up and down the ladder. It's really aching now. I was hoping you might, uh, rub my back tonight, hmm?"

She felt herself drawn into his smile.

"Yes, and we both know how that will end, don't we?" Arching her eyebrows, she said, "We'll see about your back later, but now I have to finish dinner."

As he passed by, she smacked his rear with the apron and returned the smile. "And I liked Saverio's idea for the wagon."

Several days later, Saverio was called by his father to the storage area on the ground level, a damp room sitting on an earthen floor accessible only from the outside of their house. Stepping inside, Saverio stared spellbound. His father had burned the name of the family owned painting business, *Umbianchinu Mancuso*, in a semicircle onto a large chunk of wood. Below the words, he had sketched a figure of a man holding a brush making a straight, clean line on a house.

Fascinated, Saverio muttered, "*Patri*, I didn't know you could do this."

His father pointed to containers of paint on the ground. "Now you can color in the drawing. When you're done, we'll hang it on the side of the wagon."

Chapter Two

Twelve years and some months old, Saverio Mancuso was a student for the last time. He had a love for books, but other than spending time with Rosa, he knew he wouldn't miss going to school.

His father had told him a week before, "I need you more than school does. If we want to eat, and I think we do, we need the money."

His mother put up a fight for a day, but she understood the reality of their world.

Saverio could sense there was an air of excitement at school, but not because it was his last day. The interest centered on the anticipated return of a former Marinella school student who had gone on to achieve great academic success. He was the only one from the small town to have studied at the university level, and now his success as a professor of history at the University of Palermo warranted recognition and celebration.

The subject of their attention was Niccolò Campana, a tall, pencil-thin man who wore a pair of glasses perpetually resting at the end of his nose. He was a brilliant man no doubt, but Signor Campana had a peculiar habit of spelling out words, especially proper names, using his index finger on an imaginary chalkboard when he spoke.

"Hello, everyone. For those of you with whom I'm not yet acquainted, my name is Niccolò Campana." He finger-spelled on the invisible chalkboard, C-A-M-P-A-N-A, while speaking the letters aloud for everyone's benefit. "I teach history at the University of Palermo and am pleased to talk to you today about the birth of our country, The Kingdom of Italy."

All three teachers from the school, the school director, and a few parents turned out to listen as he spoke and occasionally finger spelled. He stood in front of the group aided by a map of the Kingdom of Italy attached to an easel.

"First, let's look at our own community of Marinella. I'm sure everyone knows we're right here on the northern coast of Sicily," he said, pointing to an insignificant dot on the map. "We're about twenty-five kilometers east of Palermo, P-A-L-E-R-M-O, where I was fortunate enough to study for five of the most wonderful years of my life."

Saverio looked at Rosa seated next to him and pretended to finger-spell on his own desk, causing her to giggle loudly. The director snapped his fingers toward Rosa while Saverio wagged a disapproving finger under his desk at her. Now that he had captured Rosa's attention, Saverio cast a playful smile in her direction, and decided he was on a mission to elicit as many laughs from her as he could.

Signor Campana said, "Today we're going to focus on three people who were instrumental in helping to create the Kingdom of Italy. I've been told you've studied one of our greatest statesmen to ever live, Camillo Benso, also known as the Count of Cavour, C-A-V-O-U-R. Of course, we must recognize our most beloved first King Vittorio Emanuele II, E-M-A-N-U-E-L-E. Who am I forgetting? Anyone?"

Saverio raised his hand. He said, "Giuseppe Garibaldi," as he finger-spelled G-A-R-I-B-A-L-D-I, causing others to laugh, especially Rosa, and even some of the parents.

Signor Campana either didn't notice or didn't care. He said, "Excellent, young man. Giuseppe Garibaldi was multi-faceted: a military man, a politician, and a nationalist in the name of a unified Italy."

Unimpressed, the school director stared in Saverio's direction for the better part of five minutes.

Signor Campana forged on. "No discussion of the Kingdom of Italy would be complete without first talking about the year 1815 when the rule of Napoleon, N-A-P-O-L-E-O-N, ended with the Battle at Waterloo, W-A-T-E-R-L-O-O."

The professor spoke for another hour, but his hand never tired of spelling.

Saverio decided even if the school director punished him later, seeing Rosa's smile was worth it.

A week shy of his fourteenth birthday, Saverio was already sure he could spend at least one lifetime loving Rosa. It wasn't possible for them to have always known each other, this he understood, but Saverio was certain that, for as long as he could remember, he had loved her. Perhaps others thought of it as kid love, but for him, it was real.

He leaned against the rugged stone wall outside his parents' house. Only a short distance from his home, but what may as well have been an ocean, Rosa stood huddled with her friends, Anna and Federica, before they began their walk to school.

Unable to take his eyes away, his thoughts were consumed with why Rosa captured his attention. He liked how she threw her head back when laughing or pursed her lips before making a point of argument to her friends, or even tilted her head slightly when she listened in conversation. He also loved the thick, unruly locks of black hair cascading over the smooth olive skin of her shoulders.

Without a doubt, though, he knew it was her eyes that captivated his youthful heart from the beginning. Those piercing emerald green eyes engulfed and consumed him, and he concluded there would be no better way to leave this life than by drowning in them.

He watched as the girls clustered together, moving as a single entity and chattering until all three laughed. Suddenly, a most serious expression swept over Rosa's face. She stopped to stare up at the blue sky while a few billowy clouds roamed toward the east. Her friends circled back and searched the sky until Rosa whispered something, and all three burst into laughter again. A long moment passed until she turned toward him with a smile, making the world, his world, the most special place imaginable. In that exact instant, he knew she was the girl he would someday marry.

He said, "*Bongiornu*, Rosa," wishing he were tethered to the words passing from his lips to her ears.

Her friends glanced in his direction, linked their arms with Rosa's, and made a cooing sound followed by an almost secretive giggling. They walked away from Saverio, disappearing over the hill arm in arm, but not before Rosa turned and smiled his way once again.

Her simple smile always brought him such happiness. Now there was an energy inside him expanding into the whole of the universe, the same emotion he felt every morning when he awoke and every night before he went to sleep.

Saverio spoke in a whisper. "This is how it must feel to be in love. This is love. *This, is love.*"

His father's shout ripped him from his thoughts back to the present. "Saverio, *amuninni*! Let's go! Get the wagon loaded. Daydreaming won't help us with our work, and we promised Judge Curcio we'd be finished today."

Saverio exhaled as he slid off the wall. "*Sì, Patri.*"

His father had been hired to paint the interior of the town's courthouse, and today, they would finish the six-week job. He knew his father felt fortunate to get the work. The town had little money, but the long-sitting, powerful judge who dictated all aspects of life and activity inside the courthouse walls, and sometimes outside as well, demanded it be done.

Saverio hitched Mulo to the wagon and ran his hand along the rough-hewn side of the painted sign. He hollered, "*Patri*, we're ready to go."

They rode in silence to the courthouse. He had accepted his fate; he was a painter like his father and grandfather before him. Now as a fourteen-year-old, well, almost fourteen, he could consider himself a near partner in the business and soon might even call himself a man.

They labored throughout the day, not even taking a break for lunch. Finally the work at the courthouse was completed. Despite toiling for weeks, it amounted to little income. Saverio watched as his father took the money in his hand and bowed his head.

Judge Curcio rounded the corner and interrupted his father's silent prayer. In his typical authoritative manner, his presence dominated the surroundings.

He spoke with a gravelly voice. "Gentlemen, a fine job, a fine job indeed." He turned his attention to Saverio. "On occasion I watched the activities and found you to be a diligent young man in your endeavors. I see you've learned well from your father."

Saverio remained at the courthouse to pack up the wagon. His father left, but he said nothing to his son about where he planned to go. Later, Saverio plodded along the roads, coaxing the mule to keep moving. Though he had to make a slight detour to have the chance to see Rosa at her house, he hoped the risk would be worth the effort. He knew he'd regret not taking the direct route home if Mulo resorted to his occasional stubbornness because then the journey would become a test of wills between human and intractable beast. Fortunately, Mulo's passable mood motivated the unpredictable creature to move forward in a slow cadence.

Saverio guided the animal and wagon along the beaten, uneven road past Rosa's house, pretending not to look for her. To his surprise, though, he saw his father standing with Rosa's father engaged in conversation at the front of the house. He wondered what they might be discussing and allowed his mind to sift through only positive outcomes for him and Rosa.

He waved. "*Bonasira*, Signor Favale!"

Stefano Favale responded with an almost imperceptible nod. Saverio slogged home disappointed there would be no smile from Rosa to carry with him the rest of the evening. After unloading the wagon, he sat in his usual spot on the massive slab of rock and leaned against the house, a place where at least, in his own mind, dreams came true.

Within minutes, he had mentally transported himself to his favorite corner of the world walking down a tranquil stretch of beach while a beautiful girl with the loveliest green eyes whispered, *I love you.*

Alessandro arrived home a short time later. He went straight inside without saying anything to Saverio about his discussion with Signor Favale.

Salvadora asked her husband if the work at Judge Curcio's courthouse had been completed.

He pulled the wad of bills from his pocket and handed it to Salvadora. "Yes, we're done and the judge is happy. I must find more work, but for now I've been hired to clean the town's trading center every Saturday."

"Hired by Stefano?"

"Yes. It's not the work I want, but it's the money we need," Alessandro said.

He saw his son outside staring off into the sky, and he spoke in a low voice. "Saverio rode by while I spoke with Stefano." He shook his head. "Of course, he went out of his way to pass their house on the way home."

The faraway look on his son's face led Alessandro to think of his own past, and he couldn't help but chuckle remembering the potent but helpless crazy-in-love feeling from long ago that had also dominated his young life.

He stole a glance at his wife and admired the thick black hair falling to her shoulders without a trace of gray, exactly as it had been when she was a teenager. Alessandro loved Salvadora as much as he did the day they married, if not more, though now it was a mature love and not so feverish and intense as it was many years ago.

"Husband, what thought inside your head brings such laughter?"

He put his hand on Salvadora's arm. "I was thinking about the pretty girl I fell in love with long ago."

"You mean that gangly girl, all knees and elbows?"

"Well, by the time we married, I recall you had grown up. Am I right?"

She smiled. "And now, what does this same man think?"

"He's thinking about the gorgeous woman he's more in love with today."

"I see. And what might this kind gentleman really be after?"

Chapter Three

Rosa had the luxury of continuing with school for several years after Saverio ended his formal education. Her father, Stefano, owned the market building vendors utilized to sell produce, meats, fish, livestock, clothes, and sometimes even furniture. The rent money paid by individuals to use space inside the town's de facto trading center provided a guaranteed healthy monthly income for the Favale family.

Stefano was a tall, lean man with a face that was never completely shaved nor bearded—but always in a state between the two. Although Rosa was years away from any prospective marriage, he could see the day when a man of wealth might win his approval for her hand.

Stefano often said to his wife, Maria, "Someday our Rosa will marry a man who provides her financial security so she need never worry about money." He hoped the iteration would cause fate to make it true and waited for her agreement.

"Of course, dear," she said.

Inwardly, though, Maria wasn't convinced. She wondered, didn't love also figure into the equation? Of course, Maria loved her husband. He was a decent man, a respected individual in the community, and yes, he provided well for his family. She had to admit to her secret self, though, and not without shame, that while she loved her husband, for her the marriage had no passion, intensity, fury nor heat.

Her friend, Salvadora, had a fire in her eyes when she spoke about love and marriage. True, Salvadora and Alessandro were poor—as nearly all of Marinella was, or for that matter, all of Sicily—but Maria couldn't help but wonder if perhaps they had something more important than money.

When Maria was young, she could have picked a husband from any number of men, for she had been, and remained an uncommonly attractive woman. She was never boastful, but it was clear to anyone she had been blessed with the traits of a classical beauty: amber-colored eyes, full lips, thick, curly hair, and a lean, alluring figure.

Many years ago, her mother advised her to marry a man who would take care of her and the rest would take care of itself. Her mother had been wrong, but still, Maria had decided that when Rosa became of age to consider a suitor, she would tell her to marry a man she loved passionately and the rest would take care of itself.

Chapter Four

A few years passed, as did the weekly cleaning work at the trading center and the occasional jobs painting a house or a building's interior. Almost eighteen, Saverio still found his rock wall outside their house easy to lean on for emotional support and a sympathetic ear to his hopes and dreams.

Through the open door, he heard his father say Signor Favale hired him to paint their house.

Salvadora asked, "Is this something Saverio might do?"

"No, I think it's best if he and I work together."

Outside, Saverio nodded to himself, acknowledging it was probably Signor Favale who had suggested, and probably insisted upon, the work arrangement.

He knew in his heart Rosa's father wanted more for his daughter than for her to marry a painter, and that fact alone stood between him and his young love. While he understood the logic, he still didn't like it.

Dear God in Heaven, every time I think my Rosa might become the wife of another man, it hurts. It cuts deep like someone is gutting me with a knife and twisting it inside.

The evening's darkness was nearly complete. Saverio gave up on catching a glimpse of Rosa. He shifted his body flat on his back to watch the stars multiplying rapidly, wondering if she might be looking at the same sky. Finally, he rolled off the rock. With one last long look toward her house, he sighed and reluctantly went inside to bed.

The following day, Rosa learned from her mother their house was going to be painted. It was Saturday morning and time for the weekly visit to the bakery with friends, Anna and Federica. She was excited to share the news with someone, anyone, but in particular, with her confidants. Rosa told them of her secret plans to have fresh-squeezed orange juice in the mornings and biscotti in the afternoons for Saverio and his father, Signor Mancuso.

She said to her friends, "You won't see me until two seconds before school starts or two seconds after school ends. I'll be a homebody that week."

The young ladies entered Providenza's Bakery and, like everyone else, it was their favorite moment. Once customers crossed the shop's threshold, they were deluged with a mélange of visual treats and irresistible odors.

In unison, they sang out, "*Bongiornu*, Caterina. *Bongiornu*, Providenza."

Caterina was the face of the bakery who served the customers in front, but the heart and soul of the shop was her mother, Providenza, working in the kitchen next to the stovetop and an oversized oven.

Caterina spoke first. "Good morning, young ladies, how are you?"

Providenza, generally a bit of a grump and rarely seen by customers, always made an exception for Rosa and her friends. She popped her head around the corner, her nose and cheek dabbed with flour.

"Good morning, treasures. Look at the bread I took from the oven a minute ago."

She pointed to the open cabinet next to where Caterina stood. "It's sweet bread I made with you in mind."

No ordinary sweet bread, it was citrus infused with lemon and orange, drizzled with a sugary glaze and toasted almonds. Rosa knew the decision wouldn't be easy to make. There was also a crowded plate of Providenza's *sfinci*, her unique creation of Sicilian-style donuts stuffed with a creamy coffee ricotta cheese and a dash of cinnamon on top.

With their selections in hand, they left the bakeshop walking toward the central part of town. Inseparable, the three friends strolled down the street with locked arms, sometimes speaking in hushed tones and other times laughing aloud and talking even louder. Rosa would often guide her friends to a certain place, knowing Saverio would be working there, as was the case again that morning.

"Saverio, my mother said we're going to have the house painted. You're going to help, aren't you?"

"Rosa, I guarantee you I will be there."

She held two simple almond cookies. "I brought your favorite."

"Oh, Rosa, you didn't have to, but thank you."

She studied his handsome face, his wonderfully handsome face. "I guess we should let you get back to your work."

"Yes, I think my father is expecting me to finish here before he returns," he said and rolled his eyes.

The three girls locked arms again, continuing farther down the street.

They turned when Saverio shouted, "Rosa!"

High up in the air, he hung upside down from the top of the ladder. He shouted, "These cookies are delicious. Thank you again!"

Federica said, "He's crazy about you, Rosa."

"But who's crazier about who?" asked Anna.

"I think about him all the time. He's kind to me and funny, and obviously, look at him; he's beyond handsome."

"What does your father say?"

Rosa retreated to her thoughts.

I'm sixteen years old now. I like, and yes, I love Saverio and, regardless of what my father might think, I'm certain he'll give his approval one day.

She said, "I'm sure my father wants his only daughter to be happy."

"And your mother?" asked Federica.

"She told me I should marry a man I love with a passion and the rest will take care of itself."

She paused for a moment, then said, "I'll marry a man I love with a passion, but who in turn also loves me with a passion."

Anna said, "Let me guess, you're his passion."

Rosa hugged herself. "Yes, I am."

Chapter Five

1888

The wedding guests marched through the streets with the bride and groom leading the way while an accordion player strolled alongside the group playing festive music. They gathered at tables sitting in the shade of two massive bay fig trees.

Signor Favale had finally given his blessing to the marriage of Rosa and twenty-year-old Saverio. To celebrate the occasion, the wedding party feasted on dishes of breaded mussels, marinated artichoke hearts, fresh oysters, stuffed rice balls, slices of watermelon and prickly pear. Over the course of hours, family and friends took turns standing before Saverio and Rosa to offer congratulations and well wishes.

The music stopped when Rosa's father stood to speak. Standing between the newly-married couple with a hand on each of their shoulders, he said, "Thank you to our Lord God Almighty for this magnificent day. Friends, Maria and I want to thank all of you for being with us to celebrate the joining of our daughter Rosa to Saverio. We wish to welcome Saverio to our family, and we ask our beloved patron saint of Marinella, Sant'Agnese, to protect this young couple."

Stefano squeezed their shoulders and kissed each of them on the cheek.

Alessandro joined Stefano at the head of the table. He turned his attention first to Rosa and Saverio. Leaning over, he kissed them each on the cheek and whispered to both, "God bless this day, your day."

He straightened back up and surveyed the seated guests.

"First, Salvadora and I also wish to thank all of you for coming to witness this splendid occasion. Thank you, Maria and Stefano, for all your work to make this such a lovely and memorable event. The union of Rosa and Saverio today joins our two families forever."

Saverio wanted to listen to his father, but it was difficult with Rosa sitting next to him; she was so lovely dressed in a simple white gown. All he wanted was to hold her and be held by her. And to drink her in and to crawl inside her olive skin to hibernate for months. And—

Alessandro said, "Saverio is a good son. He possesses a keen mind and is a great help in the family business. He has always loved Rosa. I'm sure everyone saw this."

Alessandro placed his hand on his son's shoulder.

"I remember when Saverio learned we were going to paint Stefano and Maria's house a couple of years ago. He was so excited that one day he woke up much earlier than usual, long before daylight. He packed the supplies and tools and hitched Mulo to the wagon. I'm sure he wanted to be at their house before Rosa went to school. I heard the noise, but I didn't know what he was doing until he yelled, '*Patri, amuninni!* Sleeping won't get the job done.' I had to tell him, 'Son, you're one day early. We don't start the work until tomorrow.'"

He paused while the guests laughed.

"Salvadora and I are happy to see they found their one true love in each other. It's an extraordinary thing indeed when this happens."

He blew Salvadora a kiss, and everyone hooted and clapped.

"The old expression marriages are made in heaven is never more true than today. Rosa, we're happy to welcome you to our family, as well. We humbly ask for God's blessing of this marriage."

The new couple turned to each other.

"I love you."

"I love you too."

As the accordion player launched into a lively, happy tune, they kissed. People clapped and shouted; children danced, and everyone sang an old folk song.

Saverio thought about the night to come secretly wishing the next few hours would pass in an instant. He understood, though, Sicilian weddings were long, drawn-out affairs and first, tradition must play out.

With one last shout from the revelers, a slow, romantic song began.

Saverio whispered in Rosa's ear, "Would you dance with me?"

The day before the wedding, Maria had cleaned the one-room ramshackle cottage, a small almost-forgotten structure built by her parents. The foundation was made with heavy rocks, and the house sat over patchy sand only twenty feet from the sea. Over the last ten years, the little abode fell into significant disrepair, but with a bit of cleaning and straightening Maria thought it would make a charming spot for a romantic honeymoon.

The crude kitchen consisted of a broad, rock-hard piece of olivewood for a countertop. Its only companion was a bulky, iron pot sitting upside down, dormant, and unused for years. Adjacent to the kitchen was an open area with a still-functioning fireplace. A bed built up on wooden blocks sat in one corner, with a table and two chairs situated an arm's length away.

Maria opened the two wooden shutters on either side of the house to allow in fresh air. She swept the floors and put a sheet, blanket, and pillow on the bed. In case the night turned chilly, she stacked kindling next to the fireplace. As a final touch, she left a bottle of wine and a bouquet of fresh wildflowers on the table.

Maria turned a full circle to give the house a final appraisal and, finding her efforts satisfactory, she contemplated leaving a brief note. She stared outside to where the surf met the sand, hoping to draw inspiration from one of nature's finest exhibits. Listening to the gentle waves ripple onto the beach caressing rock outcroppings scattered along the shore, she put pen to paper, "Dear Rosa…"

Folding the note in half, she placed it next to the bottle of wine. Before she stood to leave, she opened the table drawer and found an old black and white photograph of Stefano and her in front of the house with six-year-old Rosa and her older brother, Damiano. Like most portraits of the time, no one smiled except little Rosa. Her innocent grin exposed the gap from her first missing baby tooth.

An image of Rosa at birth popped into Maria's mind. Her daughter seemed to be no more than a tiny premature mass of tangled black hair. When the midwife handed the baby to her, Maria instinctively hugged Rosa close to her chest, startled to see the most brilliant green eyes.

The midwife had said, "Don't worry, they'll change over to brown in a few weeks or months."

Stefano said, "Maria, with these eyes she must have come from the sea."

"I pray they never change," Maria said.

Once the wedding and festivities ended, Saverio helped Rosa into the wagon. He noted with pride he was now a part of the family painting business. The new words, "*e figghiu,*" added to the wooden board hanging on the side of the wagon signified it was now officially a father *and son* company.

Just the two of them, Saverio and Rosa sat close together moving toward the honeymoon cottage. Mulo lazily pulled the wagon down a pitted road of rock, sand, and earth. At times, the beast stopped and brayed, but Saverio coaxed the stubborn animal to move forward.

Rosa said, "I think Federica danced to every song. Did you see her? She even danced when there was no music. She wants to marry. It's all she talks about. I think everyone had a good time, don't you? I'm talking a lot. I guess I'm nervous. Are you nervous? Saverio, do you remember the first time we kissed?"

"How could I ever forget? It was the single-most important thing in my life to that point. I was fifteen and you were almost fourteen, right?"

Rosa blushed. "Yes. I'm glad my father didn't catch us."

Saverio recalled the exact moment on the day after Easter Sunday, where Marinella's residents participated in a small parade starting and ending at the trading center with a picnic in between.

He said, "It was starting to get dark and a bunch of us were behind the market building. One of your friends—I don't remember who—dared you to kiss me. You made everyone turn around, then you kissed me not once or twice, but three times."

"You do remember!"

Saverio said, "Yes, everything but walking home."

Rosa laughed.

"I remember it was the first time I thought, well, maybe, just maybe," Saverio said.

"Maybe, just maybe, what?"

"I might have a chance with you."

"Were you really in doubt?" she asked. "Oh, Saverio, there was never a chance any other way."

He loved the way she said his name, holding the *o* sound a little longer than necessary, *Saveriooo*, with her perfectly shaped lips. He leaned toward her. They kissed. Then they kissed again. When Mulo brayed, they both laughed, but Saverio had things to work out in his mind. A part of him was nervous, but he couldn't possibly allow his anxiety about their wedding night to show.

They rolled up to the little house as the sun yielded to the hills assembled along the coast. After Rosa went inside, Saverio removed the harness from the mule and left a bucket of water. He considered tying the animal to the wagon but concluded Mulo was far too lazy to wander away.

Rosa stopped in the doorway to take in the sight. The cottage had been cleaned, and fresh flowers had been left in a vase next to a bottle of wine. She sat at the table reading the note from her mother. Crying softly, she felt a hand on her shoulder.

"This is supposed to be a happy occasion," Saverio said.

She started to turn, but he held her tight, kissed her neck, and whispered, "I love you more than you'll ever know."

With a trembling hand, she held up the note. "Did you see the letter *Matri* wrote?"

"That's kind of her."

He kissed her neck again.

"Would you like a glass of wine?" she asked.

"No, I don't think so."

He nuzzled her ear, kissing it gently.

"She picked these wildflowers too. Aren't they pretty?"

He ran his fingers through her hair.

"Oh, yes. Much more than pretty."

"She even cleaned the fireplace and left the kindling for us."

"That's very considerate. Would you like a fire?"

Rosa twirled her black curly hair with her fingers. After a few quiet moments, she said, "No, I don't think so."

She stood and turned away from Saverio. "Would you help me with my dress?"

He undid the buttons in the back. They held hands and took two steps to the bed. Rosa turned Saverio to face away from her, slipped out of her garments, and studied her nakedness for a moment before placing her hand on his back.

He turned. "Rosa, I'll never forget how beautiful you are tonight."

The following morning with the sun peeking over the rim of the sea, Rosa sat in a chair beside the bed and, despite the chill in the house, she wore only her husband's shirt. Saverio stirred, blinking until the faint morning light fully awakened him.

"Love, what are you doing?" he asked.

She hugged herself. "Sitting here looking at you."

"You're cold. Give me my shirt and I'll make a fire."

Rosa stood. Saverio's shirt slid from her arms to the chair. She tilted her head and said, "Perhaps you can start a fire by kissing me again?"

Mother Nature decorated Sicily's northern coast, haphazardly dotting it with a variety of boulders, massive outcroppings, and smaller rocks and pebbles. Along a stretch of sand, Rosa and Saverio tiptoed with care under a sun hidden at times by lazy, dawdling clouds, allowing their feet to occasionally bathe in the warm water. Upon reaching a grand flat promontory extending forty feet above the water, they challenged each other in a race to scale to the top.

Saverio shouted as Rosa climbed ahead. "How is this possible? You climb like a mountain goat!"

When the race ended, he rested his head in Rosa's lap, enjoying the utter wonder of a never-ending view of the sea.

"Only one night of marriage and my husband calls me a goat."

"Never in one thousand years."

"And after one thousand and one?"

He stroked her cheek.

"Rosa, do you know why this part of the Mediterranean is called the Tyrrhenian Sea?"

"No, but I'm thinking you do. Why?"

"I read about the name's origin from the Greek historian, Herodotus. He said in the twelfth century before Christ, the Lydian people who lived in the Ottoman Empire experienced a terrible famine. Their ruler, King Atys, divided the population in two, sending one group of people under his son's rule to search for a better place to live. The Lydian people eventually settled in the Umbria region in northern Italy. Some say they still live there today."

Rosa said, "So, how did the sea get its name?"

Saverio's face lit up with a broad smile as he rolled onto his back to look directly at Rosa. "Ah, King Atys' son was named Tyrrhenus, the leader of the Tyrrhenian people, hence the Tyrrhenian Sea."

"Saverio, you're so smart. Where did you learn this?"

"Do you remember my last day at school when the professor from Palermo spoke and every time he said a name, he would spell the word in front of him?"

"Yes, he was odd and you were so funny."

"Well, at the end of class, I felt bad about making fun, so I spoke with him."

"You never told me. What a sweet thing to do."

"Well, I'm not sure about that, but we talked for a few minutes and he asked me about my interests."

"What was your favorite subject in school?"

"You mean, besides you?"

She kissed him. "Yes, besides me."

"I've always loved history. Anyway, he gave me a book about Greek historians. I read it and remembered the story. Ah, the professor's name was Niccolò Campana! He said to me, 'Young man, history is a most important subject. Keep in mind, the key to the future is remembering the past, and the two are linked forever like night and day.'"

"I love you, Saverio Mancuso."

"And I love you, Rosa Favale," he said, as he finger-spelled R-O-S-A on an imaginary chalkboard.

Watching the waves crash into the rocks below, they relaxed in quietude. Rosa ran her fingers through Saverio's thick black hair.

Closing his eyes, Saverio said, "Rosa, have you ever thought about going somewhere, I mean, living somewhere else?"

"Not really. What are you thinking?"

"I've been thinking about living in America, like your brother, Damiano. Your father said he's doing well, and I think he's proof of the opportunities that exist there. I love you and want to be with you forever, but I also want to be more than a house painter, and someday I want endless possibilities for our children."

"Saverio, that's a big subject."

"America or children?" he asked.

She said, "Well, both I guess."

"Someday, just as the Lydian people found a place to live, I think America could be our new home," Saverio said.

Chapter Six

Five years passed, and twice Rosa became pregnant, but both pregnancies ended in miscarriages. The mysteries of life and death confounded the young couple. A lack of money made consultation with a medical doctor out of the question. No matter, they didn't trust the so-called professional medical opinion anyway. Instead, Rosa spoke with Father Vittorio.

"Rosa," he said, "pray to God and live your life as the Holy Church teaches. At such time as God and God alone determines, you'll give Saverio a child."

A devout Catholic, Rosa accepted this with all her heart. She prayed to God every day and night; she attended church every Sunday and waited, then she waited more.

Saverio also wanted children, and while he didn't readily accept the science of medicine, he didn't give God much credit either. Not that he didn't believe in God. He did. Saverio attended Sunday mass with Rosa, saying the prayers and going through the rituals, but in his heart, he didn't think God cared or involved himself in people's lives. Instead, he did what he thought mattered in life: he loved Rosa and worked with his father to make what little money he could.

Saverio worried about the prospects for the next job and the next after that as the economy only worsened. Every day, the talk in town centered on people leaving for America, and Saverio became more convinced he and Rosa should be on the next ship too. With no work or prospects, they went to the cottage by the sea where they could wander the shoreline to think and talk without interruption.

"Rosa, let's make a new start where there's a chance for us and someday our children."

"If I can ever give you a child."

"Of course it will happen."

"When Saverio, when?"

The tears had started.

"Please don't cry."

"But I want it so much. I'd give anything."

"You've got to believe it will happen. I believe it, and I want our son or daughter or, who knows, maybe both, to be able to do more than paint a wall or sweep a floor. I'm sure this opportunity is in America."

"What about our parents? What will they do?" Rosa asked.

"I think they're done having children."

She playfully punched his chest. "No, what will they do if we leave?"

"Why can't they come too? They can."

"Do you think they would?"

She looked up at Saverio with a most hopeful expression.

Saverio said, "I would never have thought it possible, but it is. You're more beautiful today than when we married."

Distracted, he shook his head. "Well, you know, Rosa, they probably aren't interested, but we can talk to them. We should write Damiano a letter and ask him about life in, where is it he lives again?"

"In a place called Boston, but it's far away."

"The sooner we write a letter, the sooner we'll hear from him. I'm sure there are many places for us in America, but we can ask him all our questions, okay?"

Saverio was excited at the prospects he built up in his mind. He grabbed Rosa, twirled her around and pulled her close to kiss her neck. Rosa laughed at first, then pulled away. Her face clouded over with seriousness.

"Right now, all I can concentrate on is having a baby. Afterward, we can talk about it more. Saverio, I pray all the time about a child."

He pulled her close again. "I know, but do you remember the saying, 'God helps those who help themselves?' I think it means we must do our part too."

Rosa said, "Here? Now?"

"Yes. Right here. Right now." He caressed her cheek. "This time, you'll have a baby with your green eyes." He kissed her forehead. "And let's hope, your lovely face too."

During their sixth year of marriage, Rosa became pregnant again. She prayed every morning and every night, and many times in between. When she woke in the morning, Rosa's prayer was simple:

Dear God, thank you for allowing me to carry this baby through the night. You alone determine everything, and I pray for your continued blessings.

Before she slept at night she prayed:

Dear God, thank you for your blessings today. Through you, anything is possible. I beg you to help our child grow strong inside me and be with me again in the morning.

Rosa could feel the baby growing inside her day by day, and she knew this time it would be different. Father Vittorio spoke the truth, and now she would never stop her practice of the daily invocations. Some days Rosa even allowed herself to dream about holding their child in her arms.

Rosa took the short walk to visit and comfort her mother. The day before, her father simply collapsed at home, suffering a heart attack. She couldn't help but think about how happy her father would be if he were still alive to enjoy a grandchild sitting on his knee. Saverio said it seemed like happiness was never satisfied until it found its partner and best friend, sadness.

Stefano had been an important figure in town, and the news was met with shock and one question on everyone's minds—how can a healthy man of fifty-one years of age die so suddenly?

A few days passed and Rosa listened intently when God's own personal messenger in the form of Father Vittorio provided the answer to everyone's question at Sunday mass.

"Each of us is only guaranteed today. At any moment, our Lord may call upon you, me, any of us, or all of us. We must all live our lives in such a way that we remain true to God and His teachings and not count on tomorrow as the day to begin living a spiritually pure life."

Father Vittorio paused for effect, allowing his deep-driven voice to crash down on his flock who listened with rapt attention.

"All of you, hear me now! Waiting on tomorrow is waiting a day too long!"

There was a restlessness and uneasiness in the pews, and Father Vittorio was certain his words had reached their target.

Now he wished to show them it wasn't too late, and there was indeed still a path to being in God's good graces.

"Stefano Favale was a man who understood this and didn't wait. He lived each day as if it were his last, and he gave generously to the church in the same way. Today, our dear Stefano sits with our heavenly Father in paradise and serves as a reminder to us all that life comes and life goes, but the Lord our God and His ways are a constant. When each of you leaves church today, live your life as if your eternal spirit depends upon it. Because—it—does!"

Maria was devastated and grief-stricken. Though she had sometimes thought their marriage lacked passion, those thoughts now seemed silly. She tried to soothe her bruised conscience.

Dear God in heaven, I still loved him. He was a good and kind man.

Maria didn't have time to mourn for long. Within a week of her husband's death, she found herself in a battle to maintain ownership of the market building. Stefano's older brother, Raffaele, a wretched man possessing none of the kind qualities his younger brother had, argued the building property should stay with the man's side of the Favale family. The authorities and court agreed, and Raffaele wrested its control from Maria.

How ironic. She thought back to the church service when Raffaele pretended to be the consoling brother-in-law reassuring her, holding her hand and allowing the tears to flow freely onto his shoulder.

His words at the time now haunted her. "Maria, I vow the business Stefano built will continue and I'll endeavor to make it stronger, with you by my side."

She thought at the time it was a strange thing to say, but everything had happened so suddenly. It was only later she realized the scoundrel Raffaele had no plans to help her but had every intention of helping himself. When she thought about his words with her mind less clouded over, she had to choke back the vomit. Her dear friend and confidant, Salvadora, listened as Maria related the story.

"His comment *'with you by my side'* was that pig's way of saying, with me by his side in bed. Can you believe the audacity? No doubt, this is a man's world. Women can't vote and men helped Raffaele take what was rightfully mine. How can I fight or win when I couldn't even find an advocate to argue my case? How could I be so naïve? Salvadora, I tell you one thing now. I will never allow this business," and she waved her hands past her body, "to be Raffaele's business."

Chapter Seven

The land in Sicily hadn't been cared for properly in decades, and the lack of good farming practices ensured a diminishing yield each year from the exhausted soil. Signor Capelli had been a farmer his entire life when he lost his land in 1885 for a variety of reasons—poor soil, depressed crop prices, and lack of rain.

His two sons, Diego and Giacomo, worked with their father, but after losing their own farmland, the Capelli family began a new life as sharecroppers. They received a portion of the value of the crops minus the charges credited for seed, living quarters, and food. It was a system guaranteed to never allow anyone to get ahead, even in the best of times.

Diego, the elder of the two brothers, dutifully worked alongside his family, scratching out a meager existence until one day he'd had enough. In 1892, Diego left for America.

Younger brother Giacomo was the same age as Saverio. They had attended school together and remained close friends. Diego's travel to America was a common topic of conversation and they often spoke of the riches they could make when their own time came. The two waited for word about life in America, imagining only the best outcomes for Diego, but when he finally returned, his story didn't quite match their preconceived expectations.

With no money of his own, Diego explained how he employed a common practice of the day. "The man who hired me, everyone called him the *padrone*. I learned it was his job to take me and other people to America. He arranged my transportation and, once we arrived, they divided us into groups. Some went to work in factories, others to farms, and still others like me worked in construction. America is bigger than you can possibly imagine, and everywhere you look, people are working and building. It's nothing like here.

"I must warn you, though, it's not all good. This *padrone* was a rough character from Messina. He took us to the American boss who treated us like property. In New York, my *padrone* told me I would work in farming, but it turned out to be a lie. Once I arrived in this place called Michigan, I learned none of us could leave. They had guns and kept us locked up like animals. We went to work early in the morning, and we were brought back to a camp late at night. There was no escape."

Saverio's eyes were transfixed on Diego as he told his story. "So how did you get away?"

"I never understood why, but one day they let me and about twenty others go. And now it's almost 1895, and I'm finally home."

Giacomo said, "It's not all bad news, though, is it? Tell Saverio about the money."

With a bitter smile, Diego said, "Yes, I made money, but brother, despite what you hear about America, I can tell you the roads are not paved with gold. I know because I walked a lot of it."

Giacomo said, "I understand what you're saying, Diego, but I want a little change in my pocket too. I'm not ready to go yet, but someday when I do leave, they won't need to keep me prisoner. You can keep this life here; I'm never coming back."

Saverio had heard enough from the two brothers. "Judge Curcio is the smartest man we know. Giacomo let's pay him a visit tomorrow and see what he thinks. All we'll have to say is, Judge, what do you think about us working in America?"

All three men laughed.

By evening, still excited over the good news he selectively heard from Diego Capelli, Saverio could hardly contain himself. He relayed the conversation to Rosa, who rested in bed, expecting the baby's birth in about two months.

"Rosa, I thought it would be better for us to travel with a friend to America. It would be easier and less frightening if we have someone we can count on like Giacomo."

He paced back and forth explaining his rationale, becoming lost in a circuitous argument with himself about the best time to go. When Rosa didn't respond to a question, he turned to find her sound asleep, with her hands clasped in prayer over her belly.

Saverio kissed her on the forehead and whispered, "Rosa, I'm glad we're in total agreement."

The following day, Saverio met with Giacomo to continue discussing travel plans.

"I ask this as a friend," Giacomo said, while he and Saverio stood leaning against the wall of the market building. "Would you consider not taking Rosa and the baby with you to America?"

"No," said Saverio flatly.

"But it would be less costly if you only paid for yourself. Remember what my brother said. It'll be easier to take on more hardships without them. Once we find work and get settled, you can send for Rosa and the baby."

"If I go, Rosa and my baby go too. Giacomo, is it unacceptable for you to travel with all of us?"

Giacomo said, "Okay, my friend, it's a deal. Let's go see the judge."

Judge Curcio sat in the corner at his usual table. The restaurant, simple and unpretentious, served as a stand-in office of sorts for the judge who relished holding court to those seeking his opinion. He had a white linen napkin tucked into the tight neckline of his buttoned shirt while a handsome black jacket lay folded neatly across an empty chair beside him. A glass of red wine and a basket of bread sat in front of him while he waited for lunch.

Upon seeing Saverio and Giacomo, he asked, "Gentlemen, to what do I owe the pleasure of your company?"

Saverio explained they were thinking of going to America to find work and asked whether he had an opinion on the subject.

The judge cleared his throat and invited the young men to sit and have a piece of bread.

In a deep baritone voice, he began.

"Why yes, gentlemen, I do have an opinion on this and a great many other things."

As he spoke, he stroked the gray whiskers on his chin.

"Gentlemen," the judge addressed all males in the same manner regardless of age, "you are not alone in your desire to travel to America. I was reading only yesterday that in the last twenty years, it is estimated that perhaps as many as a million Italians have sought refuge there. Once it was the northern Italians who left but now," he arched his bushy eyebrows, "what started as a dribble, has turned into a flood of emigrants from Sicily. You will not be alone on your journey, that much is certain."

He sipped the wine and dabbed his mouth with his napkin.

"Gentlemen, the blame rests with our own hapless government. It is well established that the economic measures heaped upon us by those in control since the unification of Italy in 1861—not least of which includes the high taxes, punishing tariffs, and insignificant investment—were done in a purposeful manner. Our cousins from the north view us as an inferior civilization with people being the only product we can make in abundance." He interrupted his lecture and smiled toward Saverio. "And speaking of which, I understand you're expecting a baby of your own. Congratulations."

Saverio started to speak, but the judge's expression turned serious as he forged on.

"And now you and others look beyond the horizon for financial security. The United States, which by the way, I predict will be the next dominant world power, needs your strong and able bodies. It is a country hungry for development—namely, the construction of roads, bridges, grand buildings, and anything else your fertile imaginations can contrive."

The judge paused to inhale oxygen. Saverio pounced on the opportunity to interrupt with a question.

"Your Honor, do you think we should go to America?"

As a plate of steaming pasta with herring and fennel arrived, Judge Curcio ended the conversation.

"What I mean to say is, yes, pack your bags, board your ship, and make your fortune or die trying, for there is nothing here but sorrow and tears. Good day, gentlemen."

Chapter Eight

1895

Two months and a single day after Saverio and Giacomo cemented the idea of going to America, a frantic knocking came to the front door of Maria's house.

"Signora, Signora!"

A child's shouts interrupted another dreary day full of sad thoughts as Maria swept the bedroom's tile floor.

"Who in heaven's name is calling me?"

She dropped the broom and looked outside where Sara, a young girl who lived close by, jumped up and down, flailing her arms while she yelled, "Signora, the baby is coming. Signora, Rosa is having the baby. You must come now."

"Thank you, God," Maria said to herself.

She hastily threw a cover over the bed she used to call her own.

Maria, having lost the steady market building income, found herself forced to convert her home into a boarding house. She cooked. She cleaned. And with three paying tenants, she earned enough to keep the house. In the process, Maria gave up her own bedroom and moved into a small area off the side of the kitchen where she slept and allowed herself a few private moments each day to recall happier times.

The girl's voice called out again. "Signora, are you coming? My mother said—"

"Yes, child, I'm on my way."

Maria hurried to the best of her ability, telling Sara more than once she could no longer run as she once did. Breathless, Maria stepped into the house to find Saverio, Salvadora, and Sara's mother waiting. Within minutes, Sara and her mother went home, leaving Saverio to wander alone outside the front door.

Salvadora hugged Maria and said, "The midwife, Giovanna, arrived a short time ago."

She glanced at the door and, in a whisper, said, "Maria, please come into the kitchen."

"Is everything okay?"

Salvadora spoke in a quiet voice. "Giovanna said she expected a quick delivery, but a short time ago she said Rosa was having a difficult time with the baby's position inside the womb."

Maria's eyes filled with tears.

Salvadora pulled up her apron and wiped Maria's face. "Listen to me, no tears. You need to be strong for Rosa."

Maria's hardened lips yielded to a weak smile, a first in many months. She hurried to the bedroom, tapped on the door and entered. Rosa, soaked in sweat and mumbling words no one understood, seemed oblivious to her mother even as they held hands. Minutes turned into an hour, then two, then four. Her body had gone beyond its capacity for enduring pain. She had no reserve left for further twisting, pulling, and squeezing. Without warning, Rosa raised herself up in bed with a frenzied, almost crazed expression.

She grabbed the midwife's arm and yelled, "Do what you must, but deliver my baby now."

The fury drained from her face, and her body sagged back into the bed. Other than an occasional cry or moan, she didn't speak again.

Saverio continued pacing, first outside, then inside until he heard a baby's loud cry.

Giovanna walked out of the room grim-faced carrying an infant. She said, "Your son is fine. He's healthy and–"

Saverio managed a smile. He said, "And Rosa—"

"I'm so sorry. I did everything I could, but the delivery was too, well, it was too difficult for her."

Stunned, motionless, and in disbelief, he stared at her.

What did she say? Why would this person say something so vile on the birth of our first child?

"Rosa!"

He brushed past the newborn baby wrapped in a blanket as if it were nothing more than a bag of flour and raced into the room. Maria stepped back from the bed and braced herself against the wall for a moment before creeping away.

Saverio cradled Rosa in his arms. "Please, Rosa, please wake up. I beg you. God, I'll do anything you ask of me. Anything, anything, please give me back my Rosa. Please, God."

Soon the wailing from a grown man, a howl like the cry of an injured animal, drowned out the bawling of his hungry son. He closed his eyes and sank into a vast, unforgiving darkness.

Chapter Nine

Saverio had kept his promise to Rosa.

Only weeks prior to giving birth, she said, "If anything should happen to me, I beg you to take our child to church. I made a promise to God." She placed her hands on his chest and searched his eyes. "Please, it's important to me."

The urgency and hopefulness in her voice was a powerful force. It seemed like an easy promise to make to Rosa so young and full of life.

Whenever he recalled the conversation, his own words tormented him. "I will, but nothing will happen to you. Someday you'll be an old woman doting on your own grandchildren."

More than two years had passed since that conversation with Rosa. It was a Sunday morning, and Saverio buttoned the shirt of his young son, Tommaso.

"Please stop wiggling. We must leave now or we'll be late."

Saverio called to his mother as they stepped outside to wait in front of the house. Immediately, Tommaso tried to break his father's grip to run free. Even though the small tot couldn't go far if set loose, he would scurry from mud puddle to mud puddle haphazardly dotting the road. Dirtying his one set of church clothes wasn't an acceptable option. Salvadora pulled the door behind her and took Tommaso's hand as Saverio unhooked his finger from the back of the boy's shirt.

During the church homily, Saverio's mind drifted to the cruelty in the world. He thought how both Rosa and her father were taken from the world far too soon. Only months after Stefano died, the wretched creature most people called God was still not satisfied as he took yet again.

His own father had died unexpectedly when he fell from a ladder. Saverio remembered it as not much of a fall, perhaps eight feet at most, while working at home. Slipping from the top rung, his father fell onto his back, but seemed fine, at first leaping to his feet more embarrassed than hurt. When his father laughed, Saverio joined him. They joked about the times they'd slipped or fallen in the past, recalling the many close calls they'd had.

Later in the evening he began coughing up a small amount of blood.

Saverio recalled the last words his father spoke that evening.

"If I don't feel right in the morning, I'll go to the doctor."

But the next sunrise never came for Alessandro. During the night, he coughed up a copious amount of blood and died falling off the bed while putting his shoes on.

The sermon ended. Saverio never heard a single word from Father Vittorio. Yanked from his own thoughts as the parishioners began to stand, Saverio concluded his own silent homily.

Your Wretchedness, you're cruel and heartless, and if it were possible, I would hate you even more.

As he stood, he added an audible "Amen" to join in with the rest of the congregation.

Not long after Alessandro died, the economy sank even lower. Times had been difficult before, but now even fewer painting jobs came Saverio's way, and he found himself willing to swallow his pride in exchange for additional income. Although he despised Raffaele for cheating Maria out of the market building, Saverio felt he had no choice but to continue the Saturday cleaning work. He had completed another long day and was passing by Maria's house on his way home. She sat on the steps, resting from the endless drudgery.

"*Bonasira*. Did you see Tommaso today?" Saverio asked.

"I left him sitting with Salvadora an hour ago."

"By the way, Maria, I wanted to tell you something. After I finished cleaning the livestock area at *your* market building, I accidentally dropped a shovel full of cow or maybe it was pig shit, I really can't remember anymore, into Raffaele's boots."

"Saverio, what are you talking about?"

He said, "I know you've seen the fancy leather boots Raffaele changes into when he finishes work in your building and prances around, showing off the new-found wealth he stole from you."

"Of course, how could I forget those silly boots?"

"Well, if it brings you any satisfaction, now Raffaele's precious boots stink as bad as his own soul," Saverio said.

"You didn't?"

"Well, let's say some boots walk around shit and others were born to carry it inside them. The cretin will never figure it out."

"What did he do?" asked Maria.

"Hmm, let me think for a second." Saverio doubled over with laughter. Finally he said, "Yes, yes, the last time I saw him, he was slithering his way down the street with his nose up in the air trying to figure out where the stench came from."

"Saverio, you're terrible. Thank you."

"It was my pleasure."

After Rosa's death, Salvadora helped with Tommaso's care, as did Maria, who came to the house at least once a day, sometimes taking her grandson back to her own home. Between them both, Salvadora and Maria became Tommaso's new combined substitute mother, but they worried Saverio needed a new wife whom little Tommaso might call his mama.

While Saverio and Tommaso kicked a ball to each other in the road, Maria and Salvadora watched from inside the house.

Maria said, "It's not easy for me to say, but I must tell Saverio I want him to be happy and to take a new wife. Wouldn't it be good for him and certainly Tommaso? Every boy needs a mother, right?"

Salvadora said, "I understand how hard it is for you to say. I came to love Rosa like she was my own daughter, but yes, I agree with you."

They looked at each other and broke into tears as they hugged.

Maria stepped back. "Look at us, two old widows crying all the time. They have their whole lives in front of them. With your permission, I'm going to say something to Saverio. He must understand I want the best for him and Tommaso."

"I understand, and yes, you have my permission, but you didn't need it."

Saverio's voice sounded at the door. "Son, go put your ball away. I'll be with you in a minute."

Maria said, "Saverio, I want to tell you something."

As Tommaso scampered away, Maria took a deep breath. "I wanted you to know if you choose to take another wife, I support you. I miss Rosa too, but I want what's best for you–"

They heard a ball bounce and a gleeful squeal from a small boy somewhere in the house.

Maria sniffled. "And what's best for Tommaso."

Saverio said, "Listen, Maria, I appreciate your concern, but stop worrying. I'm fine, and so is Tommaso." He coughed. "I'm not interested in marrying again."

He turned to leave, then stopped and said, "Ever again."

At the market building the following Saturday, Saverio was finishing up his work when Raffaele suggested he forget Rosa and find himself a new wife.

Saverio could see Raffaele was making a pathetic attempt to entertain other men standing nearby when he said, "Rosa was stunning, every man here would agree, I'm sure."

As he spoke, he used his hands to signify Rosa's shapely figure.

"But she's gone now, and you need a new woman to keep you warm at night, yes?"

Saverio's blood boiled.

This bastard was her uncle.

"Have you no shame?" Saverio asked.

"Listen," he said with a sneer, "there are other women who can do for you what Rosa–"

The first punch packed years of anger, grief, and frustration behind it. Raffaele never saw it coming. One moment his face appeared normal and in the next instant, his flattened nose erupted, gushing blood. The next punch crashed into his jaw, slamming his head sideways into the wall. Through his open mouth and busted nose, pieces of teeth and blood spattered the floor, the wall, and others close by.

Barely conscious and seemingly unaware, the lump of life began a slow collapse toward the floor. Mercilessly, Saverio rained more punches down until his friend Giacomo dragged him away from pummeling Raffaele to certain death.

Like a man possessed, Saverio ran all the way to the beach cottage, collapsing against the door. He stared at a photograph of Rosa and himself, remembering the happy times he spent with the woman who possessed the most beautiful soul the world had ever known. He looked at the darkness smothering the sea, wishing somehow he might conjure his Rosa to walk out of the water and sit beside him. Banging his bloodied fist on the ground, he sobbed uncontrollably. He knew miracles never happened and they never would.

He screamed, "Why? Tell me! Why did you leave me?"

Falling to his side, he curled into a ball. "Rosa, I would trade everything to be with you."

Chapter Ten

The day after Saverio battered Raffaele, Giacomo stopped by to check on his friend. Their discussion turned to the subject of travel. Saverio had saved a modest sum of money from the scarce work, but it would take more time to save for both he and his son to go.

"Giacomo, especially after last night, I'm ready to go to America. Every place I go and every thought I have, I see Rosa. She's everywhere, but she's nowhere."

Giacomo said, "After you left last night, Raffaele surprised everyone. He's tougher than we thought. He sat up and even smiled and said to tell you he expects you next Saturday at work. I think he knows he was wrong, if you can believe it."

Saverio examined his fists with the raw, open wounds on his knuckles. "Does he? Who cares? You know, Giacomo, it's not just Rosa dying that hurts, but what does Tommaso have here? What is here for me except, if I'm lucky, a wall to slap paint on or manure to shovel? Why should we live in a place with no hope? No, we'll go to America. I need the money, so I'll clean that jackass's building, but one day I'll make decisions for Tommaso and me and never allow anyone else to control our lives again."

With a slight hesitation in his voice, Giacomo said, "Let me ask you something. Would you consider leaving Tommaso with his grandmothers until you can—"

"Never," he said defiantly. "Never, never, never. Once we leave, we're finished here."

Later in the afternoon, Saverio recalled his conversation with Giacomo when his mother said, "You can go to America and be like the other *ritornati* who go to work there and return after a year or so. Leave Tommaso with me. Maria said she'll help too. Perhaps conditions here will improve in time."

"It sounds like you and Maria and Giacomo have been planning this for a while."

His mother said, "I don't know what you mean."

"*Matri*, never mind. You see how things are. It'll never get better. If I weren't here, I would be afraid someone would take Tommaso to work in the sulfur mines. I never want to worry about that."

Saverio thought about the two-day trip he and his father had made on foot years before to the town of Sutera where his father's brother lived. Just before reaching the small town, they stopped at an enormous sulfur mining operation in Cozzo Disi.

"*Matri*, I can still see those boys in my mind. Many of them were abandoned by their families because they had no food to eat. Some were younger than I was at the time. They were naked and covered in the dust as they went down into the mine again and again carrying heavy sacks of sulfur to the surface. *Patri* said they used them because they were small enough to fit in the narrow shafts. He called them the *carusi*, the mine boys, and said the bags were heavier than some of the smaller boys.

"Some of the older boys couldn't even straighten their backs any longer and were permanently disfigured. I remember one boy who stared at me with nothing but emptiness in his eyes. I didn't know whether he hated me or just wondered why it was him and not me. I've never been able to get his face out of my mind. I know there was a reason *Patri* wanted me to see it. I never want to worry about Tommaso being taken to do the horrid work I saw."

Saverio coughed a few times, until it became more violent and his mother brought him a cup of water.

"You've been coughing a lot lately. Are you okay?"

"I'm fine. It's the thought of those horrible mines that makes me choke."

"I understand how you feel, but I worry for you and Tommaso in a strange, faraway place," she said.

Maria and Salvadora never tired of discussing ways to dissuade Saverio from leaving and taking Tommaso with him to America.

Maria said, "I still think Saverio remarrying is a good idea. Maybe a new wife wouldn't be inclined to leave her family behind in Sicily. When I see him later, I'm going to try again."

While Tommaso practiced writing his letters and numbers, Maria saw an opportunity to casually raise the subject again.

"Saverio, have you given more thought to what we discussed a while back?"

"Maria, what is it we—" He interrupted himself. "No, Tommaso, you're writing your nine backwards. Do you remember what year you were born?"

"Yes, 1895."

"Good, and the month?"

"January."

"Fantastic, and the day?"

Tommaso hesitated and finally with a broad smile, he bounced in the chair and shouted, "Ten!"

"Excellent. Let's practice writing your birth date, then we'll start over with your name, okay?"

"Yes, *Patri*."

Saverio turned his attention back to Maria.

"Sorry, Maria. Please tell me again what we discussed a while back."

Cornered, now she had to address it in a more direct fashion. "Well, I said I would completely support you if you, well, if you decided to marry again."

"Maria, I know what you're thinking, but you of all people should understand since Rosa was your daughter. There's no future in this place for us, but a life in America gives Tommaso a chance to become something other than a dirt farmer or a mine worker. If I do nothing else in life, I'll give your daughter's son a chance to succeed. I'm sure Rosa would agree with me."

As he finished speaking, he fell into a coughing fit, holding onto the table until it passed.

Saverio knelt next to Tommaso.

"Son, look at this."

He held a tattered page from a textbook with basic phrases in the English language and their translations and pronunciations. "Someday we'll learn to speak a new language."

"Okay, *Patri*."

During the night, Maria dreamed of an endless void, a vast sea of blackness where she could see nothing and only hear a faint whisper of a child's voice. Through the gloomy darkness, her body raced above the surface of the water toward the muted sound. When she arrived in the center of the abyss, she glimpsed a faint outline of a face she didn't recognize, but with the voice of a sweet, innocent child she knew to be Tommaso.

She heard his words being spoken from somewhere on an enormous ship. "*Nonna*, why can't I stay with you?" The words repeated over and over.

Now Tommaso's winsome, boyish face appeared floating over the ship staring blindly into a chasm of darkness. Maria extended her hand toward him, but she could never quite reach far enough to touch him. She felt raindrops and saw a sadness cloud over Tommaso's expression as his face began to wash into the sea. The gentle rain turned into a downpour. Maria screamed for her grandson and reached for him one more time.

She awoke from her nightmare, her heart pounding, her body soaked with sweat, and her arms extended into the air. Exhausted, she staggered from the bed and looked out into the leaden, nighttime sky, clutching herself in fear of the future.

Chapter Eleven

Saverio scaled the ladder thirty rungs high to begin the process of whitewashing the walls of the Sacred Heart of Jesus, a church dating back to the fourteenth century. A long climb, it wasn't easy with a bucket and tools strapped to his back. Reaching the top, a vicious cough seized him as he hung onto the ladder. Once the coughing subsided, a lightheadedness overtook him. He began the slow descent back down, almost as angry as he was dizzy knowing he would have to climb up once again.

Upon reaching the safety of firm ground, he began to cough again without stopping. Father Luigi placed a hand on Saverio's back, asking if he was okay.

Saverio straightened up. "Yes, I'm fine, Father, it's nothing."

The old priest coughed sympathetically as he shuffled away.

After Father Luigi disappeared, the coughing returned, this time more violently, and for the first time Saverio noticed tiny dots of blood on his hand.

The priest reappeared from around the corner carrying a cup of water. "Young man, I hope this will help. Sit for a moment and catch your breath."

He finished the work at the church, taking twice as long as he had estimated and for precious little money. Saverio experienced more coughing fits with blood and felt increasingly fatigued with more physically laborious tasks. In the space of a few months, the mysterious ailment restricted his movement and ability to do even simple, ordinary duties.

Saverio didn't believe in things he couldn't understand, including the practice of medicine. Nonetheless, his mother finally convinced him to visit a doctor.

A consultation identified the cause of his coughing, and fate cruelly turned his world upside down as the doctor's diagnosis was swift, unmerciful, and summed up in few words. "You have a cancer in your lungs. There is no cure and you won't live another year."

Saverio sat alone waiting for the doctor's return. He thought about how life was a series of events and consequences for which God received all the credit for the good, but no responsibility for the bad.

Your Wretchedness, you're a pitiless and malicious creature. You take and take and, even when you give, you take. I promised Rosa, so I bring Tommaso to church. I kneel. I cross myself. I say the words. As long as I live, though, I won't forget what you did to Rosa or my father. When my time comes, I only want to be with her again.

When the doctor returned, he said, "I'll give you medicine to help ease your pain."

"I don't need anything."

"Listen to me. I can't do anything to stop or even slow the advance of the cancer, but soon you'll need this, and more, eventually."

Saverio shook his head. "Doctor, I feel fine."

"You may feel fine now, but the day is coming when the pain will be so unbearable, you'll pray for death because that will be your only comfort."

Saverio stopped on his walk home and sat under a large shade tree to rest. Closing his eyes, he saw the face of death and smiled.

"Do you think I'm afraid of you? Listen, friend, were it not for Tommaso, I'd dance with you today."

He dragged himself along the road with thoughts focused on his son. Now more than ever, he knew there was only one escape for Tommaso—America.

Saverio spoke with Giacomo and made arrangements for Tommaso's travel. His friend was working on his own plans to go to America in September with a group of other young men from Marinella, and Saverio intended to have Tommaso on that ship.

He also wrote a letter to Rosa's older brother, Damiano, in Boston, asking about the possibility of Tommaso living with him and his family. He shared the bad news and asked for a reply as soon as possible. Time was critical. Saverio knew he had to put all the pieces of the puzzle in place before it was too late.

Just as the doctor had said, Saverio's health steadily declined. One hot July morning, a strange sensation came over him and, for a change, he felt a burst of energy. With enthusiasm, Saverio explained to his mother and Maria his plan was near completion.

He said, "I've saved the twenty-four dollars for the voyage and have the same amount to give to Damiano as a goodwill gesture. He's agreed to accept Tommaso and raise him in Boston with his family. I've done everything I can to make sure he'll have a good start in America."

Emotions aside, they found no legitimate argument to counter his logic.

Following the conversation, a tiredness overtook him. Saverio struggled to his room, carrying a handkerchief to catch the blood coming up from his lungs when he coughed. The sight terrified Tommaso, and his father tried to explain his illness, but the child understood neither the sickness nor its consequences.

"Someday you'll be with your mother and me again."

"When?"

"After you live a long and prosperous life in America where great things await you."

Tommaso cried. "I don't want to leave."

Later in the evening, while his son slept next to him in bed, Saverio wept as he brushed the boy's hair back from his sweaty forehead.

He said, "Tommaso, I'll try, but I'm not sure I won't leave you first."

Saverio was too sick to work. Eventually he sold all the painting equipment, tools, wagon, and Mulo. Fingering the currency, he felt satisfaction with the trade, hoping the money would help his mother after he and Tommaso had left Marinella on their separate journeys.

Knowing his life was ending soon, Saverio worried his son would forget him and never even know of his own mother. He bought writing paper and a small wood frame to hold the picture of Rosa and himself. While Tommaso slept, Saverio tried to capture in words everything he wished to say. Once the letter was finished, he put the picture and note in a small leather pouch and placed it on a shelf in his room before dragging himself back to bed.

His last thought before he fell asleep was that someday, Tommaso would look at the photograph and read the letter, knowing who his parents were and that they loved him dearly.

Chapter Twelve

A week before Tommaso's departure, Saverio experienced weakness and such crushing pain, he knew it would be a close race between living long enough to accompany Tommaso to the boat or his own death. Other than going with his son, he had no plans to leave his bed again. A chamber pot sat next to him, and his mother brought him food that was left uneaten.

Saverio's final days were a vicious concoction of suffering and agony. His existence was without much awareness of any activity around him, including the many hours his mother sat next to him using a wet towel to wipe away the sweat trying to cool his body.

Saverio didn't wake up when Tommaso played catch throwing a ball against the bedroom wall. When *Nonna* Salvadora called her grandson for lunch, he threw the ball one last time, accidentally knocking the leather pouch behind the shelf.

The night before Tommaso was set to leave, Saverio fought through the haze and delirium of the opium-based pain medication. His lips curled into a wicked smile as he began a silent conversation.

Hello, your Wretchedness. I'm still here. All I want from you is the strength to rise out of bed in the morning to go with my son to the boat. I ask for nothing else and I expect nothing more from you, charlatan. Then you can do with me what you will in eternity.

The following morning, the harsh light jarred Saverio from sleep without any mercy. His wasted mind and body suffered from such pain he didn't know if he would even be able to stand again. He took a swig from the bottle of painkiller, twice the normal amount, and struggled to breathe. When his feet touched the floor, he drank another shot.

Saverio was determined to walk to the port holding his son's hand. As they left the house, he thought he might be hallucinating—was this his Mulo and the wagon in the street?

Finally, he realized, this was no illusion. The man who purchased the mule and wagon returned and, in a kind act from a virtual stranger, brought it back for Saverio to use on his last ride. Saverio waved his hand to his mother and Maria to climb into the wagon.

His mother said, "Saverio, you need to ride too."

Between wheezing and coughing, he shook his head. "Tommaso will help me…walk." He patted Mulo's rump with little energy. "Old friend…one final time."

The ramble to the port took monumental effort from Saverio. Neighbors peered out from their houses, watching the skeletal figure drag himself down the road. Under normal circumstances, the walk took five minutes, but on this day it took nearly an hour.

When they arrived, Saverio struggled to drag himself into the back of the wagon, where he collapsed. He took a long draw from the bottle, coughed, and took another, emptying it of its contents, hoping he would sleep and never wake again.

His friend Giacomo and a group of young men found refuge from the heat sitting in a spot of shade provided by a rare tree near the port. By the time Giacomo walked over to the wagon, Saverio was lying motionless.

Giacomo rubbed Tommaso's head. "Hey, little man, are you ready for a big boat ride?"

Tommaso sat next to his father, holding onto his shriveled body.

Using what little strength he had left, Saverio opened his eyes to greet Giacomo and spoke in a raspy whisper. "The money…Tommaso's uncle?"

"Yes, don't worry. I'll take care of it."

His words were slurred. "Money…in his bag."

"I'll take care of Tommaso. Everything will be okay."

Giacomo continued with a quiet desperation in his voice. "Saverio, I'm sorry. God, I wish something could be done."

"It's over…for me." Saverio closed his eyes as his hand slid over to rest on his son.

Tommaso clung to Giacomo's leg, watching the adults jostle and elbow their way to stand in a line moving nowhere.

Giacomo rubbed the top of the boy's head. "That's good, Tommaso. Stick with me. We'll take this ferry all the way across the Tyrrhenian Sea. We'll play cards and have fun. Tomorrow morning when we wake up, we'll be in Naples!"

Tommaso stared at Giacomo, not comprehending what was happening.

"Next, we'll take a big ship to carry us to America and to your Uncle Damiano, okay?"

Over the next hour, Tommaso held his bag to his chest as other people dragged their belongings alongside them. Finally, he and Giacomo found themselves standing at the front of the line ready to board.

Not yet six years of age, Tommaso boarded a boat carrying a small bag and the clothes on his back, taking the first step to his ultimate destination and leaving behind everything his young life had ever known.

From the railing, Tommaso peered over the side of the boat in the direction where his father lay. In the distance, he spied his grandmothers standing next to the wagon.

Giacomo said, "Tommaso, wave at them."

Tommaso stood motionless, staring at his past.

Chapter Thirteen

No sleeping quarters existed on the ferry, but twelve rows of benches were affixed to the wood decking inside the main cabin. There was additional seating outside for passengers wishing to take in fresh air and sunshine during the voyage to Naples.

The group claimed an area inside near a window. Tommaso held Giacomo's leg looking at the four other men—Simone and his younger sixteen-year-old brother Santo who had escaped from an abusive uncle. Alberto, the simpleton son of an impoverished farmer, sat next to Santo nervously bouncing his knee, and Ottaviano, a laborer whom others simply called Gigante. Somewhere along the line, the genes of a giant had snuck into his family tree.

All had space to sit except Tommaso, who sat on the floor in front of Giacomo. Once they situated themselves, the group resorted to their old practices in Sicily, talking about the future and playing a card game called Scopa.

A short time after boarding, the vessel released from the dock and inched out to sea headed in a northeast direction. Tommaso kept his head in his hands, hiding his tears, and occasionally snuck peeks at his new companions.

About thirty minutes into the passage, the waves intensi-fied, tossing the ferry a bit. Startled, Tommaso looked up. Even at his young age, he detected a paleness in Giacomo's face.

"I've never felt like this before," Giacomo said, as he took a deep breath and tried to steady himself with his hands gripping the bench.

Simone, who spent time fishing off the coast of Marinella, said, "Take my spot and keep your eyes fixed on the horizon. It'll help you adjust to the motion."

Giacomo slid next to the side scuttle. "I know this may sound strange since we live on an island, but I'm thirty-two years old and have never been on a boat."

Simone said, "Watch the horizon and breathe in the fresh air."

Simone repositioned Tommaso to sit against his legs and placed his hand on the boy's shoulder. Tommaso bent his head back and fixed his big brown eyes on the man, who spoke in a high-pitched voice that didn't match his rough-looking exterior.

"If you feel sick, be sure to do the same. Watching the horizon plays a trick on your brain." He tapped his finger on Tommaso's forehead. "Your body moves with the motion, but not your mind. Even still, I know what it's like when the water is too rough."

Giacomo also listened to the explanation and kept his focus fixed on the point where the sky and the sea became one.

Simone smiled warmly at Tommaso. "The sea is in your veins, young man, and a few waves won't bother you." He tousled the boy's hair and laughed in a high-pitched manner not unlike the titter of a young teenager.

Tommaso closed his eyes and drifted away to the safety of sleep, but after a brief nap he awoke to a state of confusion, scrutinizing the men's faces until the new reality set in.

Santo, bored with the endless hands of cards, asked Tommaso if he wanted to go out to the deck and explore. With encouragement from Giacomo, he took Santo's hand.

"Keep an eye on him, little brother," Simone said.

Santo, tall and painfully thin as if his weight had not yet caught up with his height, suffered the misfortune of having monstrous ears that stuck out from his head almost like small wings he might use to go airborne. As the two reached the open deck, the brisk, fresh air provided a pleasant change from the staleness inside.

A few kids older than Tommaso but younger than Santo sat in a circle playing with lizards they'd captured before boarding the boat. Santo guided Tommaso to an open bench where they followed the entertainment provided by the small creatures.

One of the boys held up his four-legged reptilian prisoner. "This is the biggest one. He should be the leader of the group."

Another boy said, "Yes, but look at his tail. It's broken in half."

Still another said, "We'll let them race to see which one is the fastest. Let's line them up here."

Santo turned to Tommaso and asked, "What's wrong with your father? Is he sick?"

Tommaso shrugged, his eyes becoming moist, but stayed silent. Santo quickly changed the subject.

"Hey, when I was in school I learned that lizards like those," he motioned with his narrow chin in the direction of the boys, "are related to dinosaurs."

Tommaso turned his focus to the small brown creatures.

"Well, at least that's what I remember, but did you know they can change their color to fit their background? They do this to hide from their enemies."

A silence fell over the one-sided conversation, until Santo said, "I don't remember my parents at all, and my uncle wasn't nice to me or Simone. I used to wish I could hide myself from him. I became like the lizard and changed colors to escape from my uncle."

Tommaso stared off into the distance.

"Hey, let's go over to the railing and see how far away we are from Marinella," Santo said.

Tommaso's hopes were dashed when he found he could see nothing more than a hint of the rugged mountains edging along parts of the coastline.

Santo spotted tears welling in Tommaso's eyes. He said, "Okay, watch this."

He used the index fingers from each hand to hold his ears flat against his head and puffed up his cheeks.

When he let go of his ears, they flung forward while Santo made a whooshing noise, hoping for a reaction from Tommaso. No laugh. No smile.

"Well, let's go inside and find out what the others are doing."

Tommaso dropped to the deck sitting cross-legged, staring at the distant coast. Unable to think of anything else to do, Santo sat next to him and waited in silence. Almost two hours passed, and the late afternoon sun grew into early evening setting low on the horizon. As the air began to cool, Santo was relieved when his new young friend stood ready to return inside.

A darkness began to envelop the ferry and the sea calmed to nothing more than a large flat lake. Giacomo removed a plentiful amount of bread and a hefty block of cheese from his bag. He tore two chunks of bread for himself and Tommaso and passed the bread to Alberto while Simone removed a sharp knife from its sheath to cut each person a portion of cheese.

Giacomo said, "Here, Tommaso, you must eat. Look at Gigante. He isn't wasting any of his food. Nor is he wasting any time."

Gigante looked at the others, stopping only momentarily, before shoveling another hunk of cheese into his mouth.

As the faint light of evening finally surrendered to darkness, passengers spread blankets and bags to fashion any type of bedding for the long uncomfortable night. Giacomo sprawled on the bench with a blanket thrown over Tommaso and himself. Within an hour, bodies stretched out on floors and benches in every manner conceivable as they waited for morning's arrival.

Hours later an early glimmer of light served as an alarm to awaken passengers and prompt movement inside the ferry cabin. A faint coastline appeared on the horizon, and the wayfaring commuters busied themselves repacking clothing and blankets before moving outside into the cool, morning air to view what for most of them would be a strange, new place.

In the distance, a defined landmass was beginning to take shape.

Giacomo asked, "This must be the port of Naples, right?"

Alberto scratched his head. "I never studied geography in school. Maybe this is Rome?"

Tommaso listened to the conversation and wondered if they had arrived at the place his father often spoke of, *L'America*.

Gigante hoisted Tommaso onto his massive shoulders. "Little man, welcome to Naples!"

As Tommaso watched the port of Naples come into view, his father took his last breath. The walk to the port the day before had exhausted what little strength he had left and, upon his arrival back home, neighbors walked over to help lift Saverio out of the wagon and carry him into the house.

He never regained consciousness. Saverio left his earthly domain and went to a place where Rosa appeared to him as she did on the night of their wedding.

He heard her sweet voice.

"Saverio, let's go swimming in the sea."

The brilliant blue water with deep green swells encircled her, yet it was clear and translucent. He could see her feet didn't touch bottom, as if she were floating.

She tilted her head and called again, "Come over here to me."

Saverio stepped into the water, sensing its immediate comfort and warmth. He had never felt so young, so alive, and so vigorous.

"Rosa, where have you been?"

"I've always been here."

He couldn't see where her eyes ended and the sea began.

"I don't understand where we are. Rosa, I'm afraid."

"You have nothing to fear. Soon, you'll understand everything. Here, hold my hand. The water is warm and will bring you pleasure."

"Oh, God, I missed you."

She touched his face. "Saverio, I've always been with you."

"I'm worried about Tommaso."

"My love, you need never worry again."

Saverio took Rosa's hand, and as the water covered his head, absolute contentment consumed him.

Chapter Fourteen

A crew member shouted their arrival in Naples. "Attention. We'll begin disembarking portside in the next few minutes. Make sure you take all your personal belongings."

While they waited along with forty some-odd passengers, Giacomo and the other men's preoccupation now focused on the next step, their voyage on board the German steamship, the SS *Grabow*, taking them to America. Several passengers began to push and shove to position themselves as close to the exit as possible.

Giacomo scooped Tommaso and his bag under one arm and inched forward with the crowd. Even though it had been less than a day, Giacomo sensed immediate relief when he stepped on the ground, real solid ground, the kind that didn't move, with rock, dirt, and earth beneath his feet. He eased Tommaso down and sat next to him.

The young boy kneeled and opened his small bag, searching the contents with his hands until he found the sweet bread his grandmothers gave him for the trip. Tommaso removed the crumbling loaf from the wrapping paper and held it with out-stretched arms toward Giacomo, searching his eyes for approval.

"You should eat some before these hungry men take all of it," Giacomo said.

He took a bite and, one by one, each person, starting with Santo, asked Tommaso for a little. By the time it made its way back to the boy, only a small piece remained. He swallowed it in one bite and smacked his lips.

They continued their walk, bags and suitcases in tow, under a hot baking sun. Almost ready to take a rest, Giacomo caught his second wind and yelled to the others that he could see the SS *Grabow*, a 395-foot, 4,000-ton German steamer with the older single-screw type propulsion. Rusty and antiquated, it was sandwiched between two shiny and significantly larger, more modern steamers.

The *Grabow* lacked the state-of-the-art amenities of the newer steamships, and the voyage would take a day or two longer. Nonetheless, it sat proudly, indifferent to those truths, with a long gangway extended portside like a welcoming hand to greet passengers. While lacking the luster and newer technology of its cousins, it made up for the shortcomings in one regard—the less expensive fares were a critical and decisive factor for most of the simple peasants set to travel on it.

Hundreds of people camped out where the *Grabow* berthed, including three men resting beside a humongous trunk.

Alberto approached the group. "Is there room in there for me to sleep?" he asked.

One of the men responded, "Actually, we use it to carry our tools and supplies."

Giacomo said, "Sorry, that's my friend's attempt at humor. We were talking about the boarding procedures. Have you traveled on one of these ships before?"

They learned the veteran seafarers had already been to America, with this being their third trip, and described themselves as marble sculptors.

The same man who spoke before, said, "We met an American who told us he would sponsor our travel, because of the interest in hand-sculpted Italian marble artwork. We were skeptical, but it turned out to be true. The American imports the raw marble from Tuscany, and there are rich people in New York who pay tidy sums of money for," he held up his hands, "marble artwork sculpted by these. They come to the shop to watch us work. We carry all our tools with us, mallets, chisels, files, rubbing stones; everything here in the big hut, as we call it."

Giacomo asked, "Why don't you stay?"

"Well, we like making money, but our home is Italy. We'll continue this way until the Americans fall out of love with us."

Giacomo asked for advice on the boarding process, then thanked the kind gentlemen for their help. They walked until they found a spot to squeeze into under an enormous shade tree where groups of other travelers also camped out.

Simone volunteered to find a ship crewman while the others set their suitcases and duffle bags in the dappled sunlight and began playing Scopa.

A few minutes into the game, Gigante took pity on Tommaso. He said, "Hey, little one, do you know how to play this card game?"

He shook his head.

"Come here and I'll teach you. It's easy. If we can play it, anyone can."

Alberto said, "He's right, Tommaso. My father told me when I was a baby, my mother dropped me on my head. I'm not smart, but sometimes I win this game."

Santo asked, "Did your father say how many times your mother dropped you?"

"He told me the story many times. Maybe it happened more than once. I don't remember."

Giacomo said, "Poor Alberto. It's your turn, friend."

Gigante held out his arm to Tommaso. "Okay, sit on my lap and you can watch what I do when it's my turn. The game is simple. I'm winning already. The object is to take tricks during the game, like this." Tommaso watched closely as Gigante gathered the cards in one broad motion. "Since I'm the winner this time, I sweep up all the cards over to me."

The game was interrupted when Simone returned and said, "We need to move in the direction of the dock. We have to check in first and give them our names, then we go to a different place to start our medical examinations. We'll have to push through this crowd first."

It was only mid-morning, but the temperature was climbing to near record high. People's clothes, their tops, underclothing, and even pants were soaked with sweat and sticking to clammy skin. Skinny mules and skinnier horses surrendered themselves to their wagons waiting to escape the sun and away from the incessant annoyance of countless biting flies.

As the group made their way toward the dock, they saw various men standing on benches or wagons shouting to the mass of people in an attempt to sell a variety of products. The area was full of dishonest types keen on taking money from victims naïve enough to believe any absurdity.

One swindler scanned the crowd for patsies to sell what he described as an ancient and proven concoction to prevent seasickness when, in fact, it was nothing more than ground orange peels.

Another man claimed he had magical hats in his possession that could help a person learn a new language in weeks or even days. The man was attempting to work his own magic to convince a group of men he told the truth.

He said, "I understand your skepticism, and I didn't believe it until I tried it myself. I wore this hat for a week. I even slept with it on my head, and I learned all the letters and numbers in English with ease, one, three, four, A, B, C, three, four, A, B, three, nine, and ten. As quick as you can kick a cat, I did. I can speak courteously, Good morning, how are you, I am good to meet you, and these are but a few examples. Why, I could go on for days."

"Tommaso, don't believe everything you hear," Giacomo said and pulled the boy along with him.

They continued walking toward the *Grabow* only to be confronted by yet another pitch. The flimflammer was dressed in a cheap suit and bowtie. He sold what he claimed to be the latest in American clothing fashion, telling passersby they would be more likely to succeed if they adopted the styles he recommended. He stood on a bench and carried a cane in his left hand, rapping it loudly on the wooden board beneath him to emphasize the finer points of his pitch.

"I have the finest in American apparel you'll find anywhere. I receive it directly from my cousin in the great city of Baltimore, America, who sells ensembles, well, let's say, fit for a king. Now, let's take you for example, young man," he said, pointing to Alberto. "Step right up here, sir. Yes, you with the grand sniffer."

The salesman's words met with scattered laughter. A group of people began to cluster when Alberto climbed up to stand on the bench.

"Sir, you're a perfect example. Good God, man, in America, what kind of a chance do you think you stand? Why, when the people of New York City see you dressed in this potato sack you call clothing, they'll laugh you right back onto the ship.

I've seen it a hundred times, I have. People return here from America in tears wishing they had bought my clothing."

He put a fine exclamation point on his statement by rapping his cane twice on the bench. A considerable crowd had formed to listen to the slick-talking opportunist. Alberto stood before him as the perfect victim, and as the throng began to press closer, Gigante scooped up Tommaso.

"Now, young man, I have a fine jacket that would make all the difference in the world for you. Why, you'll have them eating out of your hand. My goodness, you do have a rather large smeller, don't you? May I ask, sir, have you ever had a seagull take up residence there?"

The grifter was cruising now. His shtick was working and the crowd roared. The simple-minded Alberto also laughed.

"Goodness, friend, you could house an entire flock of seagulls inside those commodious chambers you call nostrils."

Gigante passed Tommaso off to Giacomo. "I think we've heard enough from him."

He took a few quick steps, bounding onto the bench and towered over the con man.

Grabbing the cane, he tapped the rogue on top of the head, and spoke in a husky voice. "Sir, if I don't buy your fancy duds, will these people in America also laugh at me?"

Gigante dropped the cane onto the bench, and when the man bent over to retrieve it, he gave him a kick in the rear end and sent him sprawling to the ground.

The crowd laughed louder than ever and cheered Gigante. In the time it took a hen to lay an egg, the chiseler had lost his audience.

Now it was Gigante's turn to perform and he bellowed, "And give my regards to your cousin in the great city of Baltimore, America."

Gigante put Tommaso on top of his shoulders and led the hapless Alberto away to safety. People slapped the giant on his back and hailed him as their new hero.

The group from Marinella escaped the legion of shysters without losing any money. Upon reaching the wharf, they provided their names to a ship clerk, who said regulations required all passengers to go through a medical screening before boarding to ensure they met the strict standards set by American authorities.

The Italian-speaking clerk also said, "You won't be boarding for a while because the crew is busy loading cargo into the lowest level of the ship."

He directed the group to the medical screening area roped off to one side of the wharf where more than one hundred wretched heat-stricken people stood in line.

While waiting, they heard more about what to expect from one salty character who stood in front of them. Placing a hand on Tommaso's head, the man began his speech.

"This is my second trip to America and, if it seems chaotic, it's because it is. You're dealing with people who speak any number of languages. Most are first-time travelers like yourselves who don't know what to do or when to do it, but there's no reason to get your bowels in an uproar. There's a system in place to get everyone on board. Besides, they won't leave while otherwise sane people are lined up ready to pay good money to crawl inside this gigantic floating commode they call a ship."

The man leaned in close to share a secret with his new-found friends to the exclusion of everyone else waiting in line.

"I learned this after I arrived in America the last time, and by the way, I guarantee you these other dimwits standing here don't know about this. It's the responsibility of the shipping company to conduct a thorough physical examination of each of us. You know why?"

They all shook their heads.

He leaned in even closer to Tommaso and lowered his voice. "What about you, do you know why?"

Tommaso also shook his head.

The man straightened back up. "Well, I'll tell you why. It's because when we arrive in America, anyone with a sickness or abnormality can be held up and eventually sent back here, but the shipping company pays for their return. You understand me? It's a ticket they can't sell to another passenger, so they have good reason to check us out here and now."

He winked at Tommaso. "That's what I call inside information, but let's keep it our little secret. Is that okay with you?"

Tommaso nodded, but he hadn't understood anything about the last twenty-four hours. He wondered when his father might reappear and take him back home.

The line inched along in relative silence until a man, woman, and child left the examination area sobbing. Word passed around the girl was found to have trachoma, a chronic and highly contagious eye infection. Barred from boarding the ship, her parents were left to figure out whether the father should go ahead without his family.

During the next few hours, other passengers were denied boarding for various medical reasons, leaving those waiting in fear of their own examination findings.

Giacomo and Tommaso were the first of the group to reach the front of the line. While they waited for their turn, a ship clerk, in accordance with U.S. Immigration, recorded a detailed account of each passenger for the ship's manifest, including name, age, sex, country of citizenship, point of embarkation, occupation, how much money and how many bags each person carried, and whether the traveler was literate.

Giacomo held Saverio's letter in his hand with details about Tommaso and who he would eventually live with in Boston. He began to explain the circumstances, but the clerk, more scrivener than fact-checker, seemed unconcerned. Giacomo slipped the letter back into his pocket and pushed Tommaso forward into the examination area.

Holding hands, they walked up to the male nurse, who instructed both to remove shirts and shoes and roll up their pant legs for physical inspection. The examiner checked their scalp, eyes, ears, nose, mouth and teeth, and required each to perform a brief series of various movements with their arms and legs. As the nurse examined Tommaso's ears, Giacomo crossed his eyes and stuck his tongue out at him and saw a flicker of a smile flash across the young boy's face.

In a mechanical manner, the nurse said, "Move along."

Giacomo, surprised the examination had been so quick, asked, "We're done? We passed?"

"Yes. Next," the nurse said.

Giacomo almost gushed with excitement. "Tommaso, he says we can go. *Amuninni!*"

They stood in a line to have their bags fumigated by a steam process, ensuring no unwanted vermin such as lice and bedbugs were carried onboard. No one had mentioned this step in the process, and Giacomo was dismayed that the steaming nearly ruined his suitcase due to the high heat and moisture.

After six long hours, the entire group was reunited, and everyone from Giacomo's group passed with the only issue being Santo's large, protruding ears.

Santo said, "Tommaso, it's these ears of mine. They always get me in trouble. Luckily, a supervisor was called over to take a look at these things." He bent over laughing for a moment. "Do you know what he said?"

Tommaso shook his head.

"He yelled at the nurse who first examined me, 'You think this is a beauty contest? Well, it's not. Now let's get these people moving through here.'"

Santo pulled on his ears and said, "Now Tommaso, me and my friends are ready to go to America."

Giacomo held the stamped and numbered tickets for both himself and Tommaso signifying they had passed medical screening, their luggage had been fumigated, and they had been assigned to a specific compartment and bunks in steerage. Cleared to board, Tommaso held Giacomo's hand, and the rest of the group walked up the gangway where a crew member checked off each name on the passenger ship manifest.

Late arriving first and second-class passengers were still boarding, and the crew extended welcoming pleasantries and assistance with their baggage.

As steerage passengers, Tommaso and the others boarded with neither fanfare nor courtesy and carried their own luggage. Before making a right turn down into the bowels of the ship, they listened to a ship officer describe the vessel in detail to a dapper man dressed in fine clothes, sipping wine from a stemmed glass.

The officer, speaking with the pure Italian Florentine accent, concluded his remarks to the debonair man. "This old tub, as our captain affectionately refers to her, has made many successful voyages across the Atlantic, and I'm quite confident she'll make many more. It's true the *Grabow* is older, but she'll be around for years to come."

The Marinella group along with dozens of other bottom dwellers bunched together as they moved below the main deck and waterline adjacent to the ship's steering equipment. According to the steward who directed them to their assigned area, each of the four compartments was capable of holding 205 passengers.

The change was immediate as they crowded in. Bright sunshine and fresh air gave way to relative darkness and a dank staleness in the air. Individual bunks were jammed close together vertically and horizontally with each bedding rack containing a rolled-up cushion and a pillow doubling as a life preserver. There was so little space between the racks a passenger in one bunk could touch another with ease.

Giacomo lifted Tommaso, placing him in the top bunk. He said, "It sounds like from what that officer said, this will be our home for the next twelve days."

For a few hours they waited, lying or sitting on their bunks as more people filled an area growing smaller with each new arrival. With trunks and bags crammed in, there was little space to even walk in the narrow aisles.

Giacomo said, "Santo, you studied arithmetic in school. If each of the compartments holds 205 people and there are four compartments, how many does that make?"

"Let's see. That's 820 altogether, but it smells like a lot more."

Shouting over the noise and bedlam, Santo said to his young neighbor. "Hey, Tommaso, let's explore this hole we're in, okay?"

They slid through the narrow aisles getting in other people's way as they attempted to settle into their new homes. Santo studied people as he passed by, pointing out his observations to Tommaso.

He said, "Look. It's mostly men, not as many women, and you're one of the few kids. This is a big day, Tommaso. You know why?"

Tommaso shook his head.

"It's because a lot of people are traveling on a one-way ticket. They're never going back—"

He stopped himself from finishing his thought, and quickly changed the subject.

"Hey, look at those two old men over there. They don't seem too bothered by all the noise, do they?"

Santo softly punched Tommaso's arm. "Can you hear them snoring? It's like they're taking a nap under a tree without a care in the world."

He wrapped his arm around Tommaso, while watching the activities unfold. Some passengers sat, stood, and circled to sit again, trying to find comfort in their new temporary world while other pensive types fidgeted with things already checked and secured twice before.

At various times, bells clanged, whistles blew, and men shouted orders, adding stress and anxiety to hearts and minds already saddled with worry. Their faces displayed the full spectrum of human emotion, each etched in turn with a competing mixture of happiness, sadness, excitement, and anguish. A number of heads were bowed in prayer, anxiously mumbling the words to the Rosary while fingers rolled the beads back and forth.

The first argument-turned-fight broke out when two men began a petty disagreement over a game of dominoes. Neither man would back down. One punch turned into a second, then a third. Their noise interrupted Gigante's concentration playing Scopa. He told them to quiet down and when they didn't, he reluctantly stood.

Santo elbowed Tommaso. "Hey, watch this."

Gigante ambled over to the men. Without speaking a word, he wrapped his massive hands around the front of each man's face, enveloping their skulls with fingers almost touching at the back of their heads. He picked both would-be brawlers up in the air. "Stop fighting or next time I'll crack your heads open like eggs."

Gigante dropped the frightened pair of men onto their backsides and walked away.

Santo leaned over to Tommaso. "That's the lesson. Don't ever make Gigante mad."

Tommaso looked up to Santo, his eyes wide with surprise, though not fear. He swallowed and simply nodded.

After exploring each of the four steerage compartments, they began the trek back to their bunk area. The designated female bathroom was now being used for storage and the women's sign lay on top of a box filled with ossified dirty diapers. The men's washroom was crowded with both genders in various stages of undress standing near tubs of brownish seawater for bathing. People lined up waiting turns to use the toilet.

The confined space reeked of bowel movements and wafting flatulence from guts housing rebellious digestive gases. The air reeked of month-old sweat; it reeked from passengers' cloth bags filled with decayed animal flesh, rotted potatoes, and fetid cheese.

Struggling to escape the fetor, Santo kept a firm grasp on the scruff of Tommaso's neck. He dragged the boy behind him shoving his way through the human cargo.

Tommaso crawled up into his bunk and listened to a woman and two young girls sing a song about angels who protect and care for all God's children. Despite the commotion, the excitement, and the anxiety, Tommaso succumbed to sleep.

He awakened sometime later to a ship steward's booming voice. "Normally the first meal service takes place after we get underway, but due to additional cargo still being loaded, we won't launch until midnight. The service of dinner will begin shortly. As a reminder, bring the pail and utensils assigned to each of you when you boarded."

The pushing and shoving began immediately to secure a position as close to the steward as possible. With assigned dinner gear in hand, Giacomo and Tommaso found themselves in the middle of the swarm.

The steward's voice rang out again. "Tonight, dinner includes a generous scoop of meat and potato stew. There's also bread and remember to bring your cups for fresh water to drink."

Some groans were heard from those who had to push their way back to their bunks for their drinking cups. Others quickly filled the vacuum created as the mere mention of stew seemed to generate new excitement and more jostling for a better place in line.

Tommaso held his dining utensils close to his chest and stared straight ahead.

Giacomo said, "A bowl of hot stew sounds good compared to the bread and cheese we had for the last few days, right?"

Tommaso nodded.

One man passed by poking at the contents in his bowl. He said to no one in particular, "What did he call this again, shit stew?"

Upon reaching the front of the line, they were greeted by a kettle of thin, brownish-colored liquid containing an unknown combination of animal by-products. Appetizing or not, Tommaso's empty stomach audibly growled at the sight of a bowl filled with any kind of food.

Chapter Fifteen

A few minutes before midnight, those still awake felt the vessel being pulled from the wharf by a tug guiding the steamer into deeper waters. Once separated from the tug, the engine engaged to three quarters power, turning the single screw and propelling the *Grabow* in a westerly direction.

Giacomo, unable to sleep, listened to a veteran passenger explain the ship's planned course.

"First, we'll pass close to the island of Sardinia. From there, we move westward toward the Strait of Gibraltar. Then we say goodbye to our beloved Tyrrhenian Sea and enter the vast Atlantic Ocean. Some day if we're lucky," he laughed uneasily, "we'll arrive in New York."

Even with relatively smooth waters, Giacomo experienced a bout of nausea an hour after getting underway. He fought the sensation, but soon the gentle sway of the ship got the better of him. When he knew he could no longer reach the toilet in time, he learned firsthand why the crew placed chamber pots in strategic locations in the steerage compartments. Alberto joked the vomit looked like the stew served earlier in the evening. All the men chuckled except Giacomo who, having no food left in his stomach, continued retching clear bile.

The following morning, unsympathetic passengers encouraged Simone to summon a steward to help Giacomo and rid themselves of a most annoying problem. Despite the calm sea and little discernible rise and fall of the vessel, he was one of the unlucky few with zero tolerance for any kind of motion out of his control. A pleasant steward allowed Giacomo up on the deck to take in fresh air and sun. The change in scenery brought him relief, and he even managed his first smile in eight hours. Afterward, he returned to his compartment and ate a bowl of thick oatmeal for breakfast.

Giacomo's short-lived respite ended as he sat in his bunk. Seeing the men's bathroom signage hanging by a single screw and swinging back and forth in rhythm with the roll of the ship didn't help. Once the nauseous feeling took hold again, he turned in his bunk to face away from the pendulum, but soon beads of sweat began forming on his forehead, and only taking deep gulps of air by mouth seemed to satisfy the need for oxygen. Not fifteen minutes later, he leaned over the all too familiar chamber pot. When he finished, Gigante slung Giacomo over his shoulder and carried him back to the deck.

He began wandering from starboard to port side repeating the process time and again. The same helpful steward, Dimitri Marsala, a short, stout man from southern Italy, gave Giacomo a ginger root-based tea, unfortunately, everything that went down his throat came back up a few minutes later.

The kind-hearted steward escorted the pitiful passenger to the medical office.

The physician, a busy and self-important man, said, "There's little to be done for his kind. Let the poor louse remain on deck for a longer period of time."

Dimitri said, "Yes, Doctor. I gave him some ginger tea but—"

"Steward, listen to me carefully. I don't want to be bothered every time a wretch in steerage throws up. Fresh air is always the best medicine."

Standing outside the door, Giacomo hung his head when he heard the doctor's words. Resigned to his state of misery, he wandered aimlessly on deck praying the malady would somehow go away on its own.

During daytime hours with decent weather, small groups of steerage passengers were herded to stand in a limited area of open deck space for fifteen precious minutes each day gulping in fresh air and feeling the warmth of the sun.

Not-so-lucky groups, though, including Tommaso, Alberto, and Gigante, shared their cherished few minutes on deck the first day while crew members butchered a variety of animals for the passengers' meals. They visited briefly with Giacomo who sat listless, staring at the horizon, seemingly unaware of the slaughter taking place nearby.

Having learned his lesson, Giacomo refused dinner the second night.

Nonetheless, Dimitri felt sympathy for Giacomo. He said, "Listen, my friend, I'll be in violation of the rules by allowing you to sleep up here on the deck at night, but I hope the open air will help you acclimate to the movement of the ship. If you wish, I'll make up some bedding for you to sleep on, but please promise me you'll return to your bunk below if you can."

Giacomo would have agreed to anything except for eating and drinking. His head felt heavy like a cannonball. It was difficult to think clearly about anything that went on around him.

Dimitri said, "It's going to be chilly by morning. An extra blanket might help, but please don't walk around up here or I'll get in trouble. Do you understand?"

Giacomo labored to answer. "Yes, I'll walk around some."

Dimitri shook his head. "No, no Giacomo, don't leave here, don't walk on deck. Please. Do you understand?"

The second time, Dimitri's request sank in. Giacomo said, "Yes, I'll stay here." He touched Dimitri's arm. "Thank you, my friend."

The temperature plummeted overnight, but despite the chill, Giacomo sweated through his clothes so stinking of perspiration and vomit he couldn't stand the repugnant odor from his own body and breath.

During his allotted time on deck the following day, Tommaso sat with Giacomo for a few minutes. He didn't understand the suffering yet was unable to shake the fear of having seen something eerily similar with his own father, an image still fresh in his mind.

With Santo nowhere to be found, Tommaso left Giacomo and wandered toward the entrance to steerage, but not before a group of four older boys from first class accosted him.

One of the bullies grabbed Tommaso and asked, "How would you like to go for a swim?"

They formed a circle and pushed him from boy to boy.

The oldest, a pear-shaped, pimply-faced juvenile and the apparent leader of the group said, "Who wants to throw this little punk into the sea?"

Tommaso shook from fear, petrified they might push him overboard. He told himself not to cry, but as the circle edged closer to the side of the ship, he wet his pants.

The same miscreant said, "Now look what you've done, little baby. Do you want to wear a diaper or take a bath in the sea? Tell us now, sissy, before it's too late."

Santo, who had been searching for his young friend, spotted three of the ruffians holding Tommaso on his back while the pear-shaped boy let globs of spit drop from his mouth onto Tommaso's face. Unable to fight back, he closed his eyes until he heard Santo's voice in the distance.

"Hey, stop it!" Santo shouted.

Tommaso heard the distinct sound of running feet approaching. He watched Santo dive onto two of the boys holding him down. At first, Santo seemed to get the better of the two, but when a third jumped on Santo's back, the tide turned. Pinned to the ground by a much larger boy, Tommaso could only watch helplessly.

The leader now sat on Santo's chest. "It looks like we were picking on the wrong person."

He pinched one of Santo's ears. "We need to show elephant ears here who's the boss on this ship. Let's throw him overboard first, then we'll deal with the bed wetter."

A crew member rounded the corner. "Hey, knock it off, all of you!"

The four delinquents ran away first, and Santo stood slowly and helped Tommaso to his feet. Although physically fine, they were emotionally bruised by the attack.

When they returned to their compartment, Simone asked, "Is something wrong?"

Tommaso looked down at his pants with shame, slowly shook his head, and began to climb up to his bunk.

Santo said, "Hey, Tommaso, wait a second. We'll have to get you cleaned up."

As Santo related the story, Gigante paced back and forth, his face red with fury. He said, "If I have to, I'll tear the ship apart cabin by cabin to find those who did this to Tommaso."

Gigante barked out orders. "Alberto, help him to the toilet. Get him and his clothes cleaned up and take this canvas to wrap around him when he comes back out. Tommaso, you're going to be okay, I promise."

He unclenched his jaw and said, "Santo, let's push our way into the next group that goes up on deck and see if you can point them out to me."

With Santo's help, Gigante learned who the offenders were. Later the same day, he spied the boys sitting with men whom he presumed to be their fathers. In violation of where he could wander on deck, Gigante edged close enough to hear the group talking while they snacked on a plate of candies, sweet cakes, and slices of cheese which appeared nothing like the stew surprise he forced himself to eat. He immediately recognized one of the fathers as the man with the fine clothes who had spoken with an officer as they boarded the ship a few days before.

With surprising mobility for a big man, Gigante leapt over the railing where the group lounged. Startled, their heads snapped back in unison as each took a sharp intake of breath at the presence of the behemoth.

Pointing at the teenagers, he said, "These cretins bullied a friend of mine, threatening and spitting on a five-year-old boy."

He pointed directly at the boy who acted as the ringleader. "You. Which one of these men is your father?"

The pear-shaped boy slowly straightened his finger to point sideways at the well-dressed man sitting next to him.

"Okay, that's a start. You may think you're tough picking on a little boy, but you're nothing but a punk."

The father started to stand. "Who do you think—"

Gigante pressed his thumb against the man's forehead, forcing him to return to the back of his chair. "If you or anyone else here moves again, I *will* throw you overboard, just as pimple face here threatened to do today to a frightened little boy. I'll say this only once. Leave my friends alone. If you don't, I can be a bully too, and I always start with the biggest people." He poked his finger back toward the father. "Understand this, fancy man. I'll be coming for you first. I hope for your sake this makes sense."

Gigante stared at each as they cowered in silent fear.

Finally, the well-dressed man spoke. "Until now, it had been a splendid voyage. I find you to be most discourteous, but I shall instruct the youngsters to cease their mischief. And now sir, I wish you a good day."

Picking up the plate of food, Gigante shoveled all the candies into his front pocket. He stuffed an unopened bottle of wine into his back pocket, grabbed the largest piece of cake from the plate, and crammed it into his mouth in one bite. He looked back at the group for a moment to see if anyone would challenge him. No one did.

Gigante wiped his mouth with the back of his hand. "And a good day to you, sir."

In a single fluid motion, he turned and hurdled the railing.

Later in the evening, Gigante called Tommaso over to his bunk. "Those boys won't bother you again, I promise. Since Giacomo is sleeping on the deck, you can stay in this bunk next to me."

Gigante jammed his hand into his pocket. "Those boys said they're sorry, and they wanted you to have a piece of candy too. Now you'll have sweet dreams tonight, okay?"

The boy launched himself forward, hugging the giant man.

Gigante felt the fear, anxiety and helplessness pour from the small boy's heart and returned the hug, patting him clumsily on the head. "Okay, Tommaso, time for bed."

Giacomo's vulnerability to motion sickness had reached a near-critical stage. Practically immobile, he clung to the railing and occasionally raised his head to catch a glimpse of the sea, cursing it in what remained of his ravaged mind. His condition was beyond fatigue and dizziness; now his speech was slurred and his tongue was a white, swollen lump of tissue.

He lost everything inside him long ago, including his dignity. Although not thinking with clarity any longer, he still knew he should drink something, but couldn't bring himself to face the inevitable nausea.

By day six and well into the vast Atlantic Ocean, matters for Giacomo worsened. The near-perfect weather took a marked turn for the worse as clouds began to thicken and the wind picked up. Over the next hour, the western horizon darkened with angry black clouds multiplying in a steady, relentless effort to dominate the entire sky.

Rain pelted Giacomo's head and back as he hung to the side of the ship, and when he cared enough to look, he noticed the much larger waves. Within the hour, sea water crashed over the sides as the ship rocked up and down unpredictably.

In one of his last moments of sanity, Giacomo wished for the strength to jump over the side and drown himself in the ocean. He wondered about his friend Saverio and longed to trade places with him as death seemed a better, more palatable thought and his only means to relief. His feverish brain struggled to form basic thoughts.

Oh, God, I wish I had listened to my brother and stayed home. I want to die.

Dimitri was securing various items on the deck. When he saw Giacomo, he rushed over and shouted to be heard over the driving wind and rain. "Captain's orders! Everyone must return to their compartment immediately."

Giacomo mumbled incomprehensibly due to his swollen tongue, lolling his head back and forth.

"I'm sorry, my friend, but you must go below. I wish there was something I could do."

Depleted of any strength, somehow Giacomo managed to cling to the railing, refusing to let go. Over the noise of the wind and rain, Dimitri shouted for another steward's assistance. The two stewards argued for a minute.

Dimitri turned back to Giacomo and yelled, "Okay, you don't have to go back down below. I can let you stay up here on deck in a locked storage room."

His unfocused eyes stared blankly in Dimitri's direction. In an extreme state of delirium, his brain begged for hydration.

Dimitri said, "Let me help you. Please, we must leave this area."

Giacomo's body went limp, flopping to the deck. The stewards dragged him to a nearby room filled with cleaning supplies and canvas material.

Dimitri spread out the canvas and rolled Giacomo's body onto it. "You can stay in here. I'll check on you and let your friends know where you are."

As Dimitri spoke, Giacomo groaned and attempted to raise himself up, but instead collapsed to the canvas in an awkward position.

The other steward stomped out of the storage room stopping at the doorway. "Dimitri, he's probably dead. You can stop playing nursemaid and get back to doing your real job."

Chapter Sixteen

It was almost midnight. The *Grabow* bobbed along like a tiny cork through the violent storm, buffeted about by unrelenting savage winds and walls of waves taller than the vessel itself. The captain and crew, along with terrified passengers, worried whether the *Grabow* would be able to survive the heavy drenching rain and gale-force winds that pounded the ship.

The captain had to shout his orders to be heard. "Shut the access to all decks below. Position the crewmen to ensure passengers stay in their rooms. No one is allowed out until I give the all clear, and I mean no one. Chief Officer, make sure every crewman understands."

Meal service was discontinued in steerage and access to the upper deck was blocked due to the heavy rain and waves washing over the ship. Steerage was now a prison.

The storm's intensity grew as Tommaso held onto the cushion in his bunk in near total darkness, rising and falling with the ship. At times, trunks and chamber pots slid across the floor, crashing into the bulkheads.

There had been little motion sickness in their compartment apart from Giacomo, but now everything changed. What began with one caused a chain reaction from which there could be no protection.

Massive bolts of lightning momentarily relieved the total darkness, providing a flicker of light for the sick to locate a chamber pot or toilet. At one time it was embarrassing to be sick in front of others, but a full twelve hours into the massive storm, no one cared anymore. The tin pails used for meals now contained the aftermath of meals.

Tommaso sat in his bunk unaffected and pretended to be in his father's grasp being swung around and around. He could hear his father's laughter, and despite the horrible sound and smell, Tommaso smiled because, with his eyes closed, he no longer sat prisoner on a ship at sea, but lay cradled in his father's loving arms.

He heard the groans and watched as Simone, Santo, and Alberto joined the others in a chorus of pleas for a reprieve. As far as he could see, only he and Gigante had escaped the ravages of the tempest.

The young boy had learned the practice of saying prayers from his grandmothers. They told him God always listens, yet he wondered if even God listened in the middle of such a storm.

He closed his eyes, pressed his hands together over his chest, and said, "Dear God, please make the storm stop and help Giacomo and everyone to be better."

Tommaso opened his eyes, and with the aid of lightning saw Santo for a split-second hanging onto the side of his rack. Their eyes locked for a single moment, but Santo was no longer Santo and he no longer smiled.

Tommaso reached into his bag and removed a small wooden soldier. Bearded and fierce looking, a sword hung at his side and a shield guarded his chest. One arm was broken off at the elbow. His father had explained the soldier lost his arm in one of the many battles he had fought. When another flash of lightning illuminated the surroundings, Tommaso thought he could see his father's face on the soldier.

He turned on his side squeezing the toy in his hand. A sleepiness overtook him, and he fell into a deep slumber.

Walking beside his father, he asked, "*Patri*, where are we going?"

"Walk with me to the sea."

Happy to be at his father's side again, he skipped along.

"Yes, there's your mother."

A woman Tommaso had never seen before smiled at him.

"Did you know your mother is always here?"

He reached out to touch her.

"*Matri*?"

His father said, "Someday we'll all be together."

Tommaso reached again, but they seemed to glide away effortlessly atop the waves.

"Please, *Patri*. Please, *Matri*."

The same waves passing through his parents crashed into Tommaso, knocking him back to the beach.

He awoke to the sounds of baggage sliding back and forth between the rows of bunk racks like out-of-control skaters on an icy lake. Chamber pots rolled over, crashing into walls, spewing their thick molasses-like contents. Occasional earth-shaking thunder trumped all sounds, proving even at its edge, the mammoth storm refused to go quietly.

The never-ending night finally passed, and early the following morning, Tommaso sat up in his bunk, staring at the doorway leading to the deck. It was now standing open and a subtle light filtered down to reveal a checkerboard of vomit and waste with misery strewn in between. The first hint of fresh air drifted into the steerage section as passengers shielded their eyes from the strange light while the movement of the ship slowed to a long up-and-down rocking motion. Passengers began to stir and attempted to find their footing.

"Let's get out of here before they change their minds," Gigante said. He swept Tommaso up with one arm and raced to where other liberated passengers staggered about trying to regain a sense of equilibrium and a sliver of humanity.

From the bowels of the ship, others shuffled through the exit, still pale and dizzy, joining the cabin class passengers in the light of day. Few had been spared the torture of the storm. In spite of the differences in their various economic stations, they found common ground as fellow club members who had endured and survived the two-day nightmare.

Simone, Santo, and Alberto made their way to the open deck, finding Gigante with Tommaso, watching the sunrise.

Santo raised his hands to the sky and shouted, "Thank you, thank you, God."

After a few moments, Santo eyeballed Tommaso. "You're one tough kid. How did you do it?"

Simone interrupted. "We have to find Giacomo."

Before their search could get underway, a crewman began shouting to the steerage passengers on deck. "We need all the men to form a fire line. We'll pass buckets of sea water along to each other to wash everything out. First let's push everything not bolted to the floor to one side and direct the water the other way to wash out this mess."

The weary passengers hung their heads.

"Okay, come on, step up. We need everyone to help do what you can. It's in your own best interest. The sooner we begin, the sooner you'll have your happy home again."

They poured sea water on the floors, enlisting others to help mop the waste away. It took the better part of the daylight hours to scrub the ship's lower compartments to a modest degree of cleanliness.

On the upper deck, the ship captain mingled with the passengers. "In all my thirty years at sea, this was without a doubt the most violent storm I've ever experienced."

Crew members served a late breakfast on the open deck for the cabin class passengers who chose to dine outside. The captain ordered music from a phonograph player for their enjoyment while the crew served coffee and juices. The now-calm seas, light winds, and blue skies lifted spirits, and a general mood of relief and happiness prevailed.

Their duties accomplished below, Simone and Gigante scurried to the storage room and found Dimitri tending to Giacomo, who was lying on his side, eyes rolled toward the back of his head.

"Giacomo, can you hear me?" asked Gigante.

Giacomo raised his hands upward, reaching out to something or someone, in the final effort of his life. Gigante folded Giacomo's colorless hands over his chest and covered his face with the canvas.

They returned to their compartment, finding Tommaso on the bunk with his eyes closed. In a whisper, Gigante spoke about Giacomo's death and of a service to be held on deck the following day, unaware that Tommaso could hear every word. Unseen by the others, the young boy hid his face and tears under a blanket. When the announcement for dinner came, Tommaso sat up and grabbed his pail, cup, and utensils.

Gigante said, "My little friend, I'm sorry to tell you Giacomo died."

Tommaso stared at the floor.

"I wish I knew something more to say."

The others watched for a reaction. Without any sign of emotion, Tommaso slid off the bunk to his feet and walked toward the serving line. The men looked at each other not knowing what to do.

"He must have ice in his veins," Santo said.

"Don't be too sure. He's been through a lot," Gigante replied.

The brief funeral ceremony took place on the upper deck away from other passengers. The chief officer asked if anyone wanted to say something about Giacomo. To a man, their attention shifted to the ground until Gigante stepped forward.

"Giacomo, you were a good man, a proud man who only wanted a chance to succeed in life. You were like a brother to us, and we shall miss you. Goodbye, friend."

The big man stepped back and wrapped his arm around Tommaso. Without fanfare or further ceremony, the stewards slid Giacomo's body into the sea and, except for Dimitri, the crew walked away.

He said, "Thank you for saying something about your friend. I begged the doctor to check him earlier. After Giacomo died, the doctor became angry with me."

Dimitri slammed his fist on the railing. "He said I should have given him more information. No one goes up against him except the captain, but the chief officer backed me up in private and said he knew I had tried to get help."

He bit his lip before continuing. "Later, the doctor calmed down and said dying of sea sickness was unheard of, even though a person may feel like he's going to die. However, people do die of dehydration, and I don't know, maybe in a way he willed himself to death. I'm sorry."

"We know you did your best. Giacomo was sick the moment he stepped on this cursed ship," Simone said.

"This will be the last voyage I work," Dimitri said.

"Is it because of what happened?"

"No, I already had plans to go to San Francisco. I'm going to work for my uncle on a fishing boat, but it's people like our good doctor on board here that make the decision easier."

Dimitri rubbed Tommaso's head and walked away.

Late at night, after making sure that Tommaso was asleep in his bunk, the group spoke in hushed tones about what might happen now that Saverio's best friend was dead.

Simone said, "Giacomo was supposed to meet the boy's uncle. Now we'll help Tommaso find him, right everyone?"

They all nodded in agreement except Alberto, who said, "What if we have to leave before he gets there?"

"That's not an option. We must find his uncle," Simone said.

Chapter Seventeen

The captain of the *Grabow* stood proudly on the bridge of his ship. Even with the storm and the late departure, they were going to arrive within a day of their original schedule, and they had lost only one passenger. Per the captain's log, "The death was due to the passenger's irrational refusal to drink liquids or follow the ship's strict medical advice when succumbing to mild symptoms of nausea because of motion sickness."

The first stop for the *Grabow* occurred midmorning in Lower New York Bay where, following standard operating procedures, the ship was placed in quarantine until inspectors boarded. Once the brief medical examinations of cabin class passengers were conducted, they alone would be cleared to enter America.

The ship steamed through the Narrows to Upper New York Bay on its way into the New York Harbor where the tip of Manhattan Island came into view.

Tommaso perched on his bunk, dutifully holding his bag, waiting to be told to do something—stand in line, stay here, walk there, leave the ship. He had no idea what to do, so he sat watching other passengers pack their belongings. Tommaso, like most others in steerage, didn't understand their ordeal was only beginning.

Gigante said, "Tommaso, leave your bag on your bunk. Let's go up on deck to see this giant statue everyone is talking about."

He lifted Tommaso up to see the huge copper figure. A hush came over the passengers when the Statue of Liberty appeared in all its glory. The eerie quiet ended as cheers erupted with shouts of joy and wonder. Families, strangers, young and old, clapped and danced, celebrating as this magnificent woman welcomed them to the new world carrying a torch to guide them on their continuing journey. Gigante clapped with the rest of the crowd on deck and Tommaso did likewise, although he wasn't sure why.

Dimitri approached the Marinella group. "Tommaso, best wishes to you here in America."

He handed the boy a small wooden carving of the *Grabow*, and although it was no larger than a half dollar coin, it had extraordinary detail.

"I carved this myself." He turned the ship over and pointed to his initials DM. Smiling, he said, "That's me, Dimitri Marsala."

Simone asked, "When will you go to San Francisco?"

"I'll be paid in two days. Then I leave."

"Thank you again for helping with our friend," Gigante said.

"You're welcome. I'm sorry he suffered so."

Dimitri walked away, but Tommaso gave chase, hugged him around the legs, and whispered, "*Tanti grazii.*"

The cabin class passengers pushed forward in one direction and were greeted by their loved ones. Those from steerage took a different course pouring across a pier with their baggage in tow toward barges.

Santo said, "I won't miss that ship, will you?"

Tommaso simply shook his head.

Since Ellis Island was unable to accommodate larger ships, an immigrant official divided them into groups of thirty and packed them onto barges to be ferried to the island. A nametag was pinned to each passenger with a number corresponding to the ship manifest detailing the information of each person aboard the *Grabow*.

Passengers went to the upper level while their baggage was loaded on the lower deck of the barge. An interpreter stationed at Ellis Island was their first contact and guided them to an intimidating red brick building where their fate would be decided. Another official barked commands at the immigrants. "This is the baggage room. Leave your suitcases and trunks here."

Shouting over the clamor, the official pointed to each type of bag and sometimes forcibly separated a suitcase from a traveler to demonstrate to others they were to leave everything. Tommaso dropped his bag, wondering if he would see it again.

They were guided through a doorway leading into the Registry Room where government officials speaking the strange language known as English would make decisions affecting entire lifetimes. Expressions of awe were common as interpreters spoke rapidly in various languages.

"Proceed up these stairs. You'll be met by another official."

Three men began running, taking the stairs two at a time.

"Hold on, hold on!" The official cautioned them. "This is not a race. There are no extra points for being first. Walk up the stairs and wait for further instruction."

The official repeated the instructions in Italian, Sicilian, and Greek. The same anxious men restarted their climb at a similar pace. Tommaso watched in confusion, not under-standing the immigrants were running from something as much as they were to something, and a few cautionary words weren't going to slow down those escaping from hopelessness to hopefulness.

Tommaso and Santo gazed upwards at the steep stairwell, astounded at the height of the climb. They joined in with the mass of humanity ascending the winding staircase.

As they entered the Registry Room, with its vaulted ceil-ings, Tommaso kept hold of Simone and gaped at all the re-markable sights. He stared at two Finnish boys in traditional Lapland clothing who stared back at him. They were the same height as Tommaso and appeared to be identical twins in their costume-like clothing. He marveled at how they looked at him first, then turned to gaze at each other. It seemed as if it was one boy looking at himself in the mirror.

He wondered if they were real people, captivated by their blond hair, light-colored eyes and skin. In unison, they turned to him again and smiled. Tommaso likewise smiled, his first in America.

The Marinella group took their place in line as passengers snaked through the Great Hall awaiting medical examinations. With many hundreds of people talking over each other, the collective voices echoed off the ceiling and walls, making the surroundings more chaotic and stressful for those waiting in line.

The physicals given in Naples before the voyage in no way guaranteed passage through the American inspection, and ar-rival at Ellis Island didn't guarantee acceptance by the United States. At every turn, optimism battled with uncertainty.

In front of Tommaso and Simone, an older man who had also traveled from Sicily stepped up for examination. They listened to the doctor's questions made through an interpreter. Following the exam, the physician used a piece of chalk to write something on the immigrant's jacket lapel.

The man argued. "I may be old, but I'm not in any pain, and certainly not lame. Look at me again. I, I—"

The interpreter quieted him. "Sir, you must understand something. You didn't see it, but there is a doctor who watches everyone climb the staircase. He identified you as someone who labored up the stairs. Please step aside. The physician here said you will have to be examined further to determine if you can proceed."

Before presenting themselves to the doctor, Simone squeezed Tommaso's arm and whispered, "You're strong. There is nothing for you to worry about."

During the exam, the doctor checked each of them for shortness of breath, lameness, or any indication of a mental abnormality. No chalk was used to scrawl anything on their clothing, and Simone patted Tommaso on the back, prodding him along to the next step in the process.

He said, "Tommaso, someone is going to check our eyes to make sure everything is okay. I'll go first."

The examiner used a simple metal buttonhook to snap back Simone's eyelid looking for signs of the dreaded trachoma. It was quick. It was also quite painful. Afraid the young boy might resist, Simone kneeled to face Tommaso. He lied. "It feels like nothing. Let the man check your eye."

Simone held his hand, but to his surprise the young boy barely flinched. Fortunately for both, the examination revealed no evidence of the horrible contagion which they had heard sometimes meant a return trip to the would-be immigrant's home country.

"Santo is right. You are tougher than you look," Simone said.

After passing the medical examinations, they continued through the maze of metal railing to stand before an inspector. He peered down upon them through a pair of thick glasses while seated on a tall stool behind an imposing desk.

He rapid-fired questions through an interpreter at Simone, most of which had been posed to him before the voyage even began in Italy. The inspector used the information contained on the ship manifest as a baseline and compared Simone's present answers with what he had said before his departure.

"What kind of work are you planning to do?" the examiner asked through the interpreter.

Before the voyage and on the ship, the Marinella group had discussed how they would answer any questions concerning work.

"I'll be doing construction work in Michigan," Simone said.

"What kind of construction work?"

"Sir, I'll do any kind of construction work, it makes no difference to me. Everyone in the group I'm traveling with is doing the same."

The inspector heard similar responses a hundred times a day.

"Okay, and what about the kid you have with you? Is he yours?"

Simone reached into his pocket for the letter Saverio had written explaining the circumstance under which Tommaso traveled, as well as a ship document given to him by Dimitri reporting the death of Giacomo aboard the ship. The translator read them as the inspector turned his attention to the small boy. "So you want to live in America? What's your name?"

"My *name-a* Tommaso Mancuso."

"Hey, what's this? The kid already speaks the language! Where'd you learn to speak English?"

Tommaso looked at the man and didn't answer.

The interpreter asked Tommaso in Sicilian how he learned to introduce himself.

Tommaso responded that his father had taught him how to say his name. The interpreter translated his answer to the inspector.

"Good for you, kid, that's all right. At least you've made the effort to say your name. Okay, what's going on with these papers he gave you?" asked the inspector.

The interpreter said, "I'm reading them now. The letter from the father says he's dying and he gives permission for the orphaned boy to travel with a friend to America. The boy will meet his uncle from Boston and go to live there. This is a document from the SS *Grabow*. The man who was taking care of the boy died on the voyage."

"Tough break. Okay, kid, welcome to America. Boston's a great city. You'll love it."

Simone was rooted in place, staring dumbfounded at Tommaso until the interpreter said, "Okay, move along."

They started to walk away when the rest of the group finally caught up to them. Tommaso ran to Gigante and hugged his leg.

The inspector said, "What's going on here? It's like a family reunion. Come on, folks."

The interpreter waved them forward to the money exchange section to trade their Italian lira for U.S. dollars.

As they paraded down the stairs toward the currency exchange, Simone told the group Tommaso spoke English to the inspector. They shouted, "*Bravo*, Tommaso, *bravo!*"

The group walked out into the bright sunshine.

Simone mussed the hair on Tommaso's head, and said, "First we have to find your uncle."

"Does everyone remember Rosa's older brother, Damiano?" Simone said.

Each of the men nodded except Alberto, who asked, "Damiano is older now. What if he doesn't look the same?"

"Well, let's hope he hasn't changed much. Anyway, he's supposed to have a sign with Tommaso's name written on it," Simone said.

Santo said, "Alberto, think of Damiano with a little gray hair or maybe, no hair at all."

"Or maybe both, right?" Alberto asked.

Gigante said, "Alberto, you and I better look together, okay?"

Tommaso had never met his uncle, and the more the group talked about finding him, the more anxious he became. In his five-year-old mind, the prospect of meeting someone new was more than upsetting, it was frightening. He felt a closeness to the men. If he couldn't return to his father, he decided he would remain with his new friends. Instinctively, Tommaso sought out Gigante's hand and kept a firm grip on it.

They took a short ferry ride to a railway station in Jersey City.

Well into the evening hours, they continued to look for someone carrying a sign with Tommaso's name or any man who appeared to be searching the crowd. Once night came and the station quieted, they found a space sheltered by large trees.

Santo whispered to his brother, "We're supposed to meet the *padrone* tomorrow morning. What happens if we can't find Tommaso's uncle?"

"I don't know."

"Maybe we can take him with us," said Santo, answering his own question.

Bernardo was a forty-six-year-old man who immigrated to America from Messina, Sicily, eighteen years earlier. He had large jowls and a pockmarked face. The spindly legs looked almost incapable of supporting the weight of his rotund belly. Speaking with a heavy accent, he sometimes combined words in Sicilian and English.

Bernardo squatted in front of the group wearing well-worn dark gray trousers and a ragged open neck shirt with rolled up sleeves. Initially he spoke in Sicilian to make the newcomers feel more comfortable.

He said, "*Binvinuti, mi chiamu Bernardo.*" In an attempt to show off, he repeated the same in English. "Welcome, my name is Bernardo."

He returned to speaking his native Sicilian.

"I'll be your guide to a place called Michigan. I found good jobs for all of you on a road construction crew. It's hard labor, but who's afraid of a little difficult work? Besides, the money will be good, yes?"

Bernardo stopped talking and stared at Tommaso.

"There are five of you, but certainly you're not counting this small thing here."

Simone said, "Giacomo died during the voyage."

"Diego's brother?"

"Yes. He'd never been on a boat before and was sick from the beginning."

With a decided arrogance to his voice, Bernardo blustered, "I've been back and forth on the ocean many times. It's not an easy thing for some."

Again, Simone spoke for the group. "We're meeting the boy's uncle who's coming from a place called Boston."

"Well, Boston is a long way from here. How will you know this man?" Bernardo asked.

"Damiano comes from our own town and according to his letter, he said we would meet here at this station. We didn't find him yesterday, so—"

Bernardo's smile disappeared as he rose to his feet, interrupting Simone.

"Do you think this man will just magically appear? You simple peasants are but one small group I'm meeting. What cretin would have arranged such a mess? Such ignorance." He shook his head. "Anyway, I have my own problems. There's still another, much larger group I'm meeting later today, then a third group tomorrow. I have a schedule to keep. Find this uncle. If not, when I return with the others, we'll leave without the boy."

Gigante stood, stepping forward close to Bernardo. He spoke evenly without malice. "His father and mother died. Giacomo agreed to bring him to America to live with his uncle. We're not walking away from him. We will, as you say, find the uncle. If not, we'll talk again."

Bernardo stared at Tommaso and spit on the ground. "I guess times are getting more desperate in Sicily than even I remember. What am I to do with this boy? He can't work. Am I supposed to feed him for free?" He exhaled deeply and shook his head. "I'll return later."

The rest of the morning and late into the afternoon they continued their search, but to no avail. Damiano was nowhere to be found.

Alberto said, "What are we supposed to do? And for how long? Anything could have happened."

Gigante glared at Alberto. "Calm down, friend. We'll do all we can."

"But I'm afraid of Bernardo. What if he becomes angrier with us?"

"Don't worry about him. He's a blowhard."

Bernardo returned with a group of twenty-six men from Catania, a large city on the east coast of Sicily.

His focus immediately turned to Tommaso. "So, the boy is still here."

Simone spoke up. "We looked. We'd like to wait a little longer."

A man from the Catania group, pressed into service as their leader, spoke. "We came here for a purpose. Bernardo told us of this boy, but he's not our concern nor should he be our problem."

Gigante, who had been leaning against a wall next to Tommaso, eased over to the conversation. The Catania group, having been warned by Bernardo, could now appreciate the size of this man.

Their spokesman stammered. "We have no problem with you, but you must understand something. We must leave when the *padrone* says."

Gigante ignored him and turned his full attention to Bernardo. "What's the plan? Are we leaving now?"

"No, we'll leave first thing in the morning."

Gigante said, "Okay, we have time to keep looking. If we don't find his uncle, the boy's father sent money with Tommaso and he can pay his own passage with us."

Bernardo spat on the ground again. "I'll be no nanny to this boy."

Gigante, now visibly angry, and towering over the much smaller Bernardo, poked his finger into his chest and backed him against a bench.

"I don't remember anyone asking you to be his nanny. Schedule or not, we aren't leaving this boy alone."

Bernardo found an escape.

"Okay, okay, I have a plan. In Detroit I know of a man and his wife who have an orphanage. I can talk to them. Maybe they can take the boy in, but I give no guarantees."

Gigante said, "Ah, there is a small heart inside you somewhere."

The Marinella group began their search again, even though it seemed to be in vain. They discussed various ideas about what to do with Tommaso. A collective decision was made. They wouldn't abandon the boy. If Damiano didn't come by morning, Tommaso would travel with them.

Chapter Eighteen

Damiano Favale had been in America for fourteen years and owned a thriving butcher shop in Boston. When he received the letter from Saverio, with whom he was barely acquainted, he was willing to help due to necessity, but not love. Since the marriage of his sister, Rosa, ended in tragedy, he would take Tommaso into his home. He answered Saverio's letter with warmth, but secretly he felt indifferent to the prospect of taking in his nephew.

The day before the scheduled arrival of the *Grabow* to New York, Damiano boarded a train from Boston. He carried a small bag with a change of underclothes for himself. His wife, Serafina, used part of a cardboard box to make a sign to aid her husband in locating his nephew. She wrote the name Tommaso Mancuso in large letters on the cardboard and put it in her husband's bag. Blessed with three teenaged daughters, Serafina had given up hope of having a son and was thrilled at the prospect of bringing a boy into the house.

Late afternoon Damiano arrived in Manhattan, a place he traveled to a number of times and was well acquainted. The next day, he planned to catch a ferry to the railway station in Jersey City to meet Tommaso. Until then, his plan was to relax, have a nice dinner, and a good night's sleep.

Happy to be on his own and free of the responsibility of work for a couple of days, he sauntered along Canal Street toward his hotel, the Grand Sunset. Damiano took a shortcut through an alley to save time walking to the hotel. As he rounded the corner, he spotted two men sifting through a mound of garbage.

One of the men asked, "Sir, can you spare a little change?"

Damiano felt he didn't have a choice. He reached into his pocket and removed several coins. He took a nickel from the pile and handed it over.

The other man said, "Excuse me, you got any change for me?"

On edge, Damiano said, "No, I need the rest for myself."

"Okay, sir, I understand," he said, moving aside.

As Damiano stepped around the man, a crushing sharp pain at the back of his head managed to reach his brain for a split second before complete darkness swept over him.

Damiano lay unconscious on the ground, bleeding profusely.

The man dropped the iron pipe from his hand and sneered, "Well, my good friend, you may need the money, but I have needs too."

They dragged him into an area where the corners of two buildings met, affording the robbers the privacy they needed. One of the men turned the bag upside down, spilling the contents onto the ground next to Damiano. Finding only clothing and a piece of cardboard with a name on it, they made a quick search of his pockets and found a wallet with cash. The man they robbed remained motionless, and they were unsure if he was even alive.

"Let's go before someone comes."

They walked a couple of city blocks and stopped to count the cash.

"Can you believe our good luck? There's twenty-five dollars in here!"

"Good, get rid of the wallet."

In the narrow state between life and death, Damiano lay unconscious in a hospital bed. Slowly, his hand inched upward toward his head. He groaned at the monstrous headache that greeted him when he awoke.

The patient in the bed next to him was the first to see the once motionless body begin to stir. "I see you've decided to join us after all?"

Damiano groaned even louder. His neighbor yelled that the man was waking up. A nurse darted through a chaotic grid of patient beds.

She leaned over and asked, "Sir, can you hear me, sir?"

Damiano's unfocused eyes fluttered open. Confused, he tried to sit up.

The nurse said, "Sir, please lie back down."

Damiano's head roared with pain. He asked, "What, uh, happened? Where, where am I?"

"You're in the hospital. You have a large contusion on your head. I'll let the doctor know you're awake. Please try to rest," the nurse said. She held his hand for a few moments and left.

Several minutes later, a young, harried man rushed into the room. "I'm Dr. Crittenden. It appears you were struck on the back of the head, and for the past six days you've been a guest here in our lovely hospital."

The doctor checked Damiano's vital signs and told the nurse to let the police know the patient was awake.

After the doctor walked away, Damiano said, "I feel terrible. I think I'm going to be sick."

"Mister, you think you're sick now, wait until you see lunch," the other patient said.

Damiano groaned again and closed his eyes to shut out the light and the noise.

Early in the afternoon, two cops, one tall and skinny and the other short and plump, walked into the room accompanied by the nurse. Finding the patient asleep, the short cop said with a grumpy edge to his voice, "Hey, we were told this guy was awake."

The nurse said, "I'm sorry Officer, it appears he's fallen back asleep. Sometimes our patients do that sort of thing here."

Short cop said, "Hey, partner, would you listen to her? We're in the presence of a real comedian today. Okay, Nurse, wake him up. We've got other things to do."

"Officers, that's not our customary practice. I'll let the doctor know you're here."

"Okay, but let's hurry it up."

They learned Damiano Favale had traveled from Boston to New York to meet his five-year-old nephew from Sicily. The last thing he remembered was walking down the street. His head pounded, and the doctor told the police to give him more time as his memory may come back over the next few days or perhaps not at all.

Damiano asked the nurse to please contact his wife in Boston.

"Yes, sir, I'll be back in a moment to get the particulars and we can have a telegram sent to her."

Two days later, Serafina sat next to her husband, who was much improved and ready to leave the hospital and New York for good.

The same police officers visited again.

Short cop said, "Hey look, partner, here's our sassy nurse."

"Oh, it's you two again."

"What? No jokes for us today? Okay, Peaches, can we pretty please see our patient?"

The nurse rolled her eyes. "Follow me, Officers."

Damiano remembered cutting through an alley and being approached by two men asking for change. He told the police of his concern for his young nephew.

Short cop said, "So now you want us to go out and search for this little dago kid? Mister, what do we look like to you, some sort of a social service?"

A day later, Damiano was released from the hospital. He and Serafina took a ferry to the railway station serving Ellis Island where they learned the *Grabow* was still in the harbor, but the passengers from the voyage had long since departed.

Serafina asked, "What can we do?"

"I don't know. This ferry ride and walking around has exhausted me. Let's go back to the hotel where I can rest. Tomorrow, we'll go to the police station, and afterward, we're going home."

The following morning, Serafina clung to her husband's side as they pushed their way through the entrance to the station.

Her eyes filled with tears, she pleaded, "Officers, can you please look for our nephew?"

The pair nodded politely.

Tall cop said, "Yes ma'am, of course we can. We'll keep this cardboard we found with his name and check with the local churches and other social service programs that might know where the kid is. If we hear anything, we'll get in contact with you."

With nothing else to do, the couple left.

Short cop picked the cardboard paper with Tommaso's name off the table and stared at it for a moment.

"What's the plan?" tall cop asked.

Short cop dropped the paper into the trash and rubbed his ample waistline.

"The plan is lunch."

Damiano and Serafina began the return trip to Boston by train later that day. They rode mostly in silence, saying little to one another. Occasionally her dewy eyes looked to her husband, hoping for some words of comfort. He stroked her hand but said nothing. Over time, the memory of Tommaso Mancuso, the nephew they never met, faded away.

Chapter Nineteen

Bernardo delivered the men from Marinella, Catania and a third group from Ragusa to a road construction crew near Detroit. He said, "Don't get too comfortable. Tomorrow, you're going to a work site near a town called Grand Rapids."

Simone asked, "What will happen to Tommaso?"

"I'll take him to an orphanage house where this couple I told you about takes in boys. I need money for him too. I don't work for charity, and the man won't take this boy for free either. He's too young."

Simone took the money from the bag Giacomo brought with him and gave it to Bernardo as Tommaso hugged each of the men.

Santo said, "I think someday you'll work on a fishing boat because you never get sick."

Gigante hugged Tommaso last. He got down on a single knee and whispered, "You know about your own money hidden in the bag, right?"

Tommaso looked at Gigante teary-eyed and nodded.

"Okay, you keep that money away from everyone." He hugged the small boy. "Take care of yourself."

Gigante sniffled as he stood.

Someone from the Catania group said, "Even the behemoth cries like a baby."

The rest of the group dared not say anything except one dolt who chuckled.

Gigante feigned ignorance to the comment, but as he walked by, his fist slammed into the man's face, knocking him unconscious.

He turned his attention to the man who dared to laugh. "You still think it's funny?"

The man shook his head enthusiastically, managing to utter a convincing, "No, no sir."

Salvadora and Maria found living difficult but living alone impossible. Between the losses of husbands and children, Tommaso's departure was the ultimate blow and the last tangible connection to the past for them. Having been stripped of all other love in the world, they leaned on each other for survival.

A few weeks after Saverio died, financially-strapped Salvadora left her home and moved to Maria's converted boarding house. They found comfort sitting under the sun on the steps out front clinging to each other physically and emotionally, talking about the old days, and the conversation invariably turned to Tommaso.

"I can hear his voice," Salvadora said. "Remember how he would be so insistent and say, '*Nonna*, listen to me,' when he disagreed with something you or I said?"

"Yes. He always had to make sure you heard his point of view."

Salvadora said, "He was cute the way he would frown first, then he would say, 'Listen to me, *Nonna*. Please listen to me now.'"

"Dear Lord, I miss him," said Maria. "I can't bear it."

Salvadora put her arm around Maria's shoulder. "I can't either, but we have to. We're all we've got."

Chapter Twenty

1900

Nunzio Davanzo was a fifty-two-year-old man who emigrated from Milan, Italy, almost twenty-five years earlier. He first worked as a carpenter, saving the money he needed to have his wife, Angelina, brought over a year later. The two of them lived in Detroit and had no children of their own.

The first time Nunzio laid eyes on Tommaso, he said, "Sicily is still the trash heap, I see."

When Tommaso arrived, he had dirt caked on his hands, face, and body. His clothes were nothing more than rags.

Nunzio said, "He's a skinny thing. How old is this boy?"

"He's five, but he told me his birthday is in January," Angelina said.

"Where will I find a job for a boy this young? Why did you take him?"

"Look at him, he's precious."

"Precious or not, he has to work. I'm not running a church."

"Bernardo said if we didn't take him, he would leave him at the Detroit River with the hobos."

"You see, this is why I can never leave you to make any decisions." said Nunzio.

"I beg you. He has nowhere else to go. I'll fix him a bed and get him washed before the other boys come home from work."

Each of the boys who lived there had traveled with their families from Sicily or southern Italy for a new start in the United States. Somewhere in the journey, something went awry and sadly they found themselves at the makeshift orphanage in Detroit. Orphaned or abandoned, these boys were the castoffs no one else wanted.

The room where the boys slept was originally a carpentry workshop. In the early years, Nunzio's work as a carpenter had been quite a successful venture until a large stack of lumber crushed his hands, leaving the left one almost completely paralyzed. Since the accident, his hand served merely as a club to push open a door or to make a clumsy attempt at holding objects with a balled-up fist.

His work had become a bitter memory, and for the last fifteen years the outbuilding functioned as both storage for junk and the living quarters for the young boys. Old blankets on top of straw served as mattresses. Each boy used another blanket for cover and warmth. A stove sat in one corner of the room. In winters, they burned wood or, in its absence, coal they nicked from the railroad yard, which provided enough heat to survive the coldest nights.

Tommaso, or Thomas as Angelina called him, was the youngest child to ever live with them, and he shared a room with eight boys. They ranged in age from Thomas, just shy of his sixth birthday, to the eldest, almost fifteen. The oldest of the group staked claim to his preferred proximity to the stove, and the others fell in line, dependent on age and toughness, typically the youngest and weakest to the outside of the ring of bodies.

Nunzio and Angelina had no legal authority to do what they did. Until 1895, as many as fifteen boys lived in the small workshop. By the latter 1890s, small changes had begun taking place, most notably the movements underway to legislate child labor laws, but in spite of the changes, Nunzio made it clear he cared not one whit about people's feelings or any proposed laws. He made no apologies and felt no guilt for sending the young boys off to work and taking the money they earned.

By the turn of the new century, Nunzio found it increasingly difficult to find work for the children. Nonetheless, he was resourceful and always managed to locate some type of paid labor. Typically they worked at menial jobs for long hours, six or seven days a week. The money they made went to Nunzio, with a small part of their earnings being used to provide food and rarely a little something extra.

Angelina went along with the program for one reason—Nunzio was the boss. She had been beaten down to the point where she was, at times, almost without a mind of her own. Even though she despised the conditions the boys lived in, Angelina rarely dared to say anything to Nunzio. He was a malicious bully of a man, and she was well acquainted with his temper, having been the recipient of the back of his hand on many occasions.

If Nunzio happened to be away from home, Angelina tried to do special things for the boys like provide a little extra food to eat, but she was cautious of such activity. She had been reminded too many times that every penny spent on the boys meant one less penny for him.

In contrast to Nunzio, Angelina was an individual with a sweet disposition and a caring smile truly reflecting her innate warmth and inner beauty. She thought the best of someone even if she didn't know the person. Angelina never thought of herself as attractive—her face too long, her hair too thin, and her hips too wide, but nonetheless there was an attractiveness to her that others, save Nunzio, sensed. Left up to her to decide, the boys would live inside a real house where they would be surrounded by love, kindness, and joy.

Angelina had a soft spot in her heart for young, sweet Thomas. The others arrived when they were at least ten years of age and departed by fifteen or sooner if they left of their own accord. She knew it was through no fault of their own, but even Angelina reluctantly admitted to herself, the older boys were often jaded and cynical.

She was careful not to let Nunzio or the other boys see or hear her when she said, "Thomas, come here and sit beside me" or "Thomas, give me a hug." Her affection for the young boy was a secret that Angelina kept locked in a compartment deep inside her heart, away from Nunzio and everyone else. She knew Thomas was her gift from God.

After the workshop accident, Nunzio didn't need to work much. Instead, he found the children jobs as factory workers, farmhands, newsies, messengers, or street sweepers. They received less pay than adults but could be made to work as many hours or more. In some ways, they were better than adults because they wouldn't complain about working conditions, at least out loud. Besides, they had little to no other option.

He also negotiated the pay so he knew to the penny how much the boys owed him. Sometimes he checked on them at work and spoke to their bosses. If he saw or heard one negative comment, he dealt immediate and harsh retribution. Beatings meant nothing to Nunzio, and he was secure in the knowledge employers wouldn't say anything. They got the cheapest labor with no rules and, if Nunzio sensed a proprietor possessed a conscience or didn't favor the setup, he moved on to others who weren't so scrupulous.

Nunzio's opinions about child labor were rooted in his own upbringing. Raised from an early age by an abusive grandfather after his own parents were killed in a massive flood, he learned life was tough and no one gave a damn about him.

His grandfather had been a hardened, surly individual who hadn't liked children when he was younger and certainly had no need for any as an older man. Love and affection to him meant being neither seen nor heard, and discipline was the nearest tree branch or belt, or worse. Family discussion around the dinner table amounted to 'wash the dishes' or 'scrub the floor.' Nunzio believed he was nothing more than a bother and a burden because his grandfather told him so on a daily basis.

He was also shaped by his own experience in the immigration process. Years earlier, Nunzio and other northern Italians arrived in America, establishing themselves to a modest degree in larger U.S. cities. Twenty-five years later, their Sicilian cousins, whom Nunzio viewed as less intelligent, uncultured, and primitive, threatened the gains made by him and his fellow countrymen. While he couldn't stop their arrival, he felt obligated to do his part ensuring they remained subservient and in their place.

Chapter Twenty-One

It had been months since Salvadora and Maria had last seen their grandson boarding the ferry. An envelope from America sat unopened in Maria's trembling hands. She opened it and held the letter for both to read, but their excitement turned to heartbreak as they read about Damiano's misfortune.

"I don't understand. He never even saw Tommaso," said Maria. "What happened to our grandson?"

Salvadora stood. "Tommaso, where are you?" she screamed.

"Please come home to us, Tommaso, please come home," Maria shouted.

Their voices joined as one, resonating down the dusty road all the way to the sea and beyond.

A new family acquired Salvadora's empty house on Via Cavallo. Their eight-year-old daughter, Elena, occupied the bedroom once used by Saverio. She had wanted the bedroom at the other end of the hallway because there were a few stone blocks that jutted from the wall, making the perfect resting spot near the bed for her precious dolls.

One day when playing in her room she noticed something stuck between a shelf and the wall at the floor. Elena wriggled her little hand into the small space, but every time she pulled, the elusive object slipped from her grasp. Almost ready to give up, she focused all her attention, giving it one final yank using only her thumb and forefinger, and out came a little leather pouch.

Elena removed the contents and studied the photograph of a young man and woman. She read the letter several times and examined the photograph again. Before falling asleep that night, she reread the letter. In place of sadness, she found peace and comfort.

Over the next several days, she began to think of the man and woman as her own family with whom she might share her most private feelings. They seemed to understand her better than her own parents, and she loved the smiles on their faces. Elena decided she would keep her new family a secret all for herself.

She cautiously approached her mother one day. "*Matri*, who lived here before we did?"

"I think it was a nice young family."

"*Matri*, where did they go?"

Unwilling to admit the truth, she said, "Well, Elena, I believe they went to another town."

"Why, *Matri*?"

"You're certainly full of questions today. I think his job—"

"That's okay. *Matri*, do you know, did they have any children?"

"Dear, I think they had a boy younger than you, but I'm not sure. Now why don't you run along and play."

"Okay, *Matri*, but *Matri*, what happens when someone dies?"

Her mother spun to face Elena. "Why would you ask such a question?"

She had gone too far and was afraid her mother might find out about her secret. She fibbed. "Father Vittorio said heaven is never too crowded and everyone who's good goes there when they die. Okay, *Matri*, I'm going to play now."

Later, once she was certain her mother had forgotten the conversation, she unfolded the letter and immersed herself in its words. "Don't worry, I'll never tell anyone. I know you're in heaven and it's not crowded."

In a small mirror beside her bed, Elena practiced smiling like the beautiful woman, Rosa, in the picture.

Chapter Twenty-Two

Within days of his arrival, Thomas had begun working as a newsie selling papers on street corners. Following a breakfast of oatmeal, the workday started at seven and sometimes continued until the evening. When he returned home, dinner typically consisted of a bowl of stew reminiscent of the meals served on board the *Grabow*.

During his first month, he worked with an older boy named Paolo who said, "These are pennies, one, two, three, four, five. Five pennies are the nickel. This is the nickel. Two nickels are the dime, yes? How many pennies are the dime?"

Thomas struggled at first.

"Learn. Fast. It's ten."

Early on in his new job sometimes things went wrong. Thomas might make an honest mistake counting coins and, on a rare occasion, a customer tried to trick him into giving the wrong change back by claiming Thomas miscounted. A young child was an easy target to intimidate, especially one who spoke little English.

Each morning Thomas and Paolo walked from home near the Eastern Market to Cadillac Square, where they met a newspaper supplier, a man named Nikolai that everyone called Fats.

Fats distributed the newspapers to each of the newsies ten at a time from a wagon he sat or lay in depending on the time of day, his mood, or both. The newsies were expected to sell the papers as fast as possible and return the money to Fats, who gave each boy two cents in return per stack sold.

In Nunzio's opinion, a month of training was a reasonable amount of time to learn the trade, then he set a goal for the boy.

"You sell fifty newspapers each day. If you don't, I'll send you back and you'll work until you do."

On rare occasions, Thomas worked as late as nine at night to reach the goal, and he gave his earnings to Nunzio when he returned home in the evening. Nunzio checked with Fats to ensure no one cheated him.

Thomas learned quickly mornings and late afternoons were the busiest times, and certain street corners and diners were the best places to sell newspapers. He also learned the middle of the day to be the best time to find a good place to rest, especially if he was well on his way to meeting the fifty-newspaper goal. He was careful not to be discovered by Nunzio. Getting caught lying down on the job would end badly for Thomas or any other boy.

During his first year, he learned to count, do arithmetic well enough to make change, and speak English at more than a rudimentary level. He listened with rapt attention to how customers spoke when they bought newspapers and imitated how they pronounced the written words. Trying his best to mimic the American pronunciation, Thomas shouted the headlines, "President McKinley Shot" or "Chicago White Stockings Win Again" or "Roosevelt Becomes President."

Shortly before he left Sicily, he had begun reading the most basic words in his native language under the tutelage of his grandmothers and father. He also proved himself to be a quick study in English, learning to read with the help of Angelina.

The long and brutal hours for a young child were bad enough but adding in the cruelty of Nunzio only made matters worse when he thought Thomas or one of the boys cheated him. On one occasion, Thomas reluctantly obliged to make change for a man when he was certain he had been given a nickel and not a dime. It was the only time he was fooled because from that moment forward, Thomas never put the customer's money in his pocket until after the transaction was complete.

That evening, he turned over his money to Nunzio, then waited to eat. Angelina served dinner through an opening at the back of the house adjacent to the old workshop, now the boys' converted bunkhouse. Thomas took his bowl from Angelina and sat near the other boys.

No sooner had he taken his first spoonful of food when he felt a sharp pull on his right ear, yanking him and the bowl of stew to the ground.

Nunzio jerked him to his feet, yelling while still twisting the same ear with his good hand. "Thomas, where's my money? You stole from me."

He kept hold of Thomas's ear, squeezing harder and demanding more money. Thomas knew there was no more change in his pockets. All he could do was try to hold still.

Angelina ran over. "Please, Nunzio, he's only a child. He doesn't have your money."

Nunzio was enraged, and he pressed his face close to Thomas, who remained trapped. The putrid breath, a mixture of garlic and unbrushed teeth, enveloped Thomas's senses, causing him to cry out and forget about his aching ear.

"I spoke with Fats today. I think you bought candy with the money, sì? Now you owe me five cents." Nunzio held up a nickel. "I don't care how, get me my money tomorrow."

Fats, an immigrant who came from Russia in the 1870s, spoke little English and cared not one iota whether he did or didn't. He used the wagon not only as a vehicle to carry newspapers, pulling it like an ox, but he also lived in it. On nights when the weather was pleasant, he slept on the banks of the Detroit River using old newspapers for a pillow. In inclement weather, he pulled the wagon to an overhang between two buildings in the city.

Fats was an uncomplicated man. He asked for nothing, offended no one, and loved to talk to the young newsies. As an orphan in Russia, he ate whatever might pass for food found in the streets, or anything he could steal from an open window.

When he was fourteen years old, he hid himself on a ship in St. Petersburg not knowing nor caring where it was headed. Fats worked his way up from stowaway to any job no one else wanted, but after four years working on ships, he grew too large to comfortably live on one and found himself a home in Detroit.

Fats pulled the wagon filled with the daily newspapers as any beast of burden might, with his short powerful legs and brawny shoulders enabling him to easily lift and haul it wherever he wanted. Occasionally, a newsie or two might be lucky enough to jump in for a ride as Fats pulled his wagon toward Cadillac Square.

The day after Nunzio caught Thomas coming up short on earnings for the day, the young boy arrived early at Fats' wagon to collect his first stack of newspapers to sell. Once Thomas sold the first ten outside a diner, he returned for another stack. By this time, Fats heard what happened to Thomas the night before.

He called him over to give advice on how he might *find* money. "You see this man with coins. You bump hand and cover on ground with foot."

Thomas knew this was dishonest but felt trapped by the circumstances. Later in the day when he had an opportunity, he helped a customer pick up loose change off the ground. In the manner Fats had demonstrated, Thomas put his shoe over a nickel and helped a dapper old man retrieve the remainder of his money. The man walked away, but not before giving the well-mannered young boy a nickel for his trouble. Thomas retrieved the coin under his shoe feeling guilty. He silently promised one day he would return the nickel to the old man.

Thomas arrived home in the evening and gave Nunzio his earnings for the day, including the extra nickel.

"You understood your mistake and paid me, right?" Nunzio asked.

Thomas nodded, but he already decided to keep the other nickel a secret.

Nunzio held up a small bag to the other boys. He removed several dollar bills taken from Thomas the first day he arrived in Detroit.

"You see, here is your money." He waved the dollar bills in the air. "This is the deposit for the food and the bed, *capisci?*"

"Yes, sir, I understand."

Nunzio pushed Thomas aside to focus his attention on a bigger problem. He heard Carmelo and Matteo, two brothers left abandoned at the orphanage, had been talking too much while working on the factory canning line. The job paid each boy eight cents an hour, significantly less than the average American unskilled adult laborer, but Nunzio found the wage to be fair pay for dullards incapable of learning or bettering themselves.

Their behavior was unacceptable, and Nunzio was determined to address the problem with a show of discipline and force, as well as set an example for the others. He yanked Carmelo off the ground and bit him on his forearm. When the boy cried out, Nunzio bit him again, only harder.

"You shut your trap at work." He waved his balled-up fist while spittle flew from his mouth. "Both you and your brother stop talking. I don't want to hear this complaint about you two again."

He used his club hand to smack Carmelo across the cheek.

Nunzio walked right by Matteo. Quickly, he spun around and threw the older brother onto the ground. He slapped his hands over Matteo's ears repeatedly. Pressing his face close to the boy, he exhaled his rancid breath. Then he rubbed his coarse beard across Matteo's face causing him to cry out.

"Next time, I'll cut off your ears. You won't be able to hear your mongrel brother talk so good, right?"

Fortunately for Thomas, getting cheated or miscounting change never happened after his first year. Thomas proved himself to be quite smart. Even at the age of seven, his abilities in reading and comprehension were more advanced than most of the older boys.

Angelina spent what time she could helping Thomas with math and reading, so she knew how quickly he absorbed both arithmetic and the English language. She often told him, "Thomas, it's important you speak, read, and write English. I'll miss you when you leave, but someday you'll find it'll open doors for you."

The other boys were also surprised at how swiftly Thomas grasped the new language in his first year or so, though despite his rapid advances, he did stumble occasionally while mastering its nuances.

One morning Angelina gave Thomas a quick hug before he began his walk to work. She whispered, "Stay warm today, child."

Thomas looked up at Angelina and said, "Yes, I can feel it in the bones, the rain is coming."

She stifled a laugh and said, "No, Thomas, the expression is I can feel it in *my* bones."

"Okay. I can feel it in your bones, the rain is coming," Thomas said.

Now Angelina was unable to quiet her laughter. She said, "No, honey, it's in *your* own bones that you can feel the rain coming."

His face was contorted in confusion as he peered up at Angelina. "But I don't feel anything in my bones."

"You're too precious. We'll talk tonight about your bones and the rain."

Chapter Twenty-Three

Angelina had heard Nunzio's stories many times about his grandfather's mistreatment and abuse. Her conclusion, and one she wisely kept to herself, was that some people came away from those experiences and rejected them, while others decided to nurture and embrace the venom and pain. Early in their marriage, she realized Nunzio had decided to follow the latter.

More than once, as if practicing for a discussion he might have with others in the neighborhood concerning his civic duty, he said, "Angelina, it's true I use a bit of discipline, but I do good by these children. You see, they're no different than horses or other animals. It's not words that teach. They learn right from wrong by the whip. I know the town's people are happy, because I keep them off the streets at night with a strict curfew. Otherwise, they would roam around and cause trouble, yes?"

She said nothing, finding his beliefs to be despicable. If he said something requiring no response, it was certain she wouldn't waste her breath to say anything to a man whom she considered to be a monster.

Angelina grew up in Milan and often wondered how different life might have been for her had she never left. She came from a working-class family with nurturing parents who believed in education for all. She attended school until the age of seventeen and dreamed someday of becoming a schoolteacher herself because she loved to work with children. An excellent student with a love for life in general, Angelina had even tutored young children struggling in school.

During her teenage years, life was wonderfully idyllic. She had loving parents and the best friends a person could hope for. Every day was special, and she couldn't wait for each day of school to begin. She thought the only thing better would be the one day when she might marry a wonderful man and have children of her own to love and cherish.

Angelina thought back now to her own foolishness at falling in love with the rough-and-tumble, handsome Nunzio. He was romantic and loving when he courted her, but he changed soon after she arrived in Detroit. She realized her mistake when he revealed his true self—an angry tyrant and a wife beater.

Angelina complained to her only friend in town, Serena, an elderly immigrant neighbor from Rome.

Serena sympathized and offered advice. "I'm sorry, but he's your husband. Are you cleaning the house well and preparing his meals?"

"Yes, of course, I am," Angelina said.

"Men have needs. You're taking care of these things, aren't you?"

"Serena! Yes, I am, but he isn't the same person I met. He's changed, and I can tell he doesn't love me."

Angelina began to cry. In between the sobs, she said, "I don't care because I don't love him either. I hate him."

Serena wiped tears from her friend's face and spoke in a quiet voice.

"If this helps, know he can't read your mind. If he wants to act like the rear end of a donkey, in your mind see him as a donkey's rear."

That same night, Nunzio knocked her around because dinner wasn't on the table when he arrived home. Angelina thought of Serena's advice while sitting on the kitchen floor nursing a bloody lip. Her friend's counsel seemed even more useless than before.

Almost three years after Thomas came to live in Detroit, Nunzio took him and another boy named Biagio to meet a man about new jobs at the Great Northern Telegraph Company. Nunzio heard of a need for messenger boys to deliver telegrams. He had negotiated his cut to be a percentage of the thirty cents per telegram the company charged its customers.

It was a twenty-minute walk from home to the telegraph company. The supervisor, a man named Willie, studied Thomas the first time they met.

He said to Nunzio, "He's a pretty small boy."

Nunzio pulled Willie aside and spoke in a low voice. "I don't know how, but he's not like the other ones. He speaks good English and learned to read while selling newspapers. He can do this job."

They turned their attention back to the boys. Nunzio smacked the back of the boys' heads. "You pay attention and listen. I don't want to hear any complaints about you."

Biagio, an eleven-year-old from Sicily, was left behind at Nunzio's after his mother died and his father went to work in the copper mines in the northernmost reaches of Michigan. The other orphans called him Stick because he was skinny like a blade of grass. Biagio was three years older and a head taller than Thomas, and perhaps because he was newer to the orphanage than Thomas, he was friendly with the younger boy.

Back when they worked as newsies, Thomas asked Stick one day, "Do you like this Stick name or Biagio?"

"Stick is how those boys call me. My parents say Biagio."

Thomas picked up his stack of papers and said, "Okay Biagio, bye-bye."

Willie was a tall man with a shiny bald head and the biggest eyes Thomas had ever seen. He had a watch hanging from his jacket pocket, and he fiddled with it constantly while he talked.

"So you're going to be messenger boys and work for me? All right, my name is Willie. You need to be here every morning at eight until six in the evening."

He winked at the boys. "Every day but Sunday, that is. Okay? Follow me."

Willie took them to the back of the one-story brick building situated on the north side of Atwater Street. "You'll wait here until I call for you. Sometimes it gets busy. When a telegram comes in, you take it as fast as you can to the address. Nunzio says you know this part of town well from selling newspapers. That's good because time is important. If you don't know where an address is, you need to learn fast. I won't have the time to go around with you."

Willie peeked at his watch.

"After you deliver the message, you check to see if the person wants to reply. You understand what reply means?"

Both boys nodded.

"Now, I don't care for this, but our company policy is we don't accept tips. You understand what tips are?"

Both boys nodded again. Willie stared at them for a moment unsure and decided he better explain just in case.

"Tips are when folks give you money. You politely refuse and don't take it. You understand? I'm sorry, but it's company policy and we have to follow the rules. Sometimes, I might have you sweep in front of the building or in the office. I might think of other things too. Today only, you'll work together unless we get too busy. Starting tomorrow, each of you is going to do the telegram running by yourself."

Willie looked at his watch again and spun the chain around his fingers.

"The big boss inside likes the messengers to stand up out here." Willie shook his head and lowered his voice. "He thinks it makes us look speedy."

Thomas said, "Yes, sir."

Willie eyed Thomas, smiled, and went back inside. The boys waited outside for a while with nothing to do.

The back door swung open and Willie left the building tugging on his watch. He said, "I'll be back shortly."

As he walked away, the boys watched him tip his hat to passersby. "Good day, sir, Good day, ma'am."

Not thirty minutes later, Willie returned from the Jefferson Avenue Diner, a place serving his kind out the back door where he enjoyed his favorite breakfast of two soft yolky eggs, four thick slices of bacon, buttery biscuits on the side, and a hot cup of coffee for twenty-five cents. If his sister Mae was working in the kitchen, he might get a second cup of coffee for free.

Willie climbed to the top of the stairs and stood in front of the boys checking his watch.

"I call that a test to see what you'd do while I was gone. Now we're open for business."

Willie released a laughing rumble from deep inside while pulling two green caps from his back pocket.

"This cap must be on your head every time you meet a customer."

He put one on each boy's head. The cap for Thomas was too big.

"You'll grow into it."

He let out another good hearty guffaw.

Ten minutes later, Willie walked back out holding an envelope with an address written in large print on the front. It was their first telegram delivery.

He turned to Biagio. "You know where this address is?"

Biagio looked at the address and turned his head sideways to Thomas, who nodded.

Biagio said, "Yes, we know."

"Well, good. What are you waiting for?"

They took off running. Biagio sprinted past Thomas—his long skinny legs moved at lightning speed, covering great distances, not taking single stairs, but leaping several at a time. He easily outdistanced Thomas until he reached an intersection waiting in doubt whether to turn or go straight. When Thomas caught up, he would set them on the proper course. Once again Biagio accelerated forward shouting to his smaller sidekick behind him to run faster.

They raced down Gratiot Avenue all the way to Clyde's Fish Market. The boys waited, watching Clyde's lips mouth each word as he attempted to slog his way through the message.

A heavy-footed woman stomped her way over, making quick work of the telegram. She shouted, "Thanks be to God. What a blessing!"

Confused, Clyde continued grappling with the words.

The woman said, "Hand me that, you old goop. You'll be here all day to Sunday trying to make sense of this note."

Clyde stopped moving his lips a few seconds after she ripped the paper from his hand. He gawked at his wife, Bernice.

She bellowed, "Don't you get it? Says here we've got ourselves a grandbaby in Cleveland. Oh, we do rejoice!"

She turned away hollering the news to anyone who would listen.

Thomas asked, "Sir, any reply?"

Clyde shook his head slowly, his lips still moving while he wrestled with the difficult written words in his mind.

The boys turned and sprinted back to the telegraph office. Though unspoken, they both wanted to impress Willie with how fast they completed the round trip. Willie stepped outside when Biagio sailed through the air covering the five steps in one leap with Thomas scuttling up them one by one behind him.

Willie howled. "Hey, boys, what kept you?"

The boys worked up a sweat from running, but they didn't mind because it felt good to be free from hauling newspapers from street to street. The remainder of their first day went about the same, without much time to stand around, and sometimes another telegram was waiting for them upon their return.

As they walked home that evening, they agreed being a messenger was better than working as a newsie where they had to compete with too many hungry kids around every street corner hawking newspapers at two pennies a piece.

Biagio said, "Tomorrow we run alone. Not as fun, right?"

"No, it's going to be different tomorrow."

They arrived home at half past six tired, sweaty, and hungry. Seated on the stoop, Nunzio gazed up from his newspaper at the boys standing outside.

He hollered. "Angelina, get out here."

She hurried from the kitchen and said, "Oh, boys, look at how dirty you are. Let's get you both cleaned up, then I'm going to get your stew."

Nunzio asked, "Any problems at work today?"

In unison, the boys said, "No, sir."

"I'll check with Willie."

As Angelina and the boys turned toward the outdoor wash basin, Nunzio said, "You see how I make sure they have their jobs? I help them to grow up and protect them. Not many men can do these things, what I do for all of them."

Angelina stood motionless, remaining silent.

Finally, Nunzio said, "Don't stand there staring at me like a dumb cow. Get their dinner."

Days of being messengers ground on one by one, six days a week, ten hours a day. On Sunday mornings, Nunzio assigned chores around the house. He reasoned that, since he gave them a place to live and food to eat, they owed him at least that much in return.

"You don't have to do anything I didn't do when I was a boy. I worked on the farm with my grandfather, and he wasn't a nice person like me."

Nunzio supervised their work while sitting on the front or back stoops of the house. "I work hard to find each of you jobs. I wonder sometimes, how can you keep this job? You're all lazy. I worked much harder than you as a boy."

He had them clean and do work everywhere except inside his own house. They were never allowed inside his home and, besides, Nunzio believed it was important for Angelina to have a purpose in life too.

At the telegraph company, Biagio and Thomas devised a system to make the workload as fair as possible.

Biagio said, "Okay, we always say the truth. Too much running for one boy is not fair, right? When one runs a long way, the other boy must put his hand out for the *telegramma, si?*"

"Right!" Thomas agreed, and they shook hands sealing their deal.

Thomas had been tested a few times with the no tipping policy. Offered as much as a nickel on a few occasions, he always politely refused.

One day, though, an elderly man screamed at Thomas from his front porch for not accepting the offer of a nickel. "This is an insult to me. You never refuse something from an adult when it's offered to you. I'm going to report you to the authorities."

The old man berated Thomas, chased him into the yard, and pushed him to the ground, standing over him while continuing his crazy tirade. Flapping his arms like wings, he said, "The chick bows to the hen and the hen bows to the rooster, but all bow to the farmer. Do you understand I'm the farmer and you're the chicken?"

He repeated it over and over until Thomas wriggled out from under the man's legs and ran as fast as he could, not stopping and not looking back as the man continued yelling.

"You come back here now. You're not the farmer. Come back here, little chicken. I'm the farmer!"

Thomas, breathless and speaking in spurts, tried to explain what happened. "Mr. Willie, this man, well, he tried to give me money. I said no thank you, but he pushed me down. He yelled at me about a chicken and a rooster and—"

Thomas doubled over, trying to catch his breath.

Willie shook his head and removed his watch from his pocket.

He said, "Boy, that old kook yells at everyone. Didn't you know? He's crazier than a two-tailed cat."

Thomas could hear Willie continue laughing even after he went back inside.

While Biagio was delivering a telegram, Thomas thought about his work as a runner versus being a newsie. He missed the opportunities to read while selling newspapers, but that work meant more interaction with Nunzio, who sometimes talked nonstop for hours leaning against Fats's wagon.

Depending on his mood, Nunzio might yank on Thomas' ears, or kick him in his rear end when he wasn't looking. The worst thing in Thomas's opinion, though, was the biting. He acted like a rabid dog and bit him on the arm or shoulder, sometimes for no reason at all.

The biting made him think of Angelina. He wished she wouldn't try to help him whenever Nunzio was angry with him about something. Sometimes Nunzio yelled and hit her and he could hear Angelina crying in their house. It made him wonder if he bit her too.

Chapter Twenty-Four

In September 1905, heavy rain pounded Detroit, flooding the streets. Willie allowed the boys to wait inside the rear office door with a caution.

"Don't move from here." He wound the stem of his watch for a moment, then leaned over and said in a whisper, "Even though the boss drags as much water in as anyone, he doesn't like anybody else doing it."

Thomas and Biagio's clothes, shoes, hats, and bodies were completely soaked through. Not wanting to cause any trouble, they used the palms of their hands to wipe the pools of water back out the door. When Thomas got called for the next job, he read the writing on the envelope noting with disappointment the address was farther away than he had ever delivered a telegram before.

Twenty minutes of running through pouring rain in several inches of standing water left him waiting on the front porch of a stately home supported by massive columns. He stood before two enormous doors, removed his cap, and squeezed the water out while he waited for someone to answer. A minute turned into two, and Thomas wondered how many people lived in such a grand home. He continued waiting, imagining it took several minutes to walk from one end of the house to the other.

When the door finally opened, Thomas wiped the water from his eyes to find a stylish older gentleman standing before him dressed in a fine suit and tie. Thomas recognized him as the person he took the nickel from a few years before and wondered if the man remembered him.

"Good morning, youngster. How may I help you?"

"Yes, yes, sir, a, a telegram for you, sir."

Thomas removed the soaked envelope from his back pocket.

"Why don't you come in out of the rain?"

Thomas entered and followed the man to a nearby table walking on his tiptoes. Even still, his shoes squeaked with every step on the shiny wood floor. Frightened and cold, he shivered as he stared at the puddle of water forming beneath him.

The man said, "No need to worry over a little water on the floor. Trees are rained on every day all over the world and they seem to be fine with it."

He removed his reading glasses from his coat pocket and sat down. Studying Thomas for a moment, he asked, "How old are you, my boy?"

"I'm ten, sir."

"Goodness gracious!"

Thomas waited while the man read the message.

He looked at Thomas and said, "This is great good news."

"Yes, sir. Any reply?"

"I think not, at least for now. In any event, I'm going into town." He peered out the window from his chair. "What do you know, the rain has stopped. I have something for you, for your hard work."

He reached into his coat pocket and removed a twenty-five-cent piece.

"No thank you, sir, I can't accept it."

"That's right, company policy. I'm thinking you work for Willie, correct?"

Thomas shivered. "Yes, sir."

"Do you have a slicker?"

"No, sir."

"Okay, let's go talk to Willie first. Would you mind bringing my shoes from over there by the stairs? My back is hurting something fierce this morning."

Thomas glanced at the man's stocking feet.

The old man coughed. "Yes, I suppose I'm off to a bit of a slow start today. Someday you'll learn that old age is a scornful lover indeed."

"Yes, sir."

Thomas carried the two-toned dress boots to the man.

"What might your name be?"

"Thomas, sir."

"I'm Floyd Abernathy." They shook hands. "It's indeed a pleasure to make your acquaintance."

"Yes, sir."

"Thomas, let's go for a ride in my new motor car. Have you ever ridden in one?"

"No, sir. I must run back to work."

"Yes, I know, but today you can ride to work. Don't worry, I know Willie. He won't mind. I bet I can get you back to work as fast as you can run, if not faster."

He winked at Thomas and said, "I drive quite well for being elderly. Now, what do you say? Let's go to the carriage house."

Thomas followed the man down a wide hallway adorned with colorful paintings and statue heads perched on mahogany tables. Despite maintaining his balance on tiptoes as he walked, his shoes squeaked, sounding a rhythmic beat. They stopped suddenly when Mr. Abernathy poked his head around a corner leading to another grand hallway.

"Rachel?" he half shouted.

A female's voice answered. "Yes, sir?" A short, slender woman appeared. "Yes, sir?" she said again.

"I do apologize, but it seems we've left a bit of rain in the foyer and hallway."

"I'll take care of it right away, sir," she said.

"Thank you, Rachel."

As she walked past, Mr. Abernathy spoke again. "By the way, this is my new friend, Thomas."

"Why, Thomas, it's nice to meet you."

"Yes, ma'am."

"Can you believe he's ten years old and delivering telegrams in these conditions?" Mr. Abernathy asked.

Consumed with worry that Willie would be angry if he took too long, Thomas stared at the floor.

Rachel's face suddenly appeared as she bent over to take a closer look. "Why, you're a pitiful little thing, aren't you, Thomas?"

"Yes, ma'am."

"Well, I think you're adorable."

She used her apron to wipe the rain from his face.

"We're going into town now. I'll be back this evening," Mr. Abernathy said as they restarted their journey.

The old man sat down heavily in the driver's seat. Thomas hesitated, worried about his soaking wet clothes and shoes.

"Thomas, don't fret over a little water. All aboard now."

He climbed into the car. Surprising himself, he said, "Mister, I must tell you something."

"Oh, what might that be?"

"A long time ago, I helped you collect coins you dropped on the ground and I kept a nickel for myself. I'm sorry, but I want to repay you."

"I see." Mr. Abernathy scratched his chin and thought how pitiful the young waif appeared.

"Well, young man, I appreciate your candor, and we shall chalk the incident up to one of life's lessons. Since you seem to have learned something of value by admitting your transgression and I'm still no worse for the wear, let's forget it happened. As for repayment, consider yourself debt free as of this moment. Is that agreeable to you?"

"Yes, sir."

To Thomas' delight, they zoomed away from the house at a surprisingly fast pace. He stood in the open-air runabout vehicle holding onto the seat behind him.

Mr. Abernathy said, "There are only a few of these around, but I can see the day when everyone will have a motorized vehicle. What do you think?"

Thomas couldn't believe his luck to be riding in a real automobile. The car came to a stop in front of the telegraph office, and Mr. Abernathy sounded the hand-held bulb horn a few times. When Thomas laughed, the old man smiled and squeezed the horn again for good measure. Thomas crouched to jump out, but the man put his hand on the young boy's shoulder and told him to wait.

Willie exited the front office door. His expression of disbelief focused on Thomas, who sat not just in any motor car.

"Uh, good morning, Mr. Abernathy. How are you today, sir?"

"I'm fine Willie, and yourself?"

"Mr. Abernathy, may I help you with something?"

The horn also caught the attention of Henry Traynon, the general manager of the telegraph company branch office, who stepped out to join Willie on the front steps. Thomas and Biagio rarely saw Mr. Traynon, even the few times they waited inside the building.

Traynon said, "Good morning, Mr. Abernathy. Is there something we can help you with?"

"Why yes, there is. Your employee here is soaking wet and shivering."

Willie interjected. "Yes, sir, he's a scrappy young thing."

"Yes, Willie, I'm quite sure he is. Please wait here, Thomas."

Mr. Abernathy tottered over to the men where they spoke for a few minutes. Thomas watched Mr. Abernathy speak while the other men nodded in unison and occasionally glanced in his direction.

Willie said, "Thomas, come over here."

Thomas wondered if the man told Willie about the nickel he stole a few years back and thought about Nunzio yanking his ear or biting his arm, or worse.

Mr. Abernathy said, "Thomas, these gentlemen are agreeable with you accepting a gratuity from me. Do you understand what a gratuity is?"

"No, sir."

"Well, in the common vernacular, it's called a tip."

Wide-eyed, Thomas looked at Willie.

Willie nodded. "It's all right, Thomas, and say thank you."

Mr. Abernathy reached into his pocket and removed a silver dollar coin.

"Thomas, thank you for your service today."

Beaming from ear-to-ear, Thomas said, "Thank you, sir!"

"Now I need to get to the bank."

He tipped his hat. "Gentlemen, my best to you. Thomas, it was a pleasure making your acquaintance. You have all the makings of a fine young man."

"Yes, sir."

Thomas continued to be mesmerized by the shiny silver coin, unable to break his fixation from it.

After Mr. Abernathy drove away, Thomas squeezed the dollar coin in his hand before finally holding it up to Willie.

"Mr. Abernathy gave that to you. Now go on out back. We already have another telegram waiting for you."

Thomas walked away and stared at the coin. He held a whole dollar in his hand all for himself and couldn't wait to tell Biagio about the money and the car ride. Thomas thought this might be his best day since arriving in America.

Willie and Traynon went inside through the front door.

"Mr. Traynon, these good deed doers are changing everything," Willie said.

"Yes, the times, they're certainly changing."

"Do you think Mr. Abernathy will do what he said and get these laws changed one day and we can't even have these kids working here anymore?" Willie asked.

"Yes, I do. If the President of the Detroit Savings Bank can't do it, no one can."

"What do you think will happen?"

"Oh, someday the laws will change and Mr. Abernathy and all his rich banker friends will eat their dinners at posh restaurants while that dago boy or one like him watches through the window with an empty stomach."

Willie bristled at the term dago. He was certain a derogatory term for his own kind wasn't far from Mr. Traynon's mind at the same moment. He had no memory of being born into slavery in rural Tennessee during the Civil War, but his mother told him on the day of their freedom, she walked north by foot with him strapped to her back and didn't stop until they reached Detroit. Willie had been the recipient of hateful names all his life, and he wanted no part of that for him or anyone else.

Thomas kept the coin inside his shoe the rest of the day, taking it out only when he and Biagio walked home. Something strange happened when they arrived; Nunzio seemed happy. He rested on a stool next to the house fiddling with a cane pole and tangled fishing line. Angelina dropped scoops of stew in two bowls, and they began eating with the other boys next to their bunkhouse. Thomas no sooner sat down when Nunzio called for him.

"I spoke with Willie today. He said you rode in a fancy motor carriage."

The other boys bunched together, happy Nunzio's attention focused elsewhere.

"You have something to tell me, yes?"

Thomas realized Nunzio knew about the dollar coin and, even though Willie said it belonged to him, he removed his shoe and handed over the coin.

Nunzio said, "Better to tell the truth, sì?"

"Yes, sir."

Thomas walked away thinking at least he kept the dollar for one day when a sharp pain stung his back. He spun to see Nunzio swinging the cane pole at him again, but Thomas dove for the ground and Nunzio missed. Now enraged, Nunzio reared back with the pole and hit him over and over, quitting only when he ran out of breath.

Angelina dropped the ladle and dish into the wash basin and rushed over. "Nunzio, stop it."

He spun to face Angelina and swatted her across the face.

"Shut up, you old cow."

She fell to the ground holding her face while Nunzio went back to the stool and sat down.

"Any money at the job is my money!" He pointed the cane pole at the group of boys seated together and pushed himself up to stand.

They cowered together horrified at the sight of Thomas on the ground coiled into a ball protecting his face with his hands.

He stomped closer to the group, waving the cane. "Nobody keeps my money."

Nunzio turned back to his stool and swatted Thomas again before he sat. Breathing heavily from meting out discipline, he yelled at Angelina, "Get me something to drink."

Later in the evening, Thomas was glad to take his shoes off when he went to bed. The waterlogged and wrinkled skin on his feet itched badly. He used one foot to scratch the other, alternating back and forth. The one good thing about the itchy feet was they made him forget about the welts on his back, and after he covered himself with his blanket, he continued scratching his feet.

Federico, the boy next to him, kicked at Thomas. "Stop your scratching. If you scratch like a dog, you sleep outside like a dog."

All the other boys, except Biagio, laughed and made barking sounds while Federico and two other boys grabbed Thomas and pushed him outside, slamming the door in his face. They barked and called him a dog. Thomas walked over to the sink and drank water from a pail.

Through a window, he could see Nunzio inside wearing only trousers held up by suspenders with his gut hanging over his pants. He was pacing back and forth carrying a bottle in his hand. When Nunzio threw it, he heard the glass breaking and Angelina cry out. Thomas remained frozen, unsure what to do. He wondered, what could he do?

Rage boiled inside him when he thought of Nunzio the bully and the situation with Federico. He returned to the bunkroom and realized his own hands were balled into fists. Thomas had never felt such anger toward Nunzio, sadness for Angelina, and shame over the entire situation he found himself in. A piece of wood was wedged under the bottom to hold it in place. He pushed against the door with all his might.

Biagio said, "Wait. I move the block."

Federico said, "Stick, why let the dog inside?"

Thomas ignored Federico and crawled under his blanket, still seething.

The bully wasn't finished with his torment. "This dog needs to go to school."

He yanked Thomas from the bed, backing him against the door. "Bad dog, bad dog!"

Thomas's rage grew as he thought of Angelina in her own home, beaten and defenseless against a horrible slob of a husband. An image formed in his mind. Federico, someday a grown man and a bully like Nunzio, would be mistreating his wife and children. The thought pushed him to a level of fury he'd never experienced before.

Federico grabbed Thomas by the throat. "Dog, listen to me."

Thomas had reached his limit and swung his closed fist straight up, striking Federico under his nose. The young bully had an expression of shock as his head snapped back and blood spurted from his nose. He fell to the floor and cupped his hands to his face.

Thomas leaned over Federico. He spoke slowly and with deliberation. "I am not a dog. I am a boy and my name is Thomas Mancuso. I want to sleep. Do you understand me?"

Federico held his nose and whined.

Thomas repeated his question, only this time louder. "Do you understand me?"

Between sobs, Federico whimpered, "*Sì, sì.*"

Stunned, the other boys lay on their bedding witnessing the sudden transformation. Thomas covered himself with a blanket and closed his eyes, not saying another word.

The following morning Thomas was viewed in a whole new light. He had grown bigger in the past five years, but he was still smaller than the others. No matter, overnight his reputation was transformed. No longer the easy target to bully, he was now viewed as brooding and unpredictable, and one to be left alone.

Thomas noted the bruise on Angelina's left cheek while he waited for a bowl of oatmeal.

She said, "I'm sorry about the whipping and your dollar, Thomas."

"The coin isn't important, but I was worried about you."

"Thomas, don't concern yourself with me. I can take care of myself."

Angelina gave Thomas a quick hug and quietly said, "I'm terribly sorry."

As they walked to the telegraph office, Biagio spoke non-stop about the previous evening. "The other boys were talking about you. You surprised everyone and now they're afraid of you." He turned to eye Thomas and said, "Especially Federico."

Thomas shrugged. "Who's up first today, Biagio, me or you?"

Chapter Twenty-Five

As Mother Nature dictated every year, the weather turned colder in November.

A light snow had begun falling as Willie walked past the boys on the back stairs waiting for the next telegram assignment. "Some people are predicting it'll be a bad winter this year. Well, I guess so. Why, it's not winter yet, but it's already snowing. Sometimes, I think my mother carried me in the wrong direction."

He smiled, displaying a dazzling set of white teeth and said, "What I'm saying, boys, is instead of coming north, my mother should've turned south."

He shook the flakes from his overcoat, shivered, and walked inside.

"I like Mr. Willie. He's very wise," said Thomas.

He and Biagio hugged to keep themselves warm while they waited for the next assignment.

They agreed that in weather this cold, it was better to be running than standing on street corners, stuffing newspaper inside their clothes to keep warm.

They let go of each other when Willie said, "Telegram!"

Biagio looked over Thomas' shoulder while they scanned the address.

"I delivered here before. I'll take it." Biagio said.

Defying gravity, at least for a moment, he launched himself in a single leap over all five steps. Ignoring the accumulating snowflakes, his feet skimmed across the ground as his lanky legs began pumping him forward. Thomas marveled at how fast Biagio ran and turned around waiting for Willie's reaction.

"Boy, that rascal can run. He might be faster than the African cheetah cats I've been reading about. I read yesterday about these men who hunt them. Doesn't it seem a shame to kill an animal just for that spotted fur?"

"Yes, sir."

Several blocks away from the telegraph office, an older man named Arthur was unloading the last of the fruit and vegetable crates. The wagon was perched atop a steep incline and held in place by a stone block lodged behind a back wheel.

Arthur's helper, Samuel, released the mule from its harness and took the lead in hand to guide the animal to one of the few remaining stables still operating inside the central part of Detroit.

At the back of the wagon, Arthur hurriedly lifted the last and heaviest of the crates to carry inside. He knew the freezing cold was doing the produce no good and it wasn't helping his old bones either. Needing only a few more inches to clear the top of the wagon, he staggered back and lost his balance when the bottom of the crate snagged the side. The crate dropped to the ground with a deafening crash, echoing off walls and sounding like a gunshot. The terrified beast brayed and kicked, rocking the carriage violently. The rear wheel slipped around the block holding it in place, and the heavy wagon started its descent.

Samuel tumbled to his rear end hooting at the sight of Arthur lying on his back with a smashed pumpkin next to the side of his head. Laughing hysterically, he kicked his feet in the air and rolled onto his side.

Arthur shouted, "The wagon is rolling away."

Regaining his composure, Samuel jumped to his feet, but the wagon was picking up speed fast. He yelled a warning. "Look out. I can't stop it!"

Biagio tore across a small park where the next left turn would bring him to Doctor Clarkson's office. From there, he knew it was mere seconds to reach his destination. He heard a loud boom like a gunshot. Pretending he was being chased by a bank robber, Biagio sprinted faster, hoping to outrun his pursuer. When he neared the corner to make his turn, he felt his cap sliding from his head. With his one free hand, he reached up to grab it.

The wagon reached full speed rolling backwards down the hill, aiming directly at a panic-stricken young woman gripping a baby stroller in front of her. A man walked out of Wilson's Apothecary to the street corner and screamed at the lady, who stood petrified with fear at the sight of the charging wagon. In one motion, he dropped his package and grabbed her hand fixed to the stroller handle. He yanked her and the baby out of the way, saving them both from certain disaster. The wagon hit the curb making an awful sound, narrowly missing mom and baby, while turning sideways and launching itself airborne.

Biagio rounded the same corner and took his final breath. In a split second, his eyes filled with terror and his mind emptied of thought, as the half ton wagon slammed into him with such force it crushed his rib cage, shattered his leg bones, nearly separated his head from his shoulders, and propelled his already lifeless body into the air.

The wagon followed closely, flying into a building's solid concrete and brick foundation not two feet from the boy, splintering into pieces of wood and metal that rained down on passersby fifty feet away.

People screamed in horror seeing the way the young boy's body lay twisted in such a grotesque manner. His head was bent to one side, blood oozing from every orifice, and his closed fist still clutched tightly around the crumpled telegram.

The mother squeezed the baby to her chest. Still in shock, her body involuntarily twitched. She babbled, "My baby, oh, dear Lord, I, I don't know. My God, I didn't see, where, where did it come from?"

The man who saved her and the baby sat on the curb vomiting his breakfast between his feet.

A cap with the words Great Northern Telegraph Company written across the front lay nearby stained with droplets of a deep red color. Someone recognized the boy's cap and sent for Willie.

Thomas, who waited out back, heard only part of the conversation, but enough to know something dreadful had happened, and he prayed his friend Biagio was okay. Willie told Traynon about the accident and rushed back outside, catching sight of Thomas sprinting down the street.

Willie yelled, "Wait up, son, wait up."

His voice never seemed to quite catch up as he rounded the corner.

Thomas pushed his way through the crowd to find his best friend's mangled body lying on the ground.

Willie appeared a few minutes later and stumbled through the crowd. "Please, ma'am, excuse me, excuse me, please, sir."

Somebody said something about these poor children being forced to work, but Willie kept excusing himself and pushed to the front. He staggered back at the horrid sight and put his hand on Thomas's shoulder, who sat frozen next to Biagio.

Someone in the crowd said, "It's not right what these children are made to do."

Willie said to no one in particular, "We give these kids jobs so they have a place to sleep and food to eat. They don't have anyone."

The crowd grew quiet when Thomas leaned over and held Biagio's clutched hand in his own. He pried the stiffening fingers apart to take the blood-stained envelope. Thomas wiped his hand on his pants, raised himself to his feet, and stumbled through the crowd as it parted to allow him to pass.

In an eerie silence, their eyes followed him as he walked, with head bowed, to the doctor's office a mere fifty feet away. He handed the bloodied envelope to the doctor standing in the doorway.

Thomas turned and walked away slowly. The sun peeked through the clouds, but he could see only darkness. The shifting wind now blowing gently from the south brought neither comfort nor warmth; instead he felt only a chill. Turning the corner and safely out of the crowd's sight, he opened the floodgate to his emotions as a deluge of tears fell to the ground.

It was early evening when a Detroit policeman visited Nunzio to ask about burying Biagio. Nunzio seethed, frustrated because he couldn't browbeat the man as he did other people.

He said, "I do a good thing, finding them jobs and providing a place to sleep. The boy wasn't mine. All the people who pretend to care, let them bury him."

The policeman said, "People don't like what you're doing. Okay, maybe there's no law against it now, but I don't like what you're doing either. Detroit is changing, and you better change too. Mister, I'll be watching. If I so much as catch you spit on the sidewalk, I'm taking you to jail." He poked Nunzio in the chest. "You understand me?"

Nunzio's humiliation was complete. He'd been humbled in front of Angelina. Worse, he'd been shamed in front of the boys. Nunzio never felt rage like this before and, with the absence of Biagio, Thomas was going to be his outlet when he returned from work.

A gloomy darkness had settled over Detroit by the time Thomas began his walk home. In spite of the cold, he dragged himself along in no hurry, wondering why something so awful happened to his only friend in the world who never hurt anyone.

Sitting on the bank of the Detroit River, Thomas listened to men's voices in the distance while they warmed themselves by a fire.

If Fats were somewhere close by, he might have a chance to talk, but realized with the cold temperature, the fat man was in his wagon next to a building someplace downtown, probably sound asleep. Thomas shivered as the frigid wind blew across his body and knew it was time to head home when the hobos at the campfire started fighting over a pair of shoes.

He walked upon the frozen earth listening to the leaves crackle under his shoes and watched every breath each time he exhaled. Thomas decided he would go straight to bed without eating dinner or listening to the other orphans' pointless conversations.

When he arrived, Thomas found it strange that the boys sat huddled together outside in the cold instead of staying close to the stove inside. He sensed danger in the way they looked at him as he leaned over the outside basin to wash his hands and face in a bucket of ice-cold water. Setting his worry aside, he turned toward the bunkhouse.

Nunzio came outside holding a walking cane and pointed toward Thomas. "Come over here."

He stood before Nunzio and stared at the ground. "Yes, sir?"

Without warning, Nunzio swung the cane, hitting Thomas square on the side of his face. He dove to the ground shrieking as Nunzio stood over him striking his back repeatedly.

Angelina scrambled over. "He's been through enough. Leave him alone."

"Shut up, you pile of dung." He struck her on the side of the neck, then turned his rage back on Thomas.

Nunzio was in a savage mood and yelled in an almost incomprehensible manner. "The trouble you and the others cause. For all the good I do, I should throw you in the garbage. Now the police blame me."

He wiped the spittle from his chin. "They blame me for finding you jobs. Blame me for the room, for the bed, the fire, the food."

He struck Thomas on the back. "How do you like this?"

He swung the cane again. "People say it's bad for children to work. I worked as a child. Do they feed you? Give you a bed? Where are these people who pretend to care?"

He swung the cane with all his might, striking Thomas on the back several times. With each blow, Thomas screamed in pain.

Nunzio yelled loud enough for neighbors to hear. "Where are you people now? Tell me. Where? Where are you?"

He turned to the boys. "Maybe tomorrow you mutts can go back to Sicilia. You can beg for food there."

Nunzio grabbed Angelina by the hair, dragging her to the house. Thomas pulled himself up to his hands and knees. He touched his face with two fingers and hurt so much inside and out, he thought of joining the hobos by the river and leaving this nightmare forever. He tried to stand but collapsed to the ground. Thomas heard Nunzio inside the house shouting in his native Italian.

A few minutes later, Angelina reappeared outside the house carrying a bowl of stew.

Nunzio charged after her. "He'll get nothing."

He knocked the bowl away from Angelina and back-handed her with his crippled fist, dragging her up the stoop of the house and through the door.

Minutes passed until Thomas felt a hand on his shoulder.

Federico leaned over and helped Thomas to his feet and over to the wash basin. With care, Thomas soothed the wound on his face with the water.

Federico held out his bowl of food. "Here, you eat this. Nunzio said we are working together tomorrow."

Thomas leaned his shoulder against the wall. "Thank you."

Exhausted, he crawled to his blanket and collapsed into a deep sleep.

The following morning, every movement Thomas made caused pain. He stared at his reflection in a bowl of water, examining the long cylindrical-shaped bruise across his cheek all the way to his eye.

Angelina stirred a pot of oatmeal and whispered to Thomas she was sorry. "Someday, Thomas, I'll make this right for you."

She lightly touched his face, but he recoiled in pain. Angelina scanned the area for Nunzio and, not seeing him, scooped extra oatmeal into his bowl and sprinkled a bit of sugar on top.

A few minutes later, Federico and Thomas waited by the bunkhouse for Nunzio. The temperature still hovered near the freezing mark, but the weather had made noticeable improvement over the day before with no snow and plentiful blue skies. Without warning, Nunzio appeared from around the corner. "We'll go now, but first you listen to me."

He horse-collared Thomas with his good hand.

Excruciating pain shot through Thomas's back, and he cried out.

"If Willie or anyone else asks, you fell last night, you understand? You tell anyone who asks. *Capisci?*"

Nunzio raised his eyebrows, grabbing Thomas again at the shoulder and shook him when he didn't respond right away.

Thomas said, "Yes, sir, I understand."

Nunzio let go as the boy dropped to the ground in pain.

"Get up now or you'll feel the cane again."

Federico helped Thomas to his feet.

Not a word was spoken by anyone as they walked to the telegraph office. Once they arrived, Nunzio met Henry Traynon and Willie at the office entrance.

Traynon ran his fingers through his matted red hair. He said, "The times are different now, and we may not be able to employ these kids as we have in the past."

"If you don't, others will want them for work. The boy who ran into the wagon, it had nothing to do with him being young," Nunzio said pointing at the boys. "You must know these Sicilians are not like us. They can't be trained to do much and are slow-witted. So, do you want them for work or not?"

Their conversation ended. Willie and Nunzio turned toward the boys.

"This is the new one. He's called Federico. You must train him because he's dumb like the boy yesterday."

Willie said, "Federico, you speak English?"

Nunzio interrupted. "They all speak English. Some better, some not as good."

"Okay, you'll be working with Thomas today."

Willie turned his attention to Thomas and his bruised face. "What happened to you?"

Nunzio said, "The idiot tripped over his feet last night. Right?"

"Yes, I fell down last night," Thomas said.

Willie continued to study Thomas's face.

Nunzio said, "You have something else to say to Willie?"

Thomas shook his head. "No, sir."

After Nunzio left, Willie said, "Okay, Federico, here's a cap for you to wear, a little stained from yesterday, but it still works. Now you might see other messengers wearing uniforms or riding bicycles. You boys are too small for uniforms. Maybe next year we'll get a bicycle."

Later, Willie called with the first message.

Thomas moved gingerly, unable to straighten his back.

"Are you sure there's nothing the matter with you today?"

"Yes, I'm fine."

Winter officially arrived and snow fell in terms of feet, not just inches. Thomas remembered the past year and how difficult it was to run in snowdrifts. He thought about the bicycle Willie mentioned but dismissed the thought of the two-wheeled cycle helping in any way. He resigned himself to the fact he would be forced to use his body again as a human plow to deliver telegrams.

For several consecutive days, the temperature dropped below zero. Due to Willie's persistence, the boys were able to inch their way inside the door of the telegraph office. Henry Traynon knew there was no legitimate reason he could give for them to remain outside in the frigid weather; nonetheless, he was opposed to their presence indoors.

Willie said, "Mr. Traynon, they're sitting right by the door. I told them to be quiet and not to move. No one can even see them."

"Yeah, but we both know how it'll work. Today, they're by the door. Next week, they'll be sitting in the hall. It won't be long before I'll be able to smell them sitting right outside my office."

"Mr. Traynon, I'm sure they'll—"

"You see, Willie, there's a much bigger problem than just them. What is Detroit supposed to do with all these immigrants pouring in every day?"

"Well, I'm sure there's a plan—"

"Stop Willie. I don't want to hear anything else. They're your responsibility. Close the door on your way out."

Sitting alone in his office, Traynon tossed his glasses on the desk and cupped his head in his hands thinking.

Everything would be fine if all these foreigners would quit coming to my country.

He lit his first cigar of the day, hoping the smell would block the entire dirty subject from his mind.

Chapter Twenty-Six

The public outcry over young children working in unsafe conditions increased after Biagio was killed. Although the labor laws didn't change, many businesses voluntarily discontinued employing children, and even Henry Traynon's branch office of the Great Northern Telegraph Company reluctantly fell in line and joined the others. By the new year, Thomas and Federico lost their jobs. When the dismissal came, Nunzio was apoplectic and directed his anger at the crusaders and the boys.

He pounded his worthless fist on Fats' wagon, railing against the injustices of the world. "It's the same do-gooders who won't take these dogs into their homes. I give them a chance. The problem was the one idiot who ran himself into a wagon. The city should thank me, right?"

Fats fidgeted with a rabbit's foot he found in the woods near the river.

Nunzio said, "Fats, are you listening to me?

"Yes, I hear what you say."

"Shouldn't the city thank me?" Nunzio asked.

Fats refocused his attention on the rabbit's foot. "I can feel the luck it brings me."

A week after the boys stopped delivering telegrams, Nunzio seemed to be happier almost with a bounce to his step as he sauntered up to his house.

He knew the old days were gone; nevertheless, Nunzio beamed with pride. "See what I've done? In only five days, I found new work for those two to shovel snow off the streets in front of the businesses. They will pay me for the work because they know it's a good deal. There are men with wagons to haul snow away, but these boys can move snow also. It takes longer, but the men cost much more."

Angelina said, "That's difficult work for young boys, and it's too cold to work outside. Can't this wait until spring when it's warmer?"

"You idiot! In the spring, the snow is gone. Stop talking and bring me my lunch."

Left alone, Nunzio sat down and closed his eyes to think for a moment.

It's tiring trying to explain business deals to such a simple-minded person. This is why I'm the businessman of the family. The best part is once the snow is gone, they can sweep the streets for these same people.

Angelina had enjoyed having Thomas and Federico with her during the day when Nunzio was away scouting for jobs. It gave her the opportunity to work with Federico on writing the letters of the alphabet and reading simple sentences while Thomas focused on mastering long division and memorizing the times tables. By day three working in her secret school, she fantasized about having a table with chairs and even a chalkboard. By day five, the dream was crushed and the boys were back at work.

Thomas and Federico quickly figured out shoveling snow was hard work. Grown men struggled to move sizable drifts of snow, but for young boys, it could be almost impossible at times. On the first day, they learned moving the great volume of snow was too much for one boy alone. They found a large flat piece of wood in the alley behind the hardware store.

Thomas said, "We can take turns pushing snow onto this. Together we can drag it to the alley to dump."

They found old rope and tied it around the board and themselves to carry the snow away. Sometimes the wet snow piled up almost as high as they were tall. The work advanced inches at a time.

Some of the coldest days occurred in February, prompting Thomas and Federico to retreat to back alleys to light fires with scrap wood and stolen coal to warm their hands and feet and dry their wet shoes.

As weeks became months and seasons became years, the number of boys at Nunzio's declined. The last of the boys at the orphanage performed a variety of manual labor jobs, including picking produce and unloading or delivering goods in town. Due in part to the outcry over child labor and the demand for compulsory schooling, only two orphans, Federico and Thomas, remained. The others had left as they grew older and joined road or farming crews in another part of the state.

Eventually, even Federico departed, leaving only Thomas.

Chapter Twenty-Seven

It was not quite dawn and Angelina was in the kitchen making sandwiches for Nunzio's ice fishing trip. She worked quickly, her mind deep in thought, hoping that the sooner she finished, the sooner he would be gone.

I would make him one hundred sandwiches if it means he'll be gone for two days, and I pray the biggest fish in Lake St. Clair pulls him into the freezing water forever.

After Nunzio left with fishing gear in hand, she baked a loaf of apple bread. Not just any apple loaf; she added a mix of brown sugar and cinnamon to the recipe and drizzled a creamy glaze on top.

"Happy fifteenth birthday, Thomas!" She also set a gift on the table. "It's for you. Open it."

"Angelina, you shouldn't do this. I don't want you to get in trouble," he said.

"I have a secret stash of money. Don't worry yourself."

Looking at the pair of dark gray wool mittens, he said, "Thank you, but this is too generous."

"You only have one birthday a year. Now, go ahead and try them on."

Thomas had grown to be a handsome young man with wavy black hair and lean yet muscular arms and shoulders from the years working various manual labor jobs. His face was the perfect likeness of a father he could no longer remember.

Although the physical scars on his back hadn't faded, the beatings were memories, as any physical punishment ended when he became the last of the orphans. He sometimes wondered why the man did such horrible things and thought back to Nunzio's description of his youth on his grandfather's farm. He thought perhaps the monster inside Nunzio was the child who never got to be one and didn't want any other children to have a childhood either.

Since he was the last of the group, Thomas began thinking about his own departure someday. A co-worker and friend from a Detroit River loading dock asked, "Thomas, what keeps you living there?"

His response was measured. "It's complicated. I'm afraid of what could happen to Angelina."

"What do you owe this person anyway? You are living in a prison."

"No, I'm free to go and have been for years. I can't stand Nunzio, but there is a special kindness to Angelina. She's always treated me well. I feel like I owe her something."

Thomas gave his friend's question more thought as he walked home early that evening, worrying Nunzio might actually force him to leave. He remembered a few nights before, he sat with Angelina outside discussing, of all things, the recent invention of the electric washing machine.

She had said, "Oh, Thomas, you're kidding me, a machine that washes clothes? How on earth would such a contraption be able to scrub them clean? I would have to see one first to believe it."

When she giggled, he was certain he could see an innocent child's face laughing, no doubt, as she must have done fifty years before in Milan.

Thomas caught a quick glimpse of Nunzio sitting on the front stoop staring right through Angelina as if she weren't even there. He couldn't imagine the darkness in Nunzio's heart and mind.

Now, as he neared the house, he thought, I'm her only real family. Thoughts of Nunzio's face clouded his mind, and frightening images caused Thomas to pick up the pace. He thought again of Angelina and broke into a full-out sprint.

When he reached home, he was relieved to see Angelina alone at the front of the house shelling butter beans.

"Anything worth reading?" she asked.

Confused, he tilted his head.

"The newspaper under your arm; anything worth reading?"

"Oh, I forgot I even had it. Angelina, a wise person once told me reading is always worth the effort."

"Thank you, Thomas. You're the best student I ever had."

"You mean have."

"I always wanted to be a schoolteacher and, when you came along, I selfishly took you as my student."

"There was nothing selfish to it. Without you, I would never have learned."

She set the iron pot on the ground and exhaled a day's worth of loneliness.

"I'm sorry you never had the opportunity to go to school."

He frowned. "I do think about subjects like literature and astronomy, and I'd like to study these things someday. Yesterday I read about this scientist who said the light we see from those distant stars," he said, pointing to the sky, "is from many, many years ago, and I wonder how that is possible. The distances from all those stars to here is so vast, it's beyond my comprehension."

She said, "From the start, you've had a curious mind. You're smart too, but curiosity, I think, is much more important. I hope you never lose that."

Thomas knew the time was drawing near and soon he would leave, but he worried about Angelina. The physical punishment Nunzio inflicted on her may have slowed, but the emotional pain never ended. Thomas wondered what a man like Nunzio did to a person's spirit over a lifetime.

One crisp autumn morning Thomas returned from a night shift at the Detroit River to find Angelina sitting outside the front door folding baby's clothes she had sewed for a neighbor.

"Good morning, Angelina."

His greeting was met with silence, and only after she turned her face toward him could he tell she'd been crying.

What has he done now? Thomas thought only Nunzio could ruin a perfect, sunny start to any day.

She held her head in her hands, sniffling. "Baby clothes always make me sad. I can't help but think about the sweet child these clothes will keep warm."

Thomas sat down and put his arm around her. "Why wouldn't these clothes make you happy?"

After a minute, she sat up straight and wiped her nose.

"Thomas, would you like to hear a story?"

"Of course, yes."

"I've never told anyone this before."

Thomas swallowed. "Okay."

"A year after Nunzio and I had been living in Detroit, I became pregnant. Long before the birth, I fell in love with my unborn baby. I had such hope and anticipation, I even wondered if I was being selfish to want something that much for myself. I gave birth, but I knew right away something was wrong by the midwife's reaction. She told me he had Down's syndrome. Have you heard of this before?"

"Yes, Angelina. I'm sorry."

"Thomas, the words *Down's syndrome* meant nothing to me. All I heard was the word he, and that meant I had a son and I would help to make him the happiest person I could. The midwife was going to tell Nunzio to come in, but I asked her to make an excuse if he tried. I said I wanted a few minutes to be alone with my child. If I told you I poured a lifetime of love into my baby in those few minutes, would you believe me?"

"Yes, I would, Angelina. Of course, I do."

She sniffled. "I couldn't quite get this feeling out of my mind about what Nunzio would say. Eventually the midwife had to let him in. He kept knocking. I remember like it was yesterday, Nunzio came into the room and said he had wanted a boy and I gave him one. Thomas, he even smiled when he said it. I thought this was what Nunzio needed and now everything in our marriage would be like it was supposed to be. What a fool I was."

Angelina sobbed for a moment.

"He said he wanted to hold his son. The midwife told him the child had an abnormality called Down's syndrome. Well, his smile vanished in an instant, and he held the baby away from him like it was fish guts."

"Angelina, I'm sorry."

"He said something like, 'This cretin can't be my baby,' and practically threw him at the midwife and walked out. After she left, Nunzio returned. He referred to our child not as him but as it."

Her lips trembled.

"You don't need to say any more. I'm very sorry."

"No, I want to tell you. I must tell someone. I thought maybe it was taking Nunzio time to get used to a new baby that in his eyes wasn't perfect. I hoped everything was okay, but it wasn't. He reached over and snatched the baby by the back of his neck and left the room. I remember the baby, my baby, crying."

"Oh, my God."

"I was tired and weak. It took me time to get up and out of bed. I wrapped a sheet around me and finally made it to the bedroom door. I called for Nunzio and my baby, but by the time I reached the front stoop, that bastard was sitting outside smoking one of his stupid cigars like he didn't have a care in the world. I screamed at him. 'Where's my baby?' He walked over and dropped this sack on the ground beside me and said, 'It's dead.'"

She broke down sobbing.

"This isn't helping you, Angelina."

After a minute, she turned her face to Thomas with a frightening wild look in her eyes, one he'd never seen before.

"Thomas, he drowned my baby in the wash basin. I tried, I took him from the bag, breathed into him, and put him to my breast to make him wake up, but he was gone. I sang to him and acted like he was taking milk from me. Nunzio looked at me with those ice-cold eyes and said, 'That thing is dead and you're crazy.' He told me to put the trash back into the sack so he could throw it out."

Angelina clenched her fists and shook them.

"I ran at him and clawed and swung my fists with all my might. I wanted to kill him or for him to kill me. It made no difference. He hit me in my stomach and I thought I was going to die. I wasn't afraid, Thomas, I was happy."

"How could he be that horrible?"

"Because he's a monster. I remember he put his face right up to mine, and said, 'If anyone asks, you'll say the baby stopped breathing.' He said, 'It's the truth, isn't it? It did stop breathing.' I'll never forget his laugh."

Thomas was stunned. He had no idea what to say.

She said, "Nunzio is a terrible human being." She paused and whispered, "And I am too."

"No, Angelina, you're not a terrible person. You're wonderful."

She looked at Thomas and wiped her nose. "But I'm still here, aren't I?"

Chapter Twenty-Eight

Thomas, now almost sixteen, contemplated leaving Detroit every day. It was his concern for Angelina and her well-being that held him back. The story she related had shocked him, and her life with Nunzio seemed so grossly unfair. When he thought about the other boys who had drifted in and out of his world, he wondered if there was any fairness to life at all. He walked through an alley on his way to work, his head hung low with the weight of heavy thoughts.

He heard a familiar voice and looked up to see Willie standing at the back door of his favorite diner.

"Young man, you better pick that chin up or you'll scrape it on the ground."

"Hey," Thomas said.

"Are you feeling sorry for yourself?"

"No, but I guess I don't understand life."

"Oh, I see." Willie laughed and said, "Is that all?"

"I guess sometimes nothing seems fair."

"Hmm, life doesn't seem fair to you?"

"No, not really," Thomas said.

"Can I tell you a little something about fair?"

"Sure."

"What's fair about me having to eat out back here leaning against this brick wall because I have black skin? What was fair about that young boy who got himself run over by a wagon because he didn't have any parents and had to work? You need to get one thing straight in your head. The only kind of fair you'll ever find in this world is state and county, and don't you forget it."

Thomas lowered his head. "Okay, I won't."

Willie's tone softened. "Listen, things are always going to be uneven. It's not right. It just is." He put his arm around Thomas's shoulders. "But I'll do the best I can and you do the best you can until God almighty himself comes down here and straightens out this whole blessed mess."

Thomas walked away from the encounter convinced Willie was like the early Greek philosophers except he was a modern-day street sage.

Occasionally at work he talked to the *ritornati* who traveled back and forth to Italy, some of them for years, but Thomas decided the traveling life wasn't for him. If he closed his eyes and concentrated, he might conjure a vague image of his father's face, but he had to admit to himself he wasn't sure it was real. He could remember sitting on the house steps with his grandmothers, but they were just fragments of memories from a place long ago meaning no more to him than the Pyramids in Egypt or the Great Wall in China.

Thomas didn't consider returning to Sicily because, for him, Sicily meant nothing more than any ancient pyramid or wall. The idea of living near the sea, however, pleased him.

It was a chilly overcast Wednesday morning when a fire erupted in the Gratiot Glass factory where Thomas worked a day shift.

The factory manager shouted, "Everyone, get out! Stop what you're doing and leave now!"

Thomas grabbed his coat and joined other workers gathered outside near the rear of the building. He watched as the fire's intensity grew, and a loud explosion boomed from inside.

As the fire grew more intense, a fireman yelled, "We're all in danger. Get yourselves far away from here."

The battle to save the factory was lost even before it began. Everything inside was reduced to ashes. In the space of an hour, Thomas and a dozen others found themselves without jobs.

A light snow began falling by the time Thomas arrived home. Angelina was wrapped in her heavy coat spreading feed for the hens. He told her about the factory fire and that he was unemployed.

Angelina said, "Just as the forest fire destroys, it also causes new growth and a new beginning. Always remember that."

"I will."

"Thomas, I think this is a sign it's time for you to leave."

He smiled. "You want me to go?"

"Of course not. It's because I love you like a son that I tell you the time is here. You think about the sea because it was where you were born. It's in your blood and you can't escape it. I know you don't want to go back to Sicily, and I think I understand why."

Thomas stared at the ground.

Angelina said, "I have something for you."

She went into the house and returned a minute later holding a small cloth bag.

"Here's the money taken from you when you first arrived and something extra. I want you to take it and leave."

Thomas shook his head.

"Listen to me now. You earned this money. Nunzio thinks he knows everything, but he doesn't, and there are things he never will."

She removed an envelope from her dress pocket and clutched it close to her chest.

"In Milan, my best friend was a girl named Assunta. We went to school together, played together; we even liked the same boys. Her father was always kind to me and treated me like his own daughter. After Assunta married, her father and mother surprised everyone and left Milan and came here to America to a city called Norfolk in Virginia. Have people talked of this place to you?"

"I've heard of it."

"We've written to each other a few times over the years, and I've talked to them about you. They're older, but I heard from them about three years ago. I want you to take this letter I wrote to Assunta's father, Signor Martelli. He has a market and I believe he'll help you with finding work and to make a new life for yourself away from this. I haven't always been strong or brave enough to help you, and the fault is mine alone."

"No, that's not true."

She nodded her head.

"You did more for me than you could imagine, more than I could repay in two lifetimes. You put your trust in me and allowed me to be close to you. Since I left Milan many years ago, I hadn't felt that way until you came here. Sometimes I failed you, but I've always treasured you. I'll never forget the trust you placed in me. Don't you see, Thomas? Love is one thing, but trust is something completely different. Trust is the bow wrapped around a box of love, keeping it safe forever. I thank you for being my bow."

"Why don't you come with me to this Norfolk place and we can meet your friends together? With me, you'll be able to travel in safety and I'll take care of you."

"I know you would. It may be hard for you to understand, but I must stay here."

"Why? I don't understand why."

"Thomas, do you remember when I told you about my baby?"

"Of course."

"Well, I didn't tell you the whole story. After everything that happened, if you can believe it, Nunzio still wanted children. I never wanted to bear him another child knowing what he did. Never again. A year later, though, I became pregnant. I was upset, but I didn't tell Nunzio. You see, I learned of a way, oh, God please forgive me."

She gritted her teeth.

"It was an awful thing I did and I know I'll be judged for it, but I used something like a knitting needle to end that baby's life, and I almost ended my own. I was sick for days. Nunzio didn't care. It just meant I couldn't make him dinner for a week. Sometimes I wish my life had ended too. Because of what I did, I hurt myself and wouldn't be able to have children again.

"To this day, Nunzio doesn't know what I did, but he never had a child by me either. He told me I was a worthless old cow because I couldn't give him a son. Oh, but I sure was happy that way. Do you understand? It was my revenge. Sometimes I think God forgave me a little when you arrived. I know I'll answer for what I did. We all have our sins, and that's mine. Now I must remain here to serve my punishment."

Chapter Twenty-Nine

He sat on an ornate wooden bench at Union Station in Columbus waiting on the next train to take him to another stop in Baltimore. People were bundled in heavy coats pulling and dragging suitcases and trunks to his left and right. Languages were spoken he didn't understand, and he thought people from every corner of the world must stop here. The air was thick with a blend of cigarette and cigar smoke as people like him waited on the next chapter of their lives to unfold.

Between naps, Thomas searched his bag for another apple Angelina had packed for the trip. He smiled when he found the small wooden soldier.

Tracing his fingers over the man's stump for an arm, he whispered, "I suppose we're all damaged in one way or another."

When he looked up, he caught sight of a man far across the station sweeping the floor. It wasn't any man, but a uniquely large man. Thomas grabbed his duffle bag and raced across the slick concrete floor toward a large archway. There before him stood an older Gigante with the same huge shoulders, barrel chest, and kind face. The giant man stopped sweeping, straightened his back, and rested the broom against his side.

Thomas asked, "Do you remember me?"

Seeing the confusion, he repeated the words in Sicilian. A huge smile spread across the man's face. They shook hands for a second until Gigante enveloped Thomas in his massive arms.

"Little Tommaso, you are a grown man now," Gigante said.

He told Thomas to follow him into the janitor's storage room. Over the next hour, they caught up on each other's lives.

Gigante began telling his story in English, but within minutes reverted to Sicilian, his preferred language. "After we said goodbye, the rest of us, me, Simone, Santo, and Alberto worked on the road crew for six months. But my life changed when I met Brigida. She had come over from southern Italy about a year before me and was working as a hotel maid in Grand Rapids. One day I saw this pretty lady walking along the street. She had dropped a bag of oranges, and I helped collect them. We talked for a few minutes and I asked her if she wanted a cup of coffee. Tommaso, it was love at first sight for me.

"Brigida told me she was moving soon to live with her younger sister and husband in Columbus. It made sense. She wanted to be with family and knew she could work in any hotel. The timing was perfect because I didn't like working on the road crew. They kept us locked up like wild animals in a cage. I decided to take a chance and asked Brigida if she wanted company on her trip to Columbus. She said yes. One day I walked away from the work site. They still owed me money, but I didn't care. We arrived here and a month later, we married. Now we have four children, three girls and a boy!"

"Congratulations! What happened to the others?"

"They stayed there as far as I know. They didn't seem to mind the conditions as much."

Gigante shook his head. "I can't believe how grown up you are. I hated that you went to an orphanage; we all did, but we had no choice. We spoke of you often and wondered how you were getting along, but we didn't know how to find you."

Thomas decided to soften the truth; there seemed to be no point in making Gigante feel guilty about something he couldn't have changed. "Yes, I lived at this house with other boys. It wasn't perfect, or even great but I survived, thanks to a kind lady named Angelina, and now I'm on my way to Virginia. She knows some people from there and thinks I'll be able to find a job with them."

Gigante said, "I'm so glad to hear that, Tommaso. I knew you'd be okay." He paused. "I can't tell you how happy it makes me to speak to you in Sicilian. Our children all speak English, but it's still difficult for me. Not for you though—you sound like an American! How is that possible?"

"When I arrived in Detroit, I had to learn English to work. All the boys who lived there spoke either Sicilian, Italian, English, or all three. Angelina helped me with the language, and I guess it just came to me."

With his train's departure close at hand, Thomas said it was time to say goodbye.

"It's okay. Someone will be looking for me, and I can't hide in this closet all day."

In his best English, Gigante said, "I push the broom here, but each night I go to Brigida and the children. It's a good life."

Gigante wrote something on a piece of paper.

"Tommaso, if things don't go as you plan, this is where we live. You'll always be welcome. Always."

The announcement for Thomas's train came. They hugged again, wishing each other well.

As Thomas headed towards his train, Gigante leaned against the broom, marveling at the intelligent young man that quiet, frightened little Tommaso Mancuso had grown into. Once he saw that Thomas was safely aboard, he resumed sweeping and a small smile softened his weathered face.

Chapter Thirty

1911

After two days of captivity on trains, Thomas walked out of the Norfolk terminal into the bright sunshine carrying everything he owned, duffle bag and pallet, slung over his shoulder. The air was crisp and it felt liberating to be free from the confinement of travel.

Outside the station, a woman and two towheaded children anchored to her dress stood behind a portable wheeled produce cart. Thomas had already eaten everything—cheese, bread, and apples—Angelina packed for his trip. He searched the mound for the largest apple he could find. With breakfast in hand, he stood by a scenic inlet of the Elizabeth River. Taking in the fresh morning air, he felt an overwhelming sense of clarity and energy. Somehow, even his vision and hearing seemed sharper.

He took his first bite, making a loud crunching sound, and ate the entire fruit, core and all, not wanting to waste a single bit. Passing within six feet of a cluster of trees, he spit the seeds in a rapid-fire manner. He hit the spot he aimed for and remembered the day Fats taught him the trick of saving the seeds to the side of his mouth.

A cool December breeze blew inland across the water. He smiled to himself watching other pedestrians bundled up in heavy coats leaning into the wind, knowing by comparison this was like an early spring day in Detroit.

Twenty minutes later, he arrived downtown. The bustling streets were filled with a variety of shops, tents, and open-air markets where merchants peddled every imaginable type of product.

He stopped at a larger market stand where a woman sold *canestrato*, a cheese made from goat milk and pressed into the *canestri* or wicker baskets leaving the trademark pattern on the surface of the cheese.

"Excuse me, do you know Mr. Martelli who owns a market here in Norfolk?"

She paused for a second. "I don't think, no. You wait."

She shouted in the direction of a brick building behind her. A man stood in the doorway leaning over a crate filled with plant stems Thomas assumed were used to assemble the Americanized version of the *canestri*. The man straightened his back, stretching the tightened muscles, and peered up at his wife and Thomas.

He walked over with a curious expression. "You speak English?"

"Yes, I'm looking for Mr. Martelli who owns–"

The man cut him off. "Mr. Martelli, no, he is no longer here. He died."

Thomas thought he recognized the accent, and he spoke in the man's presumed native language. "I speak Italian."

Smiling, the man said, "No, no, I practice English. Mrs. Martelli died. She died first, then a year ago, Mr. Martelli he died too."

Thomas was crushed. It had been a gamble and he had such hopes, but Angelina had said they were older.

Thomas asked, "What happened to his market?"

"After Mrs. Martelli died, he sold to the Cavallaro family."

He pointed in a direction behind Thomas. "The market is on Main Street. Cavallaro name is on the building."

Thomas thanked the man and woman. With nothing else to do, he walked in the direction of the market.

He turned the corner at Main Street and saw a hand-painted sign reading Cavallaro Produce Market hung on the front of a brick building with a stone foundation. A young man in his early twenties unloaded empty crates from a wagon. Thomas cut across the street and, as he did so, the man's eyes turned in his direction.

Thomas no longer had a plan, but since he had caught the man's attention, he decided to stop and chat. The speech he had prepared and practiced in his head on the train was all he could think of when it came time to talk.

"Hello, my name is Thomas Mancuso, and I traveled here from Detroit. A friend of mine thought I might be able to find work through Mr. Martelli and gave me a letter to present to him."

The man cocked his head and examined Thomas for a few moments.

Thomas asked, "Do you speak English?"

The man laughed and said in perfect English, "Well, not too badly. Where are you from again?"

"I thought perhaps, well, I'm from Sicily originally, but I've lived in Detroit since 1900."

"Really? Where in Sicily?"

Thomas said, "A place called Marinella."

The man's face lit up.

"You're kidding? I'm from Bagheria. I think they are close to each other. My parents and I left when I was two. Of course

I have no memory of the place. You also came over with your parents?"

"No, I traveled with my father's friends. My parents are both dead."

"Oh, I'm sorry. What's your name again?"

"Thomas Mancuso."

"I'm Vincenzo Cavallaro. There are others from Sicily who live here. You said something about a letter for Mr. Martelli?"

"Yes."

"Excuse me, Thomas. I'm going to talk with my father."

Thomas nodded. He enjoyed the smell of the fresh fruit on display and thought about the harbor nearby.

Angelina was right. Perhaps the sea is in my blood and this could be my home.

A couple of minutes passed while Thomas watched Vincenzo speak with his father. The resemblance was uncanny. Both tall, they had thick hair and mustaches, the same facial bone structure with square jaws, high foreheads, deep-set eyes, and not a wrinkle to be found on either face. Vincenzo's hair and mustache were jet black while his father's was gray, but they were cut and trimmed exactly the same. The elder Cavallaro wore an apron and stood with his arms folded across his chest listening to his son.

They approached Thomas.

Vincenzo's father said, "I'm Antonio Cavallaro. The man you wish to meet, Signor Martelli, isn't here. After his wife died, he sold the market to me. He passed away in March."

Vincenzo jumped into the conversation waving his arm toward the brick building. He said, "Thomas, the company consisted of a bunch of tables, awnings, a wagon, and other equipment, but the most desirable part was the space for our market and–"

Antonio cleared his throat, and Vincenzo stopped talking.

"You're looking for work, I understand," the older man said.

"Yes, sir."

"You are from Marinella?"

"I was born there, but my father died when I was five. I don't remember much."

"I understand. You carry a letter?"

Thomas paused, uncertain what to do. None of this was part of the careful rehearsal he had practiced.

"Would you like to read it?"

Antonio shrugged and said, "The letter wasn't written to me, but yes, I can look. What language is this letter?"

"Sir, I don't know. I haven't opened it."

Both Antonio and Vincenzo glanced at each other while Thomas rummaged through his duffle bag to retrieve it.

Antonio asked, "And what do you know about this?"

He waved his arms past the wide variety of fruits and vegetables.

Thomas stood again. "Sir, respectfully, I don't have any experience growing produce or working in a market, but since I was five years old I've gotten myself up each morning and gone to work every single day."

He handed the letter to Antonio, who studied the handwriting on the envelope for a moment and nodded as he turned away.

Vincenzo looked at Thomas and said, "Wait a moment, okay?"

Thomas watched Vincenzo catch up to his father, and they talked while standing at the doorway to the market entrance. At times, Vincenzo appeared animated as he spoke, and a few times Antonio turned and appeared to be assessing him. The older Cavallaro put his hands up with his palms facing toward his son, then opened the envelope. He read while his son stood back in silence. Their conversation restarted after which Antonio nodded. Vincenzo walked toward Thomas, smiling.

"I think if you'd like to try, my father said we can see how you work out. When can you start?"

"I'm here now."

Thomas slung his duffle bag and pallet to the ground and reached into the wagon, pulling four crates out, placing two on each shoulder.

Vincenzo laughed and grabbed four crates for himself.

Thomas worked side by side with Vincenzo the remainder of the day. They moved tables, wood platforms, crates and shelving inside and out. Despite the chilly start, the temperature climbed to near sixty by early afternoon.

As the day wore on, Antonio told Vincenzo to begin the process of closing the market. Both Vincenzo and Thomas were sweaty from the labor.

Vincenzo said, "There's a big pot of water in the back. We can use it to cool off a bit."

Vincenzo removed his shirt and splashed water onto his face, neck, and back and went to talk with his father. Embarrassed about the scars on his back and shoulders, Thomas reluctantly took his shirt off.

Even though neither Antonio nor Vincenzo said anything, Thomas thought, this is who I am. There's nothing I can do about it.

After a short break, they resumed moving the remaining tables and crates inside. Antonio headed for the market's exit but stopped to reach into his pocket and fish out Angelina's letter. He spoke in a quiet voice to Vincenzo, who smiled and nodded at his father.

Vincenzo said, "Thomas, let me show you what we do to close up the market for the night."

Once the market was packed up, Vincenzo asked, "Where are you staying tonight?"

"I arrived this morning on the train, but tonight I thought I would throw my pallet someplace quiet under the stars."

He pointed his index finger toward the sky.

Vincenzo said, "No, it'll be chilly tonight. Please come with me. It's not much, but we have a small room in the back of our apartment where you can sleep. You can meet my wife, Carmela, and my daughter, Antonia. She's almost two years old and quite a handful. We'll have dinner, and tomorrow I'll help you find a place to live, okay?"

Carmela greeted Thomas, but the introduction was interrupted by Antonia, who ran up to her father in a tottering side-to-side fashion, squealing with excitement. Vincenzo picked her up and flipped her over.

"Antonia, I want you to meet my new friend, Thomas."

While they ate a simple dinner of pasta with tomato sauce and bread, Vincenzo spoke of their plans to grow the market.

"I've been asking my father for months to hire someone. I'm glad you came along."

The conversation turned to Thomas's trip to America and his life in Detroit. Vincenzo said he was only aware of two orphaned children, two brothers, in Norfolk, but they had been taken in by another family who cared for them as their own.

"The Sicilian way here is to help each other out. There are about forty families from Sicily, and almost all live between Twenty-eighth and Thirty-fifth Streets, where we are now." Vincenzo smiled. "I guess you can say this is our own Little Sicily."

As the conversation continued, a quiet knock was heard at the door. A young, attractive girl with long, black hair and a pretty smile entered holding a covered dish.

"Mama and Papa wanted me to bring you a pie tonight."

Vincenzo sat at the table with his hands folded over his belly and said, "Thomas, this is my baby sister, Giuseppa."

Her face flushed red.

"Brother, I'm no baby."

Carmela smiled and said, "Please tell them thank you for the pie."

"Baby sister, this is Thomas Mancuso. He's going to help us at the market."

"Yes, I know. Papa told me." She smiled at Thomas. "My friends call me Josie."

A few months before, she had read a dime novel with a heroine by the name of Josie and adopted it as her own. Her friends and teachers had all made the change to calling her Josie except for her family who, despite her best efforts, continued using her given name.

Thomas rose from the table and nodded. "It's a pleasure to meet you, Josie."

Carmela asked, "Would you like to have a piece of pie with us?"

She frowned. "No, Papa said to come back right away."

After dessert, Vincenzo remembered the letter his father had given him and removed it from his pocket.

"Thomas, I almost forgot, here's your letter. You never read it?"

"No, the friend I told you about, Angelina, wrote it for Mr. Martelli."

"You weren't curious?"

"Yes, maybe." He shrugged.

"Thomas, let me show you your room."

Thomas thanked Carmela for dinner and followed Vincenzo, who dragged one leg behind him with Antonia attached.

A few minutes later, left alone, Thomas surveyed the small room complete with a table, chair, and a flickering oil lamp next to a folded-up blanket. Thomas unrolled his pallet, extinguished the lamp, and lay down while waiting for his eyes to adjust to the darkness. His final thought was of Angelina telling him about how forest fires destroy, but also bring new growth and new life. As he fell asleep, he silently thanked her for the kindness she had shown him.

The following day Thomas worked from early morning into the evening, proving himself to be energetic, hardworking, and a quick study at the market.

In the late afternoon Josie walked into the market, and her attention immediately focused on Thomas. She spied him wearing a white apron over his clothes, and her eyes followed him as he continued working without interruption.

Antonio said, "Giuseppa, you need something at the market, yes?"

A roar of laughter from Vincenzo echoed from somewhere in the storage room in back.

She huffed at the sound of her brother. "Yes, Mama wants me to get eggplant."

She immediately began searching the market area for Thomas, who was beginning the process of carrying produce from the outside back in.

Vincenzo popped his head out, and said, "Baby sister, the eggplant is on the other side of the market."

"Big brother, I'm aware of its location. Thank you all the same."

She jutted her lower jaw out slightly as she spoke, a habit she practiced whenever she felt challenged, making her appear as someone to be reckoned with and quite fierce.

Josie strolled over to a table where at least a dozen eggplant remained. She picked one up and studied the taut, wrinkle-free skin before giving it a gentle squeeze and repeating the process several more times. Between checking each fruit, she casually glanced in Thomas's direction hoping he would turn to notice her. Finally, she chose a couple to her liking and surveyed the market again, but Thomas was nowhere to be seen.

"Giuseppa, you should go home now. It'll be dark soon."

"Yes, Papa." She walked around a table filled with yellow onions and rubbed her fingers across the slick skin of one of them. With one final look, she exhaled deeply, and said in a voice louder than necessary, "I'm going to leave now. Goodbye, everyone."

Walking home after closing the market, Vincenzo said, "Thomas, you'll stay with us again tonight. Tomorrow morning we'll leave a little early to go see a place I think you'll like. Carmela's sister and her husband have their own home with a small outbuilding at the back of the house. They used it for storage but decided a while ago to fix it up for a renter. I'm sure the cost is low and will work fine for you."

Carmela and Vincenzo's daughter, Antonia, fought sleep as long as any two-year-old might, but finally surrendered.

Now it was Carmela's turn. She rested in bed with her arm stretched over Vincenzo's chest and said, "I went into Thomas's room today to clean up a little, and I saw the envelope with the letter on the table."

Vincenzo raised his head off the pillow to peek at his wife.

"Carmela, you didn't read the letter, did you?"

"I shouldn't have, but I couldn't help myself."

Vincenzo turned toward Carmela and tickled her side.

She giggled when Vincenzo said, "You're a naughty girl."

He kissed her and rubbed his hand on her thigh.

"No, we shouldn't tonight. I don't want to wake anyone."

Disappointed, Vincenzo turned on his back again and stared at the ceiling waiting for sleep.

Carmela said, "Do you want to know what the letter said?"

"Ha, you couldn't resist, could you? Yes, please tell me."

In a whisper, she said, "Okay, the lady who wrote the letter is named Angelina, and she thought of Thomas as her own son. He came to their house when he was only five because both his parents died. I guess her husband made him work a lot. I don't think he was a good person because she said, 'even though my husband treated him poorly, Thomas was a good boy and worked every day of the week and sometimes even at night.' She said if Mr. Martelli helped him find work, it would be like helping her."

Vincenzo said, "He's quiet and never stops working. When we do talk, he's polite. There's a confidence about him, but not in a bragging way. He's going to work out. You know how my father never says anything, but I'm sure he likes Thomas too."

They remained quiet for a few minutes, allowing only their feet to touch. Carmela sighed and slowly sat up. She pulled her top off, letting it fall onto Vincenzo's face, and leaned over him to whisper into his ear.

"You'll be quiet, right?"

From his usual place in the back corner of the market, Antonio sat on a stool resting his elbows on a heavy wooden tabletop using two old barrels for support. Since the market had come under his control, Antonio claimed the choice spot as an office of sorts where he could survey the entirety of his produce market out into the road.

While preparing a sign for a daylong sale of apples, he occasionally glanced up. Thomas unloaded the crates of fresh apples while Vincenzo placed the produce piece by piece on tables they set up in front closer to the street. Vincenzo spoke nonstop, laughing at his own jokes, while Thomas remained serious and focused.

Antonio was happy his son and Thomas got along well and thought how far his family progressed in the twenty years since they emigrated from Sicily. He recalled his own time on the island, marked by poverty and hunger, and felt certain life must have dealt even harsher blows to Thomas's family for them to have sent the orphaned child across the ocean.

Chapter Thirty-One

A sense of routine settled into Thomas's new life working at the market in Norfolk. A handsome figure, he wore a crisp pair of dark trousers held up by red suspenders, a white dress shirt with the long sleeves rolled up to his elbows, and a dark bow tie.

Late mornings he guided the wagon to the wharf where he picked up produce for market, sometimes repeating the same process in the late afternoons. Initially, Vincenzo accompanied their new employee, but soon enough, Thomas was trusted to go alone, which allowed Vincenzo to remain at the market most days to do the heavy lifting his father was not as keen on doing any longer.

It had been a few weeks since Thomas settled into his new home, an outbuilding constructed of block and mortar behind Ronaldo and Olivia Caruso's house. He could almost touch the bare walls on opposite sides of the room if he stretched his arms wide. Quite cozy, it suited him perfectly.

A small wood frame for a bed sat in the corner. Any day the Carusos expected to have a new mattress, but in the meantime, Thomas used his pallet. It was the first time in his life he could remember not sleeping on the floor. There was a small wooden table and chair in one corner with an oval-shaped bowl containing water he drew from outside to fill for bathing and brushing his teeth. It was a modest space without decoration, but Thomas was thankful for a place to call his own, and for everything life had presented to him since arriving in Norfolk.

Ronaldo and Olivia Caruso were a happily married couple with two children, both under the age of six. Olivia, older than her sister Carmela by five years, could easily pass as her twin. Ronaldo was a shoemaker like his father and grandfather had been in Capaci, Sicily. Olivia and Ronaldo came to America with their parents, and after marriage, they found a small house to call home. It was an ideal location for the couple, with a ten-minute walk for Ronaldo to his shoe shop and only two blocks from Carmela's apartment where two sisters maintained their relationship as siblings and best friends.

Ronaldo liked to get into the shop early, so he and Olivia had a routine where they shared precious private time at an early breakfast before the kids awakened.

She said, "Two nights ago I got up to check on Anna and the light was on in Thomas's room out back."

Ronaldo turned to his wife. "Yes?"

"Did you hear what I said?"

"Yes. You said the light was on in Thomas's room."

"Even when you're not listening, you still hear me."

Ronaldo smiled. "It's a gift."

She shook her head. At least now she had his full attention. "Well, last night I got up to check on Anna; you know, she's having nightmares?"

"Yes."

"The light was on again in Thomas's room. It was after midnight."

"Hmm, well maybe he's having trouble sleeping. By the way, when is the mattress going to arrive?"

"Any day now, I hope. What do you think about the light on?"

"I think he uses it to see."

"Where is the rolling pin?"

"Why?"

"Because I need it to smack you on the head."

"Okay, okay, I'm kidding. I'll check to see if there's a problem."

"Please let him know I'm not spying on him."

"Are you spying on him?"

Olivia punched his arm.

"I'm getting the rolling pin myself."

Around eight o'clock in the evening, the gate at the side of the house leading to the outbuilding opened and closed. Ronaldo waited at the back door. "Hello, Thomas."

"Good evening, Mr. Caruso."

"Please call me Ronaldo. I wanted to make sure everything is good with your room, well, except for the missing mattress." He chuckled and said, "We've been told, any day now."

"It's okay. Everything is perfect. Thank you for asking."

"Well, I ask because Olivia saw your light on late at night and wanted to make sure you were comfortable."

"Oh, Mr. er uh, Ronaldo, I hope the light isn't bothering anyone. It's my only chance to read the newspaper."

"No, Thomas, you're not bothering anyone."

Ronaldo was impressed to find a young man who cared about any news, especially enough to stay up late and read it.

"What kind of books do you like?"

Thomas's face reddened. He said, "I'm sure I would enjoy any book. I, uh, I didn't attend school in Detroit."

Ronaldo said, "Listen, Thomas, don't worry about the light. It's not a problem. Good night."

Thomas returned home the following evening to find *The Time Machine* by H.G. Wells in front of the door to his room with a note from Ronaldo tucked inside that simply said "Enjoy!"

He marveled at its slick cover and ran his hand over it. He opened the book slowly, but once he did, he couldn't close it.

Later in the week, Ronaldo saw Thomas leaving for work.

He asked, "Thomas, how is the book?"

"I can't stop thinking about it. I've stayed up late reading it every night."

"That's great. I'm glad you like it."

"Ronaldo, I loved it. In fact, I've read it twice. Now I'm obsessed with the idea of time travel. Thank you for sharing the book with me."

Ronaldo recounted his conversation with Olivia later.

"Did you know Thomas read the book I loaned him twice in four days?"

"Are you talking about the same book I gave you for Christmas three years ago?"

"Well, I've been waiting for the right time."

Olivia said, "Of course you have. It's always a good idea to plan life's major decisions well in advance."

Ronaldo asked, "Have you seen the rolling pin lately?"

Chapter Thirty-Two

On a cold, sunny morning in March, Isabella wrapped herself in a heavy coat and scarf for the walk to the market. She told her husband, Antonio, she would be out doing some shopping in the morning and would come by the market. She had been wanting to invite Thomas for dinner anyway, but the constant pushing from Josie had made the inevitability of an invitation happen sooner rather than later.

"Mrs. Cavallaro, may I help you find something?" Thomas asked.

"No, that isn't necessary. I'll pick up some spinach in a moment."

"Yes, ma'am. If I can help with anything—"

Isabella interrupted. "Thomas, do you have dinner plans this Sunday?"

"No, ma'am."

"In that case, would you like to come over?"

"Well, yes, ma'am, of course. Thank you."

Vincenzo yelled from the back of the market. "Thomas, you better come hungry!"

Isabella smiled and said, "I like to cook. Trust me. There will be plenty to eat."

Thomas kept himself occupied at work, but secretly he worried over the fact he had never been a dinner guest before. He began to wonder what clothes to wear, and perhaps what to bring as a gift. In the space of a second, he decided his one pair of trousers would not do for a social call.

Antonio and Isabella lived in a two-story house on Thirty-first Street in the heart of Little Sicily. Sunday dinners were an integral part of life for them just as they had been in the old country. Meals were a time for extended families and friends to gather for hours eating various dishes of food, enjoying wine, and talking and more talking. Guests sometimes brought a side dish, but almost all the individual courses were prepared in the Cavallaro kitchen.

Isabella, a tiny woman not quite five feet tall, maintained the house under strict control as its ruler. With a loud voice, she used it to great effect in the kitchen as she barked orders at her daughter, her in-laws, and even neighbors and friends under her command as they prepared typical Sicilian dishes—*caponata*, an eggplant stew, *maccu* soup with fava beans, spaghetti *ai ricci*, served with sea urchin, couscous *al pesce*, served with clams, mussels and shrimp, various sliced fruits and for dessert, a choice of cannoli or *buccellato* cake.

Today, the soldiers under Isabella's watchful eye included neighbor Catarina, daughter Josie, daughter-in-law Carmela, and her sister Olivia. She made certain no one would go hungry on this day. Even before dinner, there was plenty to snack on. Guests enjoyed *arancine*, deep fried balls of saffron rice stuffed with ham and peas and various traditional Italian cheeses, and chickpea polenta fried to a perfect golden brown.

In the tidewater area of Virginia, the weather was often capricious. Unlike two days prior, Sunday was unusually warm. To avoid the heat of the midday sun, those who had been playing bocce eased over to the front porch to enjoy a glass of wine, snack on *arancine* and polenta fritters, and listen to each other's stories.

Everyone stopped when Antonio spoke. "A hard rain is coming, tonight or early morning."

The weather was his favorite subject, and one he predicted with uncanny accuracy. Everyone nodded in agreement. To do otherwise was foolish.

"Vincenzo, where is Thomas?" Antonio asked.

"I think he'll be here soon."

A short time later, Thomas came rounding the corner carrying a simple bouquet of fresh flowers. He wore a new pair of trousers and a shirt he had purchased only the day before, and as he walked up the steps, Vincenzo reached for the flowers.

"Thomas, you didn't have to bring me anything."

Brushing off Vincenzo's remark with a smile, he said, "Mr. Cavallaro, thank you for inviting me to spend Sunday with you and your family. These flowers are for Mrs. Cavallaro."

Vincenzo feigned a hurt look and said, "In that case, I'll ask Mama to come out."

"Mr. Cavallaro, I'm sorry for arriving late, but I stopped at the market first because I think there's a good chance for a storm tonight, and I wanted to make sure everything was secure."

When the group laughed, Ronaldo put his arm around Thomas.

"Perhaps you didn't know this, but Mr. Cavallaro is also a weather forecaster. He spoke of the coming rain a few minutes ago."

Antonio nodded at Thomas, acknowledging he had done well.

Isabella marched through the living room but continued to shout instructions to the kitchen subordinates she left behind. "Pay strict attention to the couscous. I don't want it to burn."

Isabella greeted Thomas with kisses on both cheeks and thanked him for the flowers.

She left as quickly as she arrived, bustling through the house to reestablish control over her culinary empire. Even from inside, her voice carried to the porch. "Has the water boiled yet? It's time for the pasta."

Antonio smiled at Thomas and placed his hands around his belly. "We'll have a big dinner. You'll see."

A minute later, Josie came out to the porch with a glass of wine in her hand.

"Hello, Thomas. Would you care for a glass?"

Josie wore a baby blue dress with a tiny bow at the collar and had styled her hair into a bun.

"Giuseppa, look at you. You're more lovely than ever," Ronaldo said.

She said, "Thank you," but didn't stray from her spot in front of Thomas.

"Thank you for the wine, Josie," he said.

Vincenzo asked, "Baby sister, could I have another glass of wine?"

Josie stood frozen, looking at Thomas dressed in his fine new clothes. The understated white dress shirt with the subtle thin blue striping matched perfectly with the gray trousers, creased and cuffed to ankle-length.

Finally, she turned toward Vincenzo jutting her lower jaw out. "Yes, big brother, I'm sure there's another bottle somewhere in the house."

For dinner, family and guests seated themselves around two rectangular tables as wave after wave of rich, sumptuous dishes were served. Some were more savory, others more spicy, and still others had the tang of a delicate sweetness, but they all made for an aromatic and appetizing experience. Each time Thomas finished a portion, Josie was standing behind him with a serving spoon and another helping.

This was no ordinary Sunday family dinner get-together for Josie. While the meal was being prepared, she frequently checked on the men playing bocce. Under the guise of seeing how the game was progressing, she searched the yard for Thomas.

Her mother wouldn't tolerate an inattentive part-time assistant. "Giuseppa, I need you," or "Giuseppa, where are you?" or "Giuseppa, why have you left the dough sitting out?"

Josie had intentionally seated herself at the table nearest the kitchen with Carmela, Olivia, and the children, so that she could keep an eye on Thomas in case he might want more to eat or a fresh drink. More than anything, though, she wanted to look at his handsome face. If she was only able to see Thomas once a week when she went to the market, she was going to take advantage of this time. Short of Mama or Papa putting blinders on her, nothing or nobody was stopping her today.

In Detroit, Thomas was accustomed to taking turns to clean the dishes with Angelina at the outside water basin, so it seemed only natural that he should offer to help with the dishes after dinner.

When everyone finally pushed back from the table and began to stand up, Thomas said, "Josie, may I help you in the kitchen?"

"That's kind of you, Thomas. Thank you."

Antonio said, "Thomas, I thought we might take our drinks to the front—"

Isabella placed her hand on his forearm and spoke quietly.

"Let him help Giuseppa for a minute, then he can go to the porch and discuss the weather with you."

Bowing to his wife's wishes, Antonio shrugged, grabbed an unfinished bottle of wine, and rose from the table. He walked to the front porch with the other male guests marching behind him in tight single file formation.

Thrilled to be in his company, Josie delighted in the fact he used her new preferred name, hoping it would convince her own family to make the change from the old-fashioned ethnic name of Giuseppa.

Thomas set an armful of dishes on the sink counter.

"Josie, wash or dry?"

She was with a young man alone in a room. It wasn't any man either, but Thomas, the object of her ceaseless thoughts when walking to school or brushing her hair before going to bed at night. She was nervous, and her emotions dominated her reasoning for the moment.

"Wash or dry? What's that?"

"The dishes, Josie, do you want me to wash or dry?"

Her face was beet red. "Oh, the dishes; yes, of course. Well, which do you prefer?"

Not waiting for an answer, she said, "Let me find you an apron because I'm sure you don't want your new clothes to get wet and dirty."

Josie's eyes searched the kitchen.

"Can I help you with something?" Thomas asked.

"I'm looking for an apron."

"The one in your hand will work fine."

The ladies still seated at the dining room table stifled their laughter.

Carmela whispered to Olivia, "Should we rescue her?"

"No, this is way too much fun."

Josie said, "I'm at Maury High School. It's brand-new. Well, it opened last year. I'll be a junior in the fall."

She looked at Thomas bashfully, hoping he understood her declaration to mean, I'm sixteen years old now.

"I'm not sure I've seen that school yet. Where is it?"

"It's on Shirley Avenue. It takes twenty minutes for me to walk, depending on the route I take."

Lying in bed that evening, Antonio spoke to his wife with admiration about their new employee. "He works right through the day into the evening. He's not yet eighteen, but he's a mature young man."

Isabella said, "You know, Giuseppa asks about him all the time. 'Mama, do you think Thomas is working well at the market with Papa? Is Thomas here to stay? Do you think Papa likes Thomas?'"

Antonio said, "Yes, I see the way she looks at him." He took a deep breath before the snoring began.

That night before falling asleep, Thomas thought of everything he'd experienced since his arrival in Norfolk. He liked this city, the work, and his new friends—especially Josie. At times she seemed shy around him, but he admired how she wasn't intimidated and stood up for herself in front of anyone. As far as he could tell, Josie was no ordinary girl. At the market, she took guff from no one and, even in ordinary conversation, she spoke in a manner that was more a challenge than a simple response or question. He looked forward to seeing her again. Still, he had learned a lot about life in his seventeen years and trusting happiness proved to be difficult for him. He couldn't help but wonder when it all might end.

Chapter Thirty-Three

Business grew at such a rapid pace that most days Thomas found himself hauling two larger wagonloads of product a day to market. On rare occasions, Vincenzo rode along. An early July morning was one of those exceptions.

"Thomas, business has nearly doubled over the last few years, and these kinds of deliveries are our future. It's a good problem for us to have."

He liked how Vincenzo spoke more and more of the two of them together, almost as partners.

Thomas said, "Maybe we need to think about a motorized vehicle to save time with transportation."

"We have to convince my father."

"I've been thinking about something related to the business, and it might sound a little crazy," Thomas said.

"Please, tell me."

"We're the biggest produce market in Norfolk and, to keep up with the demand, it could be time to think about another employee. We're making two significant produce runs a day and we're stretched thin now."

"Great minds think alike. So, tell me the crazy part," Vincenzo said.

"Okay, this is something I've been thinking about for a while. It involves the space next to our market that's been vacant for almost a year."

"Right."

"Well, since it's not being used, what if the owner were willing to sell it to us—"

"We could expand our produce area even larger. Great idea!"

"Yes, or we could also think of going in a different direction," Thomas said.

"What do you mean?"

"Think of it like a one stop shopping experience."

"How so?" asked Vincenzo.

"We could use the space to expand into dry goods or products from a general store or both. We could sell packaged items such as beans, flour, and grains. We could go in the direction of providing farm products like eggs, cheeses, and butter. Maybe baked items, even housewares, cookware, and dinnerware. It would be a place where customers shop for more than fruits and vegetables."

"What do you think the people from those kinds of stores will think?"

"I can guess. They'll probably see it as a threat to their livelihood."

"You're probably right. Anyway, I like it. We should talk to my father about it, but since it was your idea, you should present it."

"Vincenzo, I think it would be better coming from you."

"How about this? Let's present it together, okay?"

"Okay."

They rode in silence for a few minutes. "Vincenzo, can I ask you something?"

"Sure."

"Why did you speak up for me to your father the first day I arrived here in Norfolk? Sure, we were both born in Sicily, but you didn't know me."

"There was something about you. Maybe your story helped me trust you. You didn't even read the letter your friend sent on your behalf. I would have, but you didn't. I'm not sure why, but it made a big difference to me."

Later that afternoon, Vincenzo and Thomas approached Antonio who sat frowning as customers squeezed various produce items in search of perfection, at the same time bruising the items they left behind.

"Papa, Thomas and I talked earlier about something and we want to tell you about it."

Vincenzo explained the idea.

Antonio scratched his chin and said, "Yes, I understand. Very interesting. I'll think about it."

"Oh, and Papa, this was Thomas's idea."

Antonio wasn't a man to be rushed into a decision. His philosophy was if he liked an idea, he would think about it overnight. If he still liked the idea the next day, he might act on it after thinking about it another week or even another two or three weeks.

Sometimes Vincenzo argued with his father. "Papa, we have to decide now. It might be too late tomorrow."

Pushed to make decisions in a hurry, his father always had the same response. "The apple I pick today will taste just as sweet tomorrow."

Over a week had passed since Vincenzo and Thomas broached the idea of buying the adjacent vacant space. Late Saturday afternoon Antonio stood to take his apron off before walking home and called both over to his table to talk.

He said, "I think I would like to try this new idea we spoke of last week."

Antonio couldn't hide the grand smile and waited for a reaction.

Vincenzo asked, "Papa, why are you smiling like you know something we don't?"

"Because I have a secret to tell you."

"And now you're ready to share this secret with us?"

"Yes."

Vincenzo waved his hands in the air impatiently. "Are you going to tell us *today*?"

"Yes." The big smile returned. "Last weekend, I negotiated a price to purchase the space next door."

"Papa, that's fantastic, but that means you talked to the owner almost right away after talking with us."

Antonio said, "Yes, I did."

"But that's not like you at all. You always say, 'The apple I pick today—'"

"Son, that's true, but sometimes the apple I pick today is best eaten today. When we take ownership next month, we'll knock down the wall."

Antonio folded his apron, laid it on the table, and as he turned to leave, he said, "Thomas, I won't forget this was your idea."

Chapter Thirty-Four

The Cavallaro Produce Market more than doubled in size with the purchase of the adjacent space. No longer just an oversized fruit stand, it became more of a retail store selling a variety of merchandise with produce on the side. Its market share dominated other more specialized shops in the downtown area.

Despite the continuation of the Great War in Europe and the active U.S. involvement, the business continued to grow. By the time the war ended, produce accounted for only a fifth of the market's income. Notwithstanding the changes in its inventory, the Cavallaro Produce Market name endured—due to Antonio's dogged insistence the name remain the same.

There were other components to life in Norfolk's Little Sicily that didn't change. One was Thomas's attraction to Josie. He was certain he had fallen for her even before he first had dinner at the Cavallaro house, and nothing during the intervening years changed his mind. Josie was strong-willed but kindhearted. Most of all, he was fond of her keen sense of humor and quick wit.

Thomas liked when Josie arranged her shopping to coincide with the market closing so they could walk back to the neighborhood together. The moments he was able to spend with her were the highlight of the day for him. In private conversation, they never used the word marriage, but they talked in roundabout ways of spending their lives together beginning at some point in the future. Sometimes, their conversation turned to Thomas's life in Detroit.

"Josie, life for me was difficult to understand as a child and now as an adult all these years later, I still find the terrible conditions hard to think about. We lived in a state not much different than ordinary yard dogs. There was no opportunity for school, and we worked any kind of job this man could find for us. The work we children performed supported the place we found ourselves dumped in. It was a world turned upside down for a child."

She held his hand. "It's hard to imagine such a life."

Thomas said, "Another boy and I used to work as messengers for this telegraph company."

"How old were you two?"

"Biagio was twelve, I guess, and I was nine or so. He was my only friend where we lived."

"You never told me this."

She squeezed Thomas's hand.

"One day my friend Biagio was killed when a wagon broke loose somehow from where it sat and rolled down a hill–"

"You saw this?"

"No, I didn't see the accident, but I saw him after, and I could no longer recognize my own friend."

"Thomas, that's awful."

"I've never forgotten it, and I never will. But I do believe that, through hard work and a helping hand, like the one given to me by your father and Vincenzo, life has a way of evening out."

At that moment he thought of Willie. "Maybe the state or county fair has finally come to town after all."

"What do you mean?"

"Oh, it's something a wise man once told me."

Thomas looked directly into Josie's eyes. "I'll never allow my family to live like I did." He squeezed her hand and said, "My family will live in a real home. My wife will be treated with respect and love, and my children will go to school and learn a real skill."

Antonio was unusually pensive and anxious, first sitting, then standing, and finally pacing around his table one morning while collecting his thoughts. Something was on his mind. Thomas sat and waited.

Antonio said, "Thomas, someday I'll retire. Vincenzo and I agree, you helped make this market strong and successful. I want you to think about something. Would you like to be a part owner at a fair price?"

He hoped by making the offer, it would keep Thomas with the Cavallaro Produce Market forever, and also send a signal he hoped someday to call Thomas family.

The following day Vincenzo said, "So my father talked to you about becoming an owner in the business?"

"Your father's offer is all I've been able to think about."

Vincenzo was aware of the business proposal because it was his idea to begin with. His father was getting older, and Vincenzo liked the notion of bringing his friend, Thomas, on as a partner.

He said, "You and my sister are in love. I know it. Everyone knows it. You've been honorable with her and made yourself invaluable here at the market. Thomas, what I'm trying to say is, I hope you'll agree to being business partners." He squeezed his arm around Thomas's shoulder. "And family too."

Thomas took a deep breath and nodded. "Vincenzo, everything you say is true. Someday I'll talk to your father about Josie and the business when I'm certain I can provide for my family."

A few moments of silence passed between them.

"Vincenzo, I want to thank you because, without you, I wouldn't be here at all. You're more than my best friend. You're like a brother too."

He gave Thomas a bear hug.

"Just remember, though, you'll always be my little brother."

Chapter Thirty-Five

1920

The war was a memory for the United States, and while there had been occasional problems with inventory, primarily fruit and vegetable supply, overall the Cavallaro Produce Market thrived. It was a Saturday late in March. Thomas sat with Antonio on the front porch at the Cavallaro house while an anxious Josie helped her mother in the kitchen.

Isabella was preparing cannoli, one of her finest kitchen creations. Josie scarcely paid attention, hardly able to contain herself as the men sat on the front porch drinking wine and talking about, of all things, the weather. Exasperated, she heard them both agree, while the spring was pleasant thus far, the summer promised to be a hot one.

"Mama, how can the weather be that interesting all the time? It'll rain, it'll snow, it's sunny, it's windy; who cares! I'm getting old and all they talk about is the weather."

She peeked around the corner of the kitchen to check on Thomas, hoping they would run away that night and marry. Her mind drifted to random thoughts. It was a dream come true when Thomas came into their lives; well, her life to be exact. The first year she knew her infatuation with Thomas had grown into real love. He was kind, handsome, and intelligent, and she was sure her father approved of him.

Her mother scolded her. "Giuseppa, pay attention. Now, the secret to the perfect cannolo is the thin and crispy shell."

She was yanked from wistful thoughts and sighed. "Yes, Mama."

"Next, we take—daughter, you're not whipping the cream like I taught you."

"Yes, Mama."

Thomas took a deep breath and launched into the real subject he came to talk to Antonio about.

"Mr. Cavallaro, I want to thank you again for everything you've done for me since I arrived here. Most of all, for treating me like family. I love your daughter and I promise you I'll always provide for Josie and our children, should we be blessed someday. Will you give your permission for Josie to marry me?"

Inside the house, Josie was a mess.

"Mama, maybe they need more wine? You know how talking about the weather can make a man thirsty."

Her mother ignored the comment. Josie peeked around the corner to check again.

"Leave them to talk."

"It doesn't matter, Mama. Thomas is gone."

"I wouldn't worry so."

"Me, don't worry? Oh, why would I ever do that? Why should I worry? I've only been waiting half my life now."

She plopped down at the table and rested her chin in her hands.

"Mama, you're right. I'll be content to stay here with you and Papa and wait the other half of my life." She wrapped her hands around her head and shook it.

Antonio strolled into the kitchen with two wine glasses and an empty bottle.

Exasperated, Josie leaped to her feet and jutted out her lower jaw. "Papa, please tell me what you and Thomas talked about."

Isabella said, "Don't ask your father about his business."

"It's alright. Well, Thomas wanted to discuss an idea he had about the market and—"

"And I suppose, Papa, you and Thomas also mapped out the weather for the rest of the weekend too."

He said, "Yes. We agreed it may rain tomorrow."

Josie pushed hard for a wedding in June and settled for a date in July. They married at a filled-to-capacity crowd at the Sacred Heart Catholic Church in Norfolk.

Before she walked down the aisle with her father, she said, "Papa, I waited for what felt like an eternity, and now I want it to last forever."

She looked stunning in a flowing white chiffon and lace traditional wedding dress. They said their I do's and kissed as husband and wife for the first time. Thomas leaned over, whispering into her ear, "We'll be good together, Josie. I just know it."

Vincenzo was proud and honored to be Thomas's best man. An extrovert, a natural public speaker and one who never shied from attention, he rose to speak.

"I remember Thomas working with me the first day. I became a little worried because he never stopped moving. He was carrying tables two at a time, lifting a mountain of crates, pulling and pushing. I got dizzy watching him. I thought I might not be able to keep up. By the end of the second day, I was thinking uh-oh, what have I gotten myself into? I'm not sure I want to work this hard."

Vincenzo looked at the crowd and smiled. "I'm kidding. Everybody knows I'm kidding. I knew I could keep up. I just didn't think I wanted to."

He paused until the laughter died down. "I was also afraid with Thomas at the market, my father would figure out he might not need an extra employee and decide to get rid of me."

He laughed at his own joke. "But enough about me! There came a time when we all knew Thomas and Giuseppa were a couple. I started thinking to myself—we're friends, we work together, and well, why not be family too!"

He turned his attention to his sister. "And, of course, there's my baby sister. If it's okay with everyone, I want to take a moment to say something directly to her."

He ambled over to kneel beside her, resting his chin on her shoulder. "Baby sister?"

Josie turned to face Vincenzo. "Yes, big brother."

"I've watched over you for, what is it now? Twenty-three years or so. I know the real you as well as anyone, am I right? And I think it's time to thank you."

With a suspicious look, she said, "You're welcome, Vincenzo."

He put his elbow on the table and rested his head on his hand. "Yes, I just want to thank you for not scaring Thomas away."

Everyone had waited for Vincenzo to take a dig at his sister and howled when he did.

"We really do need Thomas at the market."

Josie laughed too and pinched her brother's cheek.

"And now look at our father sitting over there. You know why he looks relaxed with the big smile? Because he can finally stop worrying about getting you married and out of the house."

Vincenzo raised himself up to stand behind Thomas and Josie and rested a hand on each of their shoulders.

"Seriously, I love you both and I'm so happy for you. As the old saying goes, marriages are made in heaven, and today I believe this to be true."

He held up his glass of champagne. "Congratulations to Tommaso and Giuseppa; okay, okay, Thomas and Josie, and cheers, everybody!"

Later during the reception, Vincenzo and Antonio sat next to Thomas and Josie. Antonio said, "Thomas, you're a one-half owner today with Vincenzo. I'm going to retire, but I'll still come to work sometimes, and you'll pay me."

Josie squeezed Thomas's hand under the table and kissed him on the cheek.

Thomas said, "Mr. Cavallaro, we'll always leave your table in the corner of the market, and it'll be there for you to use whenever you want."

Chapter Thirty-Six

Over the next several years, business boomed for the Cavallaro Produce Market. The family-making business was also quite busy for the Mancusos. Three children came along over six years, Anthony in 1922, Tommy Jr. in 1927, and the youngest, Vincent, in 1928. Three boys filling the modest three-bedroom, one-bath house on Thirty-fifth Street at the edge of Little Sicily.

The day after Vincent was born, Thomas said, "Vincenzo, I guess it's obvious I'll never be one of the *ritornati*. I applied years ago for my American citizenship, and tomorrow it's my time to go to the federal courthouse."

On a Saturday evening two weeks later, Thomas and Josie hosted a party to celebrate his new citizenship. The living room, full of family and friends, quieted when Thomas rose to speak.

"Many years ago, a wise lady told me learning English would open doors for me. When I think back over my life, I realize how right she was, because I know one of those doors was the Cavallaro Produce Market. Without the language, I might not be here in Norfolk and probably wouldn't have been so lucky to meet Josie and convince her to marry me."

Josie snuggled next to Thomas and squeezed him around his chest.

"I'm proud to be a homeowner in the city of Norfolk where we have—how many children are we up to now, Josie?"

"It's three and that's enough!"

"Without a doubt, the proudest day of my life was the day I took an oath to become an American citizen. No one or nothing in this world is perfect, but the ideals the U.S. Constitution speaks to will always cause me to strive to be the best citizen I can. Thank you for joining me tonight in this celebration."

When everyone finished clapping, Josie jutted out her jaw and said, "I thought he might never do it and I would have to be a U.S. citizen all by myself."

The happy times came to an abrupt halt the following week when Antonio suffered a stroke and died the same evening. He was well respected, and the memorial was the largest anyone could remember in their little neighborhood. He was a day shy of his sixty-fifth birthday when he died and was laid to rest at St. Mary's Catholic Cemetery. The newspaper published a touching tribute to the larger-than-life figure who arrived in America with his wife and son in 1889 before Ellis Island opened.

At the memorial service, Vincenzo said, "My father was living proof that America is the land of opportunity. He came here as a poor man from Sicily and built a successful business and a loving home with our mother Isabella. We are touched by the presence of so many friends and family who have gathered to comfort us in our time of grief. I know he's up there looking down on us and saying thank you for taking the time to remember him today."

In the year following Antonio's death, the United States entered its worst financial crisis ever. The Cavallaro Produce Market barely survived the ugliest first years of the 1930s.

Vincenzo said, "They're calling it the Great Depression, but as far as I can tell, there's nothing great at all about it."

Business at the market was a tenth of what it had been at its height in the late 1920s. Following Antonio's death, Vincenzo and Thomas were equal partners and despite the hard times, they were still grateful for what they had.

They kept a sense of humor when one said to the other, "We've sure seen our ups and downs," and the other always responded, "Yes, and our highs and lows too."

They used their own private joke to soothe the worries and fears about the future, having heard about men jumping to their deaths over lost wealth.

"That'll never happen to us. We don't have enough money to be doing something crazy like that," Vincenzo said.

Despite their positive outlook, times did get worse. Both Vincenzo and Thomas took out loans against their homes to keep the business afloat. It was a grim and uncertain time in America and the two small business owners were not immune to the forces beyond their control. They waited for the economy to improve, as did everyone else.

Vincenzo and Thomas often found themselves talking about their own lives in the United States as naturalized citizens and about the many immigrants who had come from around the world.

"It seems to me," Thomas said, "some of these immigrants don't want to embrace the American way of life. I see it every day especially with the Sicilians who stay stuck in the ways of where they came from and are fearful to go beyond their own neighborhood and their own culture."

Vincenzo said, "I agree. I think it's just easier for some to live that way."

"I can say from experience," Thomas said, "it's critical for any newcomer in America to learn the language. A person can't progress in this world if he can't make himself understood. I've gone as far as I'll go, but it doesn't prevent me from having great hopes for my children to go to college and become professionals in a line of work of their choosing."

Thomas held the unshakeable belief that success depended in large part on fully assimilating into the American culture. He felt he had to be on guard because there were Sicilian immigrants in the neighborhood who continued with the old ways, and their influence seeped into his children's lives.

It was late Sunday afternoon when ten-year-old Anthony was playing with his friends on their street. The group came to an abrupt halt in front of the Mancuso house. They held small tree branches as play swords protecting their neighborhood from a pretend group of enemies, the kids who lived on Colonial Avenue a few blocks away.

Anthony spotted his father on the porch. He said to his friends, "*Amici*, wait here," and ran toward his father.

Thomas had heard them before using a mix of English and Sicilian that amounted to nothing more than a bastardization of the two languages. Thomas noticed over the years, the siculish or sicilianization of English words took hold and became acceptable substitutes in Little Sicily for everyday things such as *iarda* for yard, *bissinissa* for business, *stritta* for street, *carru* for car and *baccausa* for bathroom. Thomas thought the siculish speak was the lazy man's way of not taking the time to learn proper English.

Anthony, his hair slicked back with some kind of a greasy type product, mimicked the bastardized words and accented English from more recent Sicilian immigrants who, for whatever motivation, refused to assimilate.

"*Patri*, I'm protecting our *stritta*," he said, as he waved his sword like a pirate. "Everyone knows me as the *bossu* here."

"Anthony, I want you to speak English," Thomas said. "These other words are not proper in either language and have no place here. Do you understand?"

Thomas entered the house, unconsciously running fingers through his prematurely gray hair. He found Josie in the kitchen.

She said, "What's all the shouting about outside?"

"That was Anthony and his friends playing."

"He has lots of friends. It's wonderful, isn't it?" said Josie.

"Yes, I'm happy he has lots of playmates, but I don't want our children imitating those Italian movie actors with the grease in their hair, and I don't want them acting like hoodlums or using these made-up Sicilian words. Josie, they're not even proper words and only reinforce what people already think. I can hear them now, 'Those dagoes are running wild in the street and should go back to their own country.'"

Josie was stirring a pot of sauce on the stove. She said, "Thomas, come over here and try this."

"He's pretending to be like one of those *Vaselinos* from the movies with all that stuff in his hair. I want them to speak only English without the pretend accent and those mixed-up words," Thomas said.

"Here, this will make you feel better. Taste this." She held up the wooden stirring spoon to his mouth. "They're just boys having fun."

"Nobody cooks like you, Josie." He wiped his mouth with his handkerchief. "Well, I lived through the discrimination and humiliation as a boy."

"I thought it was pretty good myself." She stirred the sauce again. "You know, I can remember when you didn't even want to buy a house anywhere near this neighborhood."

"I guess I wanted to put space between us and anything connected to the attitudes that people bring from, you know, Sicily."

"Thomas, we can't control what other people think. You set the perfect example for the children by working hard and being a devoted father and husband. Besides, if you talk too much about it with them, they'll only want to do it more. I'm sure they'll outgrow it."

Josie took two steps to stand directly in front of Thomas. "By the way, you have a little sauce on your lip." She kissed him twice. "There. I got it!"

Thomas walked over to four-year-old Vincent, napping on the sofa. He put his hand on the child's shoulder.

"You're American. You speak only English. And I don't want you putting any of that mess on your head, you hear me?"

Josie said, "You're starting Vincent the right way. I'm sure everything will be fine."

Chapter Thirty-Seven

As the 1930s edged toward 1940, Thomas wasn't certain if times had gotten better or perhaps everyone had become accustomed to the shattered economy as the new norm. A new threat on another continent dominated everyday conversation—the dark shadow of war in Europe looming over the country. Reports on the remilitarized fascist regimes in Germany and Italy ruled by Adolf Hitler and Benito Mussolini alarmed people.

Thomas lamented to Vincenzo one day at work about the latest news from Europe. "These pictures and images of Mussolini shame all Americans of Italian ancestry. Yesterday Vincent came home from school and told Josie a teacher singled him out as a troublemaker because of what's going on halfway around the world. She even went as far as not allowing Vincent to play with the other kids during recess."

"What did you say to him?"

"I told him Mussolini is a crazy man. He doesn't represent us in any way. We're Americans and don't let anyone tell you any different."

"Good for you," Vincenzo said.

"I'm going to the school to speak to the principal and the teacher today. We're not changing our last name. We'll just have to change some attitudes."

On his eighteenth birthday in 1940, Anthony, the eldest of the children, talked to his father privately in the living room.

Anthony said, "Dad, I want to serve my country. I've thought about this a lot and I'm going to join the Army."

Thomas couldn't help but feel pride with the knowledge his son would make such an honorable commitment on behalf of his country by volunteering in a time of great uncertainty.

Lying in bed before sleep, Josie said, "Are you afraid for Anthony?"

"Of course, but we have to support his decision. I'm proud of him."

Josie said, "Me too, but the newspaper is full of stories about how quickly Germany is conquering other countries."

"Another war led by crazy people with plenty of ignorant followers. I hate to say it, but it looks like America will have to fight before over there becomes over here."

"Thomas, where do you think Anthony will go after his training?"

"Hopefully he'll be stationed someplace close to us. War seems inevitable and if it happens, I pray for a quick victory over those mad men so Anthony can come home soon and no more of our children or other Americans have to fight."

After Anthony enlisted, Thomas and Josie read the newspaper cover to cover every day, taking extra care to follow the news in the world. Thomas read a commentary in the newspaper saying what everybody already believed.

"Whether it wants it or not, the United States finds itself being slowly but inexorably dragged into another world war."

Lying in bed one morning, Josie said, "I hope Anthony has the time to write us a letter every so often. I just want to hear from him that everything is okay."

"Me too."

They held hands listening to a car motoring by on the road out front. As the headlights passed over the front of the house, the shadow of swaying tree branches outside danced on the bedroom wall inside.

"Josie, what do you say we take our minds off this and walk to the fireworks show tonight with Vincenzo and Carmela?"

It was a hot and sticky evening, but the newspaper promised the rain would hold off, at least allowing the fireworks show to go forward. City officials were quoted saying the celebration marking the first Fourth of July of the decade would be one to remember.

The two couples walked slowly down Granby Street toward the waterfront while Tommy Jr. and Vincent rambled a half block ahead of their parents. They neared the front of a stately colonial home complete with Tuscan style columns. Thomas spied several adults seated on the porch of the grand home and noticed a man walking, or more like staggering, through the yard toward the boys.

His speech was slurred. "Guess you boys walked over here from your little I-talian neighborhood. You going to get some pizza?" he said.

Tommy Jr. said, "No, sir, we're going to the fireworks show."

"To the fireworks show?" he said in a sing-songy voice. "Gosh, I guess they don't do that in your dago country."

While Thomas rushed forward attempting to catch up to the boys, Vincenzo stepped around Carmela and Josie to act as a barrier between them and the drunk.

"Boys, keep walking," Thomas said.

"Yeah, you keep right on walking back to your own country. I'm sure M-**u**-ss-**o**-l-**i**-n-**i** is waiting for your return."

He emphasized every vowel in the name. The man spilled some of his drink while he swung his arm to make a point.

His wife said, "Hank, honey, come back up here on the porch."

She laughed as she turned to her friends and said, "Sometimes he gets a little out of control."

Hank stepped in front of the boys. "Maybe you can eat your spaghetti with some fat meatballs too. I bet you like them."

Thomas caught up and put his hands on their shoulders. "Boys, let's keep moving."

"Sir, we're going to the fireworks show. We don't want any trouble," Vincenzo said.

"Oh, I get it. Because you speak a little English, you think you belong here, is that it?"

Hank's wife said to another man on the front porch, "Charlie, please bring my husband back up here before he does something stupid."

Hank said, "It won't be long now before all of you get shipped back to where you belong anyway. Then we'll kick your asses in Spaghetti-O-Land along with Hitler and M-**u**-ss-**o**-l-**i**-n-**i**."

Hank gesticulated wildly with his arms, spilling more of his drink as he spoke.

Thomas said, "Come on, boys, let's go."

He tried directing them around the drunk, but Hank blocked their path and bumped Thomas's chest, spilling the drink onto his shirt. He stood inches from Thomas, exhaling his alcohol-laden breath.

"Oh, sorry Mr. Guinea, but it's a hot night. Maybe it'll help cool you off a bit."

Vincenzo positioned himself to Thomas's side as Carmela and Josie looked at each other in fear.

"Uh oh, tough guy is here. I can see you're the fighter of the group, right?" He pointed his glass at Vincenzo.

Hank poured his drink on Thomas's shoe. "How about that, tough guy? You want to step up now and do something for your friend?"

In an instant, the memories of Nunzio's awful breath accosted Thomas. He tried his best to control the fury, but raw emotions churned inside him. Childhood memories, with their bitter taste of ridicule and pain, bubbled beneath the surface of his skin. Now a man, Thomas's anger stabbed at him to his core.

From the front porch, Hank's wife said, "Please come back up here, honey, and I'll fix you another drink."

"Your *daa-go* buddy here seems upset. I don't think either one of you have any fight in you. When we finally get to it, we'll mop the floor with you I-talians."

"Hello, Mrs. Snyder, it's me, Tommy Mancuso. Do you remember? I was in your class last year at Blair."

Mrs. Snyder, a stocky woman with beads of sweat rolling down her face and neck, stopped and eyed the boy.

Her face reddened as she clumped down the stairs and lumbered into the yard toward Hank.

Charlie, the man on the porch, snickered. "Hello, Mrs. Snyder," he mimicked the boy in a nasally voice.

She altered her course momentarily, spinning her wide body back toward the porch. "Charlie, shut your mouth now or I'll mop the floor with you first."

Thomas reached into his pocket. Alarmed by the sudden movement, Hank staggered a couple of steps backward, tripped and fell down in the yard.

Removing a handkerchief, Thomas looked at the drunk for a moment, then he wiped his shirt and shoes.

Mrs. Snyder mopped the sweat from her forehead.

She said, "Yes, hello, Tommy. Of course, I remember you." She shook her head for a moment. "Mr. and Mrs. Mancuso, I do apologize. Hank is never like this. I'm terribly sorry."

Thomas stared for a moment and said, "I understand, Mrs. Snyder. We should be getting along now. Good evening."

Later, Thomas told the others, "He comes into our market sometimes. He's always seemed like a polite man. I guess the alcohol brings out feelings deep inside him."

On a Thursday in July 1943, Josie rushed into the Cavallaro Produce Market with an envelope in her hand. Thomas could have recognized its color and shape from a mile away. He knew its consequence before Josie spoke and his heart sank.

"Thomas, they said our son—" She cried out, pushing the paper toward him. "They took our baby. Thomas, they said our Anthony is dead."

Thomas hugged Josie and, although he didn't want to, he took the envelope into his cold, bloodless hand. A Western Union telegram read, "THE WAR DEPARTMENT RE-GRETS TO INFORM YOU THAT YOUR SON AN-THONY BIAGIO MANCUSO WAS KILLED IN ACTION IN THE PERFORMANCE OF HIS DUTY AND THE SERVICE OF HIS COUNTRY ON TEN JULY IN GELA SICILY ITALY."

Thomas and Josie walked home clinging to each other every step of the way. Not knowing what else to do, they sat in their living room and cried until Tommy Jr. and Vincent came home from school, then they cried again. At a memorial service, Thomas closed his eyes and prayed the war would end before Tommy Jr. turned eighteen.

The following week Thomas walked to the public library and asked a kindly older volunteer librarian where he could find an atlas.

"Here you are, sir. Please bring it back to the front desk when you're done."

"Thank you, ma'am," he said, barely above a whisper.

He'd never felt so old as he turned to search for a table in a quiet corner or anywhere he could be alone. His entire life, Thomas had never looked at a map of Sicily. Cautiously, he opened the weighty cover of the book, afraid the name might leap into his field of vision before he was ready. He turned the heavy pages one at a time seeking an island he had almost driven from his mind. Thomas held his breath knowing the next page he turned would be the one he came to find but didn't really want to see.

It was a detailed map of Sicily. He scanned the page with the aid of his forefinger, careful not to touch the paper. His eyes locked on the name Gela for a second, then he closed them to block out the godforsaken place and allow his mind to think only of times when his son was still alive.

He sat with five-year-old Anthony on the living room floor teaching him to tie his shoes. He cheered twelve-year-old Anthony running the bases after slugging a home run over the right field fence at the neighborhood park. He hugged twenty-year-old Anthony in his soldier uniform for the last time before he shipped overseas.

Thomas opened his eyes and, for the next hour, tortured himself while staring at the word Gela, holding a handkerchief to his face.

Did I even think of Anthony when I woke up that morning? What was my son doing there? What were his last thoughts? How was Anthony killed? Was he alone when he died? Did he suffer?

When there were no more tears left, he retrieved a one-armed wooden soldier from his pocket. He broke its sword in half. Silently, he slid the atlas onto the librarian's desk and placed the toy alongside.

He felt suffocated and raced to the door. Pushing it open, he tore at his necktie to loosen it and take in air.

The librarian's voice sounded. "Sir, sir? You left a—"

He pushed the sound away before it could take hold and ran, slowly at first, then almost sprinting as he had when he was a boy. Crazy out of his mind, he raced down the street.

He shouted to everyone and to no one. "I don't want it. I don't want to ever see it again!"

Turning on Freemason Street, he ran without purpose. Exhausted, he finally slumped next to a tree at the edge of the road.

A few minutes passed until a young lady pushing a stroller stopped. "Sir, are you all right?"

Thomas wiped his brow. "Yes, I'm, I'm fine. I'm okay, thank you."

He stood straight and forced a smile. "Is that a boy, I mean, uh, is that a boy you have in there?"

The woman said, "Yes, this is little Stephen—"

"Don't ever let Stephen go off to war. Ever. Promise me, you'll never let him go."

Uncertain, she leaned over and placed her hand inside the stroller.

She said, "Sir, he's only six months—"

"I don't care. No matter what anyone says, don't let them take your Stephen from you. Promise me. Just promise you won't."

"Okay, I promise."

"Good. Good." Thomas straightened his tie. "I think Stephen will do great things one day."

Chapter Thirty-Eight

Early evening Thomas and Josie sat on the front porch. The heat was tolerable, the mosquitoes less so. They talked about how proud they were of both of their boys. Tommy Jr. was in his third year at the University of Virginia (UVA) in Charlottesville, and Vincent was a sophomore at the College of William & Mary Norfolk Division.

They were both home on school break disappearing with friends after a couple of hours of obligatory family time. Tommy Jr. was making excellent grades and talked about applying for UVA's Law School while Vincent focused on studies in accounting.

They reached a lull in their conversation and fell into a companionable silence. Thomas lost himself in the near cloudless sky, thinking how much he missed Anthony.

Josie lay her head on Thomas's shoulder. "I know. I know. I think about him every day. Every single day."

Thomas withdrew into his own thoughts.

Anthony was six years old. It was Christmas Eve and he was seated on the hearth with two red stockings hanging behind him, one with his name and the other for his new little brother, Tommy Jr.

"Dad, how can Santa come through the chimney when there's a fire?" Anthony asked.

Thomas had always seen a wide streak of earnestness coupled with curiosity that dominated his son's personality. "Don't worry. I'll let the fire burn out before we go to bed," Thomas said.

"Well, how does Santa fit through here anyway?" the boy said, pointing at the fireplace.

"He's magic. Santa makes himself really small."

"Okay, Dad, but what about—"

Josie interrupted his reminiscing. "Thomas, where did you go?"

He shook himself to return to the present and exhaled.

"Thomas, what are you thinking?"

They held hands while the porch swing gently swayed.

"I was thinking of Anthony and what could have been."

Josie squeezed his hand.

"Some nights I wake up and imagine Anthony in battle and wonder what he was thinking," Thomas said.

"You never told me this. Why didn't you wake me? We could have talked about it."

"Sometimes I need to work things out myself, I guess. One night I dreamed I never left Sicily and I was searching for Anthony."

"Thomas, don't talk like that. We would have never met or had any children."

"Well, it was only a dream."

"Thomas, I don't understand war. I mean, what causes such craziness in people's minds to want to do the things they do and have millions of people follow them?"

Thomas simply shook his head.

Other than an occasional voice from a neighbor's house, a quietness settled over the street. Lightning bugs decorated the evening's darkness. The sweet fragrance of honeysuckle lingered in the air.

"I want to stay like this forever," Josie said and snuggled up to Thomas.

"You've got a deal."

"Promise?"

"I promise."

"Thomas, why didn't you ever talk with the boys about what it was like for you living in Detroit?"

A lone breeze swept across the porch before retreating into the night.

"I never understood the point in going over all that with them. I've always wanted their focus to be on the future, not my past."

He paused before speaking again.

"You know, when I arrived in New York, I think in my mind I wanted to be an American right away, and I don't know why or if I even understand what that meant. I remember being on this ship and everybody crowding to the edge for a view of the Statue of Liberty. I couldn't see over other people and wondered what all the excitement was about. A man I traveled with picked me up and put me on his shoulders. I saw this huge statue of a woman holding a torch and I remember thinking, is this going to be my new mama?"

"Stop it or you're going to make me cry."

"I don't want you to cry. I said it because I want you to know how much gratitude I feel for being here with you, our children, in our own home. This is what counts. Right here. Right now."

"I'm grateful too."

Thomas placed his hand on his chest. "Except for An-thony, and he's still in here." He touched her chest. "He's in here too."

Thomas walked down Thirty-fifth Street on his way home from work, holding one end of a small rope connected at the other end to a pocket-sized puppy. Progress was slow as the tiny pup stopped every few feet to bite at the rope or chew on a stick or a leaf. Finally reaching home, Thomas began to climb the steps of the house. The puppy refused to budge.

"Oh, you need to learn how to walk up these stairs."

Josie came to the front door. "Thomas, who are you talking to?"

Her eyes dropped to the rope in his hand and the bug-eyed tiny ball of fur gazing upwards. "What's that?"

Thomas said, "It's a dog. Well, it's a puppy right now."

"What are you planning to do with it?"

"I thought I might bring Stella in and we'd have dinner."

"Oh, she already has a name?"

"Isn't she cute? I think you'll like her. I told her the whole way home my wife makes the best meatballs in town. I think she wants to try one."

Josie stared at the dog, then at Thomas, then back at the dog. Her jaw was fully extended. "Thomas, what are we going to do with a dog?"

"Wonderful; you've accepted Stella already."

Josie watched as Thomas picked up Stella and carried her up the stairs.

He looked at the grateful puppy. "I guess you need to learn to walk up steps."

Thomas stopped next to Josie.

"I never had a dog when I was a boy, and since Tommy Jr. and Vincent are at school, I thought Stella would make good company for us."

Stella wriggled to be free of one master and loved by another.

"Oh, that's what you thought? And here I was thinking all day long you were at work."

"Well, Stella was with me at work today."

"Where will she sleep?"

"I'll make up a little bed for her and she can sleep on the floor."

"In the kitchen, right?"

"Well, maybe in the bedroom at first."

"Oh, of course."

"You want to say hello to little Stella? I think she'd like to meet you."

After dinner, the new family of three sat on the front porch. Stella played with a ball of string, and within minutes it became a tangled mess twisting around her from neck to hind legs.

"The man who gave her to me said these dogs are quite intelligent."

"I have no doubt he did."

Stella rolled on her back, biting at the string.

"Thomas, what kind of dog is it?"

"They're called Boston Terriers. Some people call them the American Gentleman."

Josie bent over, untying the dog from its tangled mess.

"Can you explain to me how Stella is an American Gentleman?"

"Well, it's a nickname because they look like they're wearing a tuxedo. They're from the city of Boston."

She watched Stella fall backwards, biting at the string. "Well, I think this one comes from the city of crazy."

Thomas and Josie hosted a quiet Sunday dinner for Carmela and Vincenzo. The times had changed from the first occasion Thomas went to dinner at the Cavallaro house with so many people it required two tables to seat everyone. The small scene was more to Thomas's liking, as he had never warmed to hosting lavish or loud affairs.

"What a difference thirty-eight years makes," Vincenzo said.

"What's thirty-eight years?" Josie asked.

Vincenzo and Thomas laughed.

Carmela looked at Josie. She said, "Our boys must have a little secret."

Thomas said, "No, but Vincenzo and I were wandering down Memory Lane today, talking about the first time I went to dinner at Mr. and Mrs. Cavallaro's house."

Vincenzo said, "Yes, I can still remember baby sister here, 'Thomas, can I get you anything? Would you like another glass of wine? Thomas, another helping of lasagna?'"

Josie thumped her brother's hand and laughed, but her jaw pushed outward. "We didn't have lasagna. I remember Mama, God rest her soul, and I planned the menu, and she didn't want lasagna. And, you know, whatever Mama wants—"

Everyone finished the sentence together in unison, "Mama gets."

"Hey, baby sister, did Mama have you kissing Thomas in the kitchen on the menu?" Vincenzo asked.

"Hey, big brother, I didn't kiss Thomas that day, but I sure wanted to."

It was a tradition at least twice a month to play contract bridge after dinner, a game Thomas first learned to play by reading a book on the subject soon after arriving in Norfolk.

He enjoyed the challenge of bridge more than playing Scopa, the old Sicilian card game he viewed as simple and pointless. Thomas taught Josie how to play, and together they taught Carmela and Vincenzo.

Some years back, they tried teams of Carmela and Thomas versus Vincenzo and Josie, but misplayed tricks on the brother-sister team always led to sibling rivalry and, inevitably, arguments.

With Thomas's agreement, one evening Carmela said, "Better to know thine enemy. In other words, Vincenzo, you're on my team. Thomas and baby sister are the other team."

Between hands, the four discussed families and all the latest news.

"Thomas, what are you hearing from Tommy Jr?" Vincenzo asked.

"He's doing well at law school. He had been thinking about specializing in patent law, but lately he's been talking about copyright law."

"Is there a difference?"

"That's what I asked. Apparently, there is. As I understand from Tommy, and it's not altogether clear to me, patent law relates to an invention of something and a copyright protects the composer or author, for example, of music or a book."

"I'm sure you're both proud, as you should be. How's my godson, Vincent?"

"He'll graduate in the spring with an accounting degree and probably try for his CPA right away."

"Is he getting married anytime soon?"

"Not until after college. I should say hopefully that's the plan."

Chapter Thirty-Nine

Their youngest son, Vincent, slipped a tie around his collar. "Mom, what do you think of this tie with the graduation gown?"

"Wonderful, handsome, extraordinary! Now we need to go downstairs because your father is on his way home and will pick us up out front."

"Can we drive by Anne's to pick her up? I told her we would."

Driving on Hampton Boulevard, Thomas asked, "So, any plans tonight after graduation?"

He adjusted the rearview mirror of the Chevrolet Fleetmaster to better see Vincent and Anne sitting in the back seat.

"Yes, we're going to a friend's house. They're having a little party," Vincent said.

"Anne, if you're not busy this weekend, would you like to come for dinner Sunday?" asked Josie.

"Yes, ma'am. I'd love it."

First, Anne laughed, then Vincent laughed too.

Thomas glanced in the mirror. "Something funny going on back there?"

"Anne went to take her driver's license test today."

"No, Vince, don't say anything."

"She ran over the guy who was doing the driving test; well, backed over him."

"I didn't know he would walk behind the car while I was parking. I think it's as much his fault as it is mine."

Vincent said, "So now what happens?"

"I'm going back next week to repeat the driving part of the exam."

"Yeah, after he has surgery."

"He wasn't hurt. Well, not bad at least. He could still walk."

Thomas stopped Vincent and straightened his tie when they got out of the car. "I'm proud of you."

"Thanks, Dad. Now listen. I go in through this door here and you'll go in through the two glass doors over there."

Josie asked, "Do you have your cap?"

"Yes, it's right over here with my gown. Hmm, well, it was in the car. Let's see, where is it? Oh, I've got it; here it is!"

Josie said to Anne, "Sometimes I think he would lose his head if it wasn't attached to his body."

After the graduation ceremony, Thomas and Josie said goodbye to Vincent and Anne.

"We'll see you Sunday?"

"Yes, ma'am," Anne said.

"Here, Mom, can you take my cap and gown?"

Vincent kissed his mother on the cheek.

Thomas said, "Please be careful, both of you."

They watched as Vincent and Anne walked away toward their friend's car, holding hands.

Thomas asked, "Why the sad face? What are you thinking, Josie?"

"I'm thinking how long before I'm going to lose my youngest boy."

He hugged Josie to his side. "Don't think in terms of losing a boy, but in terms of gaining a son with a job."

"Good point."

"And maybe we'll gain a daughter-in-law too. Now, let's go home and the three of us can enjoy ice cream on the front porch."

"Yes, we'd better go home and check on the trouble your Stella has gotten into."

They sat on the front porch swing eating ice cream while Stella sat in between.

"Thomas, we're lucky with our boys, don't you think?"

"Yes, we should be proud of both."

"I think they got their character from you," Josie said.

"Remember it takes two to make a baby."

Josie blushed. They kissed and she wiped a little smudge of ice cream from Thomas's cheek.

Later that night, Thomas was the first in bed. When Josie came in and saw the four-legged creature lying on its back between the pillows snoring, she asked, "Now tell me again, where is the bed you made up for Stella?"

Three years had passed since Vincent's graduation from college. Thomas and Josie were enjoying a second cup of coffee and admiring their new chrome kitchen table with its gray Formica top and extendable leaves.

He pushed down on the top, causing the table to bounce back and forth. Thomas said, "I'm not sure what's uneven, the leg or the floor."

He bent down to check the legs. "You would think in this day and age that table legs would be made even. It must be the floor. I'll slip this matchbook under the footing right here–"

The telephone rang, Stella barked, and Thomas hit his head jumping up to reach the wall-mounted telephone. He waved his hand at Josie to stay seated while he took a few steps to answer a call he hoped would be Vincent.

"Hello?"

He rubbed the back of his head.

"Dad, we're at the hospital and they're saying the baby is close."

"Is everything okay?"

"Yes. Are you and Mom coming over?"

Thirty minutes later, they walked into Norfolk General Hospital, anxious to see their first grandchild. Thomas still recollected the story Angelina told him from long ago. He wasn't a superstitious man by nature, and although it was a modern hospital with the latest technology and best-educated doctors, he made a point of rapping his knuckles on the hospital door entrance just in case.

They found Vincent pacing in the waiting room. He hugged both his parents.

"Nothing yet. Soon, I hope," Vincent said.

A nurse rounded the corner at the same time.

"Mr. Mancuso?"

Both Vincent and Thomas turned their heads to the voice.

The nurse said, "Well, okay, this time Mr. Mancuso the baby's father."

"Is everything okay?" Vincent asked.

"Yes, you have a beautiful, healthy—" A cry interrupted her. "Baby boy with a good set of lungs. Everything is fine. Come with me."

Thomas and Josie took a seat. He put his arm around her and said, "We're blessed. At the risk of sounding greedy, I pray this is the first of many more for us."

Josie said, "Doesn't sound greedy. Hopeful is a better word."

As they waited for additional news, Josie asked, "Thomas, do you think Tommy Jr. will marry?"

"Someday yes, but he's busy with his career now. I guess he doesn't have time for it."

She tickled Thomas under his chin. "Well, I'm glad you made time for it," Josie said.

"I wouldn't have had it any other way."

Vincent came around the corner holding cigars in his hand.

"Well, we have a boy. We'll call him Raymond or Ray, I guess. He was Anne's favorite uncle."

Chapter Forty

Long-term Norfolk residents could see the changes in their town over the years, particularly after the war. While downtown was still hanging on to economic viability, vibrancy was a scarce commodity and wouldn't come back for decades. Thomas also noticed the energy shifting to the suburbs and east toward the beach for the last few years.

Late Tuesday morning, Thomas and Vincenzo sat on stools leaning against Antonio's big table in the corner. Their second customer of the morning had browsed without purchasing anything.

"The youth have the energy and when they leave, you can almost feel the life force of the city going with it. Is it only me, or do you feel it too, Vincenzo?"

"Thomas, my body started feeling the loss about ten years ago!"

As time went by, modern supermarkets and department stores all but replaced the charming Cavallaro Produce Market. Thomas knew time was catching up, and the market was now a part-time deal for him and Vincenzo. They no longer hoisted or carried crates and tables around or straightened up as fast as they did in their youth. Occasionally when Thomas exerted himself, he felt a slight twinge in his chest which over time became more of a squeezing sensation.

One afternoon when he returned home from work, he walked in the front door intending to tell Josie he had decided to retire.

Josie beat him to the punch in conversation. "I've been listening to the same song blaring from that boy's window for I'm not sure how long."

"Who and what song?"

"Our new neighbors. I'm sure it's their teenage boy. Wait a second, I guarantee it'll start again, hold on, it's coming."

A second later, "Rock Around the Clock" by Bill Haley and the Comets sounded.

"Yes, I've heard of this. Vincenzo's grandson, Robert, was at the market the other day talking about this song."

Thomas stopped to listen to a few bars. "I like this sound. They call it rock and roll music. Maybe I was born in the wrong era."

"Thomas, you're kidding me, right?"

"No, we should go dancing sometime. How about right now!"

He reached for her hands and swung Josie around while Stella barked.

"See? I think Stella likes it too."

After dinner, the sun set low in the sky while they sat on their front porch swing. Thomas hadn't wanted to admit it to himself, much less Josie, but he reluctantly revealed his recent health problems.

"Well, when did you think you might get around to telling me about your chest pain?"

"I'm sorry, Josie. I kept hoping it would pass. I already have an appointment to see the doctor later this week."

Josie jutted out her jaw. "I'm coming with you to make sure you go."

"Okay, Thursday afternoon at three. I'll talk to Vincenzo tomorrow about retiring."

"Don't let him talk you out of it."

The next day, with much reluctance, Thomas started his planned speech to Vincenzo.

"I've been wanting to talk to you for a while about, well, I'm thinking of retiring–"

Vincenzo interrupted him. "Retirement? Thomas, do you know how long I've wanted you to say this? I'm an old man and have only been coming around here to spend time with you."

"Oh, well good, then—"

"Besides, people don't walk to the market anymore and chat. Now they drive their cars to air-conditioned stores, collect their goods as fast as possible, and leave without even a hello or a goodbye. The conversation, the smiles, and the friendships—they're almost gone."

"I know it. It makes me sad, but the fact is we can't compete with all the modern department stores and suburban supermarkets," Thomas said.

Thomas hugged Vincenzo, knowing a long and satisfying chapter of his life was coming to a close.

Vincenzo and Thomas shuttered the Cavallaro Produce Market doors sooner than they or anyone expected when a wealthy speculator who had been purchasing Norfolk office space gobbled up their market.

They celebrated with family and friends at the Cavallaros' house.

Thomas spoke first. "Forty-four years ago, I was a kid walking down the street with nothing more than a duffle bag hung over my shoulder and an apple in my pocket. Life is an accumulation of millions of moments. Most are scattered and forgotten, but there are those special ones I'll always remember.

"The moment I first saw Vincenzo unloading crates from a horse-drawn wagon in front of the Cavallaro Produce Market was a chance encounter leading to Vincenzo and Mr. Cavallaro taking a chance on me. And here we are today. I'm more appreciative to you both than you can imagine. Thank you, Vincenzo."

They hugged.

Thomas pointed his finger skyward.

"And thank you, Mr. Cavallaro. Enough from me. Please, Vincenzo."

"Thank you to my dear friend Thomas. Forty-five years ago, my father started the Cavallaro Produce Market, and I like to think I helped at least a little. My father worked at a dry goods store, and one day he learned that a man by the name of Angelo Martelli, an olive-skinned Irish bloke, had decided it was time to retire."

The laughter reverberated throughout the crowded living room. Vincenzo bowed his head for a moment before he continued.

"This man, who was actually from Milan had recently lost his wife. I, I don't know. I suppose he wanted to sell for his own reasons. It was a small produce store, nothing more than a fruit stand with a canopy over it. My father was nervous about the risk, and I remember he and my mother talking about it until late that night.

"Carmela and I hadn't moved to a little apartment down the street yet, and I'll never forget the next morning when we walked into the kitchen. I had little Antonia in my arms and my parents were sitting at the same table. He said, 'Vincenzo, it's time to quit your job cleaning windows. We're going into the produce business.' My father was so loved here in the community. He could have sold anything and been successful."

Tears welled in his eyes, and Carmela held his hand.

"I swore I wouldn't cry," he said, wiping his eyes. "Well, we caught our biggest break the day this handsome young man standing next to me came walking up Main Street. With a bit of a push from me, my father decided to take a chance on this youngster. You had to have known my father. He was cautious and liked to think things through for long periods of time. At the end of the first day, though, he pulled me aside and said two things to me. First he says, 'Make sure this kid has a place to sleep tonight,' and 'Vincenzo, I think you found a good one.' Coming from my father, that was huge! Well, I've always thought the same. God knows, we've seen our ups and downs."

Vincenzo teared up and stopped his speech, unable to go further.

Thomas hugged him and whispered, "And our highs and lows, big brother."

The first official day of Thomas's retirement he sat on the front porch swing with Josie enjoying a gentle breeze and the company of Stella, wedged between the two. As they sat in silence, his mind wandered back to Detroit, thinking about Angelina.

He breathed in and exhaled heavily.

"What's on your mind?" Josie asked.

"Oh, nothing."

"I can tell when something's going on up there." She ran her fingers through his hair. "I'd like to hear about it."

"Well, I was wondering about Angelina, the woman in Detroit."

"What about her?"

"I was thinking what happened to her after I left."

"I thought you said you never heard from her."

"Well, I didn't, but before we were married, I wrote letters off and on, but I never received a response. After I had been here for about five years, I guess it was around 1916 or so, I got this crazy idea about going to Detroit to check on her."

"Doesn't sound crazy to me as long as you were coming back."

She squeezed his arm.

"Oh, of course if I had gone, I would have come back. I was curious and a little worried how things worked out with her. Her husband was an awful human being, and I felt like after what she did for me, I owed her. I couldn't understand why she never answered. Sometimes I thought maybe he got his hands on those letters and tossed them away."

"Would he do that?"

"Josie, this man was capable of anything. Anyway, this guy who worked in the drug store next to our market had decided to go to Detroit to work at the Ford Motor Company. Maybe you remember him? He was tall and wore glasses. I think his name was Lawrence or Larry."

"The name sounds familiar," Josie said.

"So, I asked if he could do me a favor and go to Angelina's house. He told me he would, but after almost a year I kind of forgot about asking him until he came home to visit his folks. Oh, I remember the name of the drug store, Gooden Pharmacy, right?"

Josie said, "I do remember. We used to sing it like a jingle, 'Gooden Pharmacy, they're gooden for you and they're gooden for me.'"

Thomas said, "Yes, that's right. Well, anyway, I ran into him, Larry, I think his name was, and he told me he went to the house, but nothing more than the skeleton of the structure remained. He asked a neighbor and found out the man who lived there died in a fire right around Christmas five years before. He said a fireman thought he must have fallen asleep smoking in bed."

"Well, what about Angelina?"

"The neighbor said it wasn't but a couple of days after the fire she left carrying only a small suitcase. She said she was headed home to Italy and planned to follow her dream of being a teacher. That would have been only a few weeks after I left."

"I wish I had met her."

"I know you would've liked her. She'd be over a hundred if she were still alive today. Maybe she is. One thing for sure, I don't know what I would have done without her."

Chapter Forty-One

1956

Although it was only seven in the morning, the heat radiated throughout the second floor of the house, seeming to find the corner bedroom the best place to lodge for the day. The record July temperatures chased Josie downstairs to the kitchen to squeeze oranges for the juice Thomas loved to drink.

Feeling smothered by the heavy blanket, Thomas sat up and threw the cover off himself. Stella rolled over and stretched her legs.

He felt discomfort in his chest and collapsed against the pillows.

"Thomas, are you coming down for breakfast?"

He didn't respond.

"I guess he's sleeping the whole day through," Josie said.

Within a couple of minutes, the ache subsided and Thomas sat back up reaching for his trousers when a new pain seized him. He lay back down in the bed and closed his eyes to rest a few moments. His mind drifted to thoughts about the voyage to America and his father's friend on the ship. Thomas tried to think of the man's name or any of the other men on the ship before dozing off and losing himself in a dream.

He awakened to Josie's perfume as she leaned over him.

"I closed my eyes for a second and I was back on the ship," Thomas said.

"What are you talking about?"

His skin was pale, and a drop of sweat rolled sideways off his forehead. Josie sat down next to him on the side of the bed.

He said, "I was on this ship and I saw my mother. I don't know how, because I never saw her before other than a dream I had a long time ago. Josie, it was strange because it was the same person."

"What dream? What ship are you talking about?" Josie held a glass in her hand. "Thomas, please drink some orange juice. It'll make you feel better."

"I asked her what she was doing in the middle of the sea. She spoke Sicilian and said she was waiting for me. She called me Tommaso and said, 'It's time to come home.' I remember the sea at that moment smelled sweet. Then I woke up, Josie, and you were here."

Another sharp pain shot through his left shoulder down to his wrist and into his hand.

"What's wrong? Are you having chest pain? I'm calling Dr. Ambrose right now."

Thomas put his hand on Josie's leg. "We don't need a doctor. Please sit here with me for a minute. I promise everything will be okay."

His eyes locked with Josie's. "Thank you for being you. And for being a wonderful wife and mother too."

"Thomas, please. You're scaring me."

"You don't need to be scared."

"Is it your heart?"

Thomas smiled weakly. "No, Josie, my heart is just fine."

He squeezed her hand and closed his eyes.

Chapter Forty-Two

1963

When World War II ended, the veterans came home. Most married. Some went to work and others went to school. America became a mobile country, and many people no longer found contentment living in one place. The children and grandchildren of the Sicilian immigrants blended into the fabric of American society. The area once known as Little Sicily became like any other neighborhood with people of varied color and nationality.

Over the last several years, Vincent and Anne brought two more children into the world, a girl in 1955 and another boy in 1960 to keep the oldest, Ray, company. They lived a quiet life in a middle-class neighborhood a few blocks from the ocean in Virginia Beach. Distance-wise, they hadn't relocated far from Norfolk, yet they had moved a world away from his parents' home.

Vincent sat in the backyard wearing his shiny new blue Lycra swim trunks. He read on the product label they were made of a special new material that would dry faster. It was another product, he thought, that went well in a world consumed with quicker, faster, and greater efficiency. He hadn't officially tried them out yet, but he knew it wouldn't be long before the kids begged him to play Marco Polo in the above-ground pool.

It saddened Vincent to think his father died so young and only enjoyed a year of retirement. Years later, he still felt the pain of losing him. His father had worked unselfishly to give him the chance to succeed, far surpassing him with an education and profession.

Dad did this for us. All of it. How do I repay him? The plan makes perfect sense now. He was the orchestra conductor that guided me, Tommy Jr., and Anthony as musical instruments. He wanted me to play music to the best of my ability. Somewhere out there, sits a force greater than all of us. Sometimes the song is cut short and never allowed to play out. Like Anthony.

Vincent's thoughts were interrupted. Through the open kitchen window, Anne asked, "Vince, do you want to split a Tab with me?"

"Sure, that sounds great, thanks."

"Okay, I'll be out in a minute."

It's time to hang the flag out on the front porch. For Anthony and Dad. They were great Americans. And they're my heroes.

Anne came outside wearing a yellow one-piece halter swimsuit.

"Hey, look at you," he said.

She smiled holding a bottle of the new popular diet soft drink and did a little twirl before sitting in the lawn chair next to Vincent.

Their oldest son Ray hung onto the edge of the pool.

"Mom, can I have a swig?"

"No, it'll stunt your growth."

"Raymond, don't say the word swig. It sounds like you want to drink a beer," said Vincent.

"Okay then, can I have a swig of beer?"

The stare from Vincent toward his son cast a large shadow over the pool. No words were necessary.

Ray said, "Never mind, I'll go in for a drink of water."

"Drink water from the hose. It'll be time to head to your grandma's house soon," his father said.

"Vince, are we taking the kids to see the fireworks show at the beach this Thursday?"

"Oh, I meant to tell you. I think a couple other guys from work are bringing their families. We'll meet up at the beach."

Vincent laughed out loud. "I think we'll drive."

"What's funny?" Anne asked.

"Oh, God. I was thinking about the time when I was a kid. It was me, Tommy, Mom, and Dad and their friends, and we were going to see the Fourth of July fireworks show."

"Where? In Norfolk?"

"Yeah, you know, down by the waterfront."

"I'll take the fireworks show at the beach, thank you!"

"Anyway, we're walking down Granby Street."

"Right."

"Everything was fine except for this one guy. He was, I think, yeah, he was the husband of one of Tommy's teachers from school. This guy is in his front yard and he's sauced. He's getting on us about the neighborhood we walked from, you know, saying the usual bad names."

"Well, how did he know you were Italian, you know, where your family came from?"

"One, he saw the direction we came from in the neighborhood. Two, take a look at Tommy and me. And Mom and Dad. And their friends. Three, I mean, just look at us."

Anne laughed and said, "Okay, I get it. When was this?"

"It had to be around 1940. Let's see, it was before the war started but Anthony had already left for training. That's right, it would have been July 1941. Anyway, this guy is going on about Mussolini and we'll kick the you-know-what out of you at war. I mean, the guy was deep in the tank. Anyway, he spills his drink on Dad's shoes, and I'm sure he did it on purpose. I could tell my dad was mad, but Tommy pipes up to this lady on the porch, 'Hey, Mrs. So and So, you were my teacher at school.' This lady was built like a linebacker–"

Ray was listening to the conversation at the edge of the pool and giggled.

"Vince, stop it," Anne said.

"Okay, but I'm just saying this lady had some heft to her. Anyway, after Tommy spoke up, she started being all polite with my dad and everything kind of calmed down. Too bad because I think Dad, he was, well, let's see, if it was 1941, he was about forty-six, but I think he would have wiped that guy out. Dad had some beefy arms on him."

"I loved your dad. He was such a sweet man."

"He was the greatest. You know, my Dad was strict with us about school and studying when we were growing up."

"I bet he had to be."

"Well, I'm not that strict."

"Hold on. I think you're strict with the kids. It's good. That's how they learn, right?"

Vincent said, "I guess so. Okay, kids, get dried off. Time to go to grandma's house for dinner."

It was a Sunday tradition. Vincent and his family went to his mother's house after church. Josie followed in the ways of her own mother and prepared Sunday meals, although not as elaborately as Isabella. There was a salad, a main course like lasagna, bread, and a side of sugar snap peas or broccoli. The adults solved all the world's problems seated around the mahogany dining room table while the children watched television in another room.

"Mom, have you heard from Tommy lately?" Vincent asked.

"He called a couple weeks ago. He said both kids had the chickenpox. When one got it, Jeannie locked both in the bedroom together to play, hoping the other one would catch it and get it over with at the same time."

"Tommy married a no-nonsense woman in Jeannie, didn't he?"

"He sure did."

"I guess Tommy's working hard," Vincent said.

"He said he's busy with his practice, but he thought they would try to come visit soon."

"That would be great to get everybody together. Everyone's always so busy. What can I help you with, Mom?"

"Nothing at all. I just enjoy having your company."

As they gathered around the table and said grace, Vincent noted clear differences from the past. He sat at the one end of the table where his father used to sit. Dinners were shorter affairs, not hours long, and English was the only language spoken.

After Vincent washed the dishes and Ray helped dry, the family headed back to the beach. An immediate calmness descended upon the house on Thirty-fifth Street. Josie loved seeing the kids, but it was relaxing and peaceful once everyone left. She sat on the front porch for a few minutes enjoying the gentle breeze before it was time to head upstairs for bed.

Josie's thoughts took her back to dinners with Vincenzo and Carmela and the hours of playing bridge.

Has it been five whole years since big brother and sister-in-law died within a month of each other? I'm the last of the old gang. I wonder if anyone will remember us after we're all gone?

As was custom every night, she looked up at the sky and blew a kiss to Thomas.

He sure loved astronomy and reading about the stars and planets, always talking about the speed of light and the vast distances in space. Thomas, it doesn't matter to me; my love is faster than your old speed of light and can reach you wherever you are at this moment.

Her left knee crackled as she stood. She noticed the drawer on the cabinet next to the swing was pulled halfway out. Josie figured it to be the neighborhood kids doing a bit of ransacking. She pushed and pulled, but something blocked it from opening or closing. Reluctantly, she sat back down on the swing to figure out the problem. Shaking the drawer from side to side, it finally opened.

Josie shook her head, seeing the old ball of rope. She recalled the moment she first saw Thomas walking up the stairs to the porch carrying his first and only dog.

It's been seven years since he died. God, I miss that dear sweet man every single day.

She closed her eyes.

Thomas sat next to Josie. Anthony, in his Army uniform, sat on the other side. Little Stella lay curled on the floor. Thomas put his hand on her hand.

"You're doing well, Josie. I loved seeing Vincent and Anne today. Those grandkids sure are growing. You know whenever you need us, Anthony and I will be here for you." He chuckled. "Yes, okay, Stella, you'll be here too."

Josie awoke, not sure how long she'd been asleep, and dropped the ball of rope into the drawer. After she went inside and closed the front door, the porch swing rocked ever so gently.

Chapter Forty-Three

1975

Tony, the youngest child of Vincent and Anne, worked with his dad in the yard as they did every weekend, mowing the grass, edging the sidewalk, digging and filling holes with new plants and dirt, then more dirt.

He wiped sweat from his brow and said, "Dad, it's so hot, my sweat is sweating. I think it's time for my union five."

He sat on the picnic table and watched his father prune rose bushes. Tony turned fifteen the day before.

"Dad, what do you think about me getting my learner's permit next week?"

"How are your grades?"

"All A's and one B, and hey, if I'm going to be a safe driver, I need to practice, right?"

No response. Tony saw this as a sign his dad might cave at any moment. He figured it was time to back away and let that little seed sprout and grow.

"Hey, Dad, the movie last night was cool, didn't you think? I mean, all my friends are saying the second *Godfather* movie was even better than the first."

Vincent slipped the hand pruners into his back pocket, gathering a few cuttings from the ground while Tony wondered if his dad was even listening to him.

Vincent stopped and said, "Yes, entertaining, but the problem is people see these movies and believe anyone with an Italian last name is somehow connected to that kind of life."

He dropped the cuttings into a trash can. "Tony, what I'm saying is these movies perpetuate a stereotype, a negative one, and that part I don't care for."

"Well, it was still a great movie, right?"

"Yes, I suppose it was. Okay, if you're back on the clock, let's put more mulch around these roses."

Tony remembered Christmas in 1975 because with a permit in his back pocket, he experienced his first car accident, a minor fender bender from backing into a pole in a grocery store parking lot.

He half-shouted, "What's a stupid pole doing in the middle of a parking lot anyway?"

His older sister Jennifer was riding shotgun. "Oh, it might be holding up a light." She pointed outside the car. "You know, like the one up there. They're called light poles."

"Oh, God. Dad will flip out."

"Yep, I bet you're right," Jennifer said.

His father's new Chrysler Cordoba complete with Corinthian leather now sported a small dent in the rear end.

On the drive home, a sudden thought brought a possible reprieve to his mind. "Hey, you know what?"

Jennifer said, "No, tell me. This will be good, I'm sure."

"Maybe, just maybe, with you and Ray at home, and this being the season of peace and goodwill—"

"I know where you're going with this, and I don't—"

"No, listen. Maybe Dad will let me slide a little, maybe?"

"Yeah, maybe. Hey! Watch the curb."

A short ten minutes later, they arrived home.

"Good luck, kiddo," Jennifer said.

She left her brother standing in the driveway and slid through the side door of the house.

Tony got lucky. His dad used the relaxed and calm approach for discipline, leaving Tony sitting in the vast gray area of halfway in and halfway out of the doghouse. He also received a stern yet measured lecture focusing on the themes of paying attention and driving being a privilege, not a right.

Despite the flub with the car, Tony thought about how great it was hanging out with the whole family at home. His mother put all the photo albums on the coffee table, and everyone sat in the living room passing books to each other and sharing stories. Tony saw a few photos of his grandparents, but the comments and conversation focused on the living.

Chapter Forty-Four

In 1983, Tony graduated from Old Dominion University with degrees in Finance and Accounting, and he thought his father would have been proud of the accomplishment. His dad, an accountant his entire adult life, had provided well for the family, putting three kids through college. He had died a year earlier, a fact that was still hard for Tony to accept. His father had *beaten* the cancer by being free of the wretched disease for five years. It wasn't supposed to return, but Tony, like many others, learned the hard way that cancer was a monster that followed no rules.

Less than three months later, his dad was buried at St. Mary's Catholic Cemetery near his mother and father, Josie and Thomas, and beside a marker for his late brother, Anthony. Tony had never known his namesake uncle who died in Sicily during World War II.

Tony persevered through the devastating loss, knowing his father would have wanted him to keep moving forward. The double major had been a lot of hard work, and he hoped they would help him on his path to becoming an investment advisor. With the counsel of a professor, he began to see a road to the future where anything might be possible.

Over the next several years, Tony worked as a bank loan officer, then interned at Goldman Sachs, which led to a job as a junior financial advisor with Merrill Lynch.

In 1990, he met his future employer by accident while watching the Tidewater Tides, the minor league baseball team in Norfolk. When the Tides found themselves down by eight runs, Tony and a friend from work stopped paying attention to the game and began discussing the team's name. Tony said he didn't care much for the repetitive name, the Tidewater Tides, and soon other people in their section, tired of witnessing their team's beat down, also got involved in the discussion.

"Okay, what would you call them?" his friend asked.

Tony brushed back the thick black hair from his forehead. "They play right here in Norfolk; what's wrong with the Norfolk Tides?"

During the fifth inning, Tony went to the concession stand for a soda and a bag of peanuts. A man who had been sitting near him in the bleachers during the entire discussion now stood behind him in line.

"I think you hit the nail on the head with the name," a stranger's voice said.

Tony turned around and said, "I think it could be the only hit the Tides get today."

They ended up talking for an hour watching the game from near the concession stand, both having left their friends behind to suffer through the rout. Tony's new friend, Victor Maynard, owned a boutique investment firm, Maynard & Associates, in Norfolk. Within a month's time, Tony started a new job.

On his first day, Tony sat with his new boss for several hours.

"Tony, like we talked about a few weeks ago, being an investment advisor is more than numbers. People skills are a major component of success, including gaining a person's trust in an honest way. It's also important to listen to and understand your client's goals, needs, and tolerance for risk; not just deciding a course of action because of your own personal comfort zone."

Occasionally Vic took telephone calls and left Tony sitting in a conference area of the office. Tony observed Vic on the telephone *listening* to his clients, not talking at them. He was impressed, and he said so.

"Well, thanks. I appreciate hearing that. Now I'd like to talk a bit about the philosophy here. Tony, I asked you to join us because I could tell from our previous discussions, your resume and work experience, that you're smart, likeable, and possess a knack for doing sound analysis of how businesses and products are trending. Those qualities are also critical to your success and your clients, keeping in mind they are, after all, one and the same.

"Over the next few months I want you to focus on getting to know your clients. It may sound silly or easy or even like bull, but I don't think so, and I don't think you do either. If I did, I would tell you straight up you're at the wrong company. Building relationships will be the most important skill, and I do mean skill, you'll learn for the rest of your career. It will serve you, and more important, it will serve your clients."

"Yes, sir."

A catered lunch arrived, and before they left Vic's office, he said, "Tony, I appreciate your courtesy, but everyone calls me Vic around here. No need to be formal, okay?"

"Yes, sir, I mean, okay, Vic."

Tony knew by the end of his first day he had found a mentor in Vic and not just a job at Maynard & Associates, but a home.

A small, dynamo multimillion-dollar company, Maynard made a tremendous amount of money for its clients and advisors. Vic served clients, and he also managed the associates under him, including Tony. He and his wife Mandy had two young girls and lived in a turn-of-the-century waterfront house in the historic district of Ghent. Only five years older than Tony, Vic seemed to be so much wiser and more worldly.

Within a month after starting work, they were becoming friends. Right away, Tony could see they had things in common. They were close in age. Vic was thirty-five; Tony was thirty. Both of them were sports enthusiasts, and each maintained an active regimen in an attempt to stay physically fit.

Shorter than Tony, Vic was an inch under six feet with a stout, muscular build. He kept his light brown hair short like a Marine, although he had no military experience.

After watching their baseball team lose again, they stopped off at the family-run pub, Extra Innings, near the Tides' stadium.

"Okay, Vic, in spite of tonight, here's to the Tides."

"Yeah, cheers. Maybe it's only coincidence, but every time I go to a game and you're there, the Tides lose," Vic said.

"It's becoming a habit, isn't it?"

"Seems like it. So, Tony, you have family in town?"

"Not anymore. I have a brother and a sister. I'm the youngest. My father passed away in eighty-two, and my mom moved back to her childhood home in Edenton, North Carolina a few years ago."

"I'm sorry about your dad. He must have been young."

"Thank you. Yeah, he was just shy of his fifty-fifth birthday when cancer got him."

"Cancer is a scourge on humankind, no doubt about it. Where are your brother and sister?"

"Ray's the oldest. He's a trial attorney with the Department of Justice. His wife, May, is a dance instructor, and they have one daughter. They live in one of those classic brownstones in the Georgetown area of Washington, D.C. I would say other than Ray working eighty hours a week and the unfortunate rhyming of their first names, life is swell for Ray and May."

Vic laughed and said, "I knew a guy who did that right out of law school and worked his butt into the ground. He went into private practice and now he makes a ton of money, but he's working the other end of himself into the ground. How about your sister?"

Tony said, "My older sister Jennifer is engaged to an airline pilot. She's an executive with Hilton Hotels, and although her home office is in California, she's constantly hopscotching around the country because as she likes to say, 'We have hundreds of Hilton hotels around the globe and I plan to see them all.'"

"That's funny. Are you all close?"

"Well, they both travel all the time and we don't see each other much. In fact, the last time all three of us kids were together with my mom was at my father's funeral."

"Wow, you're kidding?"

"No. Sometimes I think it was more than my father being buried that day. It seems like the family began drifting apart, and my father's family history was also buried along with him."

"I understand."

"As the story goes, my grandfather came over from Sicily when he was little, but no one ever really talked about it, and we kids never asked, so when my dad died, it's like…I don't know, like the vault door to that part of the family got locked for good."

When Tony drove home that night, his conversation with Vic replayed in his head. Thoughts about family, missed opportunities, old conversations, and good times and bad churned in his thoughts. He vowed to himself that he would call his mom and siblings during the week.

Chapter Forty-Five

2010

The business of Maynard & Associates grew rapidly in the 1990s. With the booming economy, the staff outgrew the small space in a less than prestigious part of town. Their new office, although situated in an older four-story brick building on Duke Street in downtown Norfolk, boasted a sleek, ultra-modern interior on the top floor with excellent views of the city and the waterfront.

Several years earlier, Tony had bought a spacious three-bedroom condo in the Freemason area adjacent to the downtown area that afforded him a fantastic view of the skyline and harbor. Over the years it had been completely updated except for the guest bathroom, which was reminiscent of an era from the 1970s with its harvest gold and avocado green. Every time he walked past it only served as a reminder to call in a professional and redo the entire room.

One brisk morning in early spring, he went to a scheduled dentist appointment before work. While he sat in the waiting room, one of a dozen home improvement magazines caught his eye with pictures of remodeled bathrooms. As quietly as he could, he tore a single page of a bathroom style to his liking and stuffed it into his pocket.

Later in the afternoon, the folded page from the magazine sat on his desk when another associate, Johnstone, saw the picture. "Hey, Tony. What's up? Planning a project? I know a tile guy. Does excellent work. Show him the picture. The rest is history. Historeee. Fantastic work. Here's his number."

Johnstone checked his phone and wrote it down on the magazine page without waiting for Tony's response and left.

Johnstone, whose real name was John Stone, was the kind of person who did everything in a rapid, hypersonic manner—walking, talking, eating; the activity didn't matter, but it was always performed as if being done under a deadline. His speech was fast. In short bursts. All the time.

Over the years, Tony and the others at Maynard became accustomed to the lightning-fast speech. He answered his telephone as "Johnstone" with the long *o* sound just like in the word stone. People who didn't know him thought his first name was Johnstone and everyone at Maynard also called him that. The joke in the office was whether his wife Karen called him Johnstone too.

Ten years younger than Tony, Johnstone vowed from day one he would be the top dollar-grossing associate. He never pretended he would pass Vic, who not only had individual clients, but also advised private pension plans, endowments, and foundations. On the other hand, Tony was viewed as a viable goal to overtake, and as Johnstone did every year, he warned this might be the time he became the top associate.

"This is my year. Catching up, buddy. Nipping at your heels. Look out."

Regardless, Tony grew to like Johnstone, his contagious humor, and even the nonstop activity.

A few days later, Mandy sat in Tony's office waiting for her husband Vic to wrap up a phone call so they could go on their usual Friday lunch date.

She eyed the folded-up magazine picture of the bathroom.

"So, you're finally going to get the work done, good for you. Let me know if you need help with the color scheme," Mandy said.

Johnstone came bounding into Tony's office, uninvited, addressing two people in two separate conversations at once.

"Hey, Tony, call my tile guy yet? Mandy, how are you? He's the best, Tony. Did my kitchen. Vic in a meeting now? Hey, don't be fooled by his age. He can get after it. Lunch date with the boss today? Vic's a lucky guy. Try the new place on Bute Street. Call my tile guy. You won't regret it. Oh, and Mrs. M, the lobster bisque. Highly recommended."

Johnstone eyed Tony suggesting that now would be a good time to call, then disappeared.

Tony shook his head at the whirlwind who had just left. It was a typical example of a one-way conversation with Johnstone—a jumble of topics melded into a few seconds of time.

Mandy whispered as she tapped her finger on the paper several times. "Tony, call him. Tile guy. Guaranteed."

Vic popped his head out of his office.

"Sorry, hon, long call. You ready to go?"

Mandy said, "There's my date! Yes, sir, I'm ready."

She tapped her finger on the door. "Tony, dinner. Sunday. Our house. Don't forget. Oh. Tile guy. Call him."

Chapter Forty-Six

The last one to leave the office, he keyed in the alarm code and pulled the door behind him. Halfway down the stairwell to the first floor, Tony remembered the magazine page with the name and telephone number of the tile guy. He knew if he didn't call tonight, the project would slide by for another decade. Not so effortlessly, he climbed back up two flights of stairs to retrieve the paper.

A few minutes later, he walked into his apartment.

"Hello?"

"Hello, may I speak with Joseph Carelli please?"

"Speaking."

"Yes, my name is Tony Mancuso, and I got your number from a co-worker who recommended you for bathroom remodeling."

They agreed to meet the following Friday at noon. In his own mind, Tony started calling him *the tile guy* because of how often Johnstone repeated it.

He eyed the time displayed on his computer. If he hurried, he could make it home in two minutes, but first he needed to extricate himself from the hour-long conference call. Once free, he dashed down the stairs to the sidewalk. Tony arrived almost breathless at the front of his condominium building and found a man of about sixty with a head full of white hair seated on a brick-encased planter facing the sun.

"Mr. Carelli?"

His gaze turned up toward Tony. He spoke with a distinctly Virginia Hampton Roads inflection. "Yes, I can tell from your eyes and for sure in your face."

Tony said, "Oh, what's that?"

"No doubt about it, Italian. Well, based on your name, more Sicilian, or at least southern Italian. No, forget southern Italy. It's Sicily all the way."

"Okay, you've got me, I give up."

Mr. Carelli said, "Sorry, it's a pleasure to make your acquaintance. It's just there aren't many of us Sicilians around here anymore."

"Oh, if you mean my family, well, my grandfather came over from Sicily when he was a child and settled here in Norfolk."

"Makes sense. Please call me Joe. Shall we take a look?"

"Yes, and thanks for coming."

They reached the guest bathroom.

Joe said, "These colors were big in 1970. You kept hoping they'd come back in style, right?"

Laughing, Tony said, "Well, I can't take all the credit. I bought the place about eight years ago. So, you're thinking a change might be in order?"

"Yes, sir. And not a moment too soon."

Tony showed Joe the magazine page with his name and telephone number scribbled on it.

"I think I told you on the phone I got your number from a guy at work," Tony said.

"Let's see, what's his name?"

"John Stone. We work together a few blocks from here. Talks fast, you might remember him."

"Yes, I do remember. Kitchen work. Nice man. Talks fast. Lovely wife."

"That's him, the one and only. He calls you the tile guy."

"Oh, I do that and everything else in a house."

Joe said he didn't work as much as he used to, but if agreeable, he would start the following week and dropped the tile samples into his pocket.

They finished discussing the project and Joe said, "I'll pick up everything you've already purchased. These tiles will go beautifully with the marble on the washstand."

Tony said, "I'd love to say I picked them out, but a friend helped. She has what you call the decorator's eye."

"Nice choice. By the way, that marble on top of the washstand is Italian if I'm not mistaken."

"Yes, I've been told. It belonged to my grandparents who I'm guessing bought it here in Norfolk."

"Hang on to it. They're quite valuable."

Over the next few weeks, Tony found seeing the progress at the end of each day interesting. One day he came home at lunchtime to chat with Joe and found him to be quite knowledgeable about Sicily's culture and history.

As he had promised earlier in the week, the bathroom project was finished Saturday. Normally Tony went into the office on those mornings loving the quiet time to catch up on unfinished projects that slipped through the cracks. On this day, however, he decided to stick around home and talk more with Joe.

He surveyed the bathroom and said, "I'm glad you accepted this job. Thank you."

Joe said, "You're welcome, and, of course, thank you. Your bathroom has officially arrived in the twenty-first century."

Tony said, "This might sound crazy, but if you don't have any plans today, would you like to have lunch at a place close by? It's my treat, of course. I'd love to talk more about Sicily with you."

They sat in a booth at the Souper Bowl, a nearby casual eatery.

Joe said, "I've traveled to Sicily many times over the years. My parents were born in Palermo, a large city on the northern coast. I grew up hearing their stories, and those memories got inside me and have been a passion of mine ever since."

"That's fantastic. My experience has been the opposite. I know nothing about the place and have no stories to tell. What did your folks do when they came to the United States?"

"They were in their late twenties and were a couple of the lucky ones to escape Italy before the start of World War II. My parents were noted antagonists toward the Fascist Party, and they barely escaped with their lives. After the war, they opened a restaurant, actually a glorified sandwich joint, right here in Norfolk on Church Street called The Big Sicilian. I came along a couple of years before the shop opened."

"You're kidding. I guess my folks would have known about it and certainly my grandparents."

"Well, the sandwich shop flourished until their retirement thirty years ago."

"Did you also work there?"

"As a teen I helped out and my parents wanted me to continue with the shop, but I developed a knack for doing home improvement projects and the business sort of took off by word of mouth. With my wife, Nellie, running the business end of things and me doing the onsite work, we made quite a team. Still do."

"You didn't want to keep running the restaurant?"

"No, the fact is the restaurant business owns you instead of the other way around. My wife and I like to travel, and the home improvement line of work has allowed me to accept or reject jobs based, in part, on when and where we planned to go next."

"What is Sicily like, or what was it like?"

"Well, the short answer is it was poor back then, and it's never caught up with the progress or success of northern Italy. In fact, it was the extreme poverty in the late 1800s that led to the mass exodus of people. More often than not, the Sicilians arrived here to find conditions as bad as what they left behind with one significant difference. In America, there was a chance, a real opportunity for a better life. In Sicily, there was nothing."

They walked back to the condo in silence until Tony said, "Looking back to many years ago, I wish my family had talked more about our history when my father was alive. I should say I wish I had taken more of an interest and asked questions."

"Well, sadly it's too late to talk to your father, but nothing is stopping you from going to Sicily and getting to know the place for yourself, and you might do a bit of family research too. As my father used to say, the key to the future is remembering the past, and the two are linked forever like night and day."

Chapter Forty-Seven

Sunday mornings were a ritual for Tony. He hadn't darkened the doorway of a church since much beyond high school, and he jokingly referred to himself as a recovering Catholic. His one free morning of the week he liked to sit on his condo balcony with coffee to drink and a newspaper to read cover to cover. This Sunday was no exception.

Later that day, Tony was going to Vic's house for dinner, as he did every week or two. Vic said he could use help with installing a window air conditioner in the attic of his house, a room he converted for use as a home office. In Tony's mind, this was no small task since most of the historic homes in the neighborhood were often three stories high. If the work required a body on a ladder, he didn't want to be that guy. In fact, Tony had never met a ladder he liked.

Vic was a handy guy, and as it turned out, the whole project was accomplished in thirty minutes from the inside through an open window. Afterward, they sat outside the back of the house enjoying cold beers and looking out over the well-manicured lawn.

Tony told Vic about his conversations with Joe. "I do give Johnstone credit for coming through for me with the tile guy as he likes to say."

Vic laughed. "I have no doubt Johnstone will follow up with you tomorrow."

Mandy walked out the French doors at the back of the house with two bottles of beer.

"I'm sure you guys are exhausted after working all of ten minutes. I brought you a couple more."

Vic said, "Thanks, how about you?"

"I need wine."

"Mandy, something has awakened in Tony, and he's thinking of going to Italy to check out his family history."

The word, or rather the name of the country, captured her attention and she sat on Vic's leg.

"If you do go, I can help you with places to visit. I love, love, love Italy!"

Vic said, "I would never have met Mandy if she had decided to stay there forever."

Mandy winked. "Oh, believe me, it was tempting. I traveled to Italy one summer during college and loved it. I'm sure Vic told you right after college he backpacked in Europe for months. I guess it was a month after I returned, I met him at a party and found out we had been in Europe at the same time. Anyway, we connected right away and, as they say, the rest is history. When you're ready to go to Italy, I'll tell you about places I visited. Oh, and let me show you my pictures."

Vic said, "Uh oh, don't let her pull you into that vortex. You'll never finish looking at all those photos."

Mandy stood and popped Vic's leg with a kitchen towel.

"Tony, my offer stands, and now I hear my name being called by a fine burgundy inside the house."

Once the door closed behind her, Tony said, "She's great, she really is."

"I know it."

"You know you're the luckiest guy in Norfolk, right?" Tony said.

"My friend, I plead guilty."

Mandy was a striking woman with long, auburn-colored hair. With a face every camera loved and a voice suited for public speaking, she parlayed her talents into commercial work. At the age of fifty-one, she did occasional television commercials for a heavyweight auto dealership and a furniture and rug superstore.

Her hobby for years had been fixing Tony up on dates, but those efforts had never resulted in a successful long-term relationship and certainly not marriage.

The next morning before leaving for work, Tony stopped and looked at the guest bathroom realizing he would miss the conversations with Joe. Walking to work, he thought about a scheduled meeting with a potential new client.

Some weeks before, Tony ran into his neighbor, Bart Kaniff, a local obstetrician and also a client, in their condominium basement fitness center.

"Hey, Tony, I have a prospective investor for you. This guy was my college roommate and we've stayed friends through the years. In fact, I delivered their baby girl a couple of years ago."

"Thanks, Bart, that sounds terrific. Whatever I can do to help, I will."

"I know you will, Tony. I told him you were someone he could trust and that you've done a damn fine job with my money, and maybe half the doctors in Norfolk. I gave him your number. I hope you don't mind."

"Of course not."

"His name is Stanley Alarson."

"Wait a minute, that name is familiar," Tony said.

"Okay, how about if I said an energy drink—"

"LightningQuik? That Stanley Alarson?"

Bart said, "You're still on top of it. Hey, be expecting a call. He's a super nice guy too."

The Monday morning after he and Bart spoke, Tony's cell phone rang. Mr. Stanley Alarson, a thirty-nine-year-old husband and father of one, was also the founder of LightningQuik, a company that produced one of the hottest-selling energy drinks on the market. He recently completed a deal whereby his energy drink, the formula and name, was being acquired by a massive food conglomerate. The transaction would net him close to thirty million dollars, the bulk of which he wished to invest.

The telephone call must have been to Stanley's liking because at the end of their conversation he said, "I'll see you at Bart's Saturday night for the NBA playoffs."

Tony said, "That's right, Lakers and Suns. Looking forward to it."

Tony thought they hit it off well, and today's meeting would be the first time to discuss in detail various options he had prepared for Stanley's review and consideration. He also wanted to get further understanding of Stanley's tolerance for risk as the Great Recession continued to linger in the economy and was still fresh on everyone's mind.

Thanks to Vic, Maynard & Associates and its clients weathered the stock market crash fairly well; many of the clients suffered only minimal damage and some even netted small gains. Tony had learned long ago to listen to Vic, who was not only incredibly smart but also possessed an uncanny knack for seeing into the future with twenty-twenty vision.

In the early 2000s, Vic began recognizing a dangerous trend in the housing mortgage market. He first became concerned by the lowered lending standards along with the increasing numbers of higher risk mortgages. By 2005, he noted the dramatic rise in the percentage of lower quality subprime mortgages and surmised the great potential for delinquencies should housing prices decline. When the earliest signs of the decline became apparent in 2006, he was convinced there would be a collapse of the mortgage-related securities market that would lead to a nationwide financial disaster.

Vic persuaded his own clients and the advisers under him to park their assets in conservative, heavily safeguarded vehicles for the foreseeable future. In the end, Vic's prognostications were proven correct.

Tony gave credit to Vic for leading him to Stanley Alarson. He felt certain his client, Bart Kaniff, told Stanley that Maynard & Associates protected his money during the crash.

Late morning, Vic asked Tony to stop in before lunch for a quick chat. When he walked in, two LightningQuik drinks sat on the table.

"Have you tried it before?"

Tony said, "I guess I should."

"Mandy bought up the last of these from the gym the other day. She hoped it would help keep you awake during your meeting."

The next morning Tony briefed Vic on the meeting, thinking it went well. "Stanley's last words to me were 'Like Bart, I want my money with someone I can trust.' Vic, every associate in this office owes you, and now Stanley understands that too."

"Well, I appreciate that, Tony, but we're a team here, so no one person gets all the credit or all the blame."

"Hey Vic, remember the guy Johnstone recommended for the work in my bathroom?"

"How could I forget?"

"Well, it's strange, but I can't get something out of mind."

Tony told Vic about Joe's family history, his travels to Sicily, and how he recommended Tony explore his own roots.

"I told him about my grandfather and he said this thing, something like, 'the key to the future is remembering the past,' and now it's stuck in my head."

Vic asked, "So let me get this straight. You land one of the biggest clients yesterday and now you're telling me you're leaving it all behind for Italy?"

"No, no, but it's got me thinking. I am curious. I guess a part of me has been curious for some time."

"Listen, Tony, it's no secret you do fantastic work here. You're the guy I rely on the most, the guy I trust the most. We're friends too. Damn good friends, I think. You want to take time off and travel, go."

As Tony left the office that evening, Johnstone did his usual fake punch to Tony's gut.

"This is it! This is the year. I'm taking you out. No more number one associate for you, buddy. Serious leads on two heavy hitters. Portfolios of seven figures each. I'm stoked, Tony. Stoked!"

"Well, I knew the day was coming."

For a small guy, Johnstone was strong. He picked Tony up in a bear hug. "Yeah, me too."

Tony walked into his condo excited and a bit nervous and shot straight out to his balcony to look over the city.

Do I want to do this? Do I want to upend everything here to go to Sicily? Hang on a second. What's the big deal really? I've traveled before. I went on a cruise to the Bahamas.

He said aloud, "Yeah, I'm a real-world traveler, aren't I?"

Before going to bed, he found his passport in the bedroom closet. Flipping through the unmarked pages, he thought back to the trip to Australia that he planned to take with his old girlfriend Loretta.

A week before their scheduled departure, Loretta tore up her knee while running. In a freak accident, she didn't notice a metal plate cover missing on a sidewalk and her leg plunged into the hole awkwardly. The injury and surgery to repair knee ligaments prevented her travel. Not long after, the relationship seemed to run out of gas, or so Tony convinced himself, until their last conversation.

She said, "The fact is, Tony, you're afraid of commitment."

"Maybe there's a kernel of truth to what—"

"There's more than a kernel. There's an elephant of truth to it. You can't commit."

Tony dropped his lonely, unstamped passport into the nightstand drawer and turned out the light.

Maybe she was right. Maybe I can't commit.

Chapter Forty-Eight

For the remainder of the week Tony worked long hours well into the evening, including Friday night when he didn't leave the office until after ten. He woke up at two in the morning and wondered whether it was a noise or a dream that awakened him until his mind zeroed in on his conversation with his tile guy, Joe. In another instant the idea of visiting his mother over the weekend and doing a little research on his grandfather came to him.

He logged a few hours at the office Saturday morning before calling. "Mom, would you like company this weekend?"

"Honey, you know I'd love it. When will you get here?"

"How about dinner time? I'll stop at the place down the street from you and get Chinese takeout. The usual? Mongolian beef with fried rice?"

An hour and a half later, he unlatched the gate of the white picket fence admiring the Grandiflora roses. They were his mother's favorite because of their hardiness, continuous blooming, and with their long stems, they made excellent cuttings which she used throughout the house. Tony spotted his mother sitting on the back porch wearing her garden work clothes digging into a box of animal crackers.

She said, "You caught me. Would you like one?"

"No thanks. Remember?" He shook the bag. "We talked about getting Chinese takeout."

"I know, but I got hungry."

"Mom, when does eating dinner so early happen?"

"Son, a lot sooner than you think. Plates are on the counter inside."

Tony smiled to himself, pleased his mother still had her quick wit.

They sat in the den with photo albums spread on the floor and table. The television blared in the background with a guy selling a product guaranteed to make any scratch on a car disappear quickly and effortlessly. Unimpressed, Tony reached over and muted the television and the pitchman's opportunity to sell yet another tube of the miracle product, at least in one little corner of North Carolina.

"Mom, why didn't we ever talk about Dad's family, you know, especially about Grandfather Thomas's roots in Sicily?"

"I don't know. Your father never talked about it. He said one of your grandfather's favorite expressions was, 'The bus fare is for the road ahead, not for stops in the past.'"

"Well, did Grandma say anything about his past?"

"No, she said he always focused on the children, and he loved to listen to the kids tell stories about school and who was doing what in sports or the latest fads. I sure miss them both. She outlived your grandfather by fifteen years. I guess that's the way it'll always be. It's like by the time we wives finally get our husbands trained, they go and die on us."

The room quieted for a minute.

"Did he speak with an accent?" Tony asked.

"Not really. Maybe you heard an extra vowel on the end of certain words, but in a faint way."

Tony opened the photo album to pages containing copies of his grandfather's death certificate and newspaper obituary. The obituary spoke of a five-year-old boy who traveled to the U.S. without his parents and lived in Detroit until he was sixteen before settling in Norfolk, where he became part owner of a market. Later in the article, it said the proudest day of his life was when he became a U.S. citizen.

Tony studied the death record and focused his attention on the space for the names of Thomas's parents. They were blank.

He removed photographs from the plastic sleeves. His grandparents sat on their front porch swing on Thirty-fifth Street with a small dog stretched across their laps. Another showed his grandfather, a smiling, handsome, middle-aged man wearing a suit and tie while he stood by himself in the side yard next to a tidy vegetable garden. Tony was certain he'd seen the photograph before but hadn't paid much attention. Now the picture of his grandfather captivated him and somehow had new significance.

"Mom, do you mind if I borrow a few pages from this book?"

By eleven o'clock the small house situated in historic Edenton was dark except for the lamp sitting on the end table next to the couch. He studied the photographs of his grandparents and wondered what life was like for them. Looking at his grandfather's face, he tried to detect something, anything about the man, but accepted the grainy black and white photograph held no answer as to why he traveled to the U.S. at such a young age.

What does the clause without his parents mean exactly? I get that his parents didn't accompany their child, but why? And why did he go to Detroit first? Then later to Norfolk? So many questions, but no one to answer them.

Halfheartedly, he reached over and pulled the chain to turn off the light.

It was Monday morning. After Vic finished a conference call, Tony stopped by his office.

"Morning, Tony, how's it going?"

"Great. Uh, Vic, you remember last week I talked a little about traveling to Italy, well, Sicily?"

"Yeah, sure."

"Well, I'd like to do it."

"Fantastic. When?"

"Well, I'm not sure yet exactly, but I'm going to sort that out soon and, of course, I'll check back with you beforehand."

Vic rapped his knuckles on the desk and said, "Sounds like a winner."

Within minutes Mandy called Tony, but without any of the usual pleasantries like hello or how are you.

"Now that you're going, you're coming over on Sunday and we'll look at photos and talk about your trip. I'm excited for you."

After work, Tony did a bit of research on flights and places to visit. He read a blog by a woman who researched her family's roots after she arrived in Italy.

The blog read in part, "If you walk in off the street to a records office in Italy to accomplish a simple birth, death, or marriage query, expect a considerable wait. The best advice is to make sure you have every shred of information and personal data you can find before you begin your trip. It's critical you have the date and place of birth. Records are maintained in a government office called the *Ufficio Anagrafe*, or Registry Office. Your best bet is to make an appointment, if possible."

The blogger made Tony think about his grandfather's place of birth.

The obituary said he was born in Marinella, but the death certificate only reported Sicily, Italy. Was this place Marinella where he was actually born, or was it just the port from where he left Sicily? This is a great question for my tile guy.

Not yet eight, he went to the kitchen and fished out Joe's business card from the bright orange ceramic bowl his niece made him for Christmas one year.

From his balcony, Tony called the number and leaned against the railing, listening to the telephone ring.

"Hello?"

"Hello, Joe, this is Tony Mancuso—"

"Yes, Tony, how is everything, okay?"

"Great, thanks. Listen, I'm thinking about going to Sicily, and I wanted to kind of pick your brain a bit."

"Fantastic! Any way I can help, I will."

"Well, I wanted to see if you would meet me for lunch or dinner when you're not busy. On me, of course–"

Joe said. "I'd be delighted."

"Would Saturday be okay?" Tony asked.

"Let's see, I have a quick job to take care of that morning, but lunch would be fine, say, around one?"

Tony said, "Perfect. You want to meet at the same place or I can come your way, no problem."

"No, I'll be over your direction. Besides, Norfolk is much more interesting than Chesapeake."

Tony arrived at the Souper Bowl early, feeling a bit anxious. He wondered if Joe might say something to make him change his mind about traveling.

Shaking off his concern, he took a booth seat and ordered the biggest sweet tea available. Right on time, Joe walked in and was flagged down by Tony. They shook hands and after an exchange of pleasantries, Tony dove right into his questions.

"I've never been much of a traveler, but something has come over me. I want to understand where my ancestors came from and see what Sicily is like. Does that make sense?"

Joe said, "At one time or another I guess we all get curious about our loved ones before us. I suppose it happens at different times for different people."

"One thing you might be able to clear up for me is the newspaper obituary said my grandfather came from Marinella."

"Right, I remember."

"I got to thinking maybe this place is the port where he left and he might be from another town altogether. I've read it's vital to know the exact place of birth because, without it, there's no way to even begin a records search. So, is Marinella a real town or just a port?"

Joe said, "It's a real city; a smaller one, but it's not only a port. There's a factory that employs a couple thousand people manufacturing flash memory technology. You may have one of the cards or drives in your camera, computer, or video games. Anyway, I think it's a safe bet to say that your grandfather was from Marinella.

"The other thing is that the bigger ships carrying immigrants to the U.S. typically departed from Naples or Genoa. It's probable he traveled from one of those locations. I think you'll be on the right track if you focus on Marinella."

Tony said, "This really helps. Unless I learn something new, I'll start there. I've been using one of the online genealogy resources, but I've had no luck thus far in Marinella. I thought it might be because the records aren't computerized yet."

"Sicily is modernizing along with the rest of the world, but at a slower pace. So, it's not surprising you didn't find anything on the internet."

"I think I should be able to understand a little of the language." Tony laughed and said, "Who knows, since it's in my blood, learning the language will come naturally to me, right?"

"Let's hope. I think learning about the culture you're visiting and having basic language skills is always a positive. If nothing else, you'll be more comfortable interacting with folks."

"I've also been doing a bit of reading about Ellis Island. I'm thinking my grandfather would have come through there, right?"

"Sure, like my parents did back in 1940. An interesting place to visit, if the opportunity presents itself. It's a museum now, but as the expression goes, 'If those walls could talk.' As it is, you can sense the emotions the immigrants from all over the world may have experienced. It's a powerful place. I've read the U.S. inspectors rejected about two percent of everyone who came through from the time it opened in 1892 until it closed in 1954. About twelve million were processed there, so a significant number were rejected."

"Wow, that's two hundred forty thousand people."

"A math whiz, huh?"

Tony chuckled. "Well, it comes with the job. Why were people rejected?"

"Usually medical issues. Inspectors or doctors marked an immigrant's clothing with a letter as a code for the health issue. There were bunches of them like 'H' for heart, 'L' for lameness, 'X' for a mental issue, 'CT' for trachoma, a nasty type of conjunctivitis. Others got rejected for supposedly being an anarchist or a radical. If you have the time someday, I recommend you check it out."

"I think I will."

"You know, Tony, there was a neighborhood not too far from here where almost all the Sicilian immigrants lived, right off of Colley Avenue. It was a Little Sicily of sorts from the late 1800s on up to World War II."

"I remember going to my grandmother's house on Thirty-fifth Street as a little kid, but I had no idea about that."

After talking with Joe, Tony was excited and no longer had any doubt about going. He spent the remainder of the day reading articles online, and by bedtime a definite plan had taken shape in his mind.

Chapter Forty-Nine

With a bottle of red wine in hand, Tony took the steps two at a time leading up to the front porch of the Maynard house. The varieties and what constituted a superior wine were a complete mystery to him, so he followed a simple rule when he bought wine for Mandy. Staying within a midrange price, he made the selection based on whether he found the label interesting or unusual.

"Hello, Tony. What a pretty bottle. Thank you."

"I'm always available to share my wine expertise."

They kissed cheeks, and Mandy switched sides and kissed his other cheek.

"You need to get used to kissing both cheeks in Italy. Vic is on the back porch putting a new grill together."

"Excellent. I'll go help slow down the assembly process."

"Ha, I don't think he'll need any help with that."

Vic leaned over grill pieces and parts while holding a bottle of beer in one hand and the assembly instructions in the other.

"Hey, Vic."

Vic stood up straight, flexed his back muscles, and pushed his readers up on his head.

"You know what the problem is?" He answered his own question without waiting. "The instructions are written by someone whose first language is not English and the drawings may as well have been sketched by me. I've made an executive decision to put the darn thing together on my own. At least it'll be faster."

"If you're not at the office tomorrow, I'll assume the worst."

"We're using this today, my man. If I'm not at the office tomorrow, you won't be either."

"Well, if I got flesh in the deal, pun intended, I'm paying attention."

They finished the assembly in twenty minutes and sat under a stately old magnolia tree to talk about Tony's travel plans.

Vic said, "Of course, it's okay. In fact, I don't remember you taking a vacation before."

Mandy carried a plate of shish kebob, shaking her head at the line of empty beer bottles sitting next to the box that used to contain a grill.

"Drinking beer while assembling one of these. This has safety written all over it."

"Tony, tell Mandy about your travel plans."

"Well, with Vic's okay, I'm going to take a couple of months off."

Tony stopped. Hearing himself say a couple of months so casually shocked him.

Mandy stared at Tony. "When you take a vacation, you take quite a vacation."

Immediately doubt crept into his mind about the amount of time.

Mandy said, "I'm kidding. We were wondering this morning if you had ever taken a vacation."

"Remember? I went on that three-day cruise to the Bahamas."

Vic asked, "How long ago?"

"It was after the Super Bowl with the Broncos or who was it?"

Mandy said, "You can't even remember."

"Anyway, I'm going to a school to study Italian. The program is six class hours a day with little field trips added in. I downloaded a language course last night to start studying now."

Vic said, "I guess we know who the teacher's pet will be."

Mandy asked, "So where are you going first?"

"I'm flying into Palermo, Sicily, which is about an hour's drive to this seaside town called Trapani."

"Why did you pick Trapani?" Mandy asked.

"Because the city is not too large, but there's still a language school for me. Anyway, after I become completely fluent, ha ha, I'll go to the records office in the little town where my grandfather was born and find out everything I can about my family history. Afterward, I'm flexible and may travel in Italy, but I'm purposely keeping it open. Who knows what might happen, right?"

Vic's cell buzzed and he picked it up to take the call.

Mandy said, "I'm envious."

"Hey, let's all go together. We'd have a fantastic time," Tony said.

Vic's phone conversation was brief. He set the phone down and said, "Tony, I heard that. You're not suggesting we all go to Italy for two months and leave Johnstone in charge? Can you imagine the intensive counseling required for everyone in the office when we returned?"

"That would be quite the experience," Tony said.

"Seriously, don't be surprised when we end up visiting. Your trip awakened the travel bug in Mandy, and frankly I wouldn't mind it either."

Mandy said, "I'm ready to go, but first, you boys finish up your beers and start the grill. Assuming you don't kill us with this new contraption, we'll eat on the patio." She turned to walk away, stopped and pointed her finger at Tony. "You're still going to look at my pictures today!"

The morning was sticky hot, and his shirt was drenched in sweat and clinging to his back as he jogged toward home. Tony felt energized like a twenty-year-old kid. After running an hour, the endorphins danced in his brain playing a practical joke on his body, making him think he could run all day.

Thoughts crowded in his head with last-minute things to do at work. Italian words and phrases he studied every night clamored for more space in his overcrowded brain. It seemed hard to believe he was getting on an airplane to Sicily in two days.

He slowed to a walk thinking about what his co-worker, Tina Dawson, said to him the day before.

"Tony, why of all places would you go to Sicily? My sister-in-law said the place is dirty and there's nothing to do. I mean, why don't you think about going to Rome, Florence, Venice, or anywhere else?"

Tony wasn't going to respond, but Johnstone came to his unnecessary rescue.

"Whoa. This coming from the lady who still lives in swanky Ward's Corner. Your big night out? Dinner at Belchman's Cafe. The nightcap? Leftovers with Sparky the Wonder Dog."

Tina said, "First of all, the restaurant is Beldman's Cafe, not Belchman's, and I'll have you know they make a fantastic hearty ham casserole. Another thing, my little Sparky is a show dog quality Corgipoo. By the way, Johnstone, where did you dig up the jacket?"

"It's Member's Only. Snazzy. Right?"

"Maybe back in the eighties, but news flash, cowboy, the club closed and you're the last member."

Laughter echoed throughout the office with debate from all four corners about the best restaurants in Norfolk, what breeds of dogs make up a Corgipoo, and whether Member's Only still sold clothing.

Tony ditched the memory of the conversation at the side of the road and entered his condo building.

Chapter Fifty

Tony left Norfolk Thursday morning, connecting through JFK into Rome with a change of planes for the final leg to Palermo. All told, close to twenty hours with security, customs, and the usual assortment of delays. It felt refreshing to be walking on solid ground again through the Falcone-Borsellino Airport.

He tried his best to go to Sicily without any expectations, but it wasn't easy. It seemed like everyone from the grocery store cashier to his barber were experts on the subject and not at all shy about sharing their opinions.

A welcoming throng of family and friends crowded the greeting area with hugs, kisses, and tears of joy for the arriving passengers. There was none of that for Tony except a man relegated to the rear of the group holding a placard with his name on it.

Tony said, "Hello, uh, *buongiorno?*" like it was a question.

The driver spoke fair English, introduced himself as Francesco, and told Tony his life story as they walked to the car. "I am thirty-five years old. I drive this limousine for ten years. Is good job and I meet many persons. I live with parents. Is old for you in America, but here, is okay. I am not married. Why I don't marry? This girl, that girl, they are all pretty, but I say she can't cook like my mama. Why leave?"

Francesco asked a few questions, but Tony realized early on his driver was quite skilled in carrying on a conversation by himself. He had intended to practice Italian, but it became clear English would rule the day, or at least the sixty-minute car ride. En route to Trapani, Tony managed to sneak in one question concerning the Sicilian language since he still felt uncertain about its everyday use.

Francesco said, "Sicilian language everyone speaks here, but also Italian. English, you don't hear much. I can teach you words now. This is something you like?"

As Francesco spoke, he looked at Tony through the rear-view mirror without glancing at the highway in front of him where they happened to be traveling, Tony noticed, at a high rate of speed. He did the quick math in his head and calculated his odds of surviving the trip would be improved immeasurably if he ceased asking any more questions.

The drive from Palermo was a scary experience, with stop lights, road signs, and even lane markings appearing to be suggestions rather than hard and fast rules.

Tony was relieved when the limo came to a stop in front of the Hotel Metropole.

He seems like an okay driver, but the other thousands of drivers, who knows? I've probably just survived at least three close calls, but why would Francesco worry? He has an airbag.

Tony wiped sweat from his brow, and after several ciaos and goodbyes, he followed his luggage being carried inside by the bellhop.

At the top of his list was a shower to wash away the last twenty-four hours, in particular, the most recent hour. He read in travel guides the typical shower stall in Italian hotels was small. Stepping inside, Tony realized they couldn't be more accurate. The positive news was the water came out hot right away, and that was where the good news ended. He turned his six-foot two frame and found the water spray hit him at chest level. The shower ended up being more of a fancy sponge bath.

He left the TV running in the background to listen to Italian being spoken. Over the next half hour, he was able to catch a few words he understood.

With a map in hand, Tony went outside to explore his surroundings. He left the hotel and walked along Via Fardella, a street going straight through a good part of Trapani. As he passed by various intersections, he sometimes caught a peekaboo view of the sea, but decided it was best to remain on the same street.

I've been lost before in Norfolk. I can see the headlines now, "American Found in Trapani After Wandering Aimlessly for Weeks."

He was encouraged to note the streets and sidewalks were clean of litter, with trash receptacles on many street corners. Dog poop was a different story. It was more akin to a minefield and something to watch out for when he went running. After purchasing a few school supplies, he remembered passing a deli and turned back to get a sandwich.

Hmm, what are my chances of getting a good old red, white, and blue peanut butter and jelly sandwich?

Before going to bed, he set the alarm for eight. With the time change, he calculated his body would be waking up at the ungodly hour also known as two in the morning. School started on Monday, and Tony wondered how long the process took for the human body to adjust to a new time zone.

Saturday morning, he felt surprisingly refreshed and sat in the lobby waiting for the apartment owner to arrive.

Right on schedule, a middle-aged woman with soft brown eyes walked up to him.

"*Buongiorno, mi chiamo* Paolina."

"Yes, hello Paolina, or, uh, *buongiorno* Paolina."

Tony noted she spoke little English and apparently was unconcerned that he was unable to do much more than grunt and point in Italian. Nonetheless, she spoke nonstop and, for all he knew, she could have been talking about polar bears living at the equator. He nodded in complete ignorance, wearing a foolish grin.

Paolina waved her arm toward the hotel exit and marched purposefully, with Tony attempting to stay close behind pulling two suitcases. They arrived at a three-story building painted in a faded salmon color. Paolina held up a ring of keys, said something Tony didn't understand, and unlocked the building's exterior wooden door. She climbed the stairs with ease, checking on her new tenant each time she reached another stair landing.

Is it possible stairs are steeper in Sicily or have I aged ten years in the last twenty-four hours?

Paolina held the apartment door open and waved her hand to invite Tony inside. She led the tour, pointing to different rooms saying, bedroom, bathroom, and kitchen. The apartment had a spacious master bedroom en suite complete with a decent-sized shower. The kitchen featured a gas oven, four-burner stove, smallish refrigerator, and a washing machine tucked behind a louvered door.

Tony said, "Microwave oven?"

With a puzzled smile, she finally said, "Ah, *un forno a microonde?* No, no," and shook her head.

Excellent, I've learned the words for something not here.

Tony gestured toward the washing machine and said, "Dryer?" wondering about the possibility of a matching dryer.

She responded with machine-gun rapidity.

Hold it now. Is she saying this is the dryer?

He bent over to look closer at the dials and buttons to confirm.

Standing behind him, Paolina spoke. He turned to see her standing at an open window holding a small basket of clothespins.

Louder than necessary, he said, "Ah, *sì, sì, sì,* okay, okay," because he was excited to finally understand something.

So the dryer is a clothesline, and what I saw before was in fact the washing machine.

Paolina said something, none of which Tony understood, as she turned a handle and pulled open the windows. She pushed the wooden shutters out to show Tony the clothesline.

Okay, I'm starting to get a handle on this Italian.

Paolina gestured toward the clothespins and clothesline and spoke at breakneck speed. Finally, she said, "Okay?"

"Yes, okay, okay," Tony said.

I know how to use a clothesline. The rest of whatever she said probably wasn't important.

Paolina said, "Please, come."

Well, that part I get.

He walked over to where Paolina stood at the doorway to the balcony.

She motioned for Tony to step outside.

The view was breathtaking. From the balcony, there was an unobstructed and incredible vista of the sea. He felt like a king standing before the vast body of water extending from his feet to the horizon. "Wow" was the only word Tony uttered, which must have been understood in Italian because she smiled.

He stepped back inside and Paolina said, "Please, passport," leading Tony to guess the tour was over.

He had read that the information from his passport would be recorded or copied every place he stayed, be it hotel or apartment, based on some older Italian law. He assumed the police made routine checks, but he had no idea if it was true or how the process worked.

Paolina took a picture of the passport page with his name and identifying data. They shook hands and, just like that, she left.

The apartment was more than satisfactory, and as a bonus, the Italian language school was supposed to be close. Tony turned on the flat screen television in the living room to listen to a news channel while unpacking and nosing around. There was a well-stocked kitchen, a modern bathroom with plenty of towels, and a more than ample-sized master bedroom with a king-sized bed, and fat, fluffy pillows.

Okay, my exploration inside the apartment is complete. It's time to venture out on my own. No sense in overwhelming myself. Keep it simple. Locate the school. Pick up basic grocery items. Finally, don't get lost.

Tony went to the same deli as the day before, but this time, feeling a little adventurous, he decided to sit outside and eat. He asked the man behind the counter if he spoke English.

"Little only," he said.

They spoke for a minute in a mish mash of Italian and English as the man prepared a caprese sandwich with ciabatta bread, slices of tomato, rosemary, basil, garlic, mozzarella, and a drizzle of olive oil.

Using basic Italian, Tony asked where the language school was located.

The man pointed to the corner of the street where the school name was prominently displayed next to a large wooden door.

Okay, I'm getting the hang of this. I'm having a real conversation. What the hell, I'll go for broke.

He introduced himself. "*Mi chiamo* Tony."

They shook hands.

In reply, the man said, "*Sono* Fausto."

This is a good start. His name is Fausto. He makes great sandwiches and I'll be back.

Late afternoon, an overwhelming sense of tiredness besieged him, but he fought back, hoping to stay awake until at least eight o'clock. He opened a bottle of red wine with a grape orchard on the label he presumed to be somewhere in Italy. It tasted delicious, and Tony was pleased his strategy for selecting wines also worked in a foreign country. He took a picture of the label with his phone and texted it to Mandy to demonstrate his knowledge of fine wines now extended overseas.

Sitting on the balcony, he watched a group of people walking along the promenade by the sea. His curiosity got the better of him. He looked at the complimentary map that came with the apartment to learn the sea was called Mar Tirreno and was a part of the overall grand Mediterranean Sea.

The cool evening air blew across the balcony, and his head became heavy and sleepy with wine. He knew he had the following day to explore the city again and decided it was close enough to the artificial bedtime goal he had set for himself earlier. The pleasant breeze and the sound of the crashing waves coming through the open bedroom window worked in perfect harmony. He fell asleep before his head touched the pillow.

Chapter Fifty-One

The first day of school began in an hour, and Tony anxiously checked his supplies for the second time that morning. The notebook, dictionary, and two pencils hadn't moved from the small table by the door.

An email advised him to arrive thirty minutes early the first day for check-in. The group classes started at nine in the morning and ended at one in the afternoon. Following a one-hour lunch break, he had a two-hour private session.

He walked into the school at eight-thirty sharp. A man named Eugenio, who may or may not have said he was the school director, escorted him to a classroom. Tony was the first student to arrive. He took the seat closest to the door in case he changed his mind and decided to escape.

While he waited, he thought about the school's online grammar test he took a couple of weeks before. Regardless of the results, Tony knew that other than having memorized a long list of vocabulary words, he was only able to converse using basic phrases and a smile.

Over the next several minutes, other students wandered into the classroom, each introducing themselves in Italian. The group consisted of a young Japanese woman, two middle-aged women from France, a man about Tony's age from Switzerland, two young women from Germany, and Tony, the lone American. After a minute or two of stumbling around the Italian language, the students withdrew to the safety of their smartphones.

A woman in her twenties entered the classroom at nine on the dot. "*Buongiorno! Mi chiamo* Margherita."

She wrote her name on the board and spoke in a slow cadence, slower than what Tony heard on the television news programs he had listened to over the past few days. Margherita had long straight black hair tied into a ponytail. She wore skinny jeans, a tee shirt that shouted the word *ciao*, a pair of fun-looking high-top tennis shoes, and pink socks, and every time she turned her head to the chalkboard, her pony-tail swung from side-to-side.

Despite her pleasant manner, the classroom was all business. Tony quickly realized if he or any of the other students were waiting for the teacher to be overcome with sympathy and coo something sweet and cuddly in their own native language, he and they would be sorely disappointed.

She took turns going around the room to chat with each person.

Based on what I've heard thus far, as a group we would have no problem ordering beers and finding the bathroom, but afterward, we'd be lost.

Once Margherita's attention focused on him, Tony sat up straight and pushed the beer and bathroom from his mind. He had the advantage of being the fourth person to answer the same basic introductory questions.

"*Ciao, come ti chiami?*" Margherita asked.

"*Ciao, mi chiamo* Tony."

"*Di dove sei* Tony?"

"*Sono* Americano."

"*Sei sposato?*"

"*No, sono* single."

It was the first personal question he had been asked since his arrival. From his studies at home, he knew the Italian language adapted some words directly from English and they were perfectly understood and acceptable to use, as was the case with the word *single*.

The question and answer exercise continued with each student for a few minutes. Afterward, Margherita asked more questions, but she jumped around randomly to make a better determination of each student's Italian level.

Tony noticed he wasn't alone in the struggle. Each person seemed to be wracking his or her brain to translate or find the correct word or phrase as a response. When the teacher's attention focused on another student, he tried to follow along to the best of his ability, but in secret found himself happy to have the attention elsewhere for the moment.

Every student in the class was a beginning Italian speaker. Keiko, the young lady from Japan, was the least proficient, with Tony somewhere in the middle of the pack. Alex, the man from Switzerland, was by far the most advanced student. He was a beginning speaker, but his comprehension far outclassed the others. From the question and answer session, Tony learned Alex lived close to the Italian-speaking region of Switzerland and had developed an ear for comprehension, but strangely enough, not for speaking the language.

The morning classes flew by with a fifteen-minute break between the grammar and conversation sections. During the pause, Tony found he wanted to rest his mind. He hadn't studied a foreign language in high school or college, and doubts about his ability began to dominate his thinking.

Just before the lunch break, Eugenio returned to the classroom to discuss the after-school cultural activities. He explained in a dumbed-down Italian using basic words and plenty of pictures that there would be a cultural outing on Wednesdays and Saturdays. The school staff encouraged attendance on the field trips as a way to continue in total language immersion.

On Wednesday, the school scheduled a tour of the Church of the Souls in Purgatory, famous for the twenty life-sized wooden effigies depicting the story of Christ's Passion.

By the end of the first four hours, Tony was exhausted. Accustomed to challenging work at the office every day, he found the classroom to be somehow more mentally draining. The other students completed their schooling for the day at the one o'clock lunch break and Tony noticed how happy they appeared when they left. He couldn't help but wonder if he may have been a bit overambitious signing up for six hours a day.

With the two-hour private session looming in the afternoon, he decided to retreat to his apartment balcony to eat a thick PB&J sandwich for lunch while trying to clear the fog in his head.

He hoped the view of the sea would provide him with inspiration and motivation; however, he found himself stuck on one question: *What have I gotten myself into?*

As he understood it, the private lesson in the afternoon would focus on a review and reinforcement of the morning class work. The difference between morning and afternoon sessions dawned on him as he trudged back to school.

In the morning group classes, I shared the spotlight with six other students, but this afternoon, I am the spotlight. No hiding, no mental break, and no temporary check out.

Plus, his head ached a lot, and he felt tired. Dog tired.

As he sat waiting for his class to begin, he gave himself a self-motivational speech.

Come on, buck up. You're tougher than this.

His teacher entered the classroom.

"*Ciao Tony, mi chiamo Francesca. Come stai?*"

He realized his speech didn't help. His near flatlined brain couldn't process much, but he said, "*Mi chiamo Tony.*"

No, no, no, you idiot, she knows my name. She asked me how I am."

He lied. "*Sono bene.*"

Despite the headache, Tony displayed the best smile he could muster, hoping Francesca might allow him to put his head on the desk and take a nap like he used to do in first grade.

"*Continuamo.*"

There's my answer. No nap time.

As class was ending, he had no memory of how he made it through.

Francesca seemed pleasant enough as far as I remember. Hold it. Her name was Francesca, right? What did I call her? Oh, God, did I even call her by the right name? I have an immediate need for five, maybe six aspirin.

Tony decided to stop at the pharmacy on his way home. There were two customers in front of him with only one salesclerk working the counter. He closed his eyes for a moment to relax and direct oxygen to his brain. When he reopened his eyes a few seconds later, or maybe it was an hour, he wasn't quite sure, the line had moved nowhere. He thumbed through his workbook to review the school assignments, pretending the homework had an even remote possibility of being accomplished. The woman in front of Tony turned around and looked at the book in his hands.

"*Buonasera,*" she said.

Although it pained him, Tony returned the greeting.

He could see the woman was more than the standard attractive; she was well north of good-looking, with amber-colored eyes, long black wavy hair falling below her shoulders, and a smile he was quite sure had gently broken many hearts.

Her presence seemed to help his headache, or at least his disposition. He held up his schoolbook to show he was a student of the language.

She started to say something, but the pharmacist called for the next person, and she turned away.

Tony listened to her speak, and although she did so at the speed of light, he found her voice soothing. Hoping the help she needed took a long time, he detected a faintly sweet perfume and took a deep breath. Out of the corner of his eye, Keiko, one of his classmates appeared. She waved at him from the sidewalk outside the store.

He stepped out to talk, and they bumbled their way through basic phrases. When he returned, the store was emptied of customers. Tony asked for aspirin and was presented with a box of ten tablets for five euro.

Okay, I was hoping for the economy size bottle with five hundred, but this will get me to dinner.

He managed to utter a simple *grazie* that sounded more like a grunt in English, licked his wounds, and limped home.

Chapter Fifty-Two

By Wednesday, a routine settled into place. Only day three, Tony felt like a sponge soaking up the new language. Although still tired at the end of the day, he had adjusted to the class schedule and the new time zone. The interaction in the morning classes with Margherita and other students, and the afternoon lesson with Francesca and the spotlight made him feel like he was learning rather than just memorizing words as he had done on his own in Norfolk.

At lunch, Tony spoke with Eugenio and understood enough to confirm in his mind the importance of going on the field trip relative to the overall learning experience. Following the private session, Tony stood on the sidewalk in front of the school waiting for the field trip group to assemble. When he heard a woman's voice behind him, he turned. The lady from the pharmacy waved at him.

She spoke in a heavily accented English, "Hello again."

Tony said, "Yes, hello or *buonasera.*"

She had an exquisite smile, and in the fullness of the sun, she appeared even more beautiful than before. She was taller than he remembered from Monday, but then that awful day had scarred him, possibly for life.

She said, "You are a student, yes?"

He found something about her voice tranquil yet alluring.

"Yes, I am studying Italian."

"Why? Why do you study?"

Okay. Here goes, I can say now what I practiced at home.

She smiled and waited while Tony gathered his thoughts.

"*Mio nonno è nato a Marinella nel 1895. Vorrei studiare la storia della mia famiglia* (My grandfather was born in Marinella in 1895. I would like to study my family history)."

"Good, the Italian is good."

Tony said, "No, but I'm trying."

She made a face like she didn't understand, and Tony furrowed his eyebrows in concentration trying to think of how to say, 'I'm trying' in Italian. Other students going on the field trip gathered outside the building, including his new friend Alex. Tony waved, but he didn't want to draw his attention away from this woman.

My God, olive skin, a radiant smile framed by luscious lips wrapped around perfect teeth, and eyes. Hmm, let me think. Yes, eyes I could fall into.

"My name is Tony."

"Yes, I know."

His eyes widened in surprise until she giggled and pointed at his notebook where, across the top, he had written the name Tony Mancuso.

"Yes, that's me. Tony Mancuso."

She said, "Mancuso, it's a good Sicilian name."

"Really?"

When she smiled, the entire street block lit up.

"Yes, a very good name."

"What's your name?" Tony asked.

"I'm Michela."

"Michela," he repeated while displacing other data in his brain to clear space so he could permanently sear her name into his memory.

Tony joined the group led by their teacher, Margherita, as they migrated in herdlike fashion for the scarce few minutes it took to reach their destination, a church structure of Baroque style architecture. She explained the wooden effigies in the Church of the Souls in Purgatory took center stage Easter week, paraded through Trapani for the entirety of Good Friday. Tony recalled something being said about the building being damaged during the Second World War, but for the remainder of the tour his mind kept returning to one single word—Michela.

At the end of the first week Tony spoke with Vic.

"Are you learning much?" Vic asked.

"You know, I feel like I am."

"How are the classes?"

"It's fast-paced. I mean, it's difficult, but it's also fun. I wasn't sure how it would be with other students, but I'm enjoying the camaraderie. We're all in the same boat."

"Hey, that sounds great."

"Yeah, I feel like I'm actually beginning to be able to communicate in another language."

Tony got up early on Saturday to go for a run. The second field trip by bus to a historic site called Segesta was later in the morning, and he felt the need to exercise and clear his mind from a week of sitting in a classroom. He walked the promenade along the sea before slipping into his normal running pace. Turning the corner, he ran by a bakery and caught sight of Michela holding hands with two children, a boy and a girl. A selfish pang of disappointment stung inside him.

Tony had taken the time to read about Segesta the night before, learning it was one of the major cities of the Elymian people who arrived in Sicily around 1200 B.C. A well-preserved but never completed Doric temple sat below a hilltop amphitheater with what were described as incredible views of the surrounding valleys.

The teachers said an important part of learning any language was forcing oneself to speak it, and they discouraged students from talking in their native tongue while in school or on field trips. The rule was difficult to follow with such a limited knowledge of Italian. How to fill a full hour on a bus to Segesta presented a significant challenge.

After quizzing each other with various verb conjugations and simple questions and answers, Tony and Alex spent the remainder of the trip, taking turns, reading the official Segesta tourist pamphlet aloud. At times the pronunciation problems led to fits of laughter for the two of them. Francesca, the tour guide for the day, helped when they reached words neither understood.

Two weeks of class had been completed, and although he was quite pleased with his progress, Tony now understood he wouldn't be a one-in-a-million genius who mastered a language in weeks or months.

On Sunday, he planned to meet Alex and Keiko for dinner, an appealing idea since he missed the Sunday get-togethers at the Maynards' house. Feeling a tad homesick, Tony decided to surprise his friends with a call to catch up on life in Norfolk.

While Vic focused on Tony's progress in class, Mandy's interest centered mostly on women's fashion and style.

"How do women dress in Sicily?"

"Well, they wear, you know, clothes, I mean, dresses and pants, that kind of thing."

"That's not helpful, Tony. How about hairstyles?

"You mean, like long or short?"

"Tony, you're a lost cause. I hope you're enjoying yourself and not stuck in your apartment studying all the time."

"No, I go on the school tours. They're interesting."

"Tony, please try to have fun. We're going out to dinner later since it isn't the same here without you."

Tony walked to the designated meeting spot and waited for Alex and Keiko. He made a point of paying attention to how people dressed hoping to sound more informed when he spoke with Mandy again. The streets were crowded with well-dressed pedestrians, both young and old, male and female. He remembered his teacher Francesca saying Sunday evening was a traditional time to take a stroll down the historic corridor to see and be seen.

Keiko joined Tony first, and they tried to make conversation in Italian since her English was just as weak, and Japanese was a non-starter for him.

As they waited for Alex, Tony spotted Michela walking on the other side of the street struggling to carry two large shopping bags.

He excused himself and walked in Michela's direction, half-speaking, half-shouting. "*Ciao*, Michela."

There's that smile of hers.

Tony helped her with one of the bags and said, "I saw you at the bakery Saturday."

"Yes, on Saturdays we go."

"Was that your son and daughter?"

His question was met with an expression of part confusion and part wonder on Michela's face.

Finally, she said, "No, no children for me."

Tony pointed to his own eyes. "But I saw you with two children."

Michela studied Tony's face for a few seconds. "Ah, okay. No, the children, they're from my sister. I have no child, no children."

She looked again at Tony and pursed her lips as if trying to think of something. "I have no, how do you say, *marito*?"

"Oh, no husband. You're not married?"

"Yes, no husband. You're married?"

Tony said, "No, I have no *marito*." They both laughed. "No, I'm not married."

Tony heard a man's voice. He turned and waved at Alex.

Turning back to Michela, he said, "He's not my *marito*."

They laughed again.

"Well, they're waiting for me."

She said, "Okay" and reached for the bag.

"Can I help you with these?"

"No, it's okay."

Tony said, "Please, they're heavy."

She said, "Okay, *grazie*."

They walked to the door of her building, standing like statues while Tony tried to think of something to say.

He gathered up his nerve and asked, "Michela, would you like to have coffee or a gelato with me some time?"

There was a quiet pause. She handed the other bag to him and reached into her purse, writing her telephone number on a piece of paper, and held up her cell.

He said, "I'll call you, okay?"

"I understand, *ciao-ciao*," Michela said.

"*Ciao.*"

They looked at each other again for another moment.

"*Ciao.*"

"*Ciao.*"

Chapter Fifty-Three

While Tony got ready for school the next morning, he had only a vague recollection of the previous evening's dinner with Alex and Keiko. His mind remained stuck on one person and he decided to call Michela right after school. Although he didn't want to seem too anxious, his limited time in Trapani easily trumped everything else.

School went by in a blur. He called her while walking home but disconnected during the voicemail greeting. The notion of leaving a coherent message in Italian seemed too daunting. Instead he went for a run and, after a shower, Tony called again.

This time Michela answered with the standard Italian greeting, "*Pronto.*"

"*Ciao*, Michela. It's Tony."

"*Ciao*, Tony. School was good today?"

"Yes, it was fine. How are you?"

"I'm okay."

"Michela, what do you think about a coffee or gelato?"

To Tony's delight and surprise, she responded, "Yes, in one hour."

Tony arrived at her building and pushed the call button next to the name *Michela Amoroso*.

She wore black slacks, a gray sweater, scarf, and low heel pumps. If she wore makeup other than faint lipstick, Tony couldn't tell.

Tony was surprised Michela wore a sweater and scarf because, to him, the temperature seemed like a balmy seventy degrees. He asked, "Are you cold?"

She said, "We always dress for cool weather. The temperature is not important."

While Michela's clothing was stylish, Tony quickly realized he had underdressed a few levels in his jeans and a Norfolk Tides tee shirt.

They walked to a *gelateria* at the corner and each chose a small cup of chocolate. In Tony's opinion, ice cream from back home couldn't compare to gelato with its denser, milky texture.

He wondered how everyone stayed so slim and asked Michela.

She said, "How do you say when everyone thinks the same thing about a group of people?"

"A stereotype?"

"Yes, that's the word. In old movies, the stereotype is Italians are short and fat."

She put one hand on her hip, turned toward him, smiled, and asked, "You think I'm fat?"

Tony forced himself to not blurt out, no, I think you're perfect in every way and absolutely the most beautiful creature to ever walk the face of this Earth, and I can't believe I'm standing here next to you! Instead, he opted to keep it simple and said, "No, no," while waving his hands vigorously back and forth.

They walked along a quiet street, Viale delle Sirene, taking in the sea view. A small park with seating carved out of a stone wall lined the walkway at the end of the road.

Tony said, "You speak English well."

"No, it's not true."

"Yes, it is." He spoke at a measured pace on purpose. "I wish I could speak Italian the way you speak English."

She looked at him for a second, then the meaning became clear. "*Grazie.* I studied English in school and, and—"

"I understand. It takes time to remember."

"Yes, it takes time, yes."

Tony learned Michela came from Palermo and was the seventh of eight children. She worked as a teacher at a primary school in Trapani where she taught reading to children in the lower grades. She described the school system as underfunded due to the never-ending economic crisis in Italy which, in turn, led to reductions in money for schools.

"I like to teach the young students. They want to learn. Some teachers for the older ones think they're only babysitters because there is no interest from the students. Please come to visit my school. You can know the conditions."

Tony said, "I would love to see your school."

"I return to work in September. Now, I am on the summer break," Michela said.

Tony explained his reasons for being in Sicily. He said he learned that his grandfather's story of leaving Sicily to go to America wasn't unusual except for the part where he traveled without his parents at such a young age.

"I am trying to study the language and hope it helps people understand I do it to respect the people and the culture."

Michela said, "I understand. It's a good thing."

"Maybe if I can speak and understand a little Italian, it will help me learn why my grandfather left Sicily when he was only five years old."

She said, "Yes, five years is too young. There's a reason I think."

The conversation was a bit difficult at times due to the language barrier, but he realized while they chatted that he had absorbed a fair amount in only eleven days of class. He was also grateful Michela could speak and understand English quite well.

Tony told her about his family and background, explaining as best he could how he helped people reach their goals for savings and retirement. He told her the time away from his job was his first vacation in many years.

It hit him at that moment. He didn't miss work and, in fact, he hadn't thought of it one time the entire day.

On the return walk home, their hands brushed against each other a couple of times. Each time, they said *scusa* and laughed. They stopped at the promenade where waves crashed against the rocks along the shore. When their hands touched again, Tony took it as a sign from the universe it was time to pop the question.

"Would you like to have dinner with me this week?"

Before she could answer, he said, "I promise next time my clothes will be better."

Tony made an *x* across his chest with his hand.

"Yes, okay, let's have dinner."

"And Michela, you select the restaurant, okay?"

"Yes. I have an idea."

He pointed in the direction of his apartment. "I live in that building."

She said, "Yes, I know. I saw you yesterday. You go, no, no, you went in there yesterday."

"Why didn't you say hello?"

Michela blushed. "Because I want to see if you call me first."

"I, uh, I, no, it's okay. Never mind."

She touched his arm. "No, tell me," she said.

Now it was Tony's turn to blush. "I've only been thinking about that one thing. You know? About calling you."

Two nights later, dinner conversation focused a bit more on their personal lives. Michela never married, saying she hadn't found the right person.

"Today, in Italy, many women want a job more than a marriage and children."

She explained now at the age of forty, it became her way of life to be single, unattached, and responsible only for herself.

She asked, "Tony, you're married before?"

"No, I've never married. I guess I've always focused on my career."

"Can I ask a question?"

"Of course," Tony said.

"How old are you?"

"I have ten years on you. I'm fifty."

He looked straight at her to see if there was any reaction, any negative reaction, to be exact.

She said, "You look much younger."

He said, "Well, you look much younger than forty. That doesn't help me."

It took a second for the meaning to sink in, and when it did, she laughed with Tony.

"Does my age scare you?" Tony asked.

"It's a number. What's the American expression, something about fifty and the new thirty, right?"

"*Grazie.* I feel much younger, like a kid." He pointed to his hair. "Except the gray. Gives me away every time."

"I like this gray. Here on the sides. How do you say this part?"

She touched his head.

"Oh, it's called a temple. I have two of them."

He smiled, pointing to both sides of his head.

Michela said, "I think this gray looks good. It makes you look; I don't know. What's the word?"

"I'm hoping the word is distinguished."

"Yes." She said it slowly. "Dis-tin-guished."

They looked at each other for a few seconds without speaking.

He sensed they had a connection. Things were going well. Michela had a calmness, a maturity, and a curious nature. It was appealing to him and he wanted to see her again.

Michela also sensed a connection. After they went out for gelato earlier in the week, she had called her sister.

"I like him. He's handsome, tall, and funny. He has thick black hair and a little gray on the sides. He has the Sicilian blood from his appearance."

"When will I meet him?"

"We're going to dinner Wednesday."

"Sounds serious."

"Stop it. I'll know more in a couple of days, but I like him."

Her sister Chiara, who lived close by in the adjacent building, said, "That's the second time you've said that you like him. This one is different; I have a feeling."

"We'll see. I just met him."

"I'll come over and help you dress."

"Now my little sister is helping me dress?"

"Better than you trying on ten different outfits before settling on the first one."

"You have a point. I'll talk to you tomorrow. Good night."

"Try to get some sleep," Chiara said as she giggled and ended the call.

Once their dinner was finished, they sipped on a sweet dessert wine. Tony noted, unlike in the U.S. where dinners often seemed to be a rushed event, there was no such feeling in Sicily. He kept expecting a waiter to present the bill, but no one did. He found it to be a pleasant change and quite relaxing.

Tony wondered if his Italian improved with wine. He asked Michela because it seemed to him that she spoke English better as the evening progressed.

Michela said, "Maybe with wine we worry less about making a mistake?"

"Should I have a glass in the morning before school?" Tony asked.

After a short walk back to Michela's apartment, they stood near her door and edged closer to each other. It was a cloudless evening and appeared as if even the stars were hanging lower in the sky, watching and waiting.

I want to kiss her so much. I think she wants to kiss me too. Seems unanimous.

It was a moment to remember.

Chapter Fifty-Four

The school scheduled an organized walking tour through parts of historic Trapani on Saturday, but Tony and Michela made plans to visit Erice, an ancient town high above the city. Instead of traversing the winding roads in car or bus, they opted to take the cableway up a steep incline. Rewarded for their choice on a spectacularly clear, sunny day, they were afforded an unparalleled view of Trapani and the Egadi Islands off the western coast of Sicily.

Tony had read the medieval town of Erice, crowned by the Castle of Venus, was surrounded by defensive walls, all of which were supposed to be well-preserved. The literature wasn't wrong. He couldn't believe the excellent condition of a castle built in the twelfth century that exuded such charm and suggested at any moment a fire-breathing dragon might swoop down on them from the massive stone walls.

Tony stopped to take pictures of the castle while Michela walked to the edge of the fortress. She adjusted her sunglasses to shield her eyes as she surveyed the distant coastline near the beach town of San Vito lo Capo.

He had read other tourists' opinions, but Tony realized they were all wrong. The most spectacular sight stood right in front of him in the form of Michela. Mesmerized, he watched her gaze right, then left while she brushed away hair from her face.

She turned to Tony. "Come here to look."

He remained motionless.

"Tony?"

Finally, he realized she had spoken to him.

"Yes?"

"Come here to see this."

He climbed the fortification wall.

She asked, "You're thinking of something?"

Tony touched her cheek. "Yes, I was thinking of you. You're the most beautiful sight here."

They held hands and kissed until people's voices tore them from each other.

They made their way to Piazza Umberto, the town's central plaza, and selected a casual diner with a choice of sandwiches.

"My father is sick, and I go to visit him tomorrow."

"I'm sorry. Has he been sick for long?"

She closed her eyes.

"Yes, he has a disease. It's his breathing. It's emph-y-sema," she said slowly. "I'll be with my parents for one week."

She looked at Tony questioningly.

Although he was disappointed she would be out of town his last week of school, he said, "Michela, believe me when I tell you, I understand. I still miss my father every day."

Their conversation took a pause while they sipped on drinks. Michela touched Tony's hand.

She asked, "Do you have plans after school?"

"I have an appointment at the records office in Marinella. I'm driving there on Sunday and I may stay for the week depending on what I learn."

"Do you have a hotel?"

"Yes, the Albergo Mercure. Have you been to Marinella?"

"Yes, a long time ago with my parents. I don't remember much," Michela said softly.

They strolled through Erice window shopping and later rode the cable car back to Trapani, holding hands for the ten-minute trip.

"So, we're going to your sister's house now?"

"Yes, okay?"

"Of course. Tell me about your sister."

"Chiara is my youngest sister. She's thirty-four and is married to Filippo. They have two children. Remember?"

"Wow, Michela, your English is really coming along!"

"No. Do you think so?"

"Yes, I do."

"This week, when you go to school, I study, no, I studied my old books to practice English."

"Well, you're doing fantastic!"

"Thank you, I try. I tell Chiara she's a thief because I was the youngest child for six years."

Tony said, "I see. You were always supposed to be the youngest child?"

Michela laughed. "Yes, exactly. She's the thief!"

A relaxed walk brought them to her sister's apartment. As they approached, Tony could hear a raucous noise inside. The door opened to a slightly younger version of Michela. Her slender smile was overshadowed by an almost defeated expression.

She took a deep breath. "They drive me crazy today." Extending her hand, she said, "Hello, I'm Chiara. I think you say Claire in English, yes?"

Tony said, "Yes, that sounds right."

He was reminded of the story he just heard when Michela said, "Yes, this is my sister the thief."

Chiara said, "You're this guy my sister talks about always."

Michela's face turned red. She quickly changed the subject. "Next week, Tony goes to Marinella to study the history of his family."

"This is exciting, yes?" Chiara asked.

"Yes, I'm excited."

Michela said, "Okay, Tony, now we speak in Italian for your practice."

The two sisters' rapid conversation about their father's declining health was interrupted by her children who ran into the room dragging a chain of stuffed animals tied together. They stopped in front of Tony.

Michela said, "Lucia, Leonardo, please say hello to my friend, Tony Mancuso."

They both eyed Tony suspiciously for a moment. He tried to sound formal when he spoke to them in Italian.

"Good afternoon, pleased to meet you."

In unison, they said, "Good afternoon."

Leonardo asked, "Can you count to ten?"

"Yes, I can. In English or Italian?"

"In English!"

Lucia said, "And say the days of the week!"

"Their uncle gave them a book in English. He said we need to study it before we all have to learn Chinese," said Chiara.

Tony smiled, not quite sure if she was joking.

A few minutes after they arrived, Chiara's husband Filippo came home from playing soccer at a local club.

Chiara said, "He plays and I prepare dinner. It's okay because Filippo cannot cook. Today we have Pasta alla Norma for dinner. Do you know this dish?"

"No, at least not yet."

"Okay, it's pasta with fresh tomatoes, eggplant, basil, and ricotta cheese."

Tony said, "It smells wonderful. By the way, your English is excellent, Chiara."

"Thank you, I read these words today to say them to you."

Over dinner, the conversation went too quickly for Tony, and on occasion Michela stopped the chatter to catch him up.

Tony had lost count of how many glasses of wine he drank. His head reeled. In combination with the Italian and Sicilian being spoken, it felt like the merry-go-round ride had gone too long and he needed to step off.

Toward the end of the evening, Tony said, "I drank too much wine, and now all the languages, Italian, Sicilian, English and Chinese sound the same."

It was the best Italian he had spoken since starting school, and everyone laughed.

As Tony and Michela walked toward their apartments, they held hands and stole the occasional kiss at street corners.

They stood together for a long moment at the front door to her building.

Tony said, "What a party. I won't be drinking for a week!"

"Do you think my family is crazy?"

"No, I like your family, but you're my favorite."

They spoke every day on the phone, and Tony hid his disappointment when he heard Michela wouldn't be coming home the following weekend. It seemed lonely without her, even though they had only met a few weeks before.

On the final day of school, Tony said goodbyes to his teachers and friends.

Alex said, "I wish you good luck. Also with Michela."

"How, uh, did you know? Tony asked.

"Friend, sometimes the truth is easy to see."

Chapter Fifty-Five

Sunday around noon, Tony drove his rental, a powerful Range Rover, on the highway from Trapani east to Marinella. With no traffic issues, the trip would take less than two hours. He couldn't resist jamming down on the accelerator to race along the curvy coastal road but, unlike other drivers, once he reached city traffic in Marinella, he obeyed all the *recommendations* suggested by the posted signs and traffic lights.

Tony thought about calling Michela when he reached the hotel. They had spoken the day before, but he still missed her voice. He knew he was falling in love. His mind was never far from thoughts about her, and he wondered what she thought of him.

Michela arrived home Sunday after a difficult week watching her father's deteriorating condition. Even though he still flashed a moment or two of his old energy and priceless sense of humor, the decline in his health over the last month was obvious and significant. She sipped on a cup of tea, sitting by the window in her apartment looking toward Tony's old street.

It took forty years to find a man I really love. What if I did something crazy like surprise Tony at his hotel or, better yet, I waited for him in his room?

The decision to not return to Trapani until Sunday was difficult. She had been torn not knowing how much time remained for her father. Despite the progression of the disease, her father jokingly asked for a cigarette, which she steadfastly refused.

"No, but I'll give you a hug for free."

"Thank you. Your sister tells me you're seeing a man, an American?"

When she said yes, he smiled.

"I hoped you would meet a nice man."

"*Patri*, he is nice, and perhaps you can meet him soon."

"Will I meet him before you marry?"

"Now you're being silly."

"Well, your sister told me how you look at this American."

Michela held her father's hands. "This is enough excitement for one day. I love you, and I want you to sleep now."

His eyes were half-closed, but he clung to Michela's hand as she pulled away. "Please listen to me, precious one. Don't hide your feelings. Nurture them. Promise me."

Monday morning, the hotel concierge said, "Signor Mancuso, I want to ensure you make success in your research. Giuliano will guide you to the *Ufficio Anagrafe*. Parking is difficult, but you can walk there in fifteen minutes."

As they walked along Via Tirreno, the main road through town, Giuliano, a man about Tony's age, spoke to the various sites and their significance. He said the town changed for the better when the high-tech manufacturing plant opened in 1990, which led to new housing, shiny new cars, and an overall feeling of more wealth. Now rumors abounded the plant might be sold to a Chinese manufacturer or closed altogether.

Giuliano spoke Italian slowly, and at times he repeated words for Tony's benefit. "We're not a tourist town like other places. When the big plant opened, we couldn't believe our good fortune. Now people say there's a reason not to believe. They say Marinella is always going to struggle."

They turned onto Via Roma and ended up facing an elongated nondescript building.

"This is the Registry Office."

Tony thanked Giuliano and gave him a ten euro note for his help.

"Thank you, but first we must enter the building, and that can be difficult."

As Giuliano predicted, a locked door barred their entry. After several minutes someone left, and Giuliano caught the door with his foot.

Tony said, "I can see you play soccer pretty well."

Once inside, they found the inner door was also locked. Giuliano knocked, but a woman seated in an interior office ignored them while maintaining steadfast attention to a pile of documents stacked on the table in front of her. They waited several more minutes until someone left. Giuliano caught the door with his foot again and held it open for Tony.

As Giuliano spoke, the woman's focus shifted between the two men standing before her. Tony unfolded the photocopy picture of his grandfather standing next to the garden and placed it on the table.

Using words he had practiced over and over, he said, "This is my grandfather. I believe he was born in Marinella in 1895 and traveled to the United States when he was five years old. I hope to learn the reason."

He thanked Giuliano, hoping his departure left her no choice, but to help.

The woman sat at the table looking at the picture with Tony's notes scribbled to the side.

Speaking in Italian again, he said, "I made an appointment for eleven o'clock today."

He pointed to where he wrote the number eleven for the hour and the day's date in large print. He looked at her anxiously.

She asked, "When was your grandfather born again?"

Tony fist pumped as inconspicuously as possible. The woman stood to her full height of five feet.

Broken floor tiles, burned-out light bulbs, and tired walls hiding behind peeling gray paint decorated the empty offices as they walked to the rear of the building. She removed a single, ancient, oversized warded lock key from her pocket to gain passage through the metal door, revealing a twelve-foot deep by thirty-foot long room with several free-standing metal shelves housing hundreds of tattered ledger type books.

She peered through glasses to focus on the paper where she wrote the birth year and climbed a three-step ladder reaching still further above her for a ledger book marked "*Nascita* 1895." Twice she yanked on the book sandwiched between 1894 and 1896 before it was freed. Stepping down the ladder, the woman slid the heavy ledger along with her. She cradled the large book to her chest. Only her eyes peering through oversized glasses were visible as she shuffled toward the table.

She thumbed through pages to the day of Tommaso's birth. Using her index finger to scan the writing, she tapped the book twice, waving Tony over. Pointing to a spot on the yellowed page, she directed his attention to the entries of births in Marinella as they occurred in chronological order.

The name, Tommaso Mancuso, jumped off the page and confirmed the date and place of his grandfather's birth. She slid her index finger down the page a few inches to other recorded names.

"Tommaso's father was Saverio Mancuso and his mother was Rosa Favale."

For Tony, all time stopped when this stranger spoke those magnificent words. Seeing the facts laid out in black and white, handwritten in old-world script, hit him with such force for a moment he became lightheaded and used his hands to steady himself, leaning on the table while experiencing the incredible joy of the moment. He breathed deeply. The powerful emotion of connecting with the past bulldozed through a wall of insignificance and indifference. Now the names and snippets of stories became real with the confirmation his ancestors were born in the same town where he was standing.

Tony wiped his cheek, and the woman looked curiously at him, her demeanor seeming to soften.

Speaking slowly, she said, "Any information on your family will be contained in these books. This is where your grandfather's birth was recorded. I'll also find the information for Saverio and Rosa's parents."

Over the next hour she lugged ledger books back and forth. Every time she found more relevant information, she tapped her finger on the pages.

"Saverio's parents were Alessandro Mancuso and Salvadora Catalano."

Thirty minutes later, more information followed. She scribbled again on a piece of paper filling up with names, places, and dates.

"Rosa's father was Stefano Favale and her mother was Maria Parrino."

She motioned for Tony to follow.

"Excuse me, but what's your name?" he asked.

She responded in English with a curious British lilt.

"My name is Camilla."

She smiled broadly, exposing two tiny rows of teeth.

Tony said, "Well, I had no idea you spoke English."

"The King's English, actually," she said and laughed at her own joke. "Of the few foreigners who visit here seeking information, almost none even try to speak Italian. I appreciate you trying because I understand how difficult it is to learn another language, but I'm proof it's possible. You're doing well. How long have you studied?"

"I studied at home in the United States through a computer program for a couple of months and I attended school in Trapani for a month."

"Good for you, Tony. Bravo!"

Camilla and Tony crowded into a dreary office, sitting across from each other at a wobbly table with a desktop computer and a bulky monitor not unlike the behemoths Americans used in the early 1990s. She appeared to be in no hurry and neither did the computer, so they waited for the sluggish machine to come online.

"I'll bet there's a story to how you learned to speak English," Tony said.

Camilla nodded. Arching her eyebrows, she said, "Would you believe a British woman who once upon a time was a sister in the Catholic Church taught me?"

"Would you believe this is the third time I've heard that story today?"

She laughed and said, "Actually, it was right after I started working here in 1968, I met Louisa."

"You've been here forty-two years? You're not even for-ty-two years old."

"Ha! Flattery will get you everywhere. Sister Louisa was the dearest, sweetest person you would ever want to meet. She was doing missionary work with the poor in Sicily, in fact right here in Marinella when I first met her. We became friends, close friends, and I dedicated a significant amount of time to studying English with her until 1990 when she died working in Carlentini in eastern Sicily after an earthquake struck. She was such a lovely person."

Michela pushed the entry intercom button to let her sister in the building downstairs. She cracked her apartment door open and returned to her bedroom to select a final pair of shoes to take with her.

"Going somewhere?" Chiara asked.

Michela maintained her focus, finally selecting a nice new pair of walking shoes she hadn't yet worn to go with the others already in the bag.

"Oh, I see. When are you leaving?"

"Tomorrow morning early. *Patri* was right. I've been run-ning away long enough. I'm not going to hide my feelings, and I'm not losing this chance with Tony."

Chiara hugged her.

It was clear from the plodding computer and snail-like pace of the internet that Marinella had not yet made the jump to the twenty-first century. After she entered a few keystrokes of new information, Camilla would stop and smile.

"Tony, this is Sicily, and now we wait."

Once the clump of digital data encoded for the old analog copper telephone lines moseyed along the information superhighway, she typed in new information. Minutes later, the printer grudgingly produced a single piece of paper entitled, *Estratto dell'atto di Nascita.*

She asked, "Do you also want copies of the birth certificates for Saverio and Rosa's parents?"

They repeated the trek back and forth between the computer and the records room. Each time Camilla climbed the ladder to locate a different book for additional information. Without fail she locked the door behind her with the carefully guarded key from her pocket and, en route back to the computer, she hummed a tune from an old children's ditty.

"What do you hope to accomplish while you're here, Tony?"

"Well, the big mystery for me is why my grandfather left Sicily when he was a young boy? The story is he didn't travel with his parents."

"I don't think these records will give you a direct answer to that question, but they might provide clues. It may be logical to conclude they died when Tommaso was young, otherwise why would he leave, correct?"

"Yes, that makes sense."

"Tony, we're past time for lunch. Let's take a break. Come back at three and we'll start with the time when you believe your grandfather went to America and work our way backwards."

"Okay. Camilla, are home addresses and professions recorded in the ledger books?"

"Of course. The information on where they lived is contained with the birth entries, but I'll write down everything for you. There may be a reference to their type of work or profession. It depends. Sometimes I've seen it recorded at the time of the person's death."

Tony left the office, but not before Camilla told him to come directly to the side door at three o'clock sharp and he could avoid the hassle of the public entrance.

The previous day he skirted by a tree-lined park while running. With nearly two hours to kill, all he had to do was find a slice of pizza to go with an empty bench under a shady tree.

While he sat with lunch on his lap, a group of three older gentlemen gathered nearby engaged in a quiet conversation. He couldn't hear their discussion but wondered if it would make a difference in his comprehension if he could. He wasn't sure.

I'm convinced life is a crapshoot. How different life would be if the wind had been blowing in a different direction a hundred or more years ago.

After lunch, Tony returned to the Registry Office and saw Camilla standing outside smoking a cigarette.

She said, "It's a nasty habit. Don't start."

"Camilla, I'd be a little late to the dance at this point in my life."

They spent the next hour in the records room while Tony watched Camilla work through the books to gather the necessary information. He found himself daydreaming about Michela when the tapping on the book sounded.

"Tony, this is your great grandfather, Saverio Mancuso. He died in 1900. He would have been, let's see, he would have been thirty-two-years old. He was a painter."

"A painter? You mean an artist?"

"No. I mean he painted houses and buildings."

"A housepainter? But, Camilla, how did he die that young?"

"The records don't say, but this is not unusual for that time because the cause of death was usually only recorded if someone died at a hospital or with a doctor in attendance."

Camilla continued her search working backwards to Tommaso's birthdate while Tony wondered about the cause of Saverio's death.

He died at such a young age. It could have been an accident, but no doubt it's somehow related to Thomas's journey to America because they both occurred the same year. But why did he travel alone to the states? There's been nothing about his mother, Rosa. Wouldn't it be logical Tommaso would have stayed with her?

He needed Michela with him to help sort out the information. He missed her and wished she could be with him to help make sense of it all.

"Tony, I'm looking in the last book for the year your grandfather was born. It's possible Rosa died elsewhere, then there would be no record here. There are many possibilities. I don't want you to be too disappointed if there's nothing, because even though recordkeeping was still quite accurate in those times, it's possible the death wasn't recorded for any number of reasons, including a clerical error."

Tony sighed. His mind retreated to speculation and conjecture.

Well, at least I know more than when I started. Maybe his mother couldn't afford to keep him or she remarried and died elsewhere or—

The familiar tapping sounded.

"Tony, your great grandmother Rosa died in 1895."

"Oh, my God, she died when he was a baby?"

"Tony, she died on the day he was born."

"Hold it. Now what? You're saying, why, what happened exactly?"

"Again, unless she died in a hospital or with a doctor in attendance, there wouldn't be any record. Let's see, it does say here she died at home and a midwife was present. Tony, it's as close to a certainty as you'll get that Rosa's death was related to Tommaso's birth."

The news was crushing. He thought he had wanted to learn the answers to his questions and, now that he had, he felt like a truck had backed over him.

Did my grandfather even know about this? His mother died in childbirth and his father died for some reason when he was five. Then Thomas traveled from Sicily to the United States.

He looked at the picture of his grandfather in the garden. With every new detail, he became more than a faded black and white image glued to a page in a photo album, and Thomas's parents and grandparents became real people too. A strange sensation came over him.

I feel a responsibility for them. These people are my people. They're my family.

"Camilla, does this road Via Cavallo where my grandfather was born still exist?"

"Yes, it's in a neighborhood close to the city hospital. You can reach it on foot in ten minutes or less."

Camilla provided directions and, although Tony's mind had already shifted to his next stop, he stooped over to hug Camilla goodbye. Something told him, though, it wasn't goodbye forever. She was a kind person, and he wouldn't forget it.

"I can't thank you enough for all of your help today."

His curiosity compelled him to walk to the neighborhood right away.

Chapter Fifty-Six

Camilla had given almost an entire workday to the project. Even though early evening and fading light made it too late in the day to explore the entire area surrounding Via Cavallo, he had been bitten by the bug. Overcome with emotion, he wanted to uncover more clues about his family.

He stood in front of the house marked number fourteen where his grandfather had been born. The thought of taking a photograph seemed rude and intrusive. He continued down the cobblestone street for a couple of minutes only to turn back like a homing pigeon returning to his loft. He leaned against the wall and closed his eyes for a moment overcome with the strangest sensation. It was as if voices were calling to him in the distance.

Tony opened his eyes and a man walked by looking curiously at him. They exchanged pleasantries, and Tony introduced himself to Guido, a middle-aged man, who said he had lived in the Cavallo neighborhood his entire life.

He told Guido his grandfather's story and asked, "Do you think any Mancusos still live on this street?"

"Mancuso is a common name. It's possible a family still lives around here, but I don't know any."

They walked along Via Cavallo while Guido discussed the neighborhood's history. He explained it had been in existence a few hundred years although the houses had been modernized, pointing to the electric and cable wires and air conditioning wall units now attached to the structures' exterior.

Tony tripped while gazing up at the houses and would have fallen, but Guido caught his arm.

"You've discovered another difference. The streets long ago were more mud than cobblestone. Now they're a bit more cobblestone than mud."

They talked for a while longer about the state of Sicily in general. Tony was struck by how friendly and helpful Guido seemed. After several minutes, Tony thanked him and returned to the hotel.

He called Michela's cell number but ended up leaving a message.

"I miss you and think about you all the time. I look up or turn a street corner and expect to see you. I've learned a lot from my visit here. I even went to my grandfather's old neighborhood. I'll tell you about it when we talk."

Later in the evening, he awoke from dozing on the bed while an American movie with dubbed Italian played. He had missed Michela's call.

"Ciao, Tony, I'm sorry I missed you and now you miss me. I want to hear about your grandfather. My father is not well. I go to see my sister. I'm missing you too. Ciao."

The following morning Tony was excited to return to the neighborhood in the full light of day. Still early, he thought first he would go for a run to take in more of the town and the waterfront. It was a peaceful hour and his mind wandered.

I'm running along the same roads and maybe even the same footsteps where Saverio and Rosa used to play.

He slowed to a walk through the park where he had lunched the day before. Tony made a mental note to call Michela as soon as he reached his room. The front desk clerk was retrieving his room key when a movement out of the corner of his eye caught his attention. He thought, what an exquisite sight. Michela sat on a sofa next to a window in the corner of the lobby.

"They told me you're running this morning."

"I was just thinking of you," Tony said.

"This morning the car made me a prisoner in Trapani and now I'm here. It's a surprise? A good surprise, I hope."

"Michela, it's the best surprise of my life."

She giggled. "Mister, you invite me to your room, please?"

"Of course."

He took her hand and helped Michela up from the sofa.

"Thank you, Mister."

Michela slid open the door leading to the balcony from Tony's room. "This is a pretty view."

"It really is, isn't it? Michela, I have to shower." He did a scrubbing motion on his chest. "How do I say that in Italian?"

"Later we'll have a lesson, but now you take a shower."

"Okay, here's the television remote control, a newspaper, and there are drinks and snacks in the fridge."

While Tony showered, he thought of Michela and how happy he was the day was shaping up to be a great one spent in the company of such a lovely woman.

He dried off and wrapped the towel around his waist. As he reached for the toothpaste, there was a knock on the bathroom door.

"Yes, uh *sì*?"

Michela opened the door wearing the hotel's thick cotton robe. It was partially undone in front to just below her navel. "Tony, do you like to go to bed with me now?"

When he squeezed the toothpaste tube, the paste gushed into the sink as the brush fell from his hand.

Laughing, she closed the door.

Like he did as a child, Tony brushed his teeth in ten seconds flat and found Michela in bed with the covers up to her chin.

She said, "Excuse me, sir, the admission of price is one towel, please."

"Uh, it's price of admission, but who cares."

So much had happened in the last twenty-four hours, it all added up to the best day of his life as they walked along Via Cavallo holding hands. Happy to take on the role of tour guide, he pointed to where his grandfather was born and his great grandparents lived.

"Tony, do you want a photograph here? You in front of your grandfather's house?"

"Yes, but I want us both in the picture."

"Also me? In the picture?"

"Of course."

Michela hugged him.

They stood together while Tony held the cell phone with an outstretched arm pointed in their direction. While Tony tried to hold the phone still, Michela reached for the photo button with her index finger. Every time she stretched the last few inches to touch it, the phone shifted slightly or her finger missed, causing one or both of them to be outside the frame. They failed so many times, the moment became comical, and neither of them could stop laughing long enough to even attempt another photo. Finally, they managed to get one decent shot.

As they looked at the picture, Michela squeezed close to Tony and whispered into his ear, "Someone was watching us from inside on the second floor."

Tony said, "I don't understand. Say it in English."

She whispered a few words, but ended up laughing, and soon Tony joined in. By the time he understood what she said, no one could be seen at the window.

They strolled over to the street where Rosa was born on Via Modestia. There was no house number that matched the old address, and the buildings appeared to have been constructed within the last few decades. They returned to Via Cavallo. Tony wanted one more chance to catch the mysterious person at Via Cavallo fourteen, but they had no luck.

They decided to return to the hotel to grab a snack and rest.

He asked, "Do you want to go to the cemetery to find the gravesites of Saverio and Rosa?"

"Yes, but I must wear different shoes."

They reached the room, and Tony looked at Michela's foot where a blister had formed.

In a pretend voice from an old war type movie, Tony said, "Soldier, you've got to take care of your feet or you're no use to us in battle."

"What does this mean, this soldier and this battle?"

"It's kind of a joke; you know, like a line from a war movie where the soldier has to take care of his feet and his boots. You understand?"

"No. They were comfortable when I bought them last week."

He used his movie voice again. "Okay, soldier, rest easy and let me see if I can help."

He rubbed her feet, kneading his thumb and knuckles deeply into her arches.

"That feels nice, Mister Soldier. Can we go tomorrow instead?"

Near the cemetery entrance late the following morning, Tony bought flowers for the gravesites of Saverio and Rosa. Since the cemetery caretaker office was locked and empty, they decided to start looking at the rear of the graveyard and work their way to the front.

Halfway through their search, Tony kneeled to study the names on two grave markers when he heard a man's voice. He looked up, surprised to find Guido from the Cavallo neighborhood.

His soiled hands carried the remains of old flowers.

Guido said, "I visit my father's grave during the week on my lunch break. I work right there," he said, pointing to a commercial building close by. "I find it's peaceful here and, of course, I still miss my father."

Tony introduced Michela and Guido. It was obvious to Tony that Guido had picked up the pace of his speech. For a moment he spoke so rapidly Tony only caught a few words and was unable to string them together to make any sense. Guido turned to Tony and spoke slowly in Italian. "After you visited the neighborhood, a woman by the name of Signora Spasaro who lives on Via Cavallo spoke to me. She wants to meet you."

"She wants to meet me?" Tony asked.

"Yes, she said she saw you talking with me, then she saw you yesterday with a woman. I'm sure she was referring to Michela. If you'd like, I'll arrange a meeting for tomorrow evening."

"Guido, is she an elderly woman who lives at Via Cavallo fourteen? I mean, where my grandfather lived?"

"Yes, how did you know?" Guido asked.

Tony and Michela shared a quick glance, thinking this was the person Michela spotted on the second floor.

Because of the excitement over Guido's news, Tony almost forgot about the reason they came to the cemetery, explaining they were looking for his great grandparents' graves. Guido asked when they died and frowned when he heard the dates.

"This cemetery replaced an older one."

Tony asked, "Where's this older cemetery?"

Guido pointed toward several buildings outside the cemetery walls. "It used to be over there until the construction."

"I don't understand. Wait, I'm sorry. Tell me again, please. Where's the cemetery now?"

Guido and Michela spoke rapidly to each other for a minute. Michela turned to Tony and explained.

"Guido said he thinks everything was moved from the old cemetery before the construction, but the records of where the graves are, how do you say, they were, what's the word, because of a fire during the war?"

"Oh, you mean the records were destroyed in a fire?" Tony asked.

"Yes, the fire destroys, or destroyed the documents."

"So, no one knows where—"

"Guido said the graves may be here, but where, he doesn't know."

The anticipation he felt a few minutes before became lost in the haze of this new discovery. He decided it was a subject best revisited another time.

They exchanged goodbyes with Guido and began a silent stroll through the cemetery. Tony randomly selected two graves and laid the flowers on the ground.

"What do you think the woman wants to talk about?" Tony asked.

Michela said, "I don't know. The person I saw in the window was old, but certainly not from the time of your grandfather."

Tony stopped and turned to face Michela. "I guess we'll find out together." He held her hands and said, "Thank you for being here with me."

They stood close together.

Michela placed her hand on Tony's face. "I'm happy." She smiled. "We are solving a mystery together," she said.

Being close to Michela and seeing her smile made him feel better. "We do make two sharp detectives, don't we? How do you say detectives?" he asked.

She took two steps back and turned sideways. "Yes, we're two *investigatori*." Pursing her lips and narrowing her eyes, Michela asked, "Do you think I make a good detective?"

Chapter Fifty-Seven

They waited near Via Cavallo fourteen standing close together holding hands.

"Guido told me this neighborhood has–"

Michela said in a low voice, "Tony, the woman is at the window."

He started to turn.

She laughed. "No, don't look now—"

From around the corner, Guido appeared.

"Sorry, I'm a little late from work," he said.

They shook hands, and Tony glanced up at the window seeing the curtains move. Guido pressed the buzzer next to the door of the house while Michela and Tony silently acknowledged to each other, *we were right!*

They waited a minute, then two.

Guido shrugged and said, "Signora Spasaro is quite old."

The door creaked open, and an elderly woman with a faint smile stood before them. She wore a simple floral print house dress that hung to mid-calf, her thinning white hair lay flat across her head, and she spoke in a voice barely above a whisper.

"*Buonasera.*"

They were invited into an immaculate home, not just uncluttered, but spotless. No articles nor objects from current day were present, but everything from a century ago—the furniture, the rugs, the black and white photographs in wooden frames, the fine china set displayed in a glass cabinet, and even the shawl draped over the chair folded with perfection. Her lilac perfume dominated the space despite the freshly brewed tea.

While her company sat in a small living room adjacent to an equally small kitchen, she walked a few steps, stopped, and smiled at her guests. She restarted at a glacial pace toward the kitchen where cups and saucers rested on the counter.

Tony felt awkward and asked, "May I help you, Signora Spasaro?"

She stopped and waved her arm to indicate no.

Signora Spasaro carried the saucers and cups on a tray to the living room and slowly restarted her journey to the kitchen and brought back a pot of hot tea.

To each of her guests, she presented rich, heavy silk napkins with an intricately woven pink and white pattern. Tony, accustomed to using leftover paper wipes from fast food sandwich joints, was afraid to even touch them fearing he might soil the beautiful piece of history.

She poured tea into each cup and returned to the kitchen to retrieve a plate of still-warm cookies filled with fig and chocolate. They were delicious, and she smiled when Tony said so.

Michela said, "I love your home. Everything is lovely; the rug, the furniture, the dishes."

"This was my parents' home and, before them, my grandparents. I have kept the house as my mother did. I'm ninety-four years old and have lived here all my life, alone since my mother died. I never married."

A surprising loud laughter, more of a cackle, leapt from her throat.

"Why the bother of it all," she said more as a statement than a question, and her lips curled into a half smile.

Tony asked, "When was your mother born?"

"In 1893 close by."

She pointed to a picture of a young girl, perhaps ten years of age with a large, almost exaggerated smile.

Signora Spasaro said, "That's my mother when she was a child. She moved here because her father never liked their old house; well, the number seventeen of the house address. The day after they moved to number seventeen, he broke his leg when he fell down the stairs. The accident confirmed his suspicion the number was bad luck, and he vowed they would leave the cursed house. Do you understand about the number seventeen?"

Tony nodded. At school, he had studied various superstitions including, the belief the number seventeen in Sicily was similar to the unlucky thirteen in the United States.

She said, "Why my grandfather bought that house, who can be sure?"

She touched her index finger to her temple and shook it slightly. "I think he was a little crazy, but his misfortune led us to be here."

She looked toward the window.

"When I saw you the other day, at first I said to myself you're Sicilian. But the way you dressed, I thought you may be from another land. I also received strong feelings, a premonition, your family is from here, yes?"

She pointed down to the floor and tapped her foot.

"Yes, my grandfather, Tommaso Mancuso, was born here."

Signora Spasaro nodded her head slowly.

A small smile escaped, and she said, "Yes, Rosa and Saverio, the parents of Tommaso."

Tony stopped breathing when he heard the names.

She reached toward the table filled with teacups and cookies and picked up a ragged leather pouch. She held it close to her chest for a few seconds and sniffled. Michela jumped to get a tissue, but Signora Spasaro waved her arm and reached into her dress pocket, removed a handkerchief, and dabbed her nose. With gnarled fingers, she caressed the leather pouch for a moment.

Signora Spasaro said, "I have a story to tell you, and I have something to give to you. It's yours, not mine. You see, my mother said she was eight years old when she came here. She slept in the room upstairs."

She sniffled again and rose from her chair, motioning with her hand for the others to follow.

"I go up and down the stairs many times a day. My doctor says this is good for me."

When she reached the halfway point, she turned to look at Tony.

"But my doctor is a young man." She shook her head and laughed. "He's only seventy-four."

They crept along behind her to the second floor and entered a bedroom.

"This was my mother's room as a child." Signora Spasaro ran her hand along a bookcase built into the wall. "She told me she found this small bag here. My mother gave it to me, but Signor Mancuso, this belongs to you."

She handed the pouch to Tony and slowly descended the stairs while the others paraded behind to the living room. Tony sat with the pouch cupped in his hands as if it might fly away.

Signora Spasaro said, "I saw you the other day alone and again with your wife taking photographs. The way you held hands and laughed took me back to a time when I was young and my whole life waited in front of me."

The skin around her eyes crinkled with a faint smile.

Quietly, she said, "Then I heard the faraway voices, and I knew why you came."

From their hotel room, Tony stared out the sliding door leading to the balcony.

Michela hugged him from behind. "Are you ready to look in the bag?"

A few hours before sunrise, Tony untangled an arm from an arm and a leg from a leg, eased himself out of bed and tiptoed across the room to the balcony. He wrapped a robe around himself to fight off the chill as he slid the door open. In the distance, empty boats rested, waiting for their captains to lead them to another day of work on the sea. Listening to the sound of quiet, sleep began to overtake him. Signora Spasaro's sweet words wandered through his mind. "Your wife, your wife, your wife…"

The warmth of the sun and Michela's soft hand on his shoulder pulled him from a deep sleep. The leather pouch lay by his side.

Chapter Fifty-Eight

A day later, Tony and Michela drove their separate vehicles to Trapani. They were there only long enough for Michela to repack clothes and shoes and leave her car. After lunch with her sister, Chiara, they headed to Palermo, staying overnight to spend time visiting Michela's family. A three-hour drive across the northern coast of Sicily brought them to a line of vehicles waiting to drive onto a ferry to take them over the Strait of Messina onto the Italian mainland. It had been a whirlwind forty-eight hours.

Tony said, "I loved meeting your parents. That's a lot of people with your brothers and sisters."

"They are, how you say, the handful?"

"Yes, I enjoyed it. Sometimes it was hard to remember who was who."

"I listened to my father talk with you. He was interested in your work."

"Your father is a sweet guy. He has a great sense of humor too."

"He liked you, and Mama did too."

"Your parents are lovely people. They made me feel so welcome."

"My mother isn't the same. She used to be happy, always laughing."

"I'm sure it's difficult for her to see the man she loves suffer."

He gently squeezed her hand while a few quiet moments passed.

"Well, Michela, do you think you're ready to meet more Americans?"

She fretted about her English. "With you it's okay, but I'm nervous with others."

"Don't worry. I wish my Italian was a tenth as good as your English."

"Yes?"

"Yes! And you'll love them and they'll love you, I'm sure."

Tony laughed.

She grabbed his leg and squeezed. "Why do you make this laughter?"

"There's nothing to worry about. Mandy can speak a little Italian and will want to speak it as much as possible. She was here many years ago and loved Italy. It'll be fine. We'll all muddle through."

"What does this mean, this muddle?"

"Hmm, I'm not sure how to say it in Italian. Let's check the translator on the phone."

Michela pronounced each letter M-U-D-D-L-E aloud in accented English as she typed the word.

He thought, everything she does, everything she says, I'm falling in love just listening to her.

Sharing a bottle of water while they waited at Florence's Amerigo Vespucci Airport, Michela said, "You spoke Italian well with my parents. You're improving every day."

"I muddled through with your parents."

"Yes, but you don't say it right," Michela said.

"How do I say–" but never finished his thought because Vic and Mandy were walking toward them.

For Tony, the reunion seemed like they hadn't seen each other in years with so much happening in the past few weeks. Mandy and Michela immediately bonded, sitting in the back seat of the SUV speaking a mix of English and Italian.

Vic caught Tony up with activities at the office.

"The economy is getting stronger, if only a little, and investors are sticking their toes back into the water, well, at least, a toe in the water."

They checked into the Sole e Girasole, a quaint bed and breakfast near the Ponte Vecchio, a medieval stone bridge built over the Arno River in the historic area of Florence. Outside the door, there were more sites and museums than could be seen in a week, a month, perhaps even a year.

As they gathered in the lobby to go to dinner, Mandy punched Tony on the arm.

"Michela is gorgeous. I love her. You're one lucky guy, Tony Mancuso."

"Believe me when I say I'm the luckiest guy in the whole world."

Over the next several days, when they weren't visiting museums and churches, Mandy and Michela went shopping. There seemed to be no end to their energy. At times they disappeared into a store for an hour, leaving Tony and Vic to drink coffee at an outdoor cafe discussing sports, business and personal lives.

"This is a crazy time, Vic. Something happened. I'm not sure where I'll end up, or rather, where *we* will end up."

"Well, take your time. I don't want to lose you from the team. Since I'm the boss, we'll be patient."

"I'll be back in the office in a couple of weeks."

"Tony, there'll always be a place for you."

The six days passed far too quickly, and now they stood together again at the airport.

Mandy said, "I don't want to leave. Vic, the girls can fly over here today. Wouldn't it be wonderful?"

Vic said, "I could certainly be talked into it."

After several hugs, kisses, and an *arrivederci* or two, Vic and Mandy left.

Michela sniffled a bit as they walked back to the car. Tony hugged her. "You'll see them again."

He wiped a tear away from her cheek.

"It's you I'm going to miss. Tony, you make me so happy."

"Please don't cry. We're together right now, and I thought we could stay in Rome for a while since I've never visited before. Are you up for that?"

"What does 'up for that' mean?"

He opened the car door for Michela and grabbed her by the waist, pulling her close.

"It means do you want to visit Rome before going home?"

They spent two days of easy driving along the coastal highway to shepherd them back to Sicily. Every bend in the road revealed sharp cliffs with breathtaking vistas of an enormous blue sea. They stopped for one night at the small seaside town of Scilla in Calabria, but the last days went by in the blink of an eye.

"I need to take care of things at work. Hey, why don't you come with me? You could. I would love it. Would you?"

"No, Tony, I can't leave now. School begins soon."

Her response punched Tony in the gut.

Michela has a life here and needs to think about getting back to work. Did I never consider that? How can she depend on me, trust me, to do the right thing?

The sudden emptiness he felt was the only thing keeping the ache deep inside him company, but the pain wasn't for him. He realized the pain came from the knowledge he wouldn't just miss Michela; he would be lost without her.

The desire, the angst, the elation, and the heartache all came together creating an emotion he never felt before.

He whispered, "This is how it must feel to be in love. This is love. *This, is love.*

Chapter Fifty-Nine

The flight from Palermo was the longest, loneliest time of his entire life.

He didn't want to be met at the Norfolk airport by anyone, preferring to take a taxi back home. Tony was greeted by a huge stack of mail sitting alongside flowers and Italian cookies on the kitchen counter, courtesy of Mandy. After a restless night, he awoke to dark clouds and pouring rain. Drinking coffee and sitting at the table with an unshaved face, uncombed hair, and unbrushed teeth, he ate cookies for both breakfast and lunch as he went through the mail. Hours passed as he dragged himself through the empty place he used to call home.

Tony was tired to the bone but, hopped up on coffee and sugar, he hung on until late afternoon time in Sicily to call.

Michela sat at the small kitchen table cold and alone. Not even a heavier sweater helped bring her warmth or comfort. The laptop sat open, and a map of an American city she had never heard of a couple of months before stared back at her.

Why didn't I go with Tony for a week? How could it hurt?

She sipped on a cup of tea looking down the street where a man she loved used to live.

Her phone buzzed.

"I'm sure by now you're sitting there in the dark eating gelato and feeling sorry for yourself."

Michela said, "Yes, and when I finish one, I'm going to eat another."

I love my sister the thief.

Chiara said, "What you need is a good dose of reality. Come over and help me go through the kids' clothes for school. Besides, there's a bottle of wine I'm getting ready to open."

Michela pulled the door behind her when the phone buzzed again. She stepped back inside thinking it was her sister wanting her to bring something.

"I'm going to help Chiara with the children's clothes. My sister is a bad influence. She has a bottle of wine," Michela said.

Tony told her he spent the day going through mail.

"You received love letters from old girlfriends?"

There was a long silence.

"Michela?"

"Yes."

"I miss you so much."

Across a vast ocean, she felt the desperation and earnestness in his voice.

"I wish I had come with you," she said.

The end of the first week about five o'clock, Tony stopped at Vic's office.

"I wanted to see if you had time to talk."

"No, I don't."

Tony was momentarily taken aback; was Vic angry about something?

"Well, not here at least, but if we're talking about a cold beer someplace else, that's another thing," Vic said with a smile that let Tony know everything was fine.

Escaping the office to go to a pub without it turning into an impromptu office party wasn't easy. They sat at a table with a bowl of pretzels and two cold beers between them.

Vic asked, "So, what's on your mind?"

"I guess I need to give it time."

"Give what time?"

"Well, the job."

"Oh, we're here to talk about the job?"

"Well, yes and no. Hell, I'm not sure, Vic. I've spent the last twenty-five years of my life being a selfish prick, and now I've got someone in my life and on my mind, day and night."

Vic said, "Well, I'm not sure about the selfish part, Tony, but the other, well?"

Tony laughed, but it hurt in his chest. Even breathing hurt.

"Listen, Tony, I hate to see you like this. What does your gut tell you?"

"To get back on a plane and pick up where we left off."

"And what's stopping you?"

"Oh, a little thing here called life and my job."

"Okay, Tony, let's cut to the chase. You've made a shitload of money working here the last twenty years or so. Now, I may not understand what you did with your money, but I imagine you have enough socked away—way more than enough—to never work another day in your life or ten more lives. Am I right?"

Tony nodded.

"If you love your job and can't get enough of it, I understand, and I'll be more than happy for you to be here. But there's more to life than the J-O-B."

He nodded again.

It was close to midnight. Sitting on his balcony, he gazed at the skyline he had memorized long ago from the comfort of a cushioned chair his body knew so well. He thought about the financial advisor profession he had mastered and his native language he spoke without even thinking.

He touched the screen on his phone. Staring back at him was an image of himself and a fantastic woman laughing uncontrollably in front of an old house in Sicily.

Glancing up at the night sky, he selected a random star for conversation.

"Just how in the hell am I supposed to decide between what I know and love and what I would love to know?"

Days turned into weeks and weeks into a month and more. The daily calls between Tony and Michela continued. The routine of the office returned, but now things were different.

I'm not who I used to be. I'm not that guy anymore. I'm not doing justice to my clients, to myself, and most important, to Michela.

Late Friday afternoon, Tony sat at his desk staring at a blank computer screen when he sensed a presence behind him.

Johnstone leaned against the door. "Tony, there's this thing. It's called a power button. Just needs a little juice. You'll have better luck. Guaranteed."

"Thanks, Johnstone."

"I'm glad you're back."

For the first time Tony could remember, Johnstone sat in his office. He wasn't sure Johnstone was even capable of sitting.

"Vic told me you met someone in Italy. I'm happy for you. I hope to meet her someday."

A few moments of silence passed between the two.

"And I want you to be you again."

They exchanged a quick glance, and Tony felt raw emotion coming up into his throat and choked a bit.

"Tony, don't let this chance go."

Johnstone disappeared with the door closing behind him.

Tony stared at the floor. The seconds dragged by. The silence was deafening.

Chapter Sixty

It was a Sunday morning, moments before the sun would rise from the east. Tony sat in his car next to lonely, forgotten headstones resting in relative darkness among the crumbling statues and tattered flowers. Closing his eyes, he thought about his grandfather's life that began in Sicily and ended here in Norfolk.

As the sun poked its head above the horizon to bring a little warmth to a cool morning, Tony eased himself out of the car and knelt, absentmindedly tugging at weeds growing between the graves. He ran his fingers along his grandfather's name etched in the stone.

"I'm sorry we never had the chance to meet. I'm also sorry I never came to visit and sit for a while. But Grandfather, or *Nonno*, if I may call you *Nonno*, I'm here now and I want to thank you. I can't begin to understand what you went through as a small child by yourself, on a ship coming to an unknown place and trying to make sense of a strange language. Thank you for making your way here and staying. It makes me love a man I never knew but wish I had."

Tony gazed at his family's gravestones. He breathed in and out slowly as the sun peeked over the church roofline in the distance. His one-way conversation restarted.

"I visited the house where you lived as a boy in Sicily. Your father wrote you a letter he wanted you to have and keep, but I don't know, I'm not sure what happened. Somehow it got lost. When I was there, I met a girl and fell in love. *Nonno*, she doesn't know it yet, but we're going to marry. Her name is Michela and she helped me with this translation."

Dearest Tommaso, our darling son ~

My hope is you understand someday that I sent you to America to have an opportunity for a better life. I'm dying from a cancer, but I want you to know a little about us. Your mother was Rosa Favale. She was sweet and kind, possessing all the good that goodness can hold. Her parents said she came from the Tyrrhenian Sea because her eyes matched the green of the sea. I loved your mother from the first time I saw her. On the happiest day of our lives, January 10, 1895, you were born. It was also the saddest day of my life because on that day, your mother died. She prayed to God every day to bring a baby into this world. Her prayer was answered, but not in the way either of us imagined. You must understand your mother would have given her life one thousand times over to bring you into this world even if it meant only knowing you for the second she did. I pray someday you'll have a family of your own, but I hope you remember we were your family once too. The photograph is your mother and I on the day we learned of you. We have more love for you than the sea holds water and always will.

Rosa Favale and Saverio Mancuso

Tony paused, cleared his throat, and spoke again.

"My hope is that for all the pain you may have felt as a child growing up alone in this world, you understand how much your parents loved you. I can't think of anything else to say, except *Nonno*, I love you too."

Tony stopped at the car door and turned back to his grandfather's grave.

"I'll always keep this letter and picture safe with me."

He sat in the car and closed his eyes for a moment.

"Arrivederci," he whispered.

Chapter Sixty-One

Tony got out of the taxi, grabbed his bag, and walked into the school building. A man in a suit and tie was leaving the school's administrative office.

In the best Italian he could manage, Tony asked, "Excuse me, could you please tell me where Michela Amoroso's classroom is?"

The man smiled. "Yes, please follow me."

They walked without speaking down the hallway until they reached the last classroom on the right.

"You must be the American."

"Yes," Tony said.

"Signor Mancuso, I'm Ignazio Ragusa, the school director."

They shook hands. He pointed to the door and, as he turned to walk away, Signor Ragusa said, "You're a lucky man."

A small window in the door allowed Tony a view of Michela standing in front of several crooked rows of desks overflowing with children. She was even more beautiful than he remembered. He knocked on the door and pushed it open. Michela turned, and the book fell from her hands to the floor.

Late in the evening, they went to the same restaurant where they dined for the first time. Tony spoke nonstop about how much he had missed her.

Michela shifted uneasily in her chair.

"Tony, I must tell you something. My life changed after you left."

"Oh?"

She hesitated for a moment.

"Something happened," she said.

"What do you mean?"

"I wasn't as careful as I should have been."

"I don't understand. Careful about what?"

"You see, I'm not drinking wine tonight."

"That's okay, we don't need to order–"

"Or tomorrow night."

She placed her hands to her stomach.

"What? You mean?"

"Yes. Are you unhappy?"

He rested his hand on her hand and kissed her on the cheek.

"Good God, of course not. I'm beyond happy—I'm ecstatic."

His lips lingered, touching her while he breathed in the beauty, the warmth, and the sweetness of her essence.

Finally, he whispered, "I love you."

He leaned back still holding her hand. "God, I missed you." He fought it, but a single tear escaped. "Why didn't you tell me?"

"Tony, I love you, but I want you to be here because you want to be with me, not because you feel like you must be."

A matching tear slid down her cheek.

"Michela, I'll never leave you again."

Chapter Sixty-Two

2015

Tony leaned back in the chair, satisfied with his day's effort, and turned the volume up to listen to music. Across the street, he caught a glimpse of a man and a small boy holding hands as they entered the corner bakery.

His mind wandered back to a time when he was young and he held his father's hand while they lazily explored the beach. A thick layer of clouds darkened on the ocean's horizon. He remembered his dad urging him to walk faster as the once dormant wind awoke from its slumber. In the space of a few minutes, it blew with such ferocity, the sand stung his face and chest until his father hoisted him onto his back to protect him on their way home. It had been decades, but Tony could still feel his father's skin from that day as he clung to his back.

A song played in the background, and a smooth, rich voice sang.

Don't know nothing that lasts forever
Everyone seems to come and go
Sharing a slice of that good country life
Then we'll roll on to another kind of show.

The four-year-old girl ran into the office, climbing onto her father's lap and rested her head against his chest. Giggling, she held his glasses to her face while she tapped on the keyboard of the computer.

Tony hugged his daughter and kissed the top of her head. He looked at a black and white photograph of a man and a woman with wonderful smiles and a tattered letter sealed in a golden-brown picture frame hanging on the wall above his desk.

She said, "*Patri*, I'm hungry."

"When your mama comes home, we'll walk to get a pizza."

She turned to face him.

"*Patri?*"

He brushed the unruly locks of thick black hair from her face.

"*Sì, amore.*"

"Is *Matri bella?*"

"*Sì, bellissima.*"

"And do you think I'm pretty too?"

Looking deep into her sea green eyes, he said, "Rosa, you're the most beautiful girl in the whole world."

About the Author

Christopher Amato is married, a proud father of three sons and grandfather to two intelligent, curious boys. He was born into a large family in Portsmouth, Virginia. His father's occupation in retail led to various stops along the way for the family of ten. In 1981 he earned a degree with honors in Criminology from Florida State University. Thanks to some nice folks in Roanoke, Virginia, who opened a tough door to pass through, he was able to secure his first job in federal law enforcement. His career as a special agent included assignments in Los Angeles, Atlanta, Washington, D.C., and Norfolk. He worked his way to a senior leadership position and after nearly thirty years, decided to retire. He and his wife began traveling to Italy to test the waters. Falling in love, they made the move full time. The former investigator, curious about his family's past, began researching the timely and timeless subject of immigration. The effort eventually resulted in the novel *A Letter from Sicily*. He has written a number of short stories and is currently at work on his second novel. Christopher lives in the beautiful walled city of Lucca, Italy, with his wife and very needy dog.

www.ingramcontent.com/pod-product-compliance
Lightning Source LLC
Chambersburg PA
CBHW051200190726
48288CB00006B/1731